Praise for Arlene James and her novels

"Arlene James has an exquisite way with words
and emotions."
—*RT Book Reviews*

"A warm, loving and engaging story."
—*RT Book Reviews* on *His Small-Town Girl*

"Delightful characters make [this] story touching
and somewhat mysterious."
—*RT Book Reviews* on *Her Small-Town Hero*

"James' engaging story points to the importance
of following one's heart."
—*RT Book Reviews* on *Building a Perfect Match*

"James' story touches the heart
and brings tears to the eyes."
—*RT Book Reviews* on *A Match Made in Texas*

ARLENE JAMES

His Small-Town Girl

and

Her Small-Town Hero

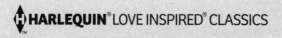

HARLEQUIN® LOVE INSPIRED® CLASSICS

Recycling programs
for this product may
not exist in your area.

ISBN-13: 978-0-373-60604-7

HIS SMALL-TOWN GIRL AND HER SMALL-TOWN HERO
Copyright © 2014 by Harlequin Books S.A.

The publisher acknowledges the copyright holders
of the individual works as follows:

HIS SMALL-TOWN GIRL
Copyright © 2008 by Deborah Rather

HER SMALL-TOWN HERO
Copyright © 2008 by Deborah Rather

www.Harlequin.com

Printed in U.S.A.

CONTENTS

Books by Arlene James

Love Inspired

The Perfect Wedding
An Old-Fashioned Love
A Wife Worth Waiting For
With Baby in Mind
The Heart's Voice
To Heal a Heart
Deck the Halls
A Family to Share
Butterfly Summer
A Love So Strong
When Love Comes Home
A Mommy in Mind
**His Small-Town Girl
**Her Small-Town Hero
**Their Small-Town Love
†Anna Meets Her Match
†A Match Made in Texas

A Mother's Gift
"Dreaming of a Family"
†Baby Makes a Match
†An Unlikely Match
The Sheriff's Runaway Bride
†Second Chance Match
†Building a Perfect Match
Carbon Copy Cowboy
Love in Bloom
†His Ideal Match

*Everyday Miracles
**Eden, OK
†Chatam House

ARLENE JAMES

says, "Camp meetings, mission work and church attendance permeate my Oklahoma childhood memories. It was a golden time, which sustains me yet. However, only as a young widowed mother did I truly begin growing in my personal relationship with the Lord. Through adversity He has blessed me in countless ways, one of which is a second marriage so loving and romantic it still feels like courtship!"

After thirty-three years in Texas, Arlene James now resides in Bella Vista, Arkansas, with her beloved husband. Even after seventy-five novels, her need to write is greater than ever, a fact that frankly amazes her, as she's been at it since the eighth grade. She loves to hear from readers, and can be reached via her website, www.arlenejames.com.

His Small-Town Girl

Then the King will say to those on His right, Come, you who are blessed of my Father, inherit the kingdom prepared for you from the foundation of the world. For I was hungry, and you gave me something to eat; I was thirsty, and you gave me drink; I was a stranger, and you invited me in.
—*Matthew* 25:34–35

To Virginia,
because friends are just chosen family, because sisterhood in Christ runs deeper than blood, because there's always lots of living left to be done and because it's never too late to find love.

Chapter One

The sweet, clean aroma of freshly harvested fields invaded the low-slung sports car as it flew along the narrow ribbon of road, its sun roof open to the autumn breeze. Tyler sucked in a deep breath, feeling the last of his tension drain away, as if a great weight had lifted from his chest. Finally.

When he'd walked out of the board meeting in Dallas, almost four hours ago now on this last day in a long and difficult week, his only thought had been to find some peace somewhere. For Tyler this meant shutting off his cell phone, climbing into his expensive cinnamon-red car and hitting the road for a good, long drive. Operating from sheer impulse, he'd headed north, avoiding the most well-traveled roads, and now he found himself in Oklahoma on Highway 81, a smooth, level two-lane stretch with little traffic for a Friday afternoon.

A blinking yellow light brought his attention to the dashboard. He depressed a button on the steering column and saw via a digital readout that at his current rate of speed he could drive exactly 8.9 miles with the fuel remaining in his gas tank. Time to pull over. A glance at the in-dash clock showed him that the hour had gone six already.

Glancing around in the dusky light of an autumn evening beginning to fade into night, he saw nothing but empty fields bisected with the occasional lazily drifting line of trees and railroad tracks running at twenty or thirty yards distant alongside the highway. Bowie, the last town he'd passed before crossing the Red River, lay many miles behind him to the south, many more than he could cover with the fuel remaining in the tank, anyway. There must be a local source of gasoline, however. People had to drive around here, didn't they? Wherever here was.

Tapping the screen of his in-dash global positioning system, Tyler noted that the small community of Eden, Oklahoma, some 2.3 miles ahead, offered a gasoline station. Confident that he would find what he needed there, he sped off.

Moments later, a female voice announced, "Right turn ahead." Seconds after that, the GPS intoned, "Right turn in two miles." Less than a minute later that changed to, "After two hundred yards, turn right. Then turn left."

Braking, he reached over and shut off the voice prompt. "Thank you, darlin'. I'll take it from here."

When he turned off the highway onto the broad, dusty street, given the appearance of the few buildings he passed, the whole place seemed deserted, and the quaint three-pump filling station that he pulled into some moments later proved no exception. The overhanging shadow of an immense tree all but obscured the faded sign that identified the station as Froggy's Gas And Tire.

Engine throbbing throatily, Tyler eased the sleek auto close enough to the door to read the posted business hours, which were 6:00 a.m. to 6:00 p.m., Monday through Saturday. Used to twenty-four-hour service, Tyler felt his jaw drop. Six to six? And closed on Sundays? Talk about turning back time.

Shaking his head, he tapped the GPS again and learned, to his chagrin, that the next nearest station could be found in Waurika, some 19 miles distant. A check on his fuel status showed a mere 6.1 miles left in his tank, thanks to his burst of speed back there, which meant… The implications hit him like a ton of bricks.

Stuck! He was stuck in the middle of nowhere. At least until six o'clock in the morning.

His intent had been to get away from the fighting, arguments and manipulation for a while, not to disappear for a whole night. He hadn't brought so much as a toothbrush with him, let alone a change of clothing. Clearly, he had to do something.

Finding solutions had become his stock-in-trade. In fact, that very trait had prompted his father to choose him over his older sister and younger brother to head the family company, much to the angry disappointment of his siblings.

Tyler reached for his cell phone. As with most businessmen, the mobile phone constituted both a necessity and an irritant for Tyler Aldrich. In the ten months since he'd been named CEO of the Aldrich & Associates Grocery store chain, it had become more headache than help, giving his family unfettered access to his ear, into which they never missed an opportunity to pour complaints, arguments and increasingly shrill demands. No doubt by now they'd filled his mailbox with as many acrimonious messages as it would hold. Nevertheless, the phone was his ticket out of here. He'd simply call for assistance—or would have if he'd had service.

Tyler sat for several moments staring at the tiny screen in his hand, disbelief rounding his light blue eyes. He'd switch to a satellite phone the instant he got back to Texas!

Even as he wondered how the people around here got along without cell-phone service, the thought of satellites calmed him. The phone might not work, but the car's satellite uplink obviously did or he'd have no GPS. Duh. He hit the button on the dashboard and put his head back, waiting for the connection to be made and an operator's voice to offer help through a tiny speaker just above the driver's door.

After Tyler identified himself and stated his problem, the customer service rep assured him that help would reach him in four to six hours. Dumbfounded, Tyler began to shake his head, wondering how he might pass the time.

He looked around him. A sheet-metal fence enclosed what appeared to be a scrap yard, flanked on one side by the filling station and on the other by a small, shingled house with a tall, concrete stoop. The house stood as dark and silent as the station. Otherwise, Tyler would have been tempted to knock on the door in hopes of rousting the station's proprietor.

With no immediate options presenting themselves, he checked out the local accommodations via the GPS.

He found just two listings, a café and the Heavenly Arms Motel.

He'd passed the motel on his way into town. Not at all up to his usual standards, it had appeared neat and clean, at least, but he could not quite resign himself to spending the night away from home when a tank of gas would have him on his doorstep before—he checked his watch—3:00 a.m. If he was lucky. Better check out that café and tank up on coffee.

A short drive around town revealed a liberal sprinkling of oil pumps across the landscape. One even occupied a bare patch of dirt next to the tiny city hall, a modern contrast to the three blocks of storefronts that seemed to comprise "downtown" Eden. Most looked as if they'd been built in the 1930s. And every one sat locked up tight as a drum, including the Garden of Eden café.

In fact, except for the old-fashioned streetlights and a few silently glowing windows of the modest homes lining the broad streets, Eden, Oklahoma, might have been a ghost town. That evoked an odd sense of loneliness in Tyler, as if everyone had a place to go except him. Well, he'd wanted peace and quiet; could be, he'd gotten more than he'd bargained for.

Easing the expensive sports car back out onto 81, he noted wryly a small sign that proclaimed, You're In Eden, God's Country And The Land Of Oil!

God apparently closed up shop at 6:00 p.m. sharp. Someone, thankfully, had forgotten to tell the local motel, though.

The low, lit sign that stood in a narrow patch of grass in front of the small motel glowed invitingly in the deepening gloom. The Heavenly Arms Motel, it read, Low Rates, Monthly, Weekly, Nightly. Family Owned And Operated.

Surely he could spend a few hours there. At the very least, he ought to find some information and possibly even assistance. All he needed were a few gallons of high-test, after all. Failing that, he could always get a room. He made a left just past the sign and pulled up beneath the overhang at the end of the main building, which looked more like a stylized ranch house than a motel lobby. A sign on the edge of the overhang proclaimed, Vacancy, which did not surprise him one bit.

Tyler killed the engine and got out of the car. The air held a crispness that he had not yet noticed in a Dallas October, which accounted for his lack of an overcoat. Bypassing a small side window to be used, according to the accompanying sign, after 10:00 p.m., Tyler followed a concrete ramp to the narrow porch that ran the length of the front of the building.

He opened the door marked Welcome and walked into a homey room complete with a polished wood floor, worn leather couches and, in the very center of the room, a six-sided game table surrounded by an equal number of chairs. A potbellied stove squatted in one corner. In another stood a chest-high, L-shaped counter with a pair of black painted doors behind it.

The far door bore a sign proclaiming it the office. The other door was marked Private. Through that door a young woman appeared mere seconds later, smiling as if greeting a lifelong friend.

"Hello. How are you?"

A pretty little thing with thick, light auburn hair that

fell from a slight widow's peak in a long braid down the center of her back, she stood no more than average height, the comfortable jeans and faded chambray shirt beneath her white bibbed apron somehow emphasizing her slight frame, just as the widow's peak emphasized the shape of her face, a slender, slightly elongated heart.

Despite delicate features and a smattering of freckles across the nose, her finest assets were large, hazel eyes—a vivid amalgam of gold, silvery-blue and muted green—thickly fringed with platinum and framed by slender brows. She wore no cosmetics and no visible jewelry, but then she didn't need to. Such beauty required no accessory beyond wholesomeness, and that she possessed in abundance.

Tyler might have brusquely stated his problem, could even have complained. Instead, he found himself returning her smile, a sense of delight eclipsing his irritation. Natural, well-used charm effortlessly oozed forth.

"Since you asked," he replied lightly in answer to her question, "I'm stranded. Yourself?"

Her smiled widened, and his spirits unaccountably lifted.

"Never better, thank you."

She untied the strings around her slender waist and lifted the apron off over her head before neatening the rolled cuffs of her long sleeves. Her thick braid swung over one shoulder, and her waist nipped in neatly where her shirt tucked into the band of her jeans. Tyler abruptly found himself thinking that he might as well spend the night.

For once he didn't have a Friday-evening engagement. Maybe, he thought, he'd even forget tomorrow's plans and stay the whole weekend. Why not? Might do his contentious family some good to wonder where he'd gotten to.

His mother didn't need an audience in order to complain about his late father's grasping second wife, anyway, and his sister and brother would just have to argue between themselves. He didn't give a second thought to the luxury stadium box where he routinely hosted guests less interested in professional football than in being seen with the right people, none of whom would ever think to look for him here.

For the first time in memory, he could simply let down his guard and be. It almost seemed foreign, such relaxation. Yet he shoved aside the niggling thoughts of responsibility, albeit responsibilities he'd strived to earn and fought to keep. Sometimes, responsibility just seemed to weigh too much. He deserved a little break, and Eden, it suddenly seemed, really did exist.

At least for the moment.

Charlotte recognized money when she saw it, especially when it stood right in front of her. One got used to all sorts in this business, from the most hopeless and downtrodden of God's children to the most flagrantly unlovable, and in her experience, those with the most money often fell into the latter category. They came in demanding more than they surely knew they could expect and often went away angry and dissatisfied, in spite of her best efforts to provide what they needed. That possibility was not what disturbed her about this particular gentleman, however.

For some reason, with barely a flick of his pale blue

gaze, he made her nervous, self-conscious in ways she hadn't felt in years. Tall and fit with stunning pale blue eyes and thick, dark hair that swept back from his square-jawed face in subdued waves, he differed significantly from their normal clientele.

For one thing, she'd rarely—okay, never—seen such a well-dressed, well-groomed gentleman. Oh, more than one well-heeled type had wandered in after finding themselves stranded, usually in the middle of the night, but something told her that even those folks operated in a social strata below this particular guest.

Other than that, though, she couldn't really put her finger on what made him so different. She only knew that he undoubtedly was, which did not mean that she would treat him any differently than she treated anyone else. Just the opposite, in fact. Her Christian principles demanded nothing less.

She ratcheted her smile up another notch and asked, "How can I help you?"

He sighed, making a rueful sound. "Unless you've got a few spare gallons of gasoline around, I guess I'll be needing a room for the night."

No surprise there. She'd heard this story before. Obviously, he should've kept a closer eye on the gas gauge. Giving her head a shake, she jerked a thumb over one shoulder.

"Sorry. That old truck out back runs on diesel. The room I can manage, though, if you can do without a kitchenette." She plunked down a registration form and pen, explaining, "Our regulars prefer them, so they're almost always taken."

"Regulars?" He sounded surprised, even skeptical.

"Most are oil-field workers who come to town periodically to service the local lines and pumps."

"You've got plenty of those around," he murmured, scribbling his information on the form.

"We sure do," she replied, taking a key from the rack hidden beneath the counter. "You're in—"

"Oil country," he finished for her, glancing up with a smile. "Or is that God's country?"

"Both," she confirmed with a smile, "but I was going to say number eight. Back row, south end. That's to your right. Your covered parking will be to the left of your door."

"Covered parking," he mused, clearly pleased by that.

"That'll be forty dollars and sixty-six cents, including tax."

Pulling his wallet from the inside pocket of his expertly tailored suit coat, he thumbed through the bills until he found a fifty-dollar bill. She unlocked her cash drawer and counted out his change while glancing over his registration form. When she got to the part concerning the make and model of his car, she understood why that covered parking had made such an impression.

Little garages, really, but without doors, the spaces were open only on one end. Her grandfather took inordinate pride in providing them for their guests, but none of them, Charlotte felt sure, had ever offered protection to anything remotely comparable to the car of— she peeked at his registration again—Tyler Aldrich. Well, no wonder. She casually shifted her gaze to the side window.

So that's what a hundred-thousand bucks on wheels

looked like. Smiling, she shoved a bunch of bills and coins at him, as if he needed nine dollars and thirty-four cents in change.

No doubt the rooms he usually rented cost ten times as much as what she had to offer. Then again, he happened to need what she had to offer.

Maybe he could afford a hundred-thousand-dollar car, but, as her grandfather Hap would say, he put his pants on just like everyone else; therefore, she would treat him like everyone else. She put out her hand.

"I'm Charlotte Jefford. Welcome to Eden, Mr. Aldrich."

"Thanks." Sliding his long, square palm against hers, he asked smoothly, "Is that Mrs. Jefford?"

Charlotte paused. Curiosity, she wondered, or flirtation? The next moment she realized that it couldn't possibly be the latter, and even if it was, it simply didn't matter. "Miss."

He smiled and let go of her hand. "Miss Jefford, then, could you advise me where I might find a meal? One that someone else prepares, that is, since the kitchenette is out of the question."

Charlotte laughed. "Easily. After dusk there's just the Watermelon Patch, about a half mile north of town. Can't miss it. Best fried catfish in the county."

He made a face. "Any chance they serve anything that's not fried?"

She considered a moment. "Beans and cole slaw." This did not seem to excite him. "They do baked potatoes on Saturday nights."

"That's a big help," he pointed out wryly, "since this is Friday."

"The truck stop in Waurika doesn't close until ten," she offered guiltily, thinking of the meat loaf she'd just pulled from the oven. "You can get a salad there." Provided he considered iceberg lettuce and a sprinkling of shredded carrots a salad.

"If I could get to Waurika, I wouldn't need a room," he pointed out with a sigh.

"Oh. Right." She bit her lip, glanced again out the window at that sleek red fortune-on-wheels and knew that her hesitation did not become her. If he'd pulled up in a pickup truck or semi, she'd have made the invitation without a second thought, had done so, in fact, on several similar occasions. So what stopped her now?

Simple appearance, perhaps? Next to his excellently groomed self, she couldn't help feeling a bit shabby in her well-worn jeans and old work shirt, not to mention the stained apron in which she'd greeted him, but that should not matter. Neither should what this smoothly handsome, well-dressed man would think about the simple apartment behind the unmarked door. The Bible taught that no difference should be made between the wealthy and the poor.

Putting on her smile, Charlotte mentally squared her shoulders and said, "You can eat here. It's just meat loaf tonight, with grilled potatoes, broccoli and greens, but at least none of it's fried."

His relief palpable, he chuckled and spread his arms. "Lead me to it. I'm starving."

Thankful that her brothers hadn't shown up for the evening meal as they did several times a week, she waved him around the end of the counter and indicated the door through which she'd entered. The unexpected company would surprise her grandfather, but she knew that he would be nothing less than gracious. They'd shared their table with hotel guests before, after all, and no doubt would do so again, though they really didn't get all that many strangers stopping in.

They had only twelve rooms, and most of their guests were locals who rented by the month or employees of one of the oil firms that paid handsomely to have rooms constantly available. Several of the truckers who routinely drove along this route stopped in on a weekly basis, usually on Tuesdays or Thursdays, but they didn't get many travelers in this area who weren't there to visit family. Strangers simply had no reason to come, which made her wonder again how Tyler Aldrich happened to be there.

Perhaps he was headed to Duncan and simply hadn't realized how far it could be between gas stations, particularly at night. If Oklahoma City were his destination, surely he'd have used the interstate to the east, while a direct trip to Lawton would have taken him through Wichita Falls. All four cities, she knew for a fact, had Aldrich Grocery stores.

Or maybe he wasn't connected to Aldrich Grocery at all.

What mattered was that he needed a little hospitality, and hospitality, as Granddad would say, was the Jefford family business. More than that, the Lord commanded it in one of Charlotte's favorite passages from the twenty-fifth chapter of Matthew.

Feeding the hungry, giving drink to the thirsty and inviting in the stranger were tenets upon which her grandparents had built their lives as well as their business. She sincerely tried to follow the example set by those two godly people. She'd just never dreamed that would mean inviting a rich man to her humble table.

Chapter Two

Tyler slipped around the end of the counter, quickly falling in behind his unexpected hostess, unexpected in more ways than one. Charlotte Jefford surprised him, not only with her pure, wholesome beauty and wit but with her warmth. He had not intended to spend the night in this place, but since he must he might as well enjoy himself.

Expecting to enter a small coffee shop or café through that private door, he felt momentarily disoriented to find himself standing in what appeared to be a dining room. For one long, awkward moment, he could do nothing more than try to take in the place.

Despite the lack of windows, the light seemed softer, warmer somehow, so that the room came across as homey and intimate if somewhat shabby. An old-fashioned maple dining set with five chairs occupied the greater portion of the room. A sixth chair stood between an overflowing bookcase and the door through which they had just entered.

Three more doors opened off the far wall, all closed

at the moment, but Tyler's attention focused on the old man who sat at one end of the oval dining table. As he bent his head over a Bible on the flowered, quilted place mat, his thinning white hair showed a freckled scalp, leaving the impression that he had once been a redhead. He looked up when Charlotte spoke, his faded green eyes owlish beneath a thick pair of glasses, which he immediately removed.

"This is my grandfather."

At the sight of Tyler, surprise flitted across the old man's lean, craggy face, replaced at once by a welcoming smile. Rising in a slow, laborious motion, he put out his hand. Tall and lean but stooped and somewhat frail, he wore a plaid shirt beneath denim bib overalls.

"Hap Jefford," he said in a gravelly voice. "How d'you do."

Tyler leaned forward to shake hands, careful not to grip those gnarled fingers too tightly.

"Tyler Aldrich. Pleased to make your acquaintance." Looking helplessly to Charlotte, who moved past the table toward the kitchen beyond, Tyler tamped down his unease and forced a smile. "I'm, uh, afraid I misunderstood the situation. I thought you had some sort of little restaurant back here."

"Goodness, no," Hap Jefford said with mild amusement, lowering himself back down onto his seat. He waved toward the chair on his left, indicating that Tyler should also sit. "Eating places are real workhouses. Time was my Lydia thought putting in a restaurant the thing to do, back when we were young enough to hold up and it seemed our boy might join the business here."

Hap shook his head, adding, "Not to be. They're both gone to the Lord now. Him first, God rest him."

Tyler hardly knew what to say to that, so he pulled out the chair and sat, nodding sagely. After a moment, he went back to the problem at hand.

"I really don't want to intrude. When your grand-daughter said I could eat here, I naturally thought—"

"Oh, don't worry," Hap interrupted. "We got plenty. She always cooks so her brothers can eat if they're of a mind. Evenings when one or the other don't drop by, we have to eat the leftovers for lunch the next day."

Tyler relaxed a bit. "Sounds as if you don't much care for leftovers."

Hap grinned, displaying a finely crafted set of dentures. "Now, I never said that. Charlotte's a right fine cook. I just don't mind a little unexpected change from time to time."

Tyler laughed. "I can understand that."

"How 'bout yourself?" Hap asked conversationally.

Not at all sure how to answer that, Tyler shifted uncomfortably. "Are you asking how I feel about leftovers or change?"

"Start with the leftovers."

Tyler had to think about that. "I don't think I've ever actually had leftovers as such."

Hap seemed shocked, but then he shook his head, grinning. "Where're you from, boy?"

"Dallas."

"Now, I'd have thought they had leftovers in Dallas," Hap quipped.

Charlotte entered just then with plates, flatware and paper napkins. Hap closed the Bible and set it aside.

"Won't be long now," she announced, placing a delicate flowered plate on the flowered mat in front of Hap. She placed another in front of Tyler.

"You really don't have to feed me," Tyler said uncomfortably as she set the third plate on the mat to Hap's right.

"Don't be silly." She reached across the table to deal out case knives. "It's ready. You're hungry. Might as well eat."

Tyler sensed that declining or offering to pay would insult both of the Jeffords, so he watched silently as she passed out forks and napkins, leaving a stack of the latter on the table.

"Iced tea or water?" she asked. "Tea's sweet, by the way."

"Water," Hap answered. Glancing at Tyler, he added, "Don't need no caffeine this time of evening."

"Water," Tyler agreed, hoping it was bottled.

"I'll be right back."

"Don't forget the ketchup," Hap called as she hurried away.

"As if," came the airy reply.

"Her grandma thought ketchup was an insult to her cooking," Hap confided to Tyler.

"It is when you put it on everything on your plate," Charlotte chided gently, returning from the kitchen with glassware and a pitcher of iced water.

"Oh, I just put it on my taters and meat loaf," Hap said with a good-natured wink at Tyler.

"And your eggs and your steak…" Charlotte retorted, placing the items on the table and moving away again "…red beans, fish, pork chops…" She stopped in the open doorway and turned to address Tyler. "He'll put it on white bread and eat that if there's nothing else on hand."

"That reminds me," Hap said with a wink at Tyler. "Don't forget the bread."

Charlotte gave him a speaking look and disappeared, returning moments later with a half-empty bottle of ketchup and a loaf of sliced bread in a plastic sleeve. She placed both on the table and went away without a word, but the twinkle in her eye bespoke indulgence and amusement.

"Thank you kindly, sugar," Hap called at her receding back. Smiling broadly, he proceeded to open the plastic and take out a slice of bread, squeeze ketchup onto the slice and fold it over before biting off half of it.

Tyler would have winced if his attention hadn't been snagged by something else. The bread wrapper bore the Rich Foods label, the private label of the Aldrich Grocery chain. Aldrich & Associates Grocery had several stores in Oklahoma, of course, and distributed some foodstuffs to independents, but seeing that label there distressed him. It took only a moment to realize why.

He didn't want the Jeffords to connect him with the Aldrich family who owned the grocery chain. He didn't see why they should, really. They might not even know that the Rich Foods brand belonged to the Aldrich Grocery chain, but it seemed very important suddenly that they not make the connection.

All his life, he'd had to worry whether he was liked for himself or his family position. Just once he wanted to know that someone could be nice to him without first calculating what it might be worth. He couldn't even remember the last time anyone had invited him, on the spur of the moment, to share a simple meal for which he was not even expected to pay.

Stunned by the abrupt longing, Tyler spread his hands on his thighs and smiled with false serenity as Hap licked ketchup off his fingers, his expression one of sublime enjoyment. When was the last time, Tyler wondered, that he had enjoyed something that much, especially something so basic?

Charlotte came in again, wearing heavy mitts this time and carrying a casserole dish. When she lifted the lid on that casserole, a meaty aroma filled the room, making Tyler's mouth water and his stomach rumble demandingly. Given a choice in the matter, he never ate meat loaf. Ground beef, in his estimation, rarely constituted healthy eating. But what choice did he have?

She brought the rest of the meal in two trips: crisp round slices of browned potato with the red skins still on, steaming broccoli and a dish of dark greens dotted with onion and bits of bacon. Simple fare, indeed, but Tyler could not remember ever being quite so hungry. Intent on the food, he startled when Hap spoke.

"Heavenly Father..."

Tyler looked up to see Charlotte and Hap with hands linked and heads bowed in prayer. Stunned, he could only sit and stare in uneasy silence.

"We thank You for Your generosity and for our guest. Bless the hands that prepared this meal and the food to the nourishment of our bodies, that we might be strengthened to perform Your will. In Jesus' name. Amen."

"Amen," Charlotte echoed, lifting her head.

Tyler gulped when her gaze collided with his. Belatedly, he realized that she had reached out to offer him a small spatula. When it finally dawned on him that she expected him to serve himself, he shook his head.

"Oh, uh, ladies first."

Smiling, she began to cut the meatloaf into wedges. Not one to stand on ceremony, Hap dug into the potatoes and plunked the platter down in front of Tyler, reaching for the ketchup. After a moment hunger trumped discomfort, and Tyler began to gingerly fill his plate.

Everything looked, smelled and, to his surprise, tasted delicious. The greens took a little getting used to, but the broccoli and seasoned potatoes were wonderful, and that was saying something, given that he employed an expensive chef and routinely dined in the finest restaurants to be found. The meat loaf, however, came as the biggest surprise.

Melt-in-the-mouth tender with a beguiling blend of flavors, it whet his appetite to a greedy fever pitch. He ate with unaccustomed gusto, and only with gritted teeth did he find enough discipline to forgo a third helping. Hap apparently possessed no such compunction, but as he reached for that third wedge, Charlotte spoke up.

"Pity no one's found a way to take the cholesterol out of beef. You can cook as lean as possible, but there's still that."

Hap subsided with a sigh. Looking to Tyler he commented wryly, "I keep telling her that no one lives forever in this world, but it seems she's in no hurry to see me off to the next." Charlotte made no comment to that, just smiled sweetly. "My first mistake," Hap went on, "was letting her take me to the doctor."

"Mmm. Guess you could've hitchhiked," she commented calmly.

Tyler found himself chuckling as Hap latched onto that gentle riposte with clownish fervor, drawing himself up straight in his chair. "You don't think some sweet young thing would come along and take me up, then?"

Charlotte looked at Tyler and blandly said, "If she happened to be driving an ambulance."

Laughter spilled out of the two men, unrestrained and joyous. Tyler laughed, in fact, until tears clouded his eyes. Whatever clever rejoinder Hap might have made derailed when the door to the lobby opened and two more elderly men strolled in.

"Y'all are having fun without us," one of them accused good-naturedly.

Hap introduced them as Grover Waller and Justus Inman. A third man identified as Teddy Booker called from the outer room, "I'm stoking this here stove. These dominoes are cold as ice!"

Hap got to his feet, eagerness lending speed if not agility to his movements. "You play dominoes, Tyler?"

"No, sir, I'm afraid not."

"You all go on," Charlotte said, "and don't stay up too late. I'll heat up some cider after a while."

"We'll be having some popcorn, too," Hap decided.

"I was hoping for carrot cake," Grover Waller said at just a notch above a whine.

"Now, Pastor," Charlotte told him, "you know you have to watch your sugar."

A belly as round as a beach ball, thin, steel-gray hair sticking out above his ears in tufts and brown eyes twinkling behind wire-rimmed glasses gave the preacher a jovial appearance that belied the mournful tone of his voice as he complained, "You've been talking to my wife."

"And she says you've got to lose twenty pounds or go back on meds," Charlotte confirmed.

He thinned his somewhat fleshy lips and hitched up the waist of his nondescript gray slacks before turning away with a sigh.

"Oh, the burden of a caring wife," Hap intoned, following the two men from the room.

"Seems to me you used to call it meddling," someone said.

"We all do until they're gone," another gravelly voice put in before the door closed behind them.

Charlotte shook her head, smiling. "They're all widowers except for the pastor," she explained. Tyler didn't know what to say to that, so he simply nodded. "They live to play dominoes, those four, and really, what else have they got to do? Well, three of them, anyway. Pastor Waller's nearly twenty years younger than the others, and he's got the church."

"I see."

After an awkward moment of silence, she rose and began to clear the table, saying, "Just let me put these in the kitchen and I'll point you to your room."

The idea of going off alone to a cold, less than sumptuous room did not appeal to Tyler. Rising, he heard himself say, "Can't I help you clean up?"

He didn't know which of them seemed more surprised. After a moment, Charlotte looked down at the soiled dishes in her arms.

"It's the least I can do after such a fine meal," Tyler

pressed, realizing that he hadn't even complimented the cook.

"I suppose your wife expects you to help out at home," she began, shaking her head, "but it's not necessary here."

"No," he denied automatically. "That is, no wife."

"Ah." Charlotte ducked her head shyly. "Well, if it'll make you feel better to help out…"

"Oh, it will," he said, lifting a dish in each hand and following her toward the kitchen. "I never expected a home-cooked meal, especially not such a healthy one." She looked back over her shoulder at that, just before disappearing into the other room. "And tasty," he added quickly, raising his voice. "Very tasty. Delicious, even."

Hearing her wry "Thanks," he stepped into a narrow room with doors at either end.

Countertops of industrial-grade metal contrasted sharply with light green walls and cabinets constructed of pale, golden wood. The white cooking range in the corner by what must have been the outside door looked as if it came straight from the 1950s, while the olive-green refrigerator at the opposite end of the room appeared slightly newer. Tyler noted with some relief that a modern thermostat for a central air-conditioning system had been mounted above the light switch on one wall. He hoped the rooms were similarly equipped.

What he did not see was a dishwasher. It came as no surprise, then, when Charlotte set down the dishes and started running hot water into the sink below the only window he had yet seen in the small apartment. Covered with frilly, translucent curtains in yellow trimmed with green, that window looked out over a small patio lit by a single outdoor light. Leaves swirled across the patterned brick, snagging on the thin legs of wrought-iron furniture in need of a new coat of green paint.

"You can put those down there," Charlotte said, indicating the counter with a tilt of her head.

Hurrying to do as instructed, Tyler looked up to find her tying that white apron around her impossibly narrow waist again. Quickly switching his gaze, he watched suds foam up beneath the running water as she squeezed in detergent.

"Better take your coat off," she advised.

He did that, then looked around for someplace to hang it before walking back into the other room to drape it over a chair. It only seemed sensible to pick up the remaining dishes before heading back to the kitchen.

Returning, he found that Charlotte had already made order out of chaos, stacking the dirty dishes as they were evidently to be washed. Glassware came first, followed by plates, flatware, serving dishes, utensils and finally pans. The leftover food had disappeared into the refrigerator, from which she turned as he entered the narrow room.

"I'll take those," she said, coming forward.

He surrendered the two plates and platter, then watched her scrape food scraps into a bucket beneath the sink, which she then sealed with a tightly fitting lid before stacking the dishes with the others. Turning, she placed her back to the counter, her gaze falling to the neatly cuffed sleeves of his stark-white shirt. Her mouth gave a little quirk at one corner as she reached for a pair of yellow vinyl gloves and pulled them on.

Wordlessly, she turned to the sink now billowing

with suds, and reached for a plate on the stack to her right. While she washed and rinsed, Tyler wandered haplessly across the room, taking in a calendar from a local propane company on the side of the refrigerator and a clock shaped like a rooster over the stove. When he turned he saw a cookie jar in the form of an owl on the opposite counter next to a small microwave and a glass-domed container covering three layers of a dark, rich, grainy cake iced with frothy white. Several pieces had already been cut from it.

"Is that carrot cake?" he asked.

She sent him an amused glance. "Of course. Want a piece?"

A hand strayed to his flat middle, but thinking of the extra time on the treadmill required to work that off, he said, "Better not."

She hitched a shoulder, handing him a wet plate with one hand and a striped towel with the other. Tyler had hold of them before he knew what was happening, but then he just stood there, confused and out of place.

Plunging her hands back into the soapy water, she asked smoothly, "Are you going to dry that or just let it drip all over those expensive shoes?"

He looked down, saw the dark droplets shining on black Italian leather and quickly put the towel to good use.

"That dish goes in the cabinet behind you," she told him, a hint of amusement in her tone. "Door on the far right."

Stepping across the room, he opened the cabinet, found an empty vertical space separated by dowels and slid the dish into it, noting that two sets of dishes were stored there, cheap dark brown stoneware, chipped in places, and the poor-quality flowered china from which he had eaten.

He realized at once that she had served him from her good plates. Both embarrassed and gratified, he left the door open and went back for more plates. A short stack of clean, wet dishes stood on the metal counter-top beside the sink.

"Looks like I'm behind," he admitted unashamedly. "But then, I've never done this before."

She smiled and added another dish to the pile. "I know."

Laughing, he got to work, making small talk as he dried and shelved the dishes. "How does a woman such as yourself come to be working in a motel?"

Looking out the window, she replied matter-of-factly, "Her parents die and she winds up living with her grandparents, who just happen to own and operate that motel."

"My condolences," he offered softly.

"It happened a long time ago," she replied evenly, glancing at him. "I was fourteen."

"Eons ago, obviously," he teased, hoping to lighten the mood. She ducked her head.

"Thirteen years."

That would make her twenty-seven, he calculated, a good age. He remembered it well. Had it only been eight years ago? At the time it had seemed that thirty would never come and his father would live forever. Yet, Comstock Aldrich had died of pancreatic cancer only nine months ago, leaving Tyler to fill his gargantuan shoes at Aldrich & Associates. After only ten months in the job, Tyler felt old and burdened, while Charlotte Jefford seemed refreshingly young and…serene.

He blinked at that, realizing just how much that calm serenity appealed to him. It fairly radiated from her pores.

"What about you?" she asked.

He studiously did not look at her. "Oh, I'm thirty-five, an executive, nothing you'd find interesting, I'm sure. You mentioned brothers. Older or younger?"

A slight pause made him wonder if she knew that he'd purposefully been less than forthcoming. "Older. Holt's thirty-six, and Ryan's thirty-four. Holt was working in the city when our folks passed, and Ryan was in college, so naturally I came here."

"The city?"

"Oklahoma City."

"Ah. And these brothers of yours, what do they do?"

"Well, Holt is a driller, like our daddy was. The price of oil these days keeps him pretty busy. He's got a little ranch east of town, too. I can't help worrying some, because that's how Daddy died." She looked down at her busy hands, adding softly, "He fell from a derrick." An instant later, she seemed to throw off the melancholy memory. "But everything's more modern now, safer, or so Holt says."

"I see."

"Ryan," she went on, warming to her subject, "he's the assistant principal at the high school. He teaches history, too, and coaches just about every sport they offer. Football, baseball, basketball, volleyball, even track." She gave Tyler a look, saying, "In a small town, you have to do it all."

"Sounds like it."

"Do you have brothers and sisters?" she asked.

"One of each. She's older. He's younger." *And they hate my guts,* Tyler thought, surprised by a stab of regret.

"Children?"

He shook his head. "Never married."

"Oh. Me, neither." She shrugged. "You know how it is in a small town, slim pickings."

He actually didn't know, and he didn't care to know. What he did care about surprised him. Put plainly, he wanted her to like him. He wanted her to like him for himself, not for social status or wealth or any of the other reasons for which everyone else liked him, because he could give them things, because his last name happened to be Aldrich.

For the first time in his life, it mattered what someone thought of him, someone who didn't know the Aldrich family, someone without the least claim to influence or wealth, someone willing to invite him, a stranger, to dinner. Someone who would take him at face value.

It mattered, even if he couldn't figure out why.

Charlotte saw her guest to the kitchen door, which opened on the same side of the building as the drive-through, and pointed across the way to his room. After thanking her profusely for the meal, he walked toward his car. Looking in that direction through the screen, she recognized her brother Holt's late-model, double-cab pickup truck as it turned into the motel lot. The truck swung to the left and stopped nose-in at the end of the building next to the pastor's sedan.

"You're late," she called as he stepped down from the cab, his gaze aimed at the man now dropping down behind the driver's wheel of that expensive sports car. Still wearing his work clothes, greasy denim jeans and jacket over a simple gray undershirt, Holt had at least traded his grimy steel-toed boots for his round-toed, everyday cowboy pair.

Tall and lean, Holt took a great deal after their grandfather in appearance, though with different coloring. A lock of his thick, somewhat shaggy, sandy-brown hair fell over one vibrant green eye, and he impatiently shoved it back with a large, calloused, capable hand as bronzed by the sun as his face was. His long legs and big, booted feet ate up the ground as he strode toward her.

"Who's that?" he asked, pulling wide the screen door and following her into the kitchen.

"Name's Tyler Aldrich," she answered. "I'm pretty sure he's one of the Aldrich grocery store family."

Holt lifted an eyebrow. "What gives you that idea?"

"Just a hunch."

She liked to shop at an Aldrich store and had often driven as far as fifty miles to do so. More than once she'd seen the large photograph of an older man identified as Comstock Aldrich affixed to a wall over the motto, From Our Family To Yours. She couldn't remember enough about that man's face to say whether or not Tyler resembled him in any way, but she'd seen the way Tyler had reacted when she'd plopped that loaf of bread on the table.

Normally, with a guest in attendance, she made hot bread or at least served the sliced variety stacked on a pretty saucer. Tonight she'd left that bread in its wrapper just to see what he would do. He'd stared as if he'd thought the thing might pop up, point a floury finger and identify him.

"Supposing he is who you think he is, what's he doing here?" Holt asked, going to the refrigerator to take out the plate of leftovers she'd stowed there earlier. "You reckon he's going to open a store hereabouts? That'd be cool."

Charlotte frowned. She hadn't thought of that possibility. After all, he'd said he was stranded, and she had no reason to doubt him. Except that just then he drove by in that flashy car of his. Apparently he had *some* gas. She turned to look at her brother, who carried the food to the microwave and set the timer.

"An Aldrich store might be very welcome," she said, "unless you're Stu Booker."

Stu had taken over the local grocery from his father, Teddy, who sat at the domino table in the front room with Hap at that very moment.

Holt turned to lean against the counter. "I see what you mean. Another grocery would put Booker's out of business." The microwave dinged, and Holt reached inside to remove the plate, asking, "Still got that carrot cake, I see."

"Yes," Charlotte muttered, "but you'll have to eat it in here. Grover's playing dominoes tonight."

Nodding, Holt took a fork from the drawer and strolled into the other room and toward the lobby, his big boots clumping on the bare floor. "I'll be back, then. Thanks, sis."

"Welcome," she answered automatically, her mind on other matters.

Should Aldrich Grocery put in a store here, the Bookers would undoubtedly suffer. It was, she decided, a matter for prayer. And perhaps a bit of subtle investigation.

Chapter Three

Charlotte glanced at her watch, more than a little miffed.

On weekdays, she started cleaning the rooms as soon as the oil-field workers left in the mornings and by this time usually could be sitting down to lunch with her grandfather. On Saturdays, she got a later start because the workmen liked to sleep in a bit before heading home to their families. Lunch, therefore, came later on Saturdays, but not normally this late.

It was already past twelve, and she still had one room left to do before she could begin preparing the midday meal, thanks to Tyler Aldrich. On a few occasions she'd had to put off the cleaning until the afternoon, but that pushed her workday well into the night as she had a weekly chore scheduled for each afternoon.

Saturday afternoons were reserved for washing and rehanging drapes. If she didn't do at least three sets of drapes each week, she'd either be a week behind or have to do it on Monday, the day she shampooed carpets. Tuesday afternoons were dedicated to outside windows,

Wednesdays to replacing shower curtains, Thursdays to cleaning oil stains off the pavement and policing the grounds. Fridays she cleaned the lobby top to bottom and did the shopping.

In this fashion, she not only cleaned every occupied room each day, she completely freshened every room once a month, while maintaining the lobby and grounds on a weekly basis and keeping their storeroom stocked. Hap did his part by handling the registration desk and banking, balancing the books, ordering supplies and helping out with the daily laundry.

She did not appreciate having her carefully balanced schedule upset. Obviously, the man had no idea what it took to keep an operation like this running smoothly. Then again, few folks did. Deciding that she was being unfair, she left the service cart on the walkway in front of number eight and rapped her knuckles on the door. She began slowly counting to ten, intending to walk away if he hadn't answered by then. She'd reached seven before the door wrenched open.

Tyler Aldrich stood there in his bare feet, rumpled slacks and a half-buttoned shirt, looking harried and ir- ritated, his dark hair ruffled. A day's growth of choc- olate beard shadowed his face. If she'd had to guess, she'd have said he hadn't slept very well.

He wrinkled his face at the glare of the sun and de- manded, "What *is* that noise?"

"Noise?" She glanced around in puzzlement.

He put a hand to his head. "Ka-shunk, ka-shunk. All night long."

"Oh, that noise. There's a pump jack out back."

He sighed. "Of course. Oil pumps. Should've figured that one."

"I'm so used to the sound, I don't even notice it anymore," she admitted, "but we don't get many complaints about it." They hadn't actually had any complaints about it until now.

"I don't suppose it would bother me if it wasn't so quiet around here," he grumbled.

Well, which is it, she wondered, saying nothing, *too quiet or too noisy?*

He put a hand to the back of his neck. "Didn't think I'd ever get to sleep, especially after those two fellows showed up about midnight."

"What two fellows?"

He waved a hand at that. "Roadside service sent them. I called before I stopped in here. Then after I decided to stay, I forgot to call back and tell them not to bother bringing me gas."

"They came at that time of night just to bring you gas?" she asked in disbelief.

"A few gallons," he muttered. "I still have to fill up."

She shook her head. The rich really did live differently than everyone else. "I hate to be an inconvenience, but I need to clean this room before I feed Granddad."

Nodding, he hid a yawn behind one hand. "Yeah, okay, just give me a few minutes to get out of your way."

"I'll be right here when you're ready," she told him politely, linking her hands behind her back. No way was she going away again. Experience had taught her that a guest would just head straight back to bed and she'd have this exercise to repeat.

Tyler gave her a lopsided grin. "Swell. Uh, listen, can I get breakfast at that café downtown?"

"Sure," she answered, and then for some reason she couldn't begin to fathom she went on. "But if you're willing to settle for lunch, you can eat with us again."

He stopped rubbing his eyes long enough to stare at her, his brow beetled. "Lunch?"

Wondering why she'd issued the invitation, she hastily backtracked as far as good manners would allow. "Just sandwiches, I'm afraid. I don't have time for anything else."

"What time is it, anyway?"

She didn't even have to look. "About ten minutes past noon."

Tyler goggled his eyes. "Noon? You're sure?" She held up her wrist, just in case he wanted to check for himself. His sky-blue eyes closed as he turned away. "I must've slept a lot better than I thought."

"You mean you're not used to sleeping till noon?" She clapped a hand over her mouth, shocked at herself. She never made unwarranted assumptions about people. Well, hardly ever. Fortunately he had not noticed.

"Not anymore," he muttered enigmatically, looking for something. Finding it, he hurried over to snatch his footwear from the floor beside the low dresser that held the television set. Plopping down in the chair that pulled out from the small desk in front of the window, he began yanking on his socks. "Sorry about this. I'll get out now and let you clean."

"No problem."

"Say, is there someplace I can buy a toothbrush and shaving gear?" he asked, rising to stomp into his shoes.

She hesitated a moment before telling him, but really, what harm could it do? "Booker's will have everything you need. Just go out here and turn right." She pointed behind her. "They're a block east of downtown."

Nodding, he stuffed in his shirttail and reached for his suit jacket. "Thanks."

He started toward her, then stopped and went back to snatch his wallet and keys from the bedside table attached to the wall. With a glance in her direction, he picked up the room key and pocketed that, too.

Did he intend to stay another night? That didn't seem like the behavior of a man who just happened to have gotten stranded by an empty gas tank. On the other hand, he'd obviously been unprepared to stay. Maybe he just needed someplace to clean up before he headed out of town. Knowing that she should give him the benefit of the doubt, she backed up as he came through the door.

He went to his car while she maneuvered the service cart into the room. A moment after that, the low-slung car rumbled to life.

She whispered a prayer as she stripped the sheets from the bed. "He's not a bad sort, Lord, but the Bookers have been here a long time, generations, and I know You look after Your own."

For the first time, she wondered if Tyler Aldrich, too, could be a believer. A shiver of…something…went through her, something too foolish to even ponder.

"Well, hello, there! Abe Houton."

For at least the fourth time in the space of the past ten minutes, Tyler put down what could well be the best, not to mention the cheapest, cup of coffee he'd ever tasted in order to shake the hand of a stranger. Dallas owned a reputation as a friendly city, Tyler mused, but tiny Eden, Oklahoma, put it to ridiculous shame.

He cleared his throat, managed a brief smile and returned the greeting. "Tyler Aldrich."

Built like a fireplug, short and squat, Abe Houton sported a fine handlebar mustache that would have made Wyatt Earp as proud as the tall brown beaver cowboy hat poised on Houton's bald head.

"Good to meet you, Tyler. Welcome to Eden. Haven't seen you around here before. What brings you to town?"

Tyler would have wondered if the shield pinned to Abe Houton's white, Western-style shirt had more to do with the question than simple friendliness but for the fact that he'd been asked the same thing repeatedly since he'd come into the Garden of Eden café. And he hadn't even had his buckwheat flapjacks yet.

When he'd sat down at this small, square table in the window, he'd intended to fill his time with people-watching while he dined on an egg-white omelet or a nice bagel with fat-free cream cheese and fruit. Unfortunately he'd become the center of attention for everyone who passed by and the healthiest breakfast he could come up with from the menu was whole-grain flapjacks. The forty-something waitress with the hairnet had openly gaped when he'd asked her to hold the butter and inquired about organic maple syrup.

Tyler looked the local policeman in the eye and repeated words he'd already said so many times that they were ringing in his ears. "Just passing through."

"Aw, that's too bad," the diminutive lawman remarked, sounding as if he meant it. "This here is a right fine town."

Tyler sat back against the speckled, off-white vinyl that padded the black, steel-framed chairs clustered around the red-topped tables. A floor of black-painted concrete and, oddly enough, knotty pine walls provided the backdrop. What really caught the eye, though, was the old-fashioned soda fountain behind the counter.

"I hope you don't mind if I ask what's so special about this town," Tyler said, truly curious.

Houton rocked back on the substantial heels of his sharp-toed brown cowboy boots, one stubby hand adjusting the small holster on his belt. The pistol snapped inside looked like a toy. Then again, Houton himself resembled a stuffed doll. Tyler had to wonder just how lethal either might be.

"Why, this is Eden, son," the little man declared, as if that answered everything. Then, with unabashed enthusiasm he added, "You should see our park."

"You mean the park at the end of the street?"

"So you have seen it! Bet you didn't notice the footbridge. My daddy helped build that footbridge out of old train rails. Prettiest little footbridge you'll ever see. Really, you should stop by and take a look."

Tyler didn't know whether to laugh or run out and take a look at this local wonder. Fortunately, the waitress arrived just then with his flapjacks, along with a dish of mixed berries, a jug of something that passed for syrup and a refill of aromatic coffee. Houton excused himself with a doff of his hat to straddle a stool at the counter, his feet barely reaching the floor.

Lifting the top edge of a suspiciously tall stack, Tyler

saw that succulent slices of ham had been sandwiched between the airy brown flapjacks. A sane, sensible, health-conscious man would remove the meat. A hungry man would just dive in. A self-indulgent one would pour on the so-called syrup and enjoy. Tyler reached for the jug, thinking that he had nothing better to do all day than work off a few extra calories.

An unexpected sense of freedom filled him as he watched the thick, golden-brown liquid flow down. Maybe, he thought, surprising himself, he'd even check out the park.

Nearly half an hour later, Tyler made his way out of the small café, nodding over his shoulder at those who called farewells in his wake. Stuffed to the gills and ridiculously happy about it, he decided that he might as well walk off some of what he'd just consumed and left the car sitting in the slanted space across the street where he'd parked it in front of a resale shop. Hands in his pockets, he strolled along the broad, street-level sidewalk, nodding at those who nodded at him in greeting, which was everyone he encountered. Even old ladies driving—or, more accurately, creeping—down the street in their pristine ten-or twenty-year-old cars waved at him. Tyler nodded back and kept an eye peeled for someplace to work up a good sweat.

He came rather quickly to the park and spied at a distance the aforementioned footbridge spanning the creek that bisected the gently rolling lawn studded with brightly leaved trees. Erosion from the banks of the creek colored the shallow water red-orange, which seemed oddly apt in this autumn setting.

Concrete benches scattered beneath the trees invited

him to sit for a spell, but he resisted the urge. Picnic tables clustered in one section of the broad space.

A few children and a pair of adult women peopled a playground near the small parking area, where carelessly dropped bicycles awaited their young riders. Tyler turned away, wondering what he was doing in Eden, Oklahoma. He pondered that as he strolled back toward his car.

A plump woman in baggy jeans and an oversize sweater swept leaves off the sidewalk in front of a small white clapboard church on the corner nearest the park. Tyler thought he recognized the sedan parked in front of the modest brick house beside it as one he'd seen at the motel last night, but he couldn't be sure. Walking on he realized that the boxy two-story building behind the church actually belonged to it, easily tripling the building's size.

He got in the car and set off to purchase toiletries, taking in the town along the way. All of Eden had been laid out in neat, square blocks that made navigation laughably simple. Turning off Garden Avenue, he meandered along Elm and Ash streets. Elm offered primarily commercial buildings, but Ash hosted the most substantial homes he'd yet seen. Constructed of brick and mottled stone, most with square or round pillars supporting deep, broad porches, none could be described as stately and all dated from the 1920s and '30s.

Noting that he'd driven into town on Pecan, he wondered if all the streets were named for trees. Turning on the GPS, he sat with the engine idling at a stop sign long enough to study a city map. It turned out that only the streets running east and west were named for trees.

The streets running north and south were named for flowers. He smiled at such fanciful monikers as Lilac, Sunflower, Iris and Snapdragon.

Marveling at the neatness and simplicity of the city scheme, he looked up. A check of his rearview mirror revealed an SUV queued up behind him. He had no idea how long it had been there, but instead of blaring the horn, as any driver in Dallas would have done instantly, the frothy-haired woman behind the wheel gave him a cheery wave. Saluting in apology, Tyler pulled out and made his way to Booker's.

The store fascinated him. Occupying a former ice house, it served as a historical microcosm of progress over the past half century, with goods ranging from a fair but mundane selection of groceries to cosmetics and cheap bedroom slippers.

He bought the necessary items, paying cash, before taking himself back to the motel, where he shaved and brushed his teeth. He put off showering in hopes of finding an adequate health club somewhere close by. Relishing the thought of working himself into a state of sweaty exhaustion, he walked over to the motel lobby in search of information.

Charlotte adjusted the heat on the heavy-duty clothes drier, set the timer on her watch, checked the load in the washer and walked back into the apartment through the door that opened from the laundry room to the kitchen. Moving swiftly, she passed through the dining room and on into the reception area. With Hap and his buddies at the domino table, she need not worry about having the front desk staffed and so turned at once toward the office. A familiar voice stopped her in her tracks.

"I wonder if you gentlemen might tell me where I can find some workout clothes and a gym?"

Laughter erupted.

Rolling her eyes, Charlotte moved at once to the counter. Justus had all but fallen off his chair, while Teddy and Hap tried to maintain some semblance of good manners, without much success. Tyler stood before the game table, his hands in the pockets of his pants as he waited stoically for their amusement to die away. At length, Hap cleared his throat.

"Only gym hereabouts is down to the high school, son."

"If you're wanting a good workout, though, you can get that out at my place," Justus teased. "I got about a hunerd head of cattle what need feeding and a barnyard full of hay ready for storage. Keys are in the tractor."

Justus chortled at his own joke, while Teddy snickered and Hap kept clearing his throat in a belated effort to remain impassive. Torn between amusement and pity, Charlotte leaned both elbows on the counter and interjected herself into the conversation.

"He looks like he's in pretty good shape to me, Justus. You never can tell, Tyler might be able to shift those big old round hay bales without a tractor."

Tyler shot her a wry, grateful look over one shoulder.

"He could get one on each end of a metal bar and lift 'em like weights," Teddy suggested with a big grin.

"Speaking of weights," Charlotte went on, addressing Tyler directly as he turned to face her. "If that's what you're interested in, I could always call my brother. He could get you into the field house."

"That would be, um, Holt?"

"Ryan. Holt's the older one."

Tyler nodded. "The driller. Among other things."

Uncomfortably aware that the other three men were suddenly listening avidly, Charlotte kept her tone light. "Exactly. Ryan's the coach—"

"History teacher, assistant principal," Tyler finished for her. "I wouldn't want to put him out."

"Well, he's your best bet," she said a bit more smartly than she'd intended. "Nearest health club is around fifty miles from here."

Tyler looked lost for a moment. Then Hap laid down his dominoes. "Here now. We could use a fourth for forty-two. Straight dominoes has me bored to tears. You wouldn't consider sitting in, would you? Least ways until Grover finishes his sermon for tomorrow."

Tyler shifted his weight from foot to foot. "I don't know how to play forty-two."

"Oh, we'll teach you," volunteered Justus, as if making amends for his teasing earlier. "Won't we, Teddy?"

"Sure thing. He can play opposite Hap."

To Charlotte's surprise, Tyler pulled out the empty chair at the table. "Does that mean we're partners?"

"That's what it means," Hap answered, obviously pleased that he'd picked up on that. Hap began turning the dominoes facedown and mixing them up. "Since I'm paired with the new kid, I get first shake." He looked to Tyler, instructing, "Now draw seven."

Hanging over the counter, her chin balanced on the heel of her hand, Charlotte got caught up in the game.

She jerked when her timer beeped. By then, Tyler had learned enough to engage in a bidding war with Justus. Ill-advised, perhaps, but gutsy.

"Two marks."

"Three."

"You don't even know what you're doing," Justus warned.

"Then your partner can take me off."

"I'm not bidding four marks. You two are nuts."

Charlotte laughed as she slipped through the door into the apartment, hearing Hap declare, "Lead 'em, partner. I got your off covered."

It wouldn't surprise her one bit if the newbie made his bid and taught a couple of old dogs a new trick or two, but why that should please her so, she couldn't say.

Chapter Four

The sun hung low over the horizon when Charlotte heard footsteps scraping on the pavement. She pulled her bulky, navy-blue cardigan a little tighter and crossed her legs before reaching over to close the Bible on the low, wrought-iron table at her elbow to keep the breeze from ruffling the pages. Picking up her coffee cup, she sipped and smiled with contentment.

This was her favorite time of day. With the work done and Granddad's dinner in the oven, she could steal a few minutes to just sit out on the patio and ponder. What would normally be a moment of supreme relaxation, however, suddenly became tinged with something else as Tyler Aldrich strolled around the corner of the building.

"Hello, there."

She shifted in her seat, uncomfortable with the way he made her feel and a little ashamed for it. Pushing the unwelcome feelings aside, she smiled in greeting. "Hello, yourself. Game's over, I take it."

He grinned. "Grover just showed up."

"Ah. Lost your seat, then."

"I don't mind. Looks like I found another one." He pointed to the chaise next to her. Like her own chair, it lacked padding and the dark green paint had flecked off in places, but he didn't seem to care. Good manners demanded that she nod, and he sat down sideways, using the elongated seat like a bench. "At least your grandfather didn't seem particularly eager to lose me as a partner."

Charlotte laughed. "He likes to win, and Grover's too polite to trounce the competition. You must've caught on well."

Tyler shrugged. "I have a good head for numbers, and it's a pretty entertaining game. Kind of like bridge. Do you play?"

"Bridge? No. Forty-two, absolutely, but usually just with the family, my brothers, Granddad and me."

"So tell me something. What is nello?" Tyler asked.

Charlotte chuckled. "Am I to understand that they wouldn't let you bid nello?"

"Never came to that. It's just something Grover said as we were playing out my last hand."

She explained that a nello bid meant the exact opposite of a trump bid. Instead of trying to catch enough tricks and count to make the bid, the nello bidder tried not to catch a single trick or point, despite having to lead the first trick.

Tyler nodded with satisfaction. "Makes sense now. I didn't have a domino larger than a trey that last hand."

"And Grover would have seen that. He does love to play nello," Charlotte put in.

Glancing around in the softening light Tyler commented, "I can't remember the last time I spent half the day playing games."

"Sounds like a case of all work and no play to me." She sipped from her mug, realizing belatedly that her hospitality lacked something. She held up the cup. "Care for coffee?"

"Decaf?"

"Sorry, no, but I've got some if you want to wait for it to make."

"Don't bother. I'm pretty content as I am." He leaned back slightly, bracing his palms on the edge of the chaise. "You're one to talk about all work and no play. I never realized how much work even a small motel can be." He waved a hand. "Hap filled me in on some of what you were doing all day."

Had Tyler asked where she was? She tried not to let the possibility feel too good or even think about why it did. This man would be gone tomorrow. Her interest in him was a matter of hospitality, nothing more. Or it should be. She couldn't imagine why it was necessary even to tell herself such things. Hadn't she learned, long ago, that she should live her life without romantic entanglements? In her experience, someone usually got hurt. Once was quite enough for her.

She managed to shrug and say off-handedly, "Well, there's always Sunday. We don't even staff the front desk then. No reason to, really. Our regular trade runs Monday through Friday."

"I'd think traffic would pick up on the weekend," he mused.

"Not really. Most of it's local. A few trucks come through. Not much else."

"Must make for a slow, easy life," he observed.

"Slow, maybe. Easy? Well, that depends."

He nodded. "Right. I wouldn't say that what you do is easy."

"Oh, it's not that hard, especially if you establish a routine. Mostly it's just time-consuming."

"Did you never want to do anything else?" he asked.

She answered without thought. "Not really. I didn't feel called to teach school or what have you. Don't see any point in waiting tables or clerking when I can do this, and trust me, I'd make a lousy secretary." She shook her head. "This always felt right for me."

"I guess your grandfather is happy about that."

"I'm not sure he's really thought about it. He loves this life, and I don't think he ever imagined I wouldn't."

"Do you?"

"Sure. I wasn't certain at first." She shrugged. "Teenagers just want to be like everyone else, you know, even when they're working so hard to be different, and living in a motel is not the same as living in a house. That bugged me for a while."

Tyler chuckled. "I don't see you as a rebellious teen."

"Not at all," she admitted, "but I had to make my peace with this life. After Gran got sick and her heart weakened, I started taking over more and more of her work, and I had the satisfaction of knowing that it gave her comfort at the end to think Granddad wouldn't be shouldering all this alone."

"I can't imagine that he's up to much of the physical work," Tyler said carefully. "Arthritis?"

"Among other things," she confirmed, "but he doesn't let it get him down."

"Yes, I noticed that. He seems, well, happy. You don't know how lucky you are that he's so upbeat."

"Oh, I'm blessed, and I know it. My mother was just the opposite, you see, always worried, always feeling slighted and threatened. I sometimes don't know what my father saw in her."

"I do," Tyler said softly, "if she looked like you."

Stunned and dangerously thrilled, Charlotte floundered a bit, responding pragmatically to what she knew had not been a strictly practical comment. "Oh. No, actually. Her hair was much darker and…b-blue eyes. She was shorter, too."

His smile tightened. "I mean, she must have been as pretty as you, as wholesomely attractive."

Charlotte gulped. Of course she'd known what he meant, but for some reason she'd made him say it, and now that he had, she felt even more flustered. "Uh, yes. Th-that is, she was quite stunningly beautiful, actually. And I should've said thank you."

"You're welcome." A grin flashed across his face, then he threaded his fingers together around one knee, saying lightly, "Sounds as if you might have had some issues with your mother."

Charlotte ducked her head. Silly of her. It had been so long ago. Still, it was not a pretty story, not one to discuss with the merest acquaintance, anyway, even one who made her want to know him better, *especially* one who made her want to know him better. And especially with a man like him. Rich, probably even spoiled. What could he possibly know or care about her life? She adopted a light, airy tone.

"Doesn't everyone have issues with their mothers?"

He chuckled. "I suppose."

She changed the subject by inviting him to speak about himself. "I seem to recall that you mentioned a brother and sister."

"That's right." Nodding, he named Cassandra, who was just fourteen months older than him, and Preston, twenty-six months younger. "We all work together."

"Really? That sounds like fun."

"Hardly," he scoffed. "All that sibling rivalry makes for a crazy dynamic, especially since someone has to be the boss."

"And that someone would be you," Charlotte murmured, somehow knowing it.

He leaned forward, forearms against his knees. "That would be me," he admitted, "and my brother and sister both resent it. When they're not fighting with each other or our mother and stepmother, they're ganging up on me."

Charlotte absorbed that for a moment, thankful that she and her brothers had always gotten along quite well, though Holt and Ryan had been known to bicker and quarrel as youngsters. Their father, she recalled, had worked hard to make them friends. Many times he had told them that if they were kind to one another they would be best friends when they grew up. Apparently Tyler's parents had not succeeded in that regard with their children.

"Sounds difficult. I notice you didn't mention your dad."

Tyler clasped his hands. "He died about nine months ago from pancreatic cancer."

Charlotte sat forward. "I am sorry."

"Thanks." He studied her as if trying to decide whether or not she was sincere before adding, "The cancer came suddenly and hit hard. His death changed everything and nothing, if you know what I mean."

Charlotte shook her head, eyebrows drawn together. Her own beloved father's death had changed everything, absolutely everything, in her family's world. She couldn't imagine it being otherwise. "I'm not sure I do."

Tyler spread his hands, looking down at them pensively. "I-I'm not sure I can explain."

"You could try," she prodded gently, sensing that he needed to talk about it.

He sat in silence for so long that she began to feel embarrassed. Then suddenly he spoke.

"My parents divorced when I was twenty-four. I wouldn't say that it was a particularly acrimonious marriage, but no one was really surprised, not even when Dad married his secretary." He speared Charlotte with a glance. "Shasta is only five years older than me, and no one will ever know what she should have looked like, if you follow me."

"I'm assuming there's plastic surgery involved," Charlotte said, disciplining a smile.

"At sixty-one, Mother is a whole lot resentful, not that she hasn't had some tasteful work done herself, you understand."

Charlotte lifted her eyebrows slightly. "Sounds as if you have a very interesting family."

"Interesting I can handle," Tyler muttered, sitting up straight. "The real problem is that ours is a family business, and everyone has seats on the board, along with some longtime employees and investors. My brother and sister and I received shares throughout the years, always on an equal basis, mind you. Mom got hers in the divorce, and Shasta inherited hers when Dad died. Throw in the fact that Dad named me CEO a month before he passed, and it makes for some, shall we say, volatile board meetings." He lifted a hand to the back of his neck, adding, "To tell you the truth, I walked out of one of those meetings yesterday. That's how I wound up here."

"Wow." Charlotte shook her head, half-relieved because Tyler hadn't come to Eden with a mind to put in an Aldrich store, half-sympathetic because his family obviously plagued rather than blessed him. "And everyone thinks that a family with all the advantages of the Aldrich grocery store chain has it made."

Tyler stiffened, a look of such affront and disappointment on his face that Charlotte caught her breath, realizing abruptly how judgmental she must have sounded. Before she could even begin to apologize, he lurched to his feet and stalked away.

For a moment, she could do nothing more than gape at his retreating back. He'd covered about half the distance to his room before she hastily ditched the coffee and leaped up to follow, without even a clue as to what she would say when she caught up to him. If she caught up to him.

He couldn't believe it. There he'd sat thinking that Charlotte Jefford had to be the most refreshing, unassuming, genuine human being he'd ever met, and all along she'd known exactly who he was. She'd probably known from the moment he'd signed the guest registration card.

He had to hand it to her, though. She hadn't let on in any fashion. Not one simpering smile had slipped out, not one admiring titter, not one desperately suggestive whisper. Until the end. Until *after* he'd spilled his guts like some needy guest on one of those tawdry psychobabble talk shows.

What on earth had gotten into him? He'd never said those things to anyone. Any complaints he made about his personal life had always come back to haunt him. Generally his family would hear of them before the words were out of his mouth, not to mention his rivals.

His circles of acquaintance nurtured some notorious gossips, so he'd learned early on to keep his personal thoughts and feelings to himself. Every word out of his mouth could be, and often was, used against him in some fashion or another. He hadn't realized until just that very moment how confining and...lonely that had become. To his perplexed shame, he'd wanted her to know him, really know him, because somehow Charlotte Jefford had felt *safe*.

Let this be a lesson to him. Not even a quiet, seemingly serene stranger stuck out here in this small town in the middle of nowhere and nothing made a *safe* confidant, not for him, not when she had known who he was all along.

The bitter depth of his disappointment shocked him. She was nothing to him, nothing at all. Yet, he could not deny what he felt. Swamped with angry misery, he did not even hear her run after him, did not hear her calling his name, until she touched him, her hand slipping around to fall on his forearm.

"Tyler!"

He turned back before he could think better of it, and found himself looking down into her troubled hazel eyes. Something wrenched inside him, something frightfully needy. Making a belated attempt to extricate himself, he stepped away. "You'll have to excuse me."

"I'm sorry," she gasped. "I'm so sorry. I'm not usually that blunt or insensitive."

His defenses firmly in place now, a ready, hard-won insouciance surged forward, burying his disillusionment. "I can't imagine what you mean."

She looked crestfallen, ashamed. "I shouldn't have implied that money made you different or could solve all your problems."

"Problems?" he echoed lightly. "What would you know about my problems, anyway?"

He winced inwardly at that last, surprised by the inexplicable need to hurt her. As she, he realized with a jolt, had hurt him.

The wideness of her mottled eyes proclaimed that his jab had hit its mark; the frank, troubled depths of them told him that she would not retaliate in kind, increasing his guilt tenfold in an instant. Like intricate quilts of soft golds, greens and blues those eyes offered comfort and warmth, as well as surprising beauty.

"I'm sorry, Tyler. I—I don't know what else to say."

Anger leaked out of him like air from a balloon.

"No, I'm sorry. I overreacted."

Unable to maintain contact with those eyes, he

looked away. The unwelcome feeling that he owed her some explanation pushed words from him.

"How long have you known exactly who I am?"

When she didn't answer immediately, he speared her with an incisive glance. She looked confused.

"You mean when did I put you together with the Aldrich grocery stores?"

"That's exactly what I mean."

She shrugged. "As soon as I learned your name. Why wouldn't I put it together? It's perfectly natural to associate one thing with another. I didn't know for sure, of course, until I saw your reaction to the bread."

"So that was deliberate," he accused, more wounded than indignant.

"Serving the only loaf of bread I had in the house?" she asked plaintively, but then she bit her lip. "No, that's not fair. It was the only loaf, but I did want to see how you'd react."

Sighing, he pinched the bridge of his nose. Could he be a bigger fool? With Aldrich stores blanketing the seven states nearest to Texas, did he really think she wouldn't put it together?

"I won't tell anyone if it's that important to you," she vowed softly.

He nodded, miserable in a way he couldn't explain even to himself. "Yeah, okay. Thanks."

She moaned. "Oh, no."

He looked up. "What?"

"I've already discussed it with my brother," she confessed, grimacing.

Tyler threw up his hands, appalled at his own behavior and apparently powerless to change it. "Well, that's just great!"

A horrible thought occurred, staggering him. Stupid as it seemed, it spoiled so much that he hadn't even realized mattered to him. Unfortunately, though, it made an awful sense. Small towns were even more notorious for gossip than Dallas society. Everyone knew it. Everyone.

"That's why they were all so friendly to me today."

Charlotte blinked, obviously taken aback. "What are you talking about?"

"The whole town must know!" he erupted. "Why else would they fall all over themselves?"

Her jaw dropped, and for some reason that just stoked his temper, that and the secret, niggling knowledge that he'd gone from overreaction to completely unreasonable. It wasn't her fault. She couldn't help who he was or what she knew. How could she know that he'd hoped to remain incognito, so to speak?

"Now, that's just silly," she finally told him, folding her arms. "Folks in Eden are naturally friendly. It has nothing to do with who your family is!"

"How do I know that?" he demanded.

The compassion warming her eyes made him want to run and at the same time to reach for her. In the end, to his everlasting shock, she was the one to reach out, wrapping her slender arms around his shoulders.

"Oh, Tyler."

She placed her bright head on his shoulder, her face turned away from him. His indignation evaporated like so much mist, leaving behind a sheepish sense of foolishness and a deep chasm of pure need.

His hands somehow landed at her waist, tentatively

clasping the delicate curves. For several long, sweet moments it felt as if some calming, invisible balm flowed across his savaged nerve endings. Like parched earth soaking up gentle rain, he absorbed the comfort that she so effortlessly offered. How had she known that he needed this when he hadn't known himself?

"I always thought it would be a terrible burden to have too much money and to be known for it," she whispered.

He sighed, confessing, "It is not a simple life, that's for sure."

After several moments, she quietly asked, "Who hurt you so badly that you would be this suspicious of people who just want to be friendly?"

He squeezed his eyes shut. *Who hasn't?* he thought. He said, "When money's involved, you never know who your real friends are. I'm not sure you can even have real friends."

She pulled away at that, folding closed the front of the oversize cardigan that she wore over a simple plaid shirt, its tail tucked primly into the belted waistband of slender jeans. "Of course you can. Not everyone is after your money."

"You wouldn't say that if you'd been around when my father lay dying," he told her, pushing a hand through his hair. "Everyone behaved like a pack of jackals, snarling and snapping over every nickel and dime of his personal fortune. Contractors, business associates, even the upper management at our own company...." Tyler shook his head remembering that even his father's broker had wrenched every penny from the estate that he could by freezing his father's accounts and dumping them into interest-bearing escrow then slapping on every management fee he could dream up.

"Charities called up begging for final bequests," he told her. "Complete strangers accosted me on the street claiming that my father had promised them money." He threw up his hands. "The blasted doctor asked for a grant to do cancer research!"

He went on, telling her the details of those awful last weeks, the words pouring out of him as if they'd been too long pent up.

Granted, Comstock Aldrich had been a formidable force, and he'd never taken a step without calculating the return in dollars and cents, but surely he'd deserved some dignity in death, some consideration of his basic humanity. Instead, everyone around him had turned into vultures, picking over the corpse before he'd even drawn his last breath. It had fallen to Tyler to hold the scavengers at bay.

Her eyes sad, Charlotte listened patiently, murmuring occasional condolences.

"That's how it is when you have real money," Tyler finished glumly.

"I'm not surprised," she admitted softly. "I always imagined it would be like that. I'd rather have Christ, frankly."

Tyler tilted his head. He didn't have the faintest idea what she meant by that. How could anyone *have* Christ? And what did that have to do with anything?

Suddenly he felt out of place, out of sync. With a pang, he realized that he'd done it again, told her much more than he'd ever told anyone.

Shocked, he backed up a step, lifting a hand to the

nape of his neck. What was it about this woman that turned him into a babbling lunatic? Gulping, he wasn't even sure that he wanted to know.

"I-I've kept you long enough," he said politely, backing away.

She started as if just coming to herself. "I have to check the oven."

"I have to…" He waved an arm. Do something. Anything. But what?

Already moving away, she lifted a finger. "Could you hold that thought for a minute? I'll be right back."

Tyler watched her move across the pavement to the kitchen door of the apartment, then stood awkwardly while she went in, the screen slapping closed behind her.

He wanted to flee—and to stay, for some inexplicable reason, except, of course, that he didn't really have anyplace to go or anything to do. And he didn't want to be alone.

For once, Tyler realized with a pang, he really wanted not to be alone.

Chapter Five

Tyler had never known a moment of real want in his lifetime, but he realized that he had somehow always been alone. Even with servants in the house and a mother who had nothing better to do than socialize and shop, he'd spent a great deal of his childhood virtually by himself.

True, he'd basically done as he pleased, and as a boy he'd often preferred to tag along with various friends and their families rather than bicker unsupervised at home with his sister and brother. There had been whole years when he'd probably slept over at a buddy's place as many or more nights as he'd slept at home, and the fact that his family hardly seemed to notice had made him feel rather bereft at times.

Tyler didn't like feeling needy, but he liked even less the idea of spending the evening alone in that shabby little room behind him. Even as he warred with himself, he wandered closer to that kitchen door.

"Sorry, Granddad," he heard Charlotte say.

Hap said something in return, but Tyler couldn't

make out the words. It had been a long time since he'd felt so much on the outside looking in. He didn't like it one bit, but he didn't move away.

Charlotte returned a few moments later with a smile on her face. "I don't know why I thought he wouldn't help himself to his own dinner," she said, pulling the door closed behind her and stepping out of the way of the screen. "He is not, as he has reminded me, helpless."

Tyler chuckled and nodded. "I take it that the domino game has adjourned."

"Only so long as it takes them to eat dinner," Charlotte said with a grin. "Justus is in there, helping himself to one of Ryan's pot pies."

"You really do always cook extra for your brothers, don't you?" Tyler said. "Or is it really for them?" He nodded toward the lobby, indicating the inveterate domino players.

She shrugged. "Them or whoever."

It occurred to him that he would have to find his own dinner tonight, and that fact made him feel lonely again. Staring off toward the highway, he pondered just why that might be since he often ate alone.

Before he reached any sort of conclusion, a vaguely familiar, dirty white pickup truck swung off the shoulder of the road and turned into the motel property. The driver did not pull into the drive-through as a motel patron would have done but came to a halt right beside them.

A tall, lean cowboy hung out the window, flipping them a wave. "Hey, sugar! You about ready there? My belly's kissing my backbone."

Tyler remembered now why that truck seemed familiar. He'd seen it there before, just last night in fact. Obviously this cowboy made a habit of stopping by to see Charlotte. Jealousy struck Tyler like a hammer blow. In the same instant he realized how ridiculous he was being.

Of course she would have a boyfriend. The wonder was that she hadn't married already. He remembered something she'd said about the pickings being slim in a small town, but that didn't mean the local male populace wouldn't realize what a gem they had in their midst. They were probably in constant pursuit. If things were different, he might well be himself, not that he had the time and freedom for personal relationships, or the inclination to pursue them. Why bother when so few people could be trusted to look past his fortune? Besides, he had a very demanding job.

His life suddenly seemed rather shallow and truncated. Had distrust completely overtaken him? Why, even his father had found the time and fortitude to get married. Twice. Tyler found himself wondering just what it would take to win Charlotte away from the cowboy.

Belatedly Tyler realized that Charlotte was speaking.

"Knock off work a little earlier," she said with a cheeky grin, addressing the driver of that truck.

Tyler had missed whatever had led up to that point, but he assumed that this was in reference to the cowboy being hungry.

"Look who's talking," the fellow drawled. "Don't tell me you've been standing around here waiting for hours on end."

"We were sitting, actually," Tyler put in, quite without meaning to. "Well, most of the time." Couldn't hurt, he mused, to let the other man know that he might have a little competition.

Charlotte laughed and waved a hand at Tyler. "Holt, this is Tyler Aldrich. He's been keeping me company, and I guess we did kind of let time get away from us. This is my brother Holt."

Her brother. Tyler didn't know whether he felt more relieved or embarrassed, which meant that he wound up being both, not that he let on. Putting out his hand, he stepped closer to the truck.

"Pleased to meet you."

"Likewise."

Holt reached across himself to shake hands, but the gesture contained a certain wariness. Tyler sensed that the eyes hidden in the shadow of that hat brim keenly assessed him. The grip of that calloused hand held a hint of warning, too, as if its owner wanted him to know that force could be brought to bear should it prove necessary.

"Come on, sprite," Holt called to Charlotte. "My dinner's waiting."

She skipped forward, brushing a hand against Tyler's forearm. "Maybe you'd like to join us? I know you haven't eaten, and the café closed at six."

Tyler smiled to himself. That was one problem solved.

"But be warned," she cautioned, "we're headed to the catfish joint."

"What's wrong with catfish?" Holt wanted to know. "We eat catfish every Saturday night."

"You eat catfish every Saturday night," she corrected. By way of explanation, she added to Tyler, "Holt takes either me or Granddad to dinner every Saturday night."

"Sometimes both of you," Holt put in.

"But not often," she clarified. "Someone usually has to stay here in case a guest drops in. It's my turn to go out this week."

"I see."

"You might as well come," she prodded. "It's either the Watermelon Patch, the truck stop up in Waurika or driving an hour or so to find another restaurant."

Tyler smiled, his decision made from the moment she'd issued the invitation. "I'd like to come along. Thank you."

Beaming, she hurried around the front end of the truck to the passenger door, Tyler following on her heels.

"After all," he said, reaching around to open the door for her, "I have to eat. Might as well do it in good company."

Perhaps the food wouldn't be particularly healthy, but no matter, and he didn't care what the tall cowboy behind the steering wheel might have to say about it. Charlotte's pleased smile gave him all the encouragement he needed, and then some.

Charlotte could not quite believe her own audacity. Imagine a man like Tyler Aldrich at a hole-in-the-wall like the Watermelon Patch. Then again, he'd rented a room in her motel and would apparently be staying a second night. She mentally shook her head. Slumming, perhaps? Or could he be as lonely as he seemed?

God knew that she wouldn't be in his shoes for anything in this world. Money like Tyler seemed to possess could only be a burden. He'd said so himself. At least she knew that her friends and family loved her for herself. She looked over at Holt, her fingertips brushing his shoulders fondly. He seemed to take that as a cue, lifting his gaze to the rearview mirror and the man in the backseat.

"Aldrich, huh? Charlotte says you're connected with the grocery stores. That so?"

She heard Tyler shift on the cloth seat. "Yeah, that's right. It so happens I'm CEO of Aldrich & Associates."

Holt let out a thin whistle, thin enough to let Tyler know that he wasn't too impressed. She cut her eyes at her brother, tempted to pinch him. What was wrong with him? Holt never behaved rudely. Perhaps he didn't trust as easily as Ryan and Granddad, but he could always be counted on to be friendly and fair, except…

She widened her eyes, remembering another time when Holt had been less than cordial, less than welcoming. He took his position as big brother to heart, and he'd never quite trusted her one serious boyfriend. To this day, Holt seemed to suspect that Jerry had broken her heart, rather than the other way around.

The implications shook her. Surely, Holt did not consider Tyler Aldrich to be a romantic prospect. The man lived in Dallas! He was passing through Eden, nothing more. Scoffing at the very idea, she fixed her big brother with a stern, wide-eyed stare.

He jerked his head at her, as if asking what he could possibly be indicted for, but she looked at him until he sighed and slumped in his seat. Smiling to herself, she turned her gaze out the window.

The rest of the drive passed in silence.

The Watermelon Patch restaurant proved to be something of a revelation for Tyler. For one thing, it sat smack dab in the middle of a real, honest-to-goodness watermelon field, though Tyler wouldn't have known that if Charlotte hadn't told him. In the dark, it looked pretty much like any empty field to him, but then he knew little about watermelons beyond when they were in season and the mark-up per unit. The building itself claimed most of his interest, though.

Cobbled together of sheet metal and weathered wood, mismatched windows, a variety of shingle types in several different colors and—amazingly—a sliding-glass door that appeared to have been salvaged from a burned-out house, the structure would not have passed any legal standard anywhere in the United States of America.

Oily smoke chugged from a leaning stack pipe on one end of the building, smudging the night sky with dirty gray and blanketing the whole area with the aromas of frying foods, while specks of light and a virtual cacophony of voices spilled out of the chinks and cracks in the walls. The whole thing looked as if it might tumble down should an errant breeze come its way.

Despite the restaurant's decrepit appearance, the joint seemed to literally jump with the movement of bodies packed inside. Automobiles of every description crowded the sandy parking area, but Holt didn't let that deter him as he angled the tall, long truck into a narrow space between a tree at the edge of the road and a massive propane tank. The tree stood so close to the passenger side of the truck that both Tyler and Charlotte had to slide across the cab to exit on the driver's side, Charlotte from the front seat, Tyler from the back.

He saw at once that he hadn't underestimated Holt's height. Tyler stood a solid six feet in his socks, but Holt had at least three inches on him, and that did not count the heels of his boots or the tall crown on that cowboy hat. Tyler doubted very much that had anything to do with why Holt removed the hat, revealing a handsome head of thick, sandy-brown hair and vibrant green eyes.

"Looks like another full house," he said, placing the hat, brim up, on the truck seat before closing and locking the door.

"Come Saturday night, you can't even find an empty chair to lay a hat on in there," Charlotte explained to Tyler.

Looping a brotherly arm around Charlotte's shoulders, Holt walked her toward the restaurant, leaving Tyler to trail along behind them. He did not think it unintentional. Wondering how long they'd have to wait before a table opened, he kept up.

In the restaurants that he normally frequented, Tyler didn't do much waiting, but he didn't mind the idea of cooling his heels a bit just now, provided he didn't do it standing alone in some dingy corner while Holt chatted up Charlotte across the room. He wouldn't put that little maneuver past Charlotte's brother, which partly amused Tyler and partly irritated him. Usually, the family members of young women cultivated his interest rather than shunned it. Perhaps that accounted for his general lack of interest.

To Tyler's surprise, they did not wait at all. Instead, a plump, fortyish, ponytailed, bleach-blond, gap-toothed waitress led them through a rabbit's warren of tables and chairs, across uneven floors, to a short bench against the back wall. Charlotte and Holt took seats on the bench. The waitress—Joanie, Tyler thought he heard her called—then shoved a narrow plank table in front of them, jostling several other patrons in the process. Next she plunked down sets of flatware tightly wrapped in paper napkins. Finally, she dragged over a chair for Tyler, its wooden legs bound up with wire to keep them from spreading.

He'd barely lowered himself onto the scarred seat when Joanie produced a pencil and pad, asking, "So what'll you folks have this evening?"

Tyler glanced around. "I, um, seem to have missed the menu."

"Oh, there's no menu, sugar," Joanie told him, cracking the chewing gum tucked into her cheek. "There's just catfish, taters, beans and slaw. All I need to know is how many pieces you want."

"Pieces?" He looked to Charlotte for clarification.

"Of fish."

"I'll have four," Holt announced decisively.

"Two," Charlotte said when Joanie looked to her.

The waitress turned her heavily lined eyes on Tyler. He picked a number for sheer symmetry's sake.

"Put me in between with three, I guess."

"How do you want those potatoes?"

"Fried," Holt answered.

"Baked," Tyler said at the same time.

They looked at each other, then away.

"None for me, thanks," Charlotte said.

"You want that spud loaded?" Joanie asked.

"Sour cream only. Fat-free, if you've got it." She gave him a bland look over the top of her pad. "Never mind."

"I'll bring y'all's tea and cornbread in a minute." She danced off, twisting and turning and smacking her gum.

Other diners shifted around in their chairs to greet the Jeffords, reaching across one another to shake hands with Tyler as Holt gave them his name. Conversation engulfed them.

"You find a buyer for that old rig yet, Holt?"

"Not looking."

"I hear Sharp's lease has expired."

Holt just shook his head at that.

"Hap keeping Ryan in line tonight, I guess."

"He's got some school deal tonight," Charlotte answered.

"More like the other way around, anyhow," Holt put in, and laughter followed.

"Did you hear that Jenny Tumm's old mother passed?" someone asked from across the room. "Died in her sleep, they say."

"She must've been a hundred," someone else observed.

"Ninety-seven," another voice contended. "I'll tell you how I know."

A recitation of names, dates and weather patterns followed, devolving quickly into various reminiscences about droughts and deluges survived, tornadoes succumbed to and a horribly late frost that had prodded the proprietor to hedge his bets with a restaurant in case his melons failed to make it again. Weather, it turned out, held a prominent place in the local, agriculture-based psyche.

Tyler listened unabashedly, caught up in the feel of community that must be particular to small-town life. Like a large family dinner, everyone talked over one another while they ate, but no one shouted in anger as often happened on those rare occasions when the Aldrich brood sat down together.

Charlotte's eye would catch his from time to time, and a small, knowing smile would curve her lovely lips, as if she saw how fascinating and foreign he found all this. He didn't try to hide his interest, only to retain a polite dignity, and to let her know that he enjoyed himself. He couldn't, in fact, recall an occasion when he'd enjoyed himself more.

Joanie returned to plunk down plastic baskets of steaming cornbread squares and tall jars of iced tea, accompanied by a bowl of sugar, another of lemon wedges and a third piled high with butter spooned out of a tub. With the possibility of bread plates dim at best, Tyler followed Holt's lead and reached for a square of that high, light, mouth-watering cornbread, his belly suddenly growling.

The bread burned his hand, but the aroma wouldn't let him put it down. Breaking off pieces with his fingertips, he poked them into his mouth, and closed his eyes as they seemed to melt on his tongue. Holt, meanwhile, slathered his piece with enough butter to guarantee a heart attack in a less fit man and scarfed it down in a single bite. He then proceeded to stir half a cup of sugar into his already sweet tea and suck the glass dry, while Charlotte looked on. Tyler held off as long as he could on a second piece of cornbread, straining his vaunted control.

Ever since his seemingly healthy father had been diagnosed with cancer, Tyler had tried to live with an eye to his own body's well-being. He'd developed an exercise routine, with the help of a private trainer, and consulted a dietitian on food choice and preparation. He'd hired a chef trained to produce whole-grain, low-fat, well-balanced dishes on a Mediterranean model with Asian influences, and routinely chose restaurants based on their ability to accommodate his preferences.

He'd limited caffeine, forsworn all but the most moderate amounts of alcohol, avoided secondhand smoke and cut out sugar and white flour. In truth, he hadn't missed a single item that he'd given up. But then he'd never eaten cornbread so sweet and soft and buttery that it all but fell apart on its way to his watering mouth or tea so fragrant and smooth that it begged to slide down his throat.

He'd already tossed prudence to the wind by the time Joanie brought a second basket of what Charlotte referred to as "corncake" to the table along with paper-lined baskets of golden fish fillets heaped atop thick slices of crisp fries, or in his case, crowded around a steaming potato the size of a football. This came accompanied with generous bowls of red beans and coleslaw and cups of creamy tartar sauce. Tyler managed to resist only the latter. The rest of it remained untouched only so long as it took Holt to pray over it.

Tyler tried not to appear uneasy when brother and

sister joined hands and bowed their heads over the rough table. He might have succeeded if the whole place hadn't gone suddenly quiet, allowing Holt's voice to carry.

"Heavenly Father, we thank You for Your bounty and seek Your blessing on this food and all those within the confines of this building. Keep us mindful of Your love and grace. We pray in the name of Your Son. Amen."

"Amens" wafted around the building. Tyler shifted, feeling uncertain. These Jeffords were sure praying people. Praying at the dinner table in the privacy of one's home was one thing, but he'd never seen anyone pray in such a public setting before. Here, however, it seemed perfectly acceptable.

Knives and forks clinked, someone laughed and conversation resumed, quickly growing to previous decibels. Holt attacked his food like a man starved.

Tyler tried to display more control, cringing a little at the grease glistening on the crispy coating of the fish. He flaked some of the breading off with his fork, but in the end he ate every piece and wished he'd ordered more. The potato, baked to perfection and heaped with sour cream, filled his mouth with warm, hearty delight. He quickly filled up, but still managed to taste the beans and slaw.

At least he intended only to taste the slaw. Surprised by the fresh flavor of the shredded cabbage and other vegetables, he ate all of the coleslaw despite the calorie-rich dressing. Only later did he reflect that the meaty, tasty beans probably comprised the most healthy part of the whole meal, but he simply didn't have room for more than a few bites.

Charlotte ate steadily, but after Holt polished off

what he'd been served, he finished her portion and sat eyeing what Tyler had left over until Joanie returned with dishes of peach cobbler swimming in cream. Too full even to be tempted, Tyler shoved his dessert across the table and watched it disappear beneath Holt's spoon while Charlotte made a fair dent in hers.

Sighing with satisfaction, Holt at last sat back, stretched out his long legs and crossed his ankles, his heels on the floor next to Tyler's chair. "Now that's what I call eating."

Tyler laughed. "I'd hate to see what you call pigging out."

"I'm a hardworking man," Holt said with mock defensiveness, his green gaze settling on Tyler. "What is it exactly that a CEO does?"

Tyler knew when he was being measured, and he also knew that a man like Holt wouldn't be impressed with mere position. He wouldn't demean himself by trying to convince Charlotte's brother that he did more than delegate. "A great deal."

"I'll bet," Holt said. Not a hint of disdain had colored Holt's voice, but neither did it contain even the barest inflection of admiration.

"I'm sure it's a huge job," Charlotte said quickly.

Warmed by her defense of him, Tyler just smiled. Tyler could feel another question hovering in the air, but he would not prompt it. Instead, he simply waited.

After a moment, a slight smile twisted one corner of Holt's mouth, but he did not disappoint. "So what's an important CEO doing in our little Eden?"

Tyler smiled to himself. "Just passing through."

"Don't take more'n a minute to just pass through," Holt pointed out.

Tyler propped his forearms against the tabletop. "Just biding my time, then."

"In Eden," Holt said doubtfully.

Tyler considered, but why dither? If pressed, Charlotte would undoubtedly repeat what he'd told her earlier. Why shouldn't she? "All right," he said. "If you must know, I'm hiding."

Holt sat forward abruptly, bracing his elbows on the table top. "From who?"

"From people who aggravate me."

"Is that a long list?"

"Long enough."

"But hopefully not growing," Charlotte said anxiously.

He chuckled. "Not lately."

Holt relaxed a bit, asking, "How long you plan on hiding out around here?"

"Oh, I don't know," Tyler answered, surprising himself. "Awhile yet."

"Well, you might as well come along to church tomorrow, then," Holt said.

The invitation sounded off-hand and casual, but Tyler knew better than that. He knew a challenge when he heard one. He knew, too, that he'd gain this man's respect only by attending church with the family the next day. Surprisingly, he found that he wanted this man's respect. That being the case, the decision seemed simple.

"Might as well. Nothing else to do, except sleep, and there's all afternoon for that."

Holt reached past Tyler, and when he drew back his

hand, he had the dinner tab tucked between two fingers. Tyler automatically reached for his wallet, but Holt waved him off.

"Naw, now, that wouldn't be neighborly."

Neighborly, as they both knew, had nothing to do with it. "At least let me pay my share," Tyler insisted.

"Not this time."

Bemused, Tyler tilted his head. "Can't I at least leave a tip?"

"You better," Joanie said from behind him, and everyone around laughed, including Holt.

Tyler had a twenty out of his pocket in a flash. Holding it up, he tilted back his head, asking, "Will this do?"

She snatched that twenty so fast her hand blurred. More laughter followed, including Tyler's own. Then a grinning Charlotte rose in the small space at the end of the bench.

Tyler rose and stepped away, allowing Holt to push back the table. Charlotte slipped around her end and came to Tyler's side. His hand moved of its own volition to the small of her back as they turned toward the exit, and it stayed there until they stepped out of the building. Holt remained inside to pay the bill at the narrow counter set up in one corner near the door.

Tyler stood in the darkness next to Charlotte, feeling sated and happy and restful. "Thank you for inviting me to join you."

"Glad you did," she said, folding her arms.

"Me, too."

He hunched his shoulders against the chill and debated the wisdom of slipping his arms around her. Holt spared him the decision by sliding back the glass door just then and stepping outside. Tyler put down his head and turned toward the truck, pleased that Charlotte stayed at his side.

Only as Holt paused at the open truck, fitting that cowboy hat onto his head once more, did Tyler fully realize what he'd done by accepting an invitation to attend church. What on earth was he going to wear?

Chapter Six

Standing next to Tyler on the pavement at the motel, Charlotte watched her brother's long legs stride toward the building. Tyler spoke to Holt as he opened the screen on the kitchen door.

"Thanks again for dinner."

Holt waved a hand negligently. "No problem. See you in the morning." He paused and looked back over his shoulder. "Provided you don't change your mind."

Charlotte sighed inwardly. What was wrong with him? Did he have to make even an invitation to church sound like a challenge?

"I won't change mind," Tyler replied evenly. She tried not to be too pleased by that. Tyler or anyone else attending church was a good thing, but it didn't have anything to do with her personally.

"You coming in?" Holt asked Charlotte. Her brother usually stopped in after dinner to speak to Hap.

"In a minute." She felt that she owed Tyler a private word. Holt had needled him all evening, and she didn't want Tyler to get the wrong impression. Holt split a look between her and Tyler, then went through the door shaking his head.

Charlotte glanced at Tyler, not quite sure what to say. "I hope you weren't offended by Holt's behavior this evening."

"Offended? Why would I be offended? Guys prod each other all the time."

He actually sounded pleased. She breathed a silent sigh of relief. "I just didn't want you to think it's because of who you are or anything."

Grinning ear-to-ear, Tyler rocked back on his heels. "Yeah, I know. Anyone hanging around his little sister would get the same treatment."

She blinked, then laughed. "True. It's nothing personal."

"Oh, it's personal," Tyler said. "Your brother wants to protect you. I can only respect that."

She sighed, saying, "I don't need protecting. I'm not seventeen, I'm twenty-seven."

Tyler's pale eyes seemed to glow. "True. For the record, I'm glad I went along. I really enjoyed myself. Thanks for inviting me."

"I'm glad, too."

"I, um, I do have a problem, though," Tyler said, rubbing his chin, "and I'm going to need some help with it."

Charlotte jerked a little straighter. "Oh?"

He held out the sides of his suit coat, saying, "I'm standing here in the only clothes I have, and I've been standing in them quite long enough. I need to come up with something for tomorrow. So what do folks wear to church around here and where can I get that?"

Charlotte hadn't even thought of such a dilemma,

but obviously he was right. The man needed a change
of clothes. She could try washing things for him, but
she'd prefer not even to touch such obviously expensive
articles. What if she ruined something? Still, she'd help
if she could. Christian charity demanded it, regardless
of his social status.

She eyed him critically for a moment, then shook her
head. "I'm sure my brothers would lend you something,
but Ryan's too wide and Holt's too tall. And Granddad—" she waved a hand dismissively "—his wardrobe's straight out of the 1950s."

Tyler seemed genuinely distressed. She imagined
that image was very important to a man in his position,
which must only enhance his need.

"What am I going to do? I don't even know what I
should be wearing. I mean, at home, I always wear a
suit and tie when I go to church."

Her ears perked up at that, glad to hear that he went
to church back in Dallas. She wondered if he was a regular attender, then pushed the thought aside in order to
tackle the more immediate issue.

"Suit and tie are fine, of course."

"But this suit needs dry cleaning," he pointed out.
"Not even a good pressing will do at this point. I can
manage the tie, but that's about it."

She tapped her foot, thinking. He could beg off, but
it was *church*. He should go. She wanted him to go. For
his own good, of course.

Oh, all right, it was more than that. In all truth, she
liked him. A great deal. She hadn't wanted to drive
away and leave him here alone tonight, and she wanted
him to go to church with the family in the morning.

So what if he would be gone before sunset tomorrow? That was just as it should be, but he still had a problem.

For the man to attend church he had to have clean clothes, and she couldn't blame him for not wanting to wear that suit for a third day.

Charlotte glanced at Tyler and found him gazing down at her patiently. "Okay," she said, embracing the project. "Let's look at our options."

"What would those options be?"

Sucking in a deep breath, she considered. "I could always wash whatever is washable."

"And I would still be stuck wearing a dirty suit," he pointed out.

"Exactly. Guess that means driving to Duncan."

Even if they'd realized earlier in the day that clothing for him would be an issue, Duncan would have been the only option. Women's clothing could be found in Eden, but not men's.

"Duncan," he mused. "How far is that?"

"About thirty-five miles."

"Ah." He looked off in that direction as if he might actually catch sight of the place. "They have a mall in Duncan, do they?"

"Uh, sure. Sort of. But all the stores in the mall will be closing…" she looked at her watch "…right about now."

"Oh." He grimaced. "Plan C, then, I guess, huh? Please say you have a Plan C."

She shook her head. "Nope. Plan B was and is to drive up to the twenty-four-hour discount store in Duncan. That's not part of the mall."

"Discount store?" he parroted doubtfully.

"You won't find anything else open at this time of night," she told him. "Not around here."

Glancing at his wrist, he smiled wryly. "You wouldn't in Dallas, either."

"Well, there you go."

He leaned forward. "There *we* go. I hope." Ducking his head, he looked up at her from beneath the crag of his brow and admitted sheepishly, "To tell you the truth, I've never done much shopping."

She rolled her eyes, half convinced that he was joking. "Oh, please. A man with your money—"

"Can hire someone else to shop for him," he interrupted flatly, averting his gaze. "I shop for investments, big-ticket items like cars and boats and property, and even then someone else has done the research for me. When it comes to clothes, I get fittings and pick out fabrics. From a grouping which my fashion consultant has already decided are appropriate."

Charlotte must have stood there with her mouth open for a full minute or more before she realized that she was gaping. Hastily she cleared her throat. "Right. Okay. I'll, um, just let Granddad know where I'll be."

Tyler heaved a great sigh of relief. "Thank you. Again. I'll get the car." He slid his hand into the pocket of his pants. "Meet you right here."

"Five minutes," she promised as they parted.

She found Hap sitting at the dining room table with Holt. As usual, Holt somehow managed to sprawl his long body over the chair without winding up on the floor. For such a hardworking man, he could look as lazy and boneless as an old hound dog, but he always said his energy all went to his brain cells at times like this. She didn't doubt it.

Charlotte bent and pressed her cheek to her grand-father's forehead. "How're you feeling?"

"Oh, I'm fine, darlin'. Don't you go worrying about me." His merry eyes twinkled. "Holt says y'all took Tyler Aldrich to dinner with you."

She glanced at her brother. "So we did. He seemed to enjoy himself."

Hap's bushy white eyebrows moved upward. "Enough to accept an invitation to church tomorrow, I hear."

Nodding, she said, "Yeah, there's a little problem with that, though, so I need to go out again for a while. Do you mind staying up until I get back?"

He twisted slightly in his chair. "Where're you going, hon?"

She could feel Holt's gaze drilling into her, and she knew what he thought, that her interest in Tyler was personal, but as she'd said earlier, she wasn't seventeen anymore. She knew her own mind, and she had a clear vision of her life and world. Tyler had no place in that world, other than a very temporary one.

"Tyler has nothing clean to wear to church tomorrow, so I'm going to help him find something at the discount store in Duncan."

"Ah." Hap grinned so wide that his dentures clacked, but he quickly shuttered his expression, glancing at Holt. Obviously they'd been discussing her and Tyler, and just as obviously Holt had made his opinion known. She wondered what he found so objectionable about Tyler, but then she reminded herself that it didn't mat-

ter. He and Hap were both wrong if they thought anything would or could come from what was, essentially,
an act of Christian charity on her part.

"He can't buy his own clothes?" Holt asked sardoni-
cally.

She folded her arms, getting to the real issue. "There
is no reason I shouldn't help him out."

"That's exactly right," Hap said, repositioning in his
chair again. "Y'all be careful, hon. I'll take care of the
desk. I'm going to be up a couple more hours anyhow."

"I'll help you," Holt added in a flat tone.

"You will get yourself home and to bed," Hap replied
good-naturedly, pointing a gnarled finger at Holt. He
flicked that same finger between himself and Charlotte.
"Neither of us need sitting up for."

"You like him," Holt accused, narrowing his eyes at
Hap. "You just want to give her a chance to start something with Mr. Big Bucks out there."

"Well, what of it?" Hap retorted, not even bothering
to deny it. "She deserves a good man, and they don't
exactly hang off the trees around here."

Exasperated at the way the men in her life seemed
to be jumping to all sorts of unwarranted conclusions,
Charlotte threw up her hands. "You're both being ridiculous," she scolded lightly, marching around the table
to drop a kiss on her brother's head. "I'm not starting
anything with anyone." She moved on to Hap, repeat-
ing the process with him. "And if I was, it wouldn't be
with him."

"Why not?" Hap demanded. "I do like that boy. He's
not such a big shot he can't rub elbows with the little
people."

"Granted, but he's a big shot who lives and works in Dallas," she reminded them, figuring that said it all.

They both knew perfectly well that she'd broken off her engagement when her fiancé, Jerry, had insisted that he couldn't make a decent living around Eden, and she'd known Jerry Moody her whole life. They'd dated for years before getting engaged, but she hadn't wanted to trade her small-town life for the big city then, and she still didn't.

Holt smiled, but she couldn't tell whether she saw relief there or something else. It simply did not matter. Not at all.

She went out without another word, ignoring the little voice in her head that whispered Tyler Aldrich, a grown man who ran a huge corporation, could surely buy his own clothes without assistance from her, had he wanted to. And provided she had been of a mind to let him.

Charlotte tried not to be impressed as she sank into the luxurious leather seat. If dinner had somehow blurred the differences between them, then this extravagant automobile served to underscore them, especially when Tyler tapped the screen of the in-dash computer. She watched as he chose a destination from those listed, state first and then city, before he turned to her.

"Address?"

"I beg your pardon?"

"The discount store, do you know the address?"

"Uh, no, actually I don't."

"How about an intersection? Anything near will work."

She racked her brain for a moment, then gave the only street name she could remember. "81 and Elder."

He chuckled. "What is it with you Oklahomans and trees? Half the streets in this state seem to be named for trees."

Charlotte shrugged, smiling. "Never thought about it."

The computer did its thing, a flashing light indicating the exact location of the discount store.

"I thought I was supposed to show you where it is," she said, wondering again why she'd agreed to this, given the suppositions of her family and the fact that he could obviously find his way around without her.

"You know that's not the only reason I asked for your help," he told her, guiding the car out onto the highway.

"Uh-huh. You don't know how to shop."

He shot her a look, smiled and said, "I've got to confess something."

She sat up a little straighter, her heart suddenly pounding. "What?"

"I've never been in a discount store in my life."

She shook her head, feeling oddly deflated. What had she expected? "It's not like you have to have a membership to get in the door or anything."

"I know that. What I don't know is what I should be looking for or where I should be looking for it. Those stores are huge. I told you, I'm used to someone else narrowing down my choices. Then I just stand there and let the tailor measure me. Even then, he usually comes to me."

"I see." She'd known people lived like that, of

course—in some other universe. "Talk about your worlds colliding," she muttered under her breath.

"What's that?"

"Nothing. Nothing at all." Which was exactly what would come of this little exercise in Christian charity, no matter what Hap might hope.

She knew the foolishness of even entertaining the possibility of getting involved with this man. Hap might think him grand, and perhaps he was, but surely everyone saw how ill-suited the two of them really were. She didn't want any part of his world, and she didn't want to be the woman that he saw whenever he decided to amuse himself by going slumming. That being the case, this little adventure could be nothing more than that. Period. In fact, she couldn't imagine why she wasted her time and energy even thinking about it. So she would stop, with a little help.

"Father," she prayed silently, *"You know I only want to do Your will, and I know that You mean for me to stay in Eden. Granddad and the boys need me, and I need them. You showed me when Jerry had to leave Eden that my place is here with my family. Don't let me be distracted by worldly things or tempted into building dreams and hopes that just aren't part of Your plan for me. Amen."*

Feeling a bit better, she settled back to enjoy the ride, and what a ride it was. They flew. At least it felt like they did, the car skimming over the ground with smooth, leashed power. Charlotte found it thrilling, but she didn't want to think about how fast they were traveling, not that she could help doing so when the computer displayed their speed in numbers two-inches high.

Seeing her unease, Tyler backed off. "Sorry. I let this thing get away from me sometimes."

She smiled her thanks for his consideration and felt comfortable enough to mention minutes later that they were approaching a known speed trap in the community ahead. He backed off a little more, and the remainder of the journey passed in companionable silence. Almost before she knew it, they hit the 81 bypass that skirted the downtown area of Duncan.

A community of some twenty-five thousand souls, Duncan provided the major shopping for Stephens county and large portions of the counties surrounding it. Still, area residents thought nothing of traveling to Lawton, Oklahoma City, Wichita Falls or even Dallas for major purchases.

Tyler parked the sports car in a remote section of a parking lot crowded with automobiles. "Hope you don't mind walking a bit," he said. "After that meal, I could use a little exercise, and I don't like to park this baby too close to others."

"No problem."

She didn't wait for him to come around the car and open the door for her, meeting him at the rear of the vehicle instead. He set the locks remotely and fell into step beside her, his hand hovering at the small of her back as it had earlier at the restaurant that evening.

That small gesture both tickled and troubled her. It had been a long time since a man had acted with any measure of gallantry toward her. On the other hand, this was not, after all, a date. She'd dated so little in the past several years that she had almost forgotten what it felt like to have a man behave with a touch of chivalry.

That's all this was, though. Nothing more. It certainly was not a romance.

Despite what her grandfather seemed to believe, Charlotte had come to suspect that God did not mean for her life to include romance, even if she sometimes secretly grieved the loss of such dreams as marriage and children of her own. She knew perfectly well that God, being the God of miracles, could yet work out those things for her, but she considered herself a realist. What she'd told Tyler earlier about the pickings being slim around Eden was the perfect truth.

All the men in her age range were either already married or had moved away. Moreover, nice, upstanding single men just did not pull out a map and decide they were going to build their lives in Eden, Oklahoma. No one ever moved into Eden unless they already had a connection there, so she couldn't expect to meet her true love walking down the street one day.

No, she was not meant for romance and marriage— she loved the life she already led. Even the work satisfied her in a very real way. Like Hap, she considered it a ministry, a way to reach out to those in need of a welcoming smile and a safe, comfortable place to lay their heads.

Yes, her life was good. Hap needed her. Her family needed her, and her work mattered. That was enough, more than most people could say about their own lives. In many ways, she mused, she was richer than even Tyler, given what he'd told her that afternoon.

As they entered the store, Tyler would have walked right past the shopping carts if she hadn't stopped to pull one out.

"You'd think I'd have gotten that one right, anyway," he muttered from the corner of his mouth as she pushed the cart down the broad aisle. "We spend a fortune on shopping carts for Aldrich stores."

He came to a stop just past the checkout lanes and looked around in puzzlement. "This is not like any store layout I'm used to. How do you ever find anything in this place?"

"It's not too difficult," she told him. "If you've been in one of these stores you've pretty much been in them all." He frowned down at her, making her dip her head. "Oh, right. You haven't been in one of these stores before."

"Not even to check the grocery prices," he said, glaring at the shelves of goods in the food section. "We have a division that keeps up with that sort of thing, though."

"A whole division? For checking the grocery prices of your competitors?"

"It's a small division," he said a tad defensively.

She strangled an unladylike snort of laughter, coughing into her hand to cover it before steering him toward the men's department. He followed her to a rack of dress slacks, looking around him like he'd never before realized where clothing came from.

Turning a tag over in his hand, he read the price and lifted an eyebrow. "I don't know whether this stuff is dirt cheap or just very poor quality."

"Sometimes both," she said before recommending a certain label. "I find these hold up better after repeated washings."

"Really? You can wash this stuff?" he asked, taking a hanger from the rack and looking over the pants.

She rolled her eyes at him before returning her attention to the selection of dress slacks. "Not everyone drops their clothes at the cleaners. What size do you wear?"

Several seconds passed before she realized that no answer would be forthcoming. She looked around to find him standing with his head bent as if in contemplation, a hand cupping the back of his neck.

"You don't know what size pants you wear?" It came out as much a statement of amazement as a question.

"I'm thinking," he said defensively. "I'm pretty sure the tailor measured me at a thirty-two. Could be thirty-four. Or was it thirty-six?"

"You could always check the label in your slacks," she suggested helpfully, getting a scowl for her efforts.

"Handmade suits don't have size labels," he informed her.

She looked away at that, hiding the lift of her eyebrows. The man was a complete alien. Undoubtedly his whole wardrobe had been handmade to fit, right down to his socks.

"You'll just have to try on several pairs," she decided, selecting a pair and holding them at his waist to judge the length. That pair went back to the rack as she reached for another. "Start in the middle with the thirty-four. We can do down or up from there as we need to."

After several trips to the changing room, he finally settled for chocolate-brown pants that were slightly larger and longer than he'd have liked, but he muttered about not having time to leave them for alteration. Charlotte bit her lip to keep from laughing.

"There is no tailor. They don't do alterations at discount stores."

"Well, how do people get the proper fit?" he asked, sounding exasperated.

"Usually they just wear them as they come."

He frowned at that and put the pants in the shopping cart.

If the slacks were a revelation for him, the shirts were a definite irritant. He turned up his nose at fabrics, styles, patterns, even buttonholes.

"I can't wear these!" he declared, dropping a sleeve in disgust.

"Oh, really?" she said mildly, parking her hands at her waist. "All the other men at church will be wearing them or something very much like them."

Color stained the ridges of his cheekbones. She hadn't meant to embarrass him, but the exchange certainly pointed up the differences between their worlds. Ignoring the white shirts, which he considered too thin, he muttered that he didn't see anything that would go with his tie.

"You can get by without a tie," she told him gently. "Some of the men around here don't even own one."

He looked at her like she must have lost her mind, but he finally opted for a pale blue shirt very near the color of his eyes. Crisis diverted, they moved on to the next item on his agenda, but Charlotte couldn't help whispering a short prayer in her mind.

Thanks, Lord, for showing me how right I am to think that this man and I have nothing whatsoever in common. She just wished the thought didn't sadden her.

Chapter Seven

After some discussion about the necessity of a coat and keeping warm, Tyler chose a nubby brown-and-gray jacket with just a fleck of orange in the tweed. The fit obviously did not please him, but he appeared somewhat mollified when Charlotte complimented him on his sense of color and style.

"Granddad and Holt couldn't put together complimentary colors if they only had two choices."

He chuckled at that, eyes dancing. "Is there a wrong color to go with blue jeans?"

"Point taken."

"Speaking of jeans," he said, craning his neck. "They're a lot more comfortable than dress clothes. Wouldn't hurt if I picked up some."

"Behind the dressing rooms."

"Ah." He headed that way, then stood scratching his ear at the shelves of folded denim. He ran a finger along one shelf. "Boot cut, boot cut, boot cut. Relaxed boot cut. Regular fit. Relaxed regular. Carpenter." He looked at her with a blatant question in his eyes.

Knowing that he must usually buy according to the designer label and current fashion—as dictated by his fashion consultant, no doubt—she stepped forward to describe the different offerings as well as she could.

"Holt wears these. Snug at the hip and thigh, wider below the knees to accommodate the tops of his boots. It's what the cowboys prefer." She moved along. "Now, Ryan wears these." She held up a pair of the relaxed style. "All the high school girls think he'd look better in the ones that Holt wears, which is why he doesn't wear them. These are still wide enough at the bottom for boots but not so snug up top." She unfolded the next pair so he could see the narrow bottoms. "These are for the left-behinds."

"Left-behinds?"

"You know, those guys left behind in the 1980s when pant legs were just wide enough to get your feet through the openings."

Tyler laughed. She folded the jeans and put them away, teasing as she did so. "You could always wear overalls like Hap."

"Uh, no."

"Then these are probably your best bet," she told him, pulling the right waist size from a stack of regular relaxed fits. He took them without a word, and while he went to try them on, she scoped out the casual knits, thinking the guy must feel like he'd wandered into an alternate universe. In a way, he had.

She shook her head, thinking about the kind of life that didn't even allow for basic shopping. As lost as he seemed to be in her world, though, she knew that she would be much more disoriented in his. The very thought gave her the willies, frankly, and she chafed at sudden gooseflesh on her upper arms.

He returned with the jeans and, to her surprise, went for three pairs, along with several polos and a Henley shirt before taking himself off to pick out socks and a package of undershorts. Evidently she'd miscalculated when she'd assumed that he would be gone by the next evening. She wondered just how long he planned to stay, but she would not ask. She had displayed quite enough unwilling interest already.

With him in control of the shopping cart now, she followed along as he browsed up and down the aisles, taking in everything from kitchenware to television sets. He spent half an hour looking at movies on DVD, and several wound up in his cart. The next thing she knew, he was looking at DVD players. She couldn't keep the questions behind her teeth this time.

"Just happen to need a new DVD player, do you?"

"Actually I thought I'd hook it up in my room back at the motel, if you don't mind."

The motel furnished only TVs with a basic satellite package of some eleven channels.

"I don't mind. You're planning to stay on for a while, are you?" She bit her lip, too late to prevent the one question she'd just decided not to ask.

"Awhile." He stopped reading the box long enough to look her squarely in the eye. "Is that okay with you?"

"Just fine." She tried to make it sound light and unconcerned, but her voice croaked, trapping her breath in her throat.

He went back to reading the package, a smile playing

about his mouth. She worried suddenly that she might be leading him on but the next instant rebuffed that idea.

Who was she kidding? Tyler Aldrich had no more interest in her personally than he did in that DVD player. He was biding his time here, nothing more. He'd admitted it to Holt. Hiding, he'd said, from people who irritated him. Her grandfather's misguided notions had her thinking that Tyler might be staying for another reason, which was clearly beyond ludicrous.

She felt relieved by that realization. Sort of. Except for a kind of amorphous sense of disappointment. Troubled, she knew she would be asking God about that in private later.

Tyler stared at the few remaining bills in his wallet, looked to the readout on the cash register display again, and reached into the pocket of his pants for his money clip. Just the weight of the folded bills within the gold clip told him that he wouldn't have enough to pay for his purchases. The thought of visiting an ATM hadn't even occurred to him. His secretary usually had a certain amount of cash delivered to him every Friday afternoon, but he hadn't been around for that delivery this particular Friday past.

Perhaps he had gone a little overboard with his purchases tonight, but he'd found the experience of shopping so novel that he'd gotten a bit carried away. Just as he'd told Charlotte, he rarely found it necessary to shop and never like this. He usually just had whatever he needed ordered and delivered.

Reluctantly, Tyler opened his wallet to retrieve a credit card. He grimaced, remembering that he carried only his company card. His personal cards remained in the wall safe back at the penthouse. He hadn't given them a thought until this very moment, his routine being to retrieve them, like an expensive personal accessory, only as he dressed to go out for a rare, purely social occasion. That bit of prudence could well prove folly, but nothing could be done about it now. He'd just have to reimburse the company.

After swiping the card, he scrawled an electronic signature on the digital pad. The teenaged clerk thanked him in a desultory fashion and handed over the receipt, which Tyler stowed within his wallet, intending to send it to his personal accountant later, the same one who paid all his bills.

Tyler followed Charlotte as she pushed the cart toward the exit. Obviously intending to leave the cart with the elderly attendant, she began gathering up the plastic bags containing his purchases. He had forgotten that even in Aldrich stores most customers carried out their own bags.

"Here," he said, shouldering his way to the side of the cart. "Let me have the bags. You get the box."

"They're not heavy," she argued as he gathered the bags.

"They're heavier than the DVD player," he replied, the weight of them dangling at the ends of his arms. She bent and picked up the box from the bottom of the cart.

They walked through a double set of automatic doors and out onto the parking lot. Halfway to the car she suddenly asked, "Have you thought about how you're going to get all this home?"

He stopped dead in his tracks and looked over his

shoulder with a sigh. "Guess I'd better go back in there and find a suitcase of some sort. Let's get this stuff to the car first."

They hurried to the far corner of the lot. He opened the trunk and got the goods stowed, then thoughtfully palmed the keys. "Can you drive a stick shift?"

She looked warily to the car. "Yes, but—"

"Okay, here's what we'll do," he interrupted, striding around to open the passenger door for her. "I'm going to drive up to the fire lane, then let you slide over to the wheel while I run back inside the store."

She lowered herself into the leather bucket, her expression troubled. Before she could voice her concerns, he closed the door and jogged around to the driver's side. She spoke as he dropped down behind the steering wheel.

"What if I have to move the car?"

"Then move it. Just come around again and pick me up." He started the engine and backed the car out of the space. "Don't worry," he told her. "It's a very forgiving transmission, built to take abuse. The worst that can happen is that you'll stall out." He saw the flash in her eye and chuckled. "I never thought you would stall. Just said it was the worst that could happen."

She smiled and pulled her braid over one shoulder. He wondered what her hair looked like down and if he would find out before he left here.

That thought nagged him as he left the idling car at the curb and literally raced back inside the store. He could almost see her with her bright, silky hair spread across her shoulders. She couldn't wear it in a braid all the time. Maybe he'd stick around until she let her hair down. At some point he'd accepted, without even considering, that he would stay on beyond the weekend, and he found a certain exhilarating freedom in that, but he couldn't really say why he'd decided to delay his departure.

Curiosity had a lot to do with it. This small-town life seemed both more complicated and at the same time infinitely more simple than his own existence. He'd thought a lot, strictly from a business perspective, about how the other half lived, so to speak, but he saw now that he hadn't gotten a very clear picture from all those studies and reports he'd read.

As he'd strolled these aisles earlier he'd told himself that it was high time he actually experienced what the average shopper did, if only to better inform his business decisions. These shoppers, after all, made up his company's market, too, but they had lives outside these stores, and understanding more about that would undoubtedly prove a huge asset. In that way, this unintended sojourn was turning out to be an invaluable learning tool. But something else kept him here, too, something personal.

He couldn't quite put his finger on it, but for some reason that he didn't really understand, he needed this time away from his own life. He needed to *not* be himself for a little while. Maybe he needed to do nothing for a time, to literally loaf around and just watch the world go by.

He actually liked spending time with the Jefford family. Even Holt, as distrustful as he might be. Tyler had the feeling that they could give him a real, honest look at what a normal, healthy family should be. For a fellow who had never even known his own grandparents except in the most peripheral fashion, that suddenly seemed important.

Perhaps that explained why the warm, patient goodness of Hap Jefford so compelled Tyler, but then so did the fierce but companionable protectiveness of a self-assured, much-adored big brother like Holt. It amazed Tyler that he should have so little in common with these folks and still find such welcome and acceptance in their company—and without the least bit of fawning. That went for everyone, including the good citizens of Eden and its environs, despite his fears on that score.

Was it any wonder that he wanted to stay just a little longer?

He located the correct aisle and spent all of three minutes choosing a cheap but adequate nylon suitcase on rollers, which he paid for with the credit card.

After waiting several long minutes to get through the express checkout line, he jogged back out to the car, still idling next to the curb, and tossed the suitcase into the back while a trio of young men in ball caps, oversized jeans and tattered athletic shoes blatantly ogled the vehicle.

"Nice ride," one of them called.

Tyler smiled as he closed the trunk. "Thanks."

"Yours?"

"Yep."

"Who's that chick driving?" another of them asked.

"I wouldn't let *my* girl drive a car like that," the third declared at the same time.

My girl, Tyler thought, surprised when a hole seemed to open up inside his chest. He couldn't remember a time when he'd thought of a woman, or had wanted to think of a woman, as *his girl*. Neither could he recall a time when the woman in question hadn't been angling for just that. Until now.

On pure impulse, he headed to the passenger door, quipping, "You're hanging out with the wrong kind of woman, then, son."

The guys laughed, elbowing each other, and Tyler dropped down into the passenger seat. Closing the door, he looked to Charlotte and reached back for the safety belt.

"Let's go."

She tilted her head, studying him for a moment as if he were some strange kind of new bug. He buckled the belt.

"Come on. Move it. I have an early appointment in the morning." He smiled to let her know that he really wanted her to drive.

After a long moment, she faced forward again. "Okay." She put the transmission in gear and pulled away from the curb.

Tyler sat back and enjoyed the ride, noting with pleasure from the corner of his eye her little nods and shrugs of approval as she worked through the gears. By the time they'd made their way through numerous traffic lights along the bypass to the open road, Tyler's grin stretched clear across his face.

"What do you think?"

"Drives like a hundred-thousand bucks," she said.

"One-forty, actually," he corrected.

She boggled her eyes at him. "You can buy a house for that, a nice house, not to mention all of the good you could do with that kind of money. Think of all the poor people in the world!"

Disappointed, even a little wounded, he looked out the window. "So you think it's wrong of me to spend that kind of money on a car, then?"

"I didn't say that. It's just—"

"What about the guy who sold me this car? The people who built it? The parts suppliers and their families? What about the immigrant worker who cleans the dealership's building at night? By buying this car I keep them all in business."

"You're right, you're right," she conceded. "It's not my place to judge you, anyway, and I'm not, truly."

"If you say so, but I'll have you know that I give away something like a third of my income every year."

She glanced over at him then, shamefaced. "I'm sorry. It's just...your kind of money is a foreign concept to people like me."

"That goes both ways, you know," he said softly. "When I look at you—" He broke off, uncertain how to phrase it.

"What?"

He wouldn't tell her that he envied her. She wouldn't believe him. He wouldn't tell her that he thought her beautiful, either. She would believe that even less, although it was the truth. Her beauty shone from the inside out with a purity that he admired in a way he couldn't even describe. He didn't want her to think that he was coming on to her, though, not after what that kid had said back there in the parking lot.

"You and your family," he said, choosing his words with honesty and care, "you're happy together. You love one another. That's something I've seen only rarely. I hope you know what it's worth."

"I do," she said, her hands tightening on the steering wheel. "Believe me, I do."

She drove on in silence. He rode beside her in quiet awareness, gradually relaxing as the miles fell away until delight somehow captured him again. He couldn't say why he found this so pleasant, but part of it, he knew, had to do with the assumption and words of that young man back there in the parking lot.

Charlotte was not his girl and she never would be. Looking at her softly lit profile against the night-blackened window, though, he had to admit that he'd been less than honest with himself about his decision to stay in Eden. He stayed because he couldn't help himself.

She drew him like a lodestone. Her honesty, her generosity, her simplicity, her contentment, they all called to him, along with some other indefinable quality that he couldn't begin to name. Despite her rough clothing and almost corny hairstyle, her lack of cosmetics or adornment of any sort, she somehow seemed to grow more beautiful every time he looked at her. He wanted to know her, to really know her.

Of course, nothing could or would come of it. Any fool knew that much. She was not the sort of woman he might escort to a business dinner or gala social occasion, and he didn't have time or the inclination for routinely hanging out a hundred and fifty miles from home. But for now, just for now, he'd allow himself to admire and to enjoy and maybe even to imagine what it might be like if she were his girl.

Unfortunately, he could never allow it to go further

than that. He didn't want to hurt her, and he knew instinctively that Charlotte was the sort of woman who would expect more than he could give her. And rightly so. He wouldn't change that or anything else about her, but in all honesty she just didn't fit into his world, which meant that she wouldn't fit into his life, either, not after he left here.

Nevertheless, they seemed to be forging a friendship, something personal and private that belonged wholly to just the two of them and this moment. He'd never had that before, not with anyone, and he wanted this time in Eden with her and her family—and away from his own.

In an odd fashion that he didn't really understand, something told him that he could go home again in a few days more whole than he'd been when he'd arrived. Surely, he could have that much before he returned to his life.

Couldn't he?

Charlotte took a guilty pleasure in being behind the wheel of Tyler's massively expensive sports car. Compared to this, Hap's old diesel truck drove like a horse and buggy. That was not what discomfited her, though.

She'd never been so aware of anyone as she was of Tyler. She felt his gaze, felt his silent regard, and after she'd insulted him, too. Money had never meant beans to her, one way or another, and now suddenly she found herself judging him at every turn just because he'd been born into a wealthy family. It made her feel small and frightened in a manner that she didn't want to examine too closely.

"Can I ask you something?" she said into the velvety silence.

"Sure."

"What's it like to grow up with all that money?"

She felt rather than heard his sigh. He turned his gaze out the window. After a moment he said, "It just is, like the color of your hair or the face you see in the mirror every morning. It's not something you think about until someone else makes an issue of it."

She bit her lip at that. "I see. I'm sorry."

He shook his head. "Honest curiosity is one thing. Envy is something else altogether." She felt his gaze on her again. "And you really don't envy me, do you?"

Unsure how best to answer that, she wrinkled her nose apologetically. "Not really."

"Mind if I ask why?"

She had to think about that. "Well, it's not as if a few extra bucks wouldn't come in handy now and then," she said carefully, "but we already have all we need and...I don't know. I guess after your folks die you learn that what's most important is family, the people you love."

Tyler studied her for a moment. "My father used to say that everyone had their own treasure. Identify that, he would say, and you'd know how to work them."

"Work them?"

"You know, get the upper hand."

"Ah. Like in a business deal."

"Yeah, like in a business deal. Except I think he'd find you a tough nut to crack."

She let her eyes leave the roadway then and settle briefly on his face. "Why's that?"

"Because what you treasure most is unassailable,"

he said softly. "If my family cared for me one fraction of what yours does for you…"

You'd be a happy man, she thought. Stricken, she concentrated on the roadway again, wishing that she didn't know half so much as she did.

Chapter Eight

"Nah, come on. We'll all go together," Holt insisted, holding open the back door to the double-cab truck. "The parking's limited over at the church."

Shrugging, Tyler pocketed his car keys and started across the pavement.

"Wouldn't want to ding up that expensive mechanical wonder of yours," Holt added as soon as Tyler stepped off.

Tyler kept his tongue fixed firmly behind his teeth, partly because Holt was right and it embarrassed him, partly because the car would have drawn more unwanted attention his way. He already felt terribly out of place.

His new clothing felt odd, too light and too big and too…textured, somehow. Compared to Holt, however, who stood there in dark, creased jeans, a plain white shirt open at the collar and a brown leather coat with a western cut, Tyler appeared overdressed. The leather jacket didn't quite match Holt's hat or boots, but Tyler had to admit that it fit the tall cowboy far better than his own tweedy sport coat fit him.

Before Tyler reached the truck, Charlotte came through the kitchen door. To Tyler's great delight, she'd left her hair loose. It hung halfway down her back in a sleek, satiny fall that put him in mind of a sunset in those glorious moments suspended between day and evening. The narrow black headband that held her vibrant hair back from her forehead emphasized the gentle widow's peak that gave her smiling face the shape of a slender heart.

Stopping in his tracks, he admired not only her hair and face but the slender length of her legs beneath her simple, straight gray skirt. He recognized her shoes with their rounded toes and delicate, modest heels, having noticed them on the shelves at the discount store. A pale peach twin set completed her ensemble. The whole of it probably cost her less than forty dollars, judging by what he'd seen last night, and he remarked fiercely to himself that she deserved better than that.

In fact, he could give her better, the very best, and would enjoy doing so, if only she would let him, which he knew without a doubt she would not.

For one thing, Charlotte wouldn't want expensive clothing. He knew only too well how she viewed his costly goods. His things didn't impress her at all, not his clothing, not his car. Instead, she made him feel a little ashamed about how he spent his money, even though he could easily afford to spend whatever he liked and gave generously to numerous charities.

It hardly mattered that he could buy Charlotte the best of everything, anyway. Designer labels could do nothing to enhance her loveliness. Charlotte's beauty came from inside and radiated outward with a purity that no amount of money could purchase.

For a long moment, Tyler stood as if mesmerized. Then the screen door banged, drawing him back to himself. Ducking his head self-consciously, he started forward again. A moment later, he realized that Hap had joined them.

Clad in shiny, threadbare brown dress slacks, a navy-blue shirt, loosely knotted gray tie, red suspenders and a dark red cardigan sweater, he parked a jaunty gray fedora on his head, cupping the brim downward in front with a slick, sweeping motion of one hand. Tyler laughed, finding an odd joy in just looking at the old fellow. He mentally shook his head as he spied the thin white socks worn with stiff black wingtips as Holt helped Hap up into the truck.

Tyler moved to Charlotte's side, asking conversationally, "Who's minding the store?"

"No one. We don't staff the front desk on Sundays, but we don't turn away guests when we're here, either."

Tyler opened the front passenger door for her, noting that even as she thanked him she slid a loaded look her brother's way. Holt's mouth fixed in a straight line. After donning a pair of sunshades, he slipped behind the wheel. Tyler climbed into the backseat with Hap, wondering if he had become a bone of contention between brother and sister. The idea pinched a little.

Overcome with the scent of cheap aftershave as soon as he shut the door, he glanced at Hap, realizing that he had never before seen the old man cleanly shaved.

His expression must have shown his shock, for Hap grinned ear-to-ear.

"Clean up good, don't I?"

"You sure do," Tyler replied, marveling at the happiness that radiated off the old man. Thankfully, Holt cracked open the window up front and quickly got them moving, bringing enough breeze into the vehicle to freshen the air.

Breathing easier, Tyler took time to study the elder Jefford. Crippled with arthritis and plagued with other ailments, he had lost his wife and only child while living a life of hard work that had apparently left him without two nickels to rub together. Given all that, Hap should have been the last man to live in such joy that it overflowed, making it a pleasure just to sit next to him. Tyler had to wonder how that could be.

Mere minutes later, Holt pulled the long truck into the grass beside the park on Mesquite Street across from the small, white clapboard church that Tyler had noticed the day before. The sign above the door declared it to be simply, First Church of Eden.

They all piled out and came together at the edge of the street. A relatively well-dressed, dark-haired man standing beneath an ancient hickory tree in front of the church waved in greeting and came to meet them as they crossed to the sidewalk. He clapped Holt on the shoulder, engulfed Charlotte in a hug, then did the same with Hap, kissing the old man on the cheek.

"How're you doing, Granddad? You look good."

Without waiting for an answer, he turned his attention to Tyler. Seeing only interest and welcome in the other man's familiar hazel eyes, Tyler put out his hand while Charlotte made the introductions.

"Ryan, this is Tyler Aldrich. He's staying with us. Tyler, this is our brother, Ryan."

Though he stood a couple inches shorter than Holt, Ryan had maybe thirty pounds on his brother, making him seem the larger of the two men. Fit and strong, with dark, chestnut-brown hair and dressed in a smart navy suit, dress shoes, striped shirt and tie, he might have been any executive anywhere.

"Good to meet you, Ty," he exclaimed, shaking Tyler's hand with both of his. People rarely addressed Tyler as Ty, not even as a boy. His mother would have objected vociferously, but Tyler said nothing. It fit somehow in this setting.

Obviously used to being in charge, Ryan moved behind the group and gently but firmly herded them toward the church, saying, "We're going to need some extra space. Sis, you go in first. Granddad, I know you want to sit on the aisle because scooting across the pew hurts you, so you come in at the back here."

"Yes, sir, Mr. Jefford," Holt teased. "Anything you say, Mr. Jefford."

"Now, don't give me any of your lip," Ryan scolded lightly, sounding more and more like the assistant principal he was. "I'm just trying to help."

While the brothers bickered good-naturedly, Tyler took the opportunity to slide into place behind Charlotte, feeling Holt fall in behind him, just like students in school. They stepped up onto the single, broad stoop and pushed into the crowded building as a group.

Surprised to find that the sanctuary contained no

foyer, Tyler spent the next fifteen minutes shaking hands and nodding at folks whose names he barely caught as the group worked their way toward the front pews. He followed Charlotte into the narrow space between the second and third pews and took a seat next to her on the unpadded bench. Holt folded himself up next to Tyler and parked the hat, which he had removed as soon as they'd entered the building, on one bent knee.

Tyler took a moment to look around him. Talk about bare bones. Walls, floor, pews, all were constructed of pale wood finished with an oil rub that had to be decades old. Only the platform at the front boasted carpet in a bright peacock-blue, which contrasted sharply with the white painted lectern, altar and three armless chairs.

An acoustic guitar had been propped against an old upright piano in one corner, and hanging fixtures of cheap, unpolished brass lit the room. The tall, narrow windows had been painted in swirls of blue, green and gold, softening the austere interior. A fresh flower arrangement of red carnations supplied the only other splash of color.

A young woman in an ankle-length black knit dress, her pale hair twisted up against the back of her head, moved forward and took a seat at the piano. She opened her sheet music and began to play softly, prompting those visiting in the aisles and over the backs of the pews to take their seats and ebb into silence.

Grover Waller, dressed in a severe black suit that did nothing to alter his jovial appearance, hurried forward and occupied one of the chairs on the platform. A tall, gaunt younger fellow and a stout middle-aged woman joined him. After a few moments, the music stopped, and the young man stepped up to welcome everyone and make announcements.

The gutters on the "education building" needed cleaning. Next Sunday everyone should bring a dish to the monthly potluck dinner. For November no potluck dinner had been scheduled due to the annual Thanksgiving feast. Sign-up sheets could be found on the narrow tables at the back of the sanctuary. The youth would be taking the church van to a movie in Duncan on the following Saturday evening. Everyone was encouraged to attend the football game on Friday and cheer on the local team at home.

Next came announcements from the congregation. First one and then another stood to proclaim good news. This one's daughter had won the lead in the school play. That one's son had been elected to student council. A plump woman with suspiciously dark hair stood to declare that she had *finally* become a grandmother. The nineteen-inch-long, seven-pound infant resided in Houston with her parents. An older couple stood to be applauded for celebrating fifty-four years of marriage. Several confessed to birthdays during the coming week, at which point the crowd spontaneously broke into congratulatory song, accompanied by the piano.

Finally Grover stepped into the pulpit to call the congregation to worship with prayer. Tyler dutifully bowed his head, but he soon found himself looking up in surprise as Grover took on the authoritative tone of a true man of God. Tyler noticed that several people had lifted their hands toward heaven. He'd never seen that before.

Tyler had attended church often enough, mainly whenever it had seemed necessary or expedient. His family held membership at one of the oldest, most notable churches in Dallas, and there had been many weddings, funerals and baptisms over the years. He'd always found it a pleasant, restful experience filled with beautiful music and formal speech. On occasion he'd even felt an odd tug at his heart, but he'd never felt this sense of community.

More revelations followed. The gaunt fellow went to strap on the guitar, while the stout woman moved to the front of the platform to lead the music. And such music! It was so exuberant that Tyler actually felt a bit uncomfortable at times, though he had to admit that those around him seemed to be having fun.

Four men took up an offering before Grover returned to the pulpit to preach because, he later joked, stepping on toes tended to close wallets. Tyler dropped a hundred dollars into the plate when it came by, wishing he could have doubled the amount, but with a mere seventeen bucks in cash left in his pocket, he'd have to visit an ATM soon. If he could find one.

Grover Waller proved to be a huge surprise. Tyler had liked the round, friendly, soft-spoken man when he'd gotten to know him the day before at the dominoes table, but Waller hadn't quite fit Tyler's idea of a clergyman. That idea changed fast. Grover didn't preach so much as he taught, didn't exhort so much as encourage, yet he was blunt to the point of shocking, at least to Tyler's way of thinking.

"Your sin is no different from the sin of the worst mass murderer in history," he declared. "In God's eyes, sin is sin, brothers and sisters. It is the great equalizer. Don't go congratulating yourselves because you don't do what some others do or because some folks think you're pretty swell. If you have not found the saving grace of Jesus Christ, you're no different in God's eyes than anyone else. And if you have received that grace, you really have no excuse for not living a life pleasing to your Heavenly Father."

The preacher went on to speak about the Holy Spirit and matters that Tyler frankly did not understand, but those first words tied up his mind to the point that he couldn't really even think about anything else. He realized with some shock that in a far corner of his mind he'd always thought that he was somehow different from everyone else. He was Tyler Aldrich.

Too often in his business dealings he'd encountered exaggerations and outright lies, so he prided himself on his honesty. God knew that he didn't steal, as so many did, padding accounts and invoices. But then why would he since he'd always had anything and everything money could buy in the first place?

Okay, he didn't outright lie, but he did expect others to take his word at face value and agree with it, which they usually did—everyone but his family, who had no respect for his position. But why shouldn't his word be accepted? He was Tyler Aldrich of *the* Aldriches, CEO of Aldrich & Associates Grocery. And here stood this man telling him that his smallest evasion was judged just as harshly by God as the worst case of mass murder.

The idea took Tyler's breath away, and suddenly the snobbery for which he had so long condemned his mother and sister seemed as much a problem for him as for them. Why should the Aldriches be better than anyone else? Could his honesty be of any more value than another man's? More valuable than Holt's or Hap's or Charlotte's? If his sin was no different than anyone else's, how could his goodness be?

And what about this grace of which Grover spoke?

Tyler paid little attention to the remainder of the service, so caught up with this idea of his sin being as bad everyone else's in the whole wide world that he couldn't concentrate on more immediate events. He considered the possibility that Grover had concocted this sermon just for him, but try as he might, the startling concept of equality in God's eyes wouldn't let him go.

You're no different in God's eyes than anyone else.

By the time he managed to shift mental gears, he and the Jeffords were standing outside beneath a darkening sky. A few people headed straight for their automobiles, but most clustered in small groups, talking and laughing.

Almost immediately a bunch of young people surrounded Ryan, who seemed quite popular with his students. They all evidently knew Hap, too, who teased and joked with them.

Several men approached Holt, stepping aside for a moment of conversation. That left Tyler with Charlotte, which suited him just fine.

A number of people engaged them in passing, several pausing to shake Tyler's hand again and thank him for visiting, and then a tall, solidly built fellow with a toddler, a girl, parked in the crook of one elbow stepped up to Charlotte. Garbed in a white shirt and tie, sans jacket, with blond hair falling rakishly over one brow, he literally radiated fondness—and something more.

"Why, Jerry!" Charlotte exclaimed, stretching upward to press her cheek to his. "I didn't expect to see you until the holidays."

"Sandy's mom is having new flooring installed at her house. We came down to help her move stuff out of the way."

Charlotte spent several moments fussing over the child, who cuddled shyly against her father's shoulder with her thumb in her mouth. "She's just so adorable."

"You're looking good."

Smiling, Charlotte rocked up onto her toes. "Thanks. So are you."

Tyler was beginning to feel left out and more than a little miffed about it. Who, he wondered, was Jerry, and what did he mean to Charlotte? Tyler sensed a history here, and he didn't like it, especially considering that light in Jerry's eyes.

"Is Sandy with you?" Charlotte asked.

"No, she's sleeping in this morning. Every little thing seems to sap her strength these days."

"Oh? I hope she's not ill."

Jerry smiled. "Actually she's pregnant again."

"How wonderful!"

"We're hoping for a boy this time."

"Wouldn't that be perfect!"

Suddenly everything changed. It was as if lightning had struck but no one felt it except the three of them, Charlotte and Jerry, who stood looking into each other's eyes, and Tyler, who stood staring at them.

"You should be a mother," Jerry said softly, and in that instant Tyler *knew,* even before Jerry guiltily switched his gaze to Tyler himself.

Ignoring Jerry's last statement, Charlotte slipped an

arm through Tyler's. "What a ninny. I was just so surprised to see you I didn't think to introduce Tyler."

She hastened to give the men each other's names without a single word of explanation. Jerry nodded in acknowledgment just as a light rain began to fall.

"I'd better get her back to her grandmother's," he said, laying a protective hand over the child's head.

"Give my best to Sandy," Charlotte called as he moved away.

Before the fellow was out of earshot, Holt joined them, people scattering in every direction. Hap headed for the truck as Ryan took off at a jog for the parking area in the rear of the building. Tyler could do nothing except hurry Charlotte toward the pickup. Holt caught up to Hap and held his arm as they crossed the street. Tyler yanked open the rear door and handed Charlotte inside, leaving the front seat for Hap this time.

"Whew! Weather's turned off nasty," Hap observed in his gravelly voice as Tyler slid in next to Charlotte.

"I'm surprised it held off this long," Holt commented.

Tyler realized that he wasn't going to get an opportunity to find out about Jerry Moody and just what the man meant to Charlotte. He felt a petty, sick resentment over that. Looking down at his damp jacket, he could only shake his head.

What was wrong with him? So Charlotte had once had a boyfriend who'd married someone else. What difference did it make? Except it did, somehow. In a very stupid, selfish, inane way, it even hurt.

They pulled up at the motel, and Holt killed the engine, declaring, "I can smell that ham from here, sis."

Tyler immediately became aware of his empty stomach. He'd skipped breakfast in order to be ready for church on time, and now he regretted that. He regretted, too, the thought of a lonely meal, and he absolutely hated the feeling of wanting to tag along with the Jeffords like some waif from another century.

Charlotte chuckled and said to no one in particular, "I guess you're smelling those potatoes and gravy, too."

"Nothing better than red-eye gravy," Hap declared, opening up his door.

Holt hurried around to assist his grandfather, but Charlotte stayed where she was for a moment, gazing over at Tyler with calm eyes. "You've got time to change, if you want, but don't take too long at it."

Tyler felt his heart thud. "I'm invited to dinner?"

"Well, of course you are," she said, hopping out of the truck, "and I expect you to eat it while it's hot." She dashed for the kitchen door, leaving him alone in the truck.

So he was *expected* for dinner, was he?

He smiled.

Funny, he'd never realized that the sun could shine even in the gloom of rain.

Chapter Nine

Ryan sat back with a satisfied sigh and patted his firm middle. "Sis, it is downright sinful the way you cook."

"I'd have to say it's delectable," Tyler remarked, smiling up at her.

He'd been doing that a lot, smiling at her, and every time her heart rate kicked up another notch. She didn't know when she'd decided to include Tyler in Sunday dinner. It just didn't occur to her not to. Even before Jerry had surprised her on the church lawn, she'd taken it for granted that Tyler would be at her dinner table. If it had seemed more important that he be there after she'd talked to Jerry, well, she wouldn't think about that now. Obviously the rest of the family had expected Tyler to join them because not even Holt had said a contrary word when Ty had walked in. Ryan especially seemed to enjoy his company.

Always less intense and more trustful than Holt, Ryan's easy, open-armed acceptance of this newcomer in their midst came as no surprise. He took after Hap in that way. Still, Charlotte wondered if perhaps Hap had said something to Ryan about Tyler, something to make Ryan think that she had feelings for Tyler or vice versa, but somehow she didn't think he had.

She thanked the men for their compliments and rose to begin clearing the table. Ty immediately jumped to his feet, but Charlotte quickly refused his help.

"No, no. I'm going to clear and stack, but the boys always wash up on Sundays. Don't you, guys?"

Holt shot to his feet and headed toward the lobby, saying, "Right after the game."

"What he means," Ryan clarified, rising more decorously, "is right after we eat the leftovers for supper." He clapped a hand onto Tyler's shoulder, saying, "You do like football, don't you?"

Tyler nodded, seemingly torn between helping her and watching the football game. Hap got up and hobbled after Holt, saying, "Come on, there, boys. We got a tradition to uphold here."

Charlotte made a shooing motion with one hand, and Tyler finally relented. She tried not to be flattered that he appeared to prefer clearing the table with her to watching the game with her brothers.

Ryan, being the more enthusiastic of the two, pushed ahead, leaving Ty to bring up the rear. Charlotte couldn't help glancing in his direction—or admiring the way those new jeans fit him.

She bowed her head, confused by her own reactions and thoughts. Could it be that God was trying to tell her something? Shaking her head, she rejected all possibility that God might intend Tyler Aldrich to become more than a pleasant interlude in her life.

She and Ty lived in two completely different worlds.

His kind of life terrified her. How awful it would be to constantly fear not fitting in. Conversely, the idea that a rich man from the big city would find her lifestyle appealing was nothing less than laughable. Besides, he'd given her no real signal that he found her more than a curiosity.

Feeling incredibly foolish, she quickly cleared the table, stowed the leftovers to be reheated later and stacked the dishes to be washed. Then she removed her apron, dislodging the headband in the process. She smoothed her hair back from her forehead, replaced the headband, tugged at her jeans and turned toward the door. Sucking in a deep breath, she pasted on a smile and went to join the men.

Holt had stretched out on one of the sofas, his booted feet propped on the arm, while Hap occupied the rocking chair as usual, and Ryan sat at one end of the remaining couch, his gaze fixed on the television screen. Tyler had taken the other end, leaving only the middle of the sofa for her, unless she chose to pull out one of the straight chairs around the game table. That seemed rude somehow, telling, so she went to sit next to Ty. No sooner did she lower herself to the cushion than Ryan jumped up, hollering with glee. At the same time Tyler leaned forward, laughing, and Holt bolted into an upright position.

"I guess our team scored," she commented brightly.

Tyler sat back, casually lifting an arm about her shoulders as he turned to address her. "That's twice in eight minutes!" He looked to Holt, exclaiming, "Now tell me the quarterback is too young."

"That doesn't mean the coach isn't too old," Charlotte pointed out.

Tyler looked at her in surprise. A smile spread slowly across his face. "You think the coach is too old, do you? I'll be sure to tell him you said so."

"You know the coach?" she asked, wondering why she should be surprised.

"Ty has a box," Ryan announced pointedly.

"You mean a private box at the stadium?" Charlotte clarified.

"It's the company's box," Tyler said lightly.

"We're all going to go down to join him for a game sometime," Holt commented in a dry tone.

Charlotte doubted that very much. For one thing, all of them never went anywhere together except church; someone had to take care of things around here. Besides, she couldn't believe that either Hap or Holt would ever willingly make the drive to Dallas. Ryan would jump all over any actual invitation, and she hoped he got one, but chances were that Tyler Aldrich would forget all about them as soon as he left here. And that was for the best.

Talk continued in a lively vein, the men arguing the merits of various elements of the team. Charlotte had her own opinions, and she quietly interjected them into the conversation. Several minutes passed before they all settled down again. Only then did Charlotte realize that Ty had never removed his arm from about her shoulders and that she'd somehow shifted closer to him.

She contemplated moving away, but she didn't want to call attention to the situation, especially as no one else even seemed to notice. After some time, she allowed herself to relax and get caught up in the enjoyment of the game and just sharing space with those dear to her. Only later did she question the wisdom of including Tyler Aldrich in that category.

Tyler sat forward on the couch and clasped his hands together between his knees, forearms resting on his thighs. The Jefford men had trooped en masse to the kitchen, looking for food now that the football game had ended. How they could even think of eating, he didn't understand, but he appreciated the opportunity to be alone with Charlotte, all the same.

Now that it was just the two of them, though, he didn't quite know what to say. The Jeffords as a whole were easy people to be around. Hap treated him almost like family, while Ryan already seemed to think of him as a good buddy. Even Holt, who at times acted like he expected Ty to make off with the family silver, obviously bore him no ill will. Their welcoming acceptance frankly floored him. No doubt they treated everyone else the same way, but Tyler still reveled in their friendship.

Only Charlotte confused him. She couldn't have been more welcoming, caring or generous, but that just seemed part of her nature. It shamed him to think that his own family would not be so accepting of a stranger. Rather than friendliness and inclusion, snobbery, conflict and rivalry characterized the Aldriches. They would look down on the Jeffords without a doubt, Charlotte included. Charlotte especially. So what was he doing here with her? What was the point? And why did her reasons for being here with him matter so much?

Tyler really wanted to believe that all the Jeffords simply liked him, that they found him special somehow, apart from his sky box and millions of dollars. But he couldn't help wondering if his wealth figured into it, although in Charlotte's case he suspected she liked him *despite* his money. Maybe that was the key. Maybe the others were willing to give him the benefit of the doubt simply because Charlotte liked him. Tyler couldn't fault them for that.

"That was a great game," she finally said.

"Oh, yeah. It's always a great game when they win."

The woman amazed him. Not only did she look like a vision, work like a Trojan, cook like a chef, treat all who came into her orbit with compassion and welcome and quietly, effortlessly order her entire family, the girl also knew a thing or two about football.

She had a coach for a brother, so Tyler supposed he shouldn't have been surprised. What really blew him away, though, was how much she seemed to actually enjoy the game for its own sake.

On the other hand, she seemed to enjoy everything in the same way—her family, her work, her faith, her whole life. That she could do so when she'd suffered so much loss and had so little made Tyler feel small and spoiled.

He admired her, but it was more than that, too. He wanted for himself what she had, her contentment, her goodness. Worse, he wanted her in his life somehow.

It was a foolish notion, but sitting next to her here on the sofa with his arm curled about her slender shoulders earlier had felt like the most natural thing in the world to him. It shouldn't have—no one could have been more out of place kicking back to watch a televised football game than the one person in the room who usually watched those home games live from a private box for twelve on the fifty-yard line.

No doubt Charlotte would feel as out of place there as he often did here, but somehow that didn't seem to matter anymore.

Glancing through the picture window to the front lawn and the roadway beyond, he saw that the rain had stopped and the sky had cleared. In perhaps an hour, night would descend. Time enough for a little exploration.

"I don't know about you, but I could use some exercise," he said, swinging his head around to look at her. She sat tucked back into the corner of the leather sofa recently vacated by Ryan, one leg curled beneath the other. Her elbow braced against the rolled arm as she toyed idly with a sleek strand of her hair. "Want to take a little walk?"

She hesitated. He could see her mind working, though what thoughts went through that fine brain of hers he couldn't have said. After a moment, she nodded. He hadn't realized that his heart had stopped beating until it started again. Straightening, he rose at once to his feet, giving her no time to rethink. Charlotte unfolded her legs and got up, moving silently to the apartment door.

He followed and listened as she explained to her family that they were going to the park. Reaching inside, she took a corduroy coat from the chair in the corner behind the door and handed it to him, then removed a smaller down-filled nylon jacket from a peg on the wall.

She threw on the dark blue nylon jacket as they walked toward the front porch. Tyler held the outer door wide as she passed through and turned toward the ramp.

"You'll want to wear that," she said, glancing back over her shoulder at the corduroy coat that he carried in one hand.

He didn't argue, just shrugged into the heavy corduroy. The temperature outside had dropped considerably. The coat smelled of Hap so must have been the old man's. Ty found it a cheery, comfortable aroma. Falling into step beside her, he strolled across the pavement. He felt good, as if enfolded in a warm hug, but something else percolated just below the surface of his mind, too.

Hope, he decided after a moment. He felt hopeful, eager, even excited. All the frustration that had driven him from Dallas only days earlier seemed distant and foreign, as if it belonged to another lifetime, another man. Smiling, he sucked in a great lungful of autumn air, content to amble along as she led him around the back of the motel and across a patch of open ground to the point where Mesquite Street came to a dead end.

The entrance to the park lay some three blocks distant, so they strolled in that direction. Despite the increasingly stark trees, the park couldn't have seemed more beautiful to him if it had been the true Garden of Eden, and he wouldn't have complained if the walk had been three miles instead of three blocks.

In ways he could not have planned or even understood before, this sojourn in Eden, Oklahoma, seemed to be exactly what he needed. The peace and tranquility alone had reenergized him, and he'd gotten a good, hard look at how the majority of the world lived. In addition to that, the Jeffords had shown him what family could be. But might there be something more to it, something deep and personal? Somehow, he had begun to hope so.

Charlotte folded her arms, holding her jacket closed against the chill. Striking out on foot like this might well be foolhardy. The rain had cleared for the moment, but those clouds in the northwest promised more. Her chief concern, however, did not involve the weather.

She shouldn't be doing this. Being alone with Tyler courted disaster. She supposed that seeing Jerry with his little daughter today had made her feel that she'd missed out on something, but that was no reason to behave foolishly. She sensed Tyler's growing interest in her, though, and right now that made him very nearly irresistible. Disaster indeed.

Tyler Aldrich could have any woman he wanted. With his wealth, connections, charm and looks, he probably found himself inundated with interested women. She was nothing more than the woman of the moment, and she'd best remember that. No one could seriously expect that his interest in her could be more than curiosity or that they could have any sort of future together.

In all likelihood he'd probably never met a less sophisticated individual than her, and as alien as he at times seemed in her world, she knew that she would be even more lost in his. The man had a private luxury box at the pro football stadium in Dallas, for pity's sake. He knew the coach personally! She wouldn't know how to behave rubbing elbows with people like that.

No, she couldn't see anything ahead for her and Tyler Aldrich, and she wouldn't set herself up for disappointment by trying to create anything. She knew, had always known, that her life lay here in Eden with her grandfather and brothers. When Tyler left this place, as he must soon do, that would be the end of it. Period.

God had surely brought him here for a purpose, however. She'd sensed some confusion on his part during the pastor's sermon that morning, and this walk seemed like a good opportunity to clear up any questions he might have about what the pastor had said. Letting her feet take care of getting them to the park, she turned her mind to the better subject.

"I keep thinking about Grover's sermon today."

Tyler zipped her a look from the corners of his eyes. "Yeah. Yeah, that was interesting."

"Anything about it strike you especially?"

He put his head down for a moment. "I've sort of been thinking about the equality thing."

That set her back enough to slow her steps. "Equality?"

"Sure. You know, how everyone's sin is really the same."

Picking up the pace again, she mulled that over. She'd never thought of it in terms of equality, but that did make a certain sense. "Hap says that the only difference between people is Jesus," she remarked.

"I wouldn't say that's the only difference," Tyler replied with a smile. "Hap may be the most gentle and caring fellow I've ever met."

Pleased, she bumped his shoulder with hers. "I meant, the only difference in God's eyes."

Tyler's brow furrowed. "You don't think God sees what kind of person Hap is?"

"Of course. I also believe that God honors the good we do," she clarified. "The point is that, since all sin is equal in God's eyes, we're all equally guilty, so we all need the grace that comes to us through Jesus Christ."

"Okay. I get that," Tyler said slowly.

She could tell from his tone that he wondered where she might be going with this, and ultimately she supposed the only way to get there was just to ask what she wanted to know. "Are you a Christian, then, Ty?"

He shrugged. "Sure. My family have been members of one of the biggest, oldest churches in Dallas for generations."

"Then you understand what I mean by grace?" she asked. He made no reply, as if he took her question to be a statement. After a moment, she went on uneasily. "I guess what I want to know is why you haven't given your pain and grief to God."

He looked genuinely confused at that. "I beg your pardon?"

She stopped, realizing only in that moment that they'd reached the entrance to the park, and turned to face him. She realized, too, that she'd spoken without thinking again, but now she had no choice except to blunder on.

"You don't seem to have yielded to God your grief over your father's death and the pain of your family's rejection," she said calmly, "and I can't help wondering why."

"The pain of my family's rejection?" he echoed, sounding genuinely confused. "Where on earth did you get that?"

She spread her hands helplessly. "From what you

said about your brother and sister resenting that your father chose you to head the company. That has to feel like rejection."

He shook his head. "Sweetheart, I wouldn't know how to behave if my family wasn't always at each other's throats."

Dismayed for him, she tried to reconcile that statement with what she knew about family. "I understand that you're all probably only now coming to grips with the loss of your father and—"

"Please. It's not like he was a big part of our lives or anything."

Now she felt confused. "But he was your father."

"Let me tell you a little story," Tyler said, leading her over to a bench, where they sat down side by side. "I was maybe ten when the maid had to see somebody about something." He shrugged. "I guess she didn't want to leave me home alone. Anyway, I wound up riding along with her in her car to this strange neighborhood, and I guess we were there for some time because I started playing baseball in the streets with a bunch of kids I'd never met before. I hit this ball straight through the front window of a house there." He made a motion with his arm, indicating the path of a line dive.

"Oh, no." Charlotte lifted her hand to hide a smile. "I broke a window once, with a pork chop."

He chuckled. "A pork chop?"

She nodded and wrinkled her nose. "It was greasy, and when I stabbed at it with a fork, it flew off my plate and through the window."

"And what did your father do?" Ty asked.

She spread her hands. "Why, he fixed it. That window was always getting broken. The kitchen was really small and we didn't have a dining room so the table had to sit right up against it."

Tyler slumped back against the bench, shaking his head. "So you broke a window and your father fixed it. No big deal. I broke a window and my father sent me to boarding school for the rest of the year."

She gasped, appalled. "He didn't! Over a window that you broke accidentally?"

Tyler made a face, shaking his head. "The window didn't have anything to do with it. What infuriated him was that he had to be called out of an important business meeting to deal with it."

"But—"

"The maid gave them the number," Tyler went on. "I begged them not to call. I even offered to buy those people a new house if they wouldn't phone my father's office."

Charlotte snickered. She couldn't help it. "You really offered to buy them a whole new house?"

His lips twitched. "Hey, I was ten. Cut me a break here."

They laughed over that, then fell silent.

"It wasn't so bad, really," Tyler said after a moment. "Those months at boarding school taught me a lot of discipline. I fared better than the maid, that's for sure. She was fired on the spot." He sent Charlotte a rueful glance. "No one called my father out of a business meeting and got away with it. Business always came first with him. Always." He picked at a piece of lint on the pocket of Hap's coat. "Toward the end of their marriage my mother used to have him dragged out on the least pretext. I assume that was why he divorced her. One thing was certain, he was never there for us, any of us."

Reaching out, Charlotte laid her hand over his. "I'm so sorry, Tyler, but I do understand. My mother was like that in a way. It wasn't that she had more important things to do but that she seemed to think everyone else was there for her and not the other way around."

He turned his hand and clasped hers palm to palm. "Maybe we're not so different after all," he whispered.

Suddenly, she very much feared that he might be right.

Chapter Ten

They sat together in silence for a while, soaking in the serene beauty of the park, hands clasped but not looking at each other.

Finally, Tyler's soft voice asked, "How did your parents die? You said something about an oil-field accident."

Charlotte cleared her throat and answered him. "In my father's case, that's right. He fell from a derrick."

"That must have been tough," Ty murmured, squeezing her hand with his.

"It was a terrible shock, but not as shocking as what my mother did," Charlotte admitted.

She rarely spoke of it. In all the years since, she hadn't found any reason to tell another person about it. Everyone in the family and around town had always known. It had become common knowledge almost from the moment it had happened.

Ty squeezed her hand again. "What did she do?"

Charlotte looked at their clasped hands. The sight of them made her feel even sadder for some reason. "As soon as she got the news about Dad, my mother swallowed a bottle of pills." She matched her gaze to his then. "With zero regard for the children she was leaving behind, she took her own life. She wrote a note, asking, 'Who will take care of me now?'"

Tyler closed his eyes. "Oh, man." He lifted his free arm and curled it around her, pulling her close to his side. "I have to wonder how the human race survives sometimes."

"I know how I survived," Charlotte said, laying her head on his shoulder and letting herself feel comforted. "My grandparents taught me to take these things to the Lord." She lifted her head again. "I want to encourage you to do the same. It's like Grover said today, His grace is more than sufficient."

Tyler chuckled lightly and brushed his knuckles across her cheek. "I'd rather that you prayed for me, frankly."

She blinked and sat up straight again, pulling her hand free. "Yes, certainly, but you can always go to God yourself, you know."

"Somehow I think your prayers might serve me better."

For a moment she stared up at him. "Why would you say that?"

He smiled down at her, his palm cupping the curve of her jaw. "I suspect you have a direct line."

Flabbergasted, she exclaimed, "But don't you see that your prayers are as powerful as mine?"

"No," he answered simply, leaning closer still. "Now let me ask you something."

"All right."

"Would you ever consider leaving Eden?"

The shift in subject threw her. She'd expected something along spiritual lines. "Leave Eden?"

His sky-blue eyes held her. "To live, I mean. Would you ever consider living anywhere besides Eden?"

She didn't have to look for the answer, but it might have been more accurate to say that she didn't want to look for it. "No!"

He drew back a little. "Why not? You never know what another place might have to offer." Obviously warming to his subject, he rushed on. "Take Dallas, for instance. You could eat out every night of the year and never visit the same restaurant twice. And shopping. Oh, my goodness. You can't imagine what the shopping is like. Even I know it's far superior to anything around here. Then there's entertainment." He waved a hand. "Anything you can think of. Lots you probably wouldn't think of, too, but never mind that."

He went on enumerating all the reasons for living in the Dallas/Fort Worth Metroplex area. "The best hospitals, museums, art galleries, pro sports, amateur sports…" He threw up his hands. "You have no idea!"

"I'm sure it's lovely," she said, mystified, "but it's not for me."

"How can you know that?" he demanded, his gaze intense.

"Well, for one thing," she pointed out, quite unnecessarily, she thought, "my family is here, and they need me, Granddad especially."

"Your brothers are adults," Tyler argued. "They want you to be happy. Your grandfather, too, no doubt."

"But I'm happy here."

"Are you?"

"Absolutely. If I wasn't, I'd be married to Jerry Moody right now." Her hand rose halfway to her mouth, but the words had already been said, although why she had said them she didn't know.

Tyler sat back with a *whump.* "I knew it." Abruptly he shifted toward her, eyes narrowing. "You're still in love with him, aren't you?"

"No!" She shook her head, feeling out of control and reckless. "Why would you think that? I just told you that I broke off our engagement."

She could see the wheels turning in his head, the cogs fitting into place behind his eyes. "You broke off your engagement because Jerry wanted to move away from here."

"Eden is my home," she said, trembling now. "I belong here."

"And you don't love Jerry?" Ty probed.

For some reason, she had to make him believe her. "No," she said firmly. "I'm fond of him, but if I loved him…if I'd loved him *enough,* I'd have married him."

Ty's nostrils flared, and she knew suddenly that he was going to kiss her. She knew as well that she must stop him. She meant to. She truly did, but at that moment she couldn't think how. Instead, everything in her focused on the descent of his head and then the pressure of his lips on hers.

Her head fell back against his shoulder, and her eyes slammed closed. Without her consent her arms rose to slide about his neck. The whole world screeched to a halt and gradually tilted. Only Tyler anchored her to its surface, his arms looped around her, holding her against him.

Once she felt the world right itself again she blinked up at him, realizing where they were and just what they'd been doing. She gasped to think that she'd sat here in this very public place in broad—okay, waning—daylight, kissing Tyler Aldrich. Kissing!

"O-h-h." She slapped a hand over her mouth.

Tyler tilted his head as if measuring the effect of that kiss. After a moment, he grinned, his white, even teeth dazzling in the deepening gloom. Her face flamed. At almost the same instant, he tenderly pushed her head back down against her shoulder, as if to spare her the embarrassment.

She sat there for several moments before she understood that he was waiting for her to speak, but what could she say? What *should* she say? Moments ticked away before a truly coherent thought formed inside her head. Only then did she drop her hand from her mouth.

"Tyler," she said, sitting up and taking a firm grip on herself, "that should not have happened."

He lifted both eyebrows. "Why not?"

"B-because…" She blanched at the breathless sound of her own voice. Making a concerted effort to appear calm and unruffled, she put her concern into carefully chosen words. "That should not have happened because I'm not the sort of woman who casually does that kind of thing."

He laughed. Laughed. Sliding back on the seat, he lifted his face and laughed out loud. She frowned, offended but somehow uncertain about it, until he chucked her beneath the chin with a curved finger.

"Sweetheart," he said indulgently, "you are not like any other woman I've ever known, but, believe me, I do understand that much about you." He placed a hand over his heart, adding, "I absolutely meant no disrespect. You have to know that."

She did. Now that her pulse rate had normalized and her brain seemed to be functioning again, she knew that while he had initiated the kiss, he had also ended it. After a relatively short period of time.

She blushed, aware that she had overreacted.

In all likelihood that kiss had told him everything he'd needed to know about her, and that would be the end of the matter.

Nodding, she looked around, relieved to note that they were quite alone. Apparently everyone else had the good sense to stay in out of the chancy weather. She turned a glance over one shoulder to take note of the clouds. Building high in the northwest, the dark gray matter now seemed to loom over them in the silvering light.

"We'd better get inside before it rains again," she stated firmly, pushing up to her feet once more. As if to reinforce that decision, a chill, damp breeze swirled around them.

Tyler stood, and they headed back in the direction from which they had come, both seemingly caught in their own thoughts.

Whatever God's reason for allowing their two universes to meld for this moment in time, Charlotte told herself firmly, that's all it was, all it could ever be, a moment in time. Tyler would soon leave, and their paths would never cross again.

If the thought pained her, that, too, would be temporary. Wouldn't it?

Tyler clasped his hands together behind him, bowed his head and worked hard at not grinning like an idiot. It took considerable effort, surprising effort. He'd have danced down that street if he could have explained the impulse, but just why he felt so happy all of sudden remained something of a mystery.

Yes, he had enjoyed that kiss—reveled in it, honestly—but he had rarely done anything so foolish. He didn't know quite why he'd done it, really. Maybe he'd just wanted to prove to himself, or her, or both of them, that what she'd said was true, that she really hadn't loved Jerry Moody. But what was the point in that? It didn't change anything.

He'd had some half-formed notion of offering her a job, thereby tempting her into his orbit, but that, he now realized, was insanity. The differences between him and Charlotte were stark, insurmountable, and even if they weren't, she had no intention of ever leaving Eden— witness poor old Jerry still pining after her despite a wife and two children. Tyler suddenly felt rather sorry for the big goof.

Obviously Jerry had needed to look elsewhere to earn a living; Tyler could understand that. He couldn't imagine how anyone might stay here for any real length of time. The place didn't even offer a decent Internet connection, to say nothing of cell service. Even with those things, Tyler mused, failing to realize that *he* had replaced *anyone* in his own mind, he could never trust his family long enough to stay out of pocket for more than a week or two.

The pity of it was that he and Charlotte simply had no real time to get to know one another. Anything beyond that remained out of the question.

Besides, if they didn't have enough against them, religion might well be an issue, too, at least for her. He didn't know what she meant by grace. Spiritual things had never figured very large in his life. He had nothing against faith, of course, it just didn't seem to apply to him.

She was right. He shouldn't have kissed her. Yet he couldn't regret it.

No woman had ever moved him like sweet, simple, unassuming Charlotte Jefford.

He thought about it as they hurried back toward the motel, the mist blowing in from the north quickening their footsteps.

She might fit him personally, but his world simply did not fit her. He couldn't imagine her doing the things his mother and sister did, sitting on charity boards and orchestrating formal dinner parties, worrying about making the proper fashion statement. Unlike Cassandra, Charlotte had no career ambitions, and she would never be content just spending money or filling her days with trips to the spa. Why, the women in his family would eat her alive.

Between Cassandra's sniffing put-downs and his mother's pointed commiseration, Charlotte wouldn't have a chance. Cassandra would murmur that Charlotte looked like a walking trash heap, her standard criticism for anyone who didn't dress to her specifications. She'd slyly attack Charlotte's education and her antecedents. His mother would simply heap pity on the poor woman until she suffocated.

He didn't even want to think about Shasta. His stepmother had been a nobody, a lowly secretary without connections or wealth, as his mother and sister all too often pointed out, before Comstock Aldrich had married her. Tyler had found, however, that the worst snobs were those who had the least about which to be snobbish. Shasta wouldn't stop at just turning up her nose at someone like Charlotte. She'd do her best to wound.

No sense fooling himself. Not one person in his life would understand what he saw in Charlotte, not even his brother, and they would undoubtedly make both their lives miserable if he should be so foolish as to try to forge some sort of relationship with her, though what that could be with a girl like Charlotte he couldn't imagine. She would expect nothing less than marriage, and that could never be for obvious reasons.

"Are you hungry?" she asked as they hurried around the back wing of the motel.

He wasn't, but he curled up his lips and nodded anyway.

"We'd better get in there before they eat it all, then," she told him, picking up the pace.

They ran the last little way, raindrops beginning to pelt them. Tyler laughed, feeling grand in spite of everything, and told himself that he deserved this vacation from his life.

He needed the renewal that he'd found here, and he

was going to take it. Beyond that… He didn't want to think beyond that. For once, for a little while, he just wanted to be happy.

Charlotte folded the dish towel and draped it over the handle on the front of the oven. Behind her, Tyler closed the cabinet door. With the last dish now safely stowed away, she reached around to untie her apron, while Ty leaned a hip against the counter.

"Thanks for your help," she said, lifting the apron off over her head. Her braid flopped against her shoulder. She reached up and pushed it away, catching the glimmer of a smile as Tyler bowed his head. "What?"

He folded his arms. "You feed me. Again. Then you thank me for drying a few dishes. Seems to me you've got it backward."

Charlotte waved a hand dismissively. "I have to cook. You have to eat. It's just logical."

"It's generous," he corrected, "and I thank you." Leaning in slightly, he added, "Another excellent meal, by the way."

She inclined her head. "You're welcome. But you're putting too fine an edge on it. You've been lots of help around here these past few days. I'd be less than gracious to begrudge you a few meals."

In truth, he'd been more than simply helpful. Not only had he lent a hand with her chores, he'd entertained Hap at the dominoes table, offered Stu Booker, the local grocer and son of Hap's friend Teddy, a line of private-label goods at rock-bottom prices, counseled Justus Inman on setting up a trust to protect the Inman family farm, befriended everyone else with whom he'd come in contact and followed around her brothers like a lost puppy.

His behavior puzzled her. Maybe he'd simply become bored, but that didn't explain why an accomplished, successful man like him continued to hang around little old Eden in the first place. He'd stopped that first night only because he couldn't find fuel for his car, but what kept him here?

After he'd kissed her she'd feared that she might be the reason why he continued hanging around, but now she thought that perhaps God was using this time to bring Ty closer to Him. A man with Tyler's resources could do much good for the kingdom of God, much good indeed.

Besides, it didn't make any sense for Ty to stay for her. He had to know as well as she did that the two of them did not suit each other. He lived in Dallas and would no doubt return there, but she would only leave Eden if God told her to, and she couldn't believe that would ever happen. Hap and her brothers needed her. That hadn't changed, nor would it.

Clearly that kiss had been a fluke, an aberration born of pity, if nothing else, and though it hurt a bit to think so, she could only conclude that it had shown Tyler in no uncertain terms that they could never have anything serious between them. For one thing, the kiss had not been repeated, which was just as it should be.

Still, the longer Tyler Aldrich lingered in Eden, the more she wondered why.

After expressing interest in the oil business on Sunday evening, Tyler had tagged along with Holt on Monday, returning that evening bedraggled and filthy in his cheap jeans and T-shirt. Despite the exhaustion stamped on his face, he'd seemed quite satisfied with himself, and Holt had grudgingly allowed that Tyler wasn't afraid of hard work. The conversation around the dinner table that night had demonstrated a fresh, incisive understanding on Ty's behalf of the laborious process of extracting crude oil from the ground.

After that experience, she shouldn't have been surprised when Ryan had shown up at her breakfast table on Tuesday morning, especially since he and Tyler had spoken on Sunday about the possibility of Ty's checking out the weight room at the high school. After downing three eggs, twice that many slices of bacon and half a pot of coffee, Ryan had left again, a casually dressed Tyler with him.

They'd returned at lunchtime, grinning and joking like little boys. The talk around the table then had been all about workout techniques and sports. Ryan had pronounced Ty good company as he'd taken his leave and headed back to the school, leaving Charlotte to shake her head in his wake.

On Tuesday afternoon and for all of Wednesday Tyler had devoted himself to helping her, and she could truthfully concur with the assessments of both of her brothers. The man did not quail at getting his hands dirty, and his quick wit and pleasant manner made working with him pure fun, especially since his understanding of routine housekeeping proved laughably basic at best.

He'd quickly caught on, however, and had exhibited such rapt attention in the laundry room that she'd invited him to do his own washing. The pride he'd taken in that stack of fresh, clean clothing still made her smile.

"Listen," he said, breaking into her reverie, "now that everything's done, I was thinking about taking in a movie."

"Ah," she said, shifting mental gears. "In that case, you'll want to head up to Duncan again. You remember where the discount store is? The theater is about a half mile farther up 81 from there. It's on the same side of the road. You can't miss it."

His teeth flashed white before he glanced away. "Yes. I see. Well, how about a little TV instead? I have a couple of videos, but if those don't appeal to you we ought to be able to find something on broadcast, don't you think?"

We. She bit her lip, realizing too late that he'd been issuing an invitation, not asking directions. "I—I really don't know. I never watch television on Wednesday evening."

He cocked his head, and though his posture did not change, she sensed a sudden tension in him. "No? Is there something else you usually do then?" His casual tone did nothing to dispel the heightened sense of interest.

"I—I usually attend the midweek prayer service at church."

"Oh." The awkwardness evaporated as quickly as it had developed. "Mind if I tag along?"

Mind? She tamped down a spurt of delight, reminding herself that his interest had nothing to do with her personally. His curiosity obviously knew no bounds, and he'd probably only invited her to watch television with him in the first place because he felt bored. Besides, no matter what kept Tyler here, she must remember that he would be leaving, probably sooner rather than later.

Becoming too attached to him, too used to his presence, too pleased by his attention would only cause her grief later. Nevertheless, no harm ever came from spending an hour in prayer with someone. She formed a polite, fond smile. "Let me get my things."

Chapter Eleven

Tyler looked around the circle of smiling faces, smoothed his damp palms on his jeaned thighs and tried not to fidget in his folding chair. He'd expected something similar to the Sunday service when he'd invited himself along with Charlotte, and things *had* started out that way. They'd congregated in the sanctuary, sung a few songs, listened to a few announcements—mostly prayer requests for those not in attendance—and then, to his shock, filed out to the fellowship hall where they'd broken into groups.

It had never occurred to Tyler that he could find himself sitting in a circle of strangers who were waiting for him to add his private concerns to their prayer lists. He glanced around the large room at the other circles. One, composed entirely of men, included both Holt and Ryan. They had waved and nodded but had not invited him to join them, no doubt knowing full well that he preferred to spend whatever time he had left here with their sister.

On Monday Holt had boldly asked him if he had any interest in Charlotte, to which Ty had replied, "For all the good that's likely to do me." Holt had grunted at that and lobbed a three-foot-long wrench at him so he could couple one pipe to another.

Ryan had been less direct but more obvious, blabbing incessantly about what a treasure Charlotte was and how they feared she would never find someone to truly appreciate her. Tyler had kept his own mouth shut, but he couldn't doubt that Ryan would give his blessing if Ty so much as hinted at wanting to pursue a relationship with Charlotte. Again, for all the good that would do him.

The participants of one of the other circles had already bowed their heads. A third group linked hands even as Tyler watched. Swiftly he turned back to his own circle, acutely aware of Charlotte sitting to his right and his lack of an answer for a personal prayer request.

"I, um… Well, I really don't have anything."

"We all have something that we need to take to God," an elderly woman noted kindly.

Tyler shifted his weight on the hard chair, feeling out of his depth. Charlotte, thankfully, came to his rescue.

"I think what Tyler means is that he wants his request to remain unspoken."

Unspoken. He remembered something about an unspoken request among those that the pastor had read from the pulpit earlier. That had seemed odd to him, but now he cravenly made the claim for himself. "Right. Un-unspoken."

Attention shifted to the person to Tyler's left, who went on at some length about the travails of his mother who was confined to a hospital. More to keep from looking at Charlotte than in real concern, Tyler focused his concentration on what the fellow had to say.

He couldn't help contrasting the poor old woman's situation with his father's. A private suite, personal nurses, limitless funds and doctors who fell all over themselves to provide the latest in treatment and technologies could not compare with crowded, shared rooms, noisy visitors, unresponsive, overworked staff, compassionate but helpless physicians and devoted families frustrated by uncaring and inadequate insurance bureaucracies.

It didn't seem fair that one experience should be better than another in the face of illness. Guilt clouded Tyler's mood until the man began to speak about his mother's sweet nature and happy spirit. Gradually guilt turned to envy, an emotion Tyler had little experience with and even less right to.

His had been a privileged existence, even if his father had been critical and distant and his mother self-absorbed. Yet he found himself coveting the obviously loving relationship that man had with his ailing mother. Uncomfortably self-conscious now, Tyler wished that he had not come.

That feeling only intensified as the group linked hands and bowed their heads. Instead of one person leading the entire group, each individual was expected to pray aloud, squeezing the hand of the person to his or her left when finished so that the prayer could continue around the circle uninterrupted. A middle-aged woman with salt-and-pepper hair across the way from Tyler began.

"Sovereign Lord God, You have told us that where

we gather in Your name, You are there also. Thank You for coming to meet us, Father, as we approach Your throne in the name of Your Holy Son…"

As she spoke, Tyler felt an unusual sensation, as if something brushed against his skin, all of his skin at the same time. Later, as others took their turns, Tyler felt a movement inside his chest, a spreading almost, as though something tightly knotted unfurled. He didn't know what to call it, but he knew that he had never felt it before.

When Charlotte began to pray aloud, her voice a soft, gentle salve to his jangling senses, he perceived a presence, as if someone stood just behind him. This so unnerved him that he concentrated with fierce determination on Charlotte's words.

"We praise You, Lord, and thank You for Your many blessings," she was saying, "but then You know our needs even better than we do. You know that Granddad's arthritis pains him more and more lately. He never complains, but I dread the coming winter for him. Please ease his discomfort and don't let the cold rob him of enjoyment. Make me a blessing to him, as You have made him a blessing to me, and show us always what You would have us do."

She paused, and Tyler waited in an agony of dread for the squeeze on his hand that would make it his turn to speak. Instead, warmth spread from his palm, up his arm and throughout his body as she went on.

"Thank You, too, for Ty. He's been such help and he's brought such enjoyment. You know his needs, Lord, better than I do, even better than he does. I just lift those up to You, heavenly Father, trusting You to fill each and every one. Bless him. Bring him peace and joy."

When that dreaded squeeze finally came, Tyler couldn't have spoken if his life had depended on it. His heart seemed to have swollen inside his chest to the point that it crowded his throat. He couldn't shake the sudden conviction that he didn't deserve the gratitude Charlotte had expressed, but what could he say to that? What could he say, period? He knew a moment of agonizing uncertainty; yet, in that same moment, a voice seemed to whisper inside his mind, and suddenly the words just flowed from his mouth.

"We are blessed whether we deserve it or not, even when we aren't smart enough to ask for it. Thank You for that. A-and—"

His mind stuttered to a stop, suddenly blank. He shifted forward, and a calming hand settled upon his shoulder, bringing clarity and ease. His first thought was that it must be one of Charlotte's brothers, come to offer support.

Apparently he hadn't fooled them one bit. He'd wanted them to think that he was just like them, that he had experienced everything they had experienced, but he'd never participated in anything like this. He didn't have closely held religious beliefs as they did, but it didn't seem to matter at all. He felt deep gratitude just then for the kindness of the Jefford family.

They had taught him so much, more than he'd even realized until just that moment. Because of them, he saw what his own family lacked. Because of them, he understood that money and position didn't matter and true happiness came from within. Because of them, he knew that God was real. He'd always believed that on some level, but now he *knew,* and for the first time he really believed that he could actually talk to God, one-on-one.

Smiling inwardly, Tyler let his chin touch his chest and spoke from his heart. "Thank You for bringing me here to Eden. Thank You for new friends and good fun, for relaxation and broadening experiences, for renewal and…just…thank You." Something unexpected touched his mind, and he blurted it without thought. "Be with my family. We all need Your blessings even if we don't know it."

He started to say, "Amen," but remembered just in time and squeezed the hand of the fellow next to him instead. For a moment silence filled the room, and then Tyler became aware of Holt's voice from across the hall.

"We bow to Your leadership, Lord, seeking to do Your will and knowing that You alone can provide wisdom and joy in our lives. We are Your creatures, Your children. Make us men You are proud to call Your own."

Not Holt, then, Tyler thought, though whoever had been behind him appeared to have silently moved off now. The fellow next to Tyler began to speak, but Holt's words seemed to have caught in Tyler's mind.

Make us men You are proud to call Your own.

With stabbing dismay, Tyler realized that he had not always been such a man. In fact, he did not really even know how to be such a man. Troubled, he mentally added a new prayer to those spoken in the circle.

Make me a man You are proud to call Your own.

* * *

The service moved back into the sanctuary. Tyler felt a warmth, an ease that he had not felt earlier. The smiles of those around him seemed softer, their laughter brighter, conversation more serene. Grover thanked everyone for coming, read a verse of Scripture, spoke a final prayer over the gathering and let the service close with a hymn.

Tyler did not catch the chapter and verse of the Scripture, but the words settled inside him.

"Therefore I say to you, all things for which you pray and ask, believe that you have received them, and they shall be granted you."

Could it really be so simple? he wondered. Was it truly just a matter of belief?

Obviously, he mused, Charlotte's faith and that of her brothers and grandfather meant more than he'd assumed. But what did it mean for him?

He looked across the room to where Holt stood shaking hands with a gentleman so elderly that his frail body seemed to curl inward over the cane against which he balanced his slight weight. Their mutual affection lit the building. Ryan, meanwhile, laughed with a fortyish couple and Charlotte hugged a middle-aged woman with tightly curled hair.

Tyler had thought these people poor. He saw no designer suit in the place, no expensive watch, no artificial beauty, but he knew that no one here was poor. They were rich in spirit, far richer than he, in fact.

Perhaps their bank balances would not impress anyone, but what did that matter? No doubt they had their own troubles, their own concerns, perhaps even secrets that would shock their friends, but they were better off in many ways than the people he knew.

He found it disconcerting, to say the least, to realize that he might well be the poorest person in the building. Any unimportant claims to wealth that he could make had come to him purely through an accident of birth. These people had found their riches in a place where he had never before thought to look. They had found their wealth in their families and friends and their faith in God.

He looked to Charlotte's brothers again. A man's man, as strong and tough as they came, Holt also had brains and an indomitable will balanced by an honest spirit. Holt had everything it took to it make in Tyler's world, but when Tyler had said as much the other day, Holt had merely laughed.

"Been there, done that," he'd said. "Won't be going there again." He'd stopped what he'd been doing then and stood tall, legs braced wide apart, dirty, gloved hands at his sides. "I am where I belong," he'd added, no shred of doubt in his voice.

At the time, Tyler had thought he, too, knew where he belonged. Now he wondered.

He thought of Hap, the single most loving individual whom Ty had ever known. Being loving hadn't seemed much like a manly attribute to Tyler until the last few days, but Hap could show him just how it should be done.

Ryan, on the other hand, might be the happiest person Tyler knew. He bore the weight of his responsibilities with delight and facility, sincerity shining from his every pore. He loved his job and his family, his students and his teams, his town and his life. Not only could Ryan succeed in Tyler's world, he could succeed in a big way, but Tyler hadn't even bothered to say as much. He'd learned his lesson with Holt.

Or had he? He sensed that he still had lessons to learn here in Eden, Oklahoma. Important lessons.

Such thoughts occupied his mind as the meeting dispersed and he escorted Charlotte to his car. Only as he reached down to open the door for her did he ask the question that had been bothering him for some time.

"Who was that behind us in the prayer circle?" Someone had noticed his distress and calmed him with a touch. He owed that person a debt of thanks. It hadn't been Holt, but it might have been Ryan. Or perhaps the pastor?

Charlotte paused with one foot in the car and one foot out. She turned a puzzled look on him. "I don't know who you mean."

"There was someone standing just outside the circle, someone right behind us."

She thought a moment. He could see her mentally placing everyone present. Finally, she shook her head. "No, I don't think so."

"He put his hand on my shoulder," Tyler insisted, but she simply stared. "Ryan, maybe. Or Grover?"

"No, I saw them both with the men's group. I'd have known if either had risen."

Tyler frowned. "Well, someone put his hand on my shoulder."

She bit her lip, then a smile tugged it free again. Shrugging delicately, she dropped down into the seat.

Tyler closed her inside and moved around the vehicle, his mind awhirl.

This place and these people suddenly had him questioning everything, especially himself.

"You did not!" Charlotte exclaimed, sure he was teasing.

The afternoon had turned fair and bright, hinting at a beautiful weekend, although the sunshine seemed fragile, almost crystalline, as if a sharp breeze might shatter it. Should Friday hold the same promise, she might start to believe and plan something frivolous like a final picnic before winter settled in. Sitting here on the patio with Tyler, sipping coffee and talking about youthful escapades, anything felt possible, anything at all.

"I did," Tyler admitted sheepishly, "I totaled the car leaving the dealership."

"What did your father do about that?" she asked, remembering that a broken window at the age of ten had resulted in a year at boarding school for Tyler. She prepared to sympathize, but Ty shrugged.

"Bought me another one."

Charlotte let her jaw drop. "No boarding school?"

"Not even a scolding."

She sagged, at a complete loss to understand. "That makes no sense whatsoever."

Ty spread his hands. "It seemed to at the time. I had a driver's license, so I had to have a car. Besides, by that age I was no bother to them any longer."

"I'd call wrecking a brand-new car a bother."

"Problems that could be fixed with money were not problems to my parents," Tyler pointed out. He lifted a hand to his temple, confessing, "The fact is, I got pretty wild there for a while, but as long as it didn't particularly disturb their lives they didn't seem to mind. Even after I graduated college and my father brought me into the company, so long as I showed up and took care of business, that was all that mattered." He went on to explain that he'd come into his trust fund by then and so had his own money.

Charlotte shook her head. "I'll hope you'll pardon me for saying so, but I'm amazed you turned out so well."

He flashed her a grin. "So you think I turned out okay, do you?"

Charlotte rolled her eyes. "Obviously."

"I don't know sometimes," he said with jarring honesty. "I think I was mostly trying to get their attention back then. Eventually I realized that my father respected just one thing, though, and I won his regard in that, at least. I think."

"Business," she surmised.

Nodding, he looked up into the sunlight. "I'm just not sure business acumen is all that should be passed from one generation to the next."

"Oh, I'm sure you'll do better with your own children," she said with sincerity, ignoring the foolish little pang that accompanied the thought.

Tyler stretched out on the chaise and crossed his ankles. "I'm not sure I'll ever have children," he told her.

"But of course you will."

"Will you, do you think?" he asked lightly.

For a moment she couldn't breathe, but then she remembered that regret and longing belied her faith. She had trusted God long ago to see to her future, and she'd accepted that the gifts she had in her grandfather and brothers surpassed any she could imagine for herself. What would she have done after the deaths of her parents without Hap and Holt and Ryan?

"These things are in God's hands," she said, "and capable hands they are."

The unmistakable sound of a car turning off the highway reached her ears, but she ignored it. Hap would take care of whoever had stopped in—guest, salesman or passerby seeking directions.

"I had a wreck once," she said, launching into the story.

Like Holt, her father had always run a few head of cattle on their place, and one day returning from town with a girlfriend of hers, they'd discovered a cow had gotten out and gone wandering around the yard. Her father had left the truck idling while he'd gone on foot to drive the cow back into the pasture. Charlotte, all of twelve, had decided to pull the truck up to the house. She'd been driving around the ranch for years, but her friend, who lived in town and hadn't known that, had panicked as soon as the truck started moving. She'd grabbed hold of Charlotte and tried to hide her face against Charlotte's shoulder.

"All I could see was black hair," Charlotte recalled with a chortle. "I tried to stomp the break but kept hitting the clutch. It didn't seem like I'd driven ten feet, but it had to be more like ten yards."

"What finally stopped you?" he asked, chuckling.

"The barn."

"It's a miracle you weren't killed!"

"You're telling me. I had to drive right past the propane tank to get there."

Hap rounded the corner of the building just then, saying, "Here they are. Ty, you got company, son."

Tyler twisted around in his seat just as a tall, slender, elegantly attired blonde walked into view. Charlotte sat up a little straighter, suddenly conscious of her shaggy sweater, rumpled shirt, faded jeans and rundown sneakers. Hoping that the hole in her left sock didn't show, she crossed her ankles primly, not that it helped anything.

The blonde might have walked straight out of the pages of a fashion magazine. The slender skirt of her moss-green suit emphasized the svelte length of her legs, while the short, belted jacket and the filmy silk blouse beneath it called attention to the feminine lushness of her figure. Her pale hair had been twisted into a sleek, sophisticated knot that could not have been accomplished without expertise while the pearls at her earlobes and the diamond at her throat fairly shouted wealth.

Charlotte's stomach dropped to the rubber-clad soles of her feet while Tyler literally groaned. The blonde folded her arms, one foot swinging out to the side in an obviously practiced pose.

"Ty?" she queried, making that single syllable sound like an indictment as well as irony. Abruptly, her focus switched to Charlotte, her subtly made-up eyes narrowing.

Tyler sighed and asked, "How did you find me?"

"If you don't want to be found, you shouldn't use your company credit card," the blonde retorted.

Ty winced. Charlotte remembered how often he'd used that card during the past few days. He'd been shopping with that card, and last night after prayer meeting he'd driven Charlotte all the way to Waurika for malts. Just this morning he'd insisted on paying his bill with it so Hap could balance the accounts. He'd remarked repeatedly that he really needed to get some cash because not everyone around here took plastic.

Somehow, though, Charlotte didn't think the credit card was the problem. The problem stood in front of them. Who was this woman? Employee? Coworker? Girlfriend?

Charlotte couldn't bear to think the latter, but the possibility could not be ignored, not with this cool blonde standing here alternately smirking and glaring at her.

Ty bowed his head, pressing thumb and fingers to his temples. Then he looked up and smiled wanly at Charlotte.

"Sorry. I haven't introduced my sister."

Sister! Charlotte felt an instant of relief, followed swiftly by dismay, which she attempted to hide with a bright smile. If Tyler's sister represented the kind of woman who moved in Tyler's world, and she no doubt did, then Charlotte could never expect to meet his standards. Only then did she realize that on some level she had hoped to do just that.

Tyler stood, indicating his sister with a wave of his hand. "Cassandra Aldrich." He looked to her and placed a hand on the back of Charlotte's chair. "Allow me to introduce my hostess, Charlotte Jefford. You've already met her grandfather, Hap."

"Charlotte," Cassandra parroted with a little smirk, her gaze sweeping over Charlotte again. "What an old-fashioned name." Tyler's shoe scraped on the patio paving, and she quickly corrected herself, smile broadening. "Classic, I should've said. My own is a classic name. Tell me, do they call you Lottie? Now *that* would be old-fashioned."

"Cut it out, Cassandra."

"Whatever do you mean, *Ty?*"

"You know exactly what I mean."

Cassandra laughed. The sound contained nothing of amusement or pleasure. "It's a little hang-up of our mother's," she said to Charlotte. "She can't abide sobriquets. That means nicknames, by the way."

"I know what it means," Charlotte informed her quietly.

If she had needed proof that she would not fit into Tyler's world, she now had it in spades, not that she had been considering any such thing. Had she? No, of course not. She knew where she belonged. When had she started to second-guess that?

"What are you doing here, Cassandra?" Tyler asked coldly.

An unpleasant expression tightened Cassandra's pink mouth. "Perhaps little Lottie and her grandpa will excuse us while we discuss it."

"That's enough!" Tyler ordered, but Charlotte quickly leaped to her feet and brushed past him.

"Come on, Granddad, I need you to watch the front desk while I start dinner."

"Charlotte, don't—" Tyler began.

"No, really, it's fine," she told him, smiling to forestall further objection. "I'll see you later?"

"Yes, of course, but—"

Ducking her head, she hurried on by him, determined not to cry. It would be stupid to cry about Cassandra Aldrich's petty cruelties, and she wouldn't think of crying for any other reason. That would be beyond foolish.

Catching Hap by the arm, she turned him away from the unpleasant scene. They made it around the corner before Hap grumbled, "Not a good thing, her showing up like that."

Not a good thing at all, Charlotte thought, but she said nothing. The lump in her throat would not permit it.

She set about preparing the evening meal at once, but even as she worked, her thoughts were with Tyler and his sister. He would leave now. She knew it.

She'd always known he would go away again, had expected every day to be his last with them. Somehow, though, she had not been prepared for her own disappointment.

Tyler Aldrich, she realized suddenly, would leave a huge gaping hole in her life when he left.

How that could be after so short a time, she simply did not know.

Chapter Twelve

"That was a nasty thing to do," Tyler hissed.

Cassandra rolled her eyes. "Oh, please. Don't tell me that Little Miss Lumberjack and Old Man Overalls are your new best friends."

"Those people have been very good to me."

"Well, duh." She cast a spurious glance toward the rooms. "You can bet it isn't every day they get an Aldrich in here."

"It doesn't have anything to do with that," Tyler vowed.

"Right. Like you really believe that."

Suddenly weary, he dropped down onto the chaise again. Sniffing, Cassandra maneuvered herself in front of a lawn chair but didn't sit. Tyler reflected glumly that this one outfit of Cassandra's probably cost more than Charlotte's entire wardrobe.

"What do you want, Cassandra?"

She folded her arms in that patented display of contempt. "I want you to do your job."

He sat back and crossed his legs. "That's what I've been doing."

She lifted her eyebrows at the jeans he wore but stayed on topic. "Sure you have. That's why no one's heard from you in a week. What did you do, turn off your phone?"

"Yes."

"Typically juvenile."

He didn't deny it. Why should he bother defending himself? Cassandra would never understand, and what difference did it make that the cell service was spotty at best?

"Do you want to criticize, or do you want to tell me why you bothered to drive all this way?"

Clearly, she hated to say what had brought her here. Whatever it was literally made her grit her teeth. In the end, though, she had no choice. One of their major suppliers had gotten hit by Immigration. They'd lost so much staff that they'd effectively been shut down.

"We have to do something," she insisted. "Quick. Or by next week we won't be able to stock our shelves."

Tyler frowned. He should have anticipated something like this. The company policy forbade dealing with domestic producers who employed illegal immigrants, but realistically even lip service took a backseat to cost. "Who is it?"

"Paxit."

Tyler's frown deepened. It would have to be their largest supplier. By coincidence, the Paxit corporate offices were in Lewisville, Texas, on the far northern edge of the greater Dallas Metroplex.

"What is the board recommending?"

Cassandra snorted. "The board recommends point-ing fingers and hanging each other out to dry, as usual. Shasta is threatening to sue someone, anyone. Preston blames you for continuing Father's policies."

Tyler shook his head. "That's novel. He usually blames me for making too many changes."

"You should have been there to handle this!" Cassandra accused, going from cynical to white-hot in the blink of an eye. She shared that trait with their late fa-ther. When all else failed, resort to anger. It didn't help that this time she happened to be right. "Mother has taken to her bed, sure we'll all be bankrupt in a week," she added petulantly.

Tyler sighed. While their father had resorted to tow-ering rage, Amanda Aldrich routinely broke down in weeping self-pity punctuated with threats of impend-ing "nervous breakdowns," which the family tended to ignore, as her husband had done.

"I've talked to Spencer-Hatten," Cassandra an-nounced, lifting her chin defiantly. "The price is steep, and there's no time to relabel, but at least we could keep the shelves filled with SH goods."

"Except that the board won't go along with that," Tyler said flatly, "because Spencer-Hatten will demand a seat, and the next thing we know they'll own us."

Her chin went up another notch. "You don't know that."

He did know it, and so did Cassandra, but she'd rather see him fail than preserve the family business. No doubt she'd cut some sort of personal deal with Spencer-Hatten. He expected nothing less.

Tyler sighed inwardly. He had been foolish and self-indulgent. Perhaps he could have justified staying over the weekend, but what excuse did he have for remaining throughout the week? The time had come to return to his life.

The thought depressed him, but he had a job to do, the job for which he had been bred and groomed his entire life. He would be better at that job now; he had no doubt. Although at the moment he didn't have the faintest notion how he would solve this problem, he knew that he would find a way.

The prayer that had whispered through his mind last night came to him again. *Make me a man You are proud to call Your own.* He intentionally added another line. *Guide me in this.*

Tilting back his head, he looked up at his sister. Her cold, steely beauty, underlaid with the bitterness of resentment, cut his heart like a knife. Suddenly he longed to take her in his arms and tell her that all would be well. It's what Holt or Ryan would have done for their sister. *His* sister would probably come out swinging if he did such a thing, provided the shock didn't kill her first.

Sorrow draped him like a shroud. He pushed it aside and rose to his feet. "Go home, Cassandra. Tell the board we'll be meeting for lunch tomorrow. Then call the caterer."

Her eyes and lips narrowed cynically. "Haute cuisine won't get you out of this one, little brother."

God will, he thought, *if I ask Him.* And he intended to do just that. Charlotte would show him how. It might be the very last thing they would ever do together, but what could be more fitting?

Cassandra pivoted on her very narrow heel and sauntered away without another word. Tyler stood where she'd left him, head bowed, until he heard a door close and the car drive away. Sucking in a deep, calming breath, he went in search of Charlotte. As expected, he found her in the kitchen, a knife in hand as she sliced carrots.

"I'm sorry," he said. "Cassandra was out of line. She usually is."

Charlotte shook her head, her bright braid swinging between her shoulder blades. He'd never told her how much he liked her hair loose. He never would now. What possible purpose could it serve except to make leaving all the more difficult?

"Don't be silly," she said. "I'd never let anything like a little nickname offend me."

"I know you wouldn't, but she intended to offend."

Charlotte turned a smile in his direction, such softness in her eyes that his heart broke. "That's not your fault."

He couldn't look into those lovely eyes any longer. It hurt too much, as did what he had to say next. "I'll be leaving early in the morning."

She turned away, her hands still on the cutting board. "Not tonight?" she asked after a moment.

One more night, he thought. One more dinner. One more moment of ease and light. Not so easy now, not so light. Still, he would stay. For one more night.

"Tomorrow," he confirmed, "early. Tonight after dinner I'd appreciate it if you would pray with me."

He heard a clunk just before she whirled and came into his arms. Closing his eyes, he held her tight for a long, sweet moment.

"I wish it could be different," she whispered, "but you know it can't."

Ty swallowed. "I know. You have to stay in Eden."

"And you must return to your responsibilities," she said, pulling away to dab at her eyes. Now that the truth had been laid bare, they would pretend no longer. "We had fun, didn't we?"

He nodded but could not speak. She turned back to the cutting board.

"Would you set the table, please? The good china, I think." She shot him a bright smile that cut him to ribbons. "We'll end as we began."

It was all he could do to lift down the plates, one by one, without shattering his composure, if nothing else.

Dinner became a family affair. Hap must have called Ryan and Holt, the latter of whom dragged in filthy from a day in the field and spent long minutes washing until Charlotte deemed him clean enough to sit at her table.

Conversation could only be described as lively, if slightly forced. Everyone laughed and joked and talked at the same time. No one inquired about Cassandra or mentioned that Tyler would be leaving, and for that he silently thanked them.

After the meal, Hap's cronies began arriving, and Holt got up to take himself off home. He gave Tyler a hearty handshake and patted Charlotte's shoulder consolingly as he went out the door. Ryan hung around long enough to have a private word with Tyler.

"How often you reckon you'll be getting back up this way?"

Tyler had been beating himself with that question all evening. He could come every now and again, surely, but to what purpose? Why make himself and Charlotte miserable by projecting hope where none existed? Sick at heart, he could only say that he didn't know when he'd be back their way.

Ryan looked disappointed by that, but then he smiled and said, "Guess it's something else to pray about."

"Yes, it is," Tyler agreed solemnly, "and I'd appreciate it if you'd do just that."

"I absolutely will," Ryan said, grasping Ty's hand warmly. "Just know that whenever you come back, you'll be welcome."

Ty had to clear his throat. "Thank you, Ryan."

With a wary look in Charlotte's direction, Ryan left to attend one of his usual school functions. By that time Hap had migrated to the lobby for his usual game of dominoes. Tyler insisted on helping Charlotte finish cleaning up.

They worked in silence, broken only by the clink of dishes and the creak of cabinet doors. Eventually nothing remained to do. Charlotte removed her apron and looked at him.

"You said you wanted to pray."

Tyler wondered if he could manage that now, and he felt a little foolish for even bringing it up. "Oh, that. It's a business thing. I shouldn't have bothered you with it."

Ignoring that, she led him back to the table. They sat down again and linked hands. He explained the situation. Her prayer surprised him. She asked for wisdom for him in figuring out how to deal with the matter, but then she asked God to give him wisdom in dealing with his family, especially his sister.

"Just help them show each other how important they are to one another."

She squeezed his hand then, but she'd given him so much to think about that his mind whirled. He could barely form a sentence. Finally he came up with, "I guess that's it in a nutshell, God. I need wisdom to deal with all of this, and I don't think I even realized that until now, so maybe we've made a start. Thank You for that. Amen."

"Amen," Charlotte whispered.

They lifted their heads just as laughter exploded from the front room.

Charlotte rose, saying, "I don't know about you, but I think I need a little of that. Want to join me? Hap will understand if you'd rather not, but I know that the others would like to see you again."

One last time, she meant. One last time. Ty would rather have done anything than walk into that room and say his goodbyes—anything except walk through the door *without* saying them.

Joining the others turned out to be a wise decision. Hap, Teddy, Grover and Justus routinely kept each other and everyone around them in stitches, and they seemed especially jovial and clever that night. Tyler took their ribbing good-naturedly, knowing it for a sign of affection, and sat in for occasional hands while one or the other of them excused himself.

Eventually the game broke up. Grover left first, but not before giving Ty a personal farewell.

"We'll miss you, son. Have a safe trip and don't be a stranger now, you hear? I'll be praying for you."

"Thank you, sir."

"None of that now. You're all but family here."

More than family by Aldrich standards, Tyler reflected morosely. "Again, I thank you."

Teddy and Justus settled for handshakes and silent nods. As soon as they'd gone, Hap immediately attempted to make himself scarce, but Tyler wasn't about to let him get away with that. Clapping a hand on the old man's shoulder, he laughingly declared, "Oh, no, you don't."

Hap grimaced and hitched himself around. "I always hate goodbyes."

Tyler hated this one, but he gamely stuck out his hand. "It's been a pleasure. One I'll never forget. Grover said I was the next thing to family, but you've made me feel more like family than anyone else ever has. I needed that."

"Shucks, son," Hap said in a voice even rougher than usual. "If you're gonna do a thing, do it right." With that he engulfed Ty in a hug.

Clasping the old man carefully, Tyler felt his eyes mist. This was what a godly man should be, he thought.

Lord, make me a man You are proud to call Your own.

After delivering a bristly kiss to Tyler's cheek, Hap turned away, his stiff, shuffling steps carrying him into the apartment.

Tyler could not remember ever being kissed by another man, and suddenly he mourned the loss. What he would have given as a child for such a simple thing as that from his father. This time in Eden just seemed chock-full of surprising treasures, and the main one stood behind him.

He puffed out a breath and, when it could not be put off any longer, turned to Charlotte. She stood with her arms wrapped tightly about her middle, a clear warning that he heeded.

"I'll be heading out early," he said, "before daylight, even. I have an important lunch meeting, and I need to prepare."

She nodded. "You'll be careful going home? You won't drive too fast?"

Home? he thought. Funny, this place seemed more like home now than Dallas did, but he nodded.

"I guess this is goodbye, then," she said softly.

Again he nodded, but long seconds ticked by and still his feet did not move toward the door. "Charlotte," he began, surprising himself by moving forward rather than away. "I truly wish—"

She interrupted by simply stepping into his arms. "What is, is, Ty." She lifted her head, her eyes swimming with tears. "I'm glad to have known you, Tyler Aldrich. I'll be praying for you."

"I'm counting on that," he told her in a choked voice, then he got out of there before he did something stupid and they both broke down.

As he walked away, he told himself that it was time he started talking to God on a regular basis, and since there was no time like the present, he looked up at the black sky, whispering, "Lord, take care of her. Take care of them all. I know You will. They're good folks and they love You."

He'd learned a little something about that himself.

* * *

Charlotte passed a sleepless night, alternately praying and wondering if Tyler slept. Did he want to go back to his old life? she asked herself. Of course he did. Otherwise, he would not do it. Would he?

At other times she wondered if she might be wrong about God's will for her, but how could that be? Her family needed her, and she needed them. She remembered how very, very sure she had been before, when Jerry had insisted that the job waiting for him in Tulsa was their future.

"Your future," she had told him firmly. "Mine is here."

And it had been. It still was. It must be.

Besides, Tyler had not actually asked her to go with him. Surely he would have if he wanted that. Yet his going felt terribly like abandonment. She prayed for acceptance, remembering her happy life before Tyler Aldrich had found himself out of gas in Eden.

She would find that contentment again. Surely she would.

Long before daylight, Charlotte had her fill of these restless thoughts. Finally, she rose from her bed to throw on her robe and pad quietly into the kitchen to make up a pot of coffee. She worked in the dark, lest she awaken Hap. About halfway through the brewing process, she recognized the throaty rumble of Ty's car engine.

The sound drew her to open the kitchen door, but then she stood behind the screen to watch the sleek automobile back out of the covered space where it had spent the majority of the past week. Could it really be a mere week since she had first laid eyes on the man from Big D?

Only the screen and the dark stood between her and one final farewell. The car rolled forward, coming to rest just outside, not a dozen yards between them. Her hand reached out to push open the screen—but, no. If she went out there now, things might be said that shouldn't be.

The car rolled forward once more, a fortune on wheels, another world on wheels. She watched the turn signal blink, then the car swung out onto the highway heading south. In moments it had disappeared as if it had never existed.

Wiping her tears from her cheeks with the sleeve of her robe, she closed the door on this short but surprisingly poignant chapter in her life.

Chapter Thirteen

The solution came to Tyler as he crossed the Red River. One moment he was asking God to help him do what he knew he must, and the next moment the dilemma that pulled him back to Dallas had been reduced to a plan of action. He couldn't imagine why he hadn't thought of it at once.

Sure of the rightness of his plan, he drove straight to the corporate office of Paxit Distributing on the northern outskirts of the DFW Metroplex, where the owner and CEO, Comer Paxton, received him into his Spartan office with obvious dread and resignation. The fellow fully expected Tyler to cancel his contract, which had been Tyler's intention in the beginning. Now he had a better plan.

In a matter of a few hours, they hammered out a deal for Aldrich & Associates to buy Paxit Distributing and hire Paxton himself to run it. That would keep Paxit operational, allow it to settle the fines levied by the government, avoid any major rupture in the lines of supply and give Aldrich & Associates greater control over its own fate.

Getting the Aldrich board to sign off might take some doing, but Tyler knew it would work out when Comer Paxton gripped his hands together, bowed his head over them and exclaimed, "This is the answer to my prayers!"

"Funny you should say that," Tyler told him, smiling. "It's the answer to my prayers, too."

Over the next short while, he watched Comer Paxton come alive. Worry and defeat seemed to fall away; hope blossomed in the man's eyes. Corresponding gladness welled in Tyler. The sheer pleasure of finding a solution that protected this man's life's work and benefited everyone in the mix came as a surprise.

So this, Tyler thought, heading toward his own corporate offices, *is joy.* Funny that he should find it in the midst of dejection. He pushed that thought away, concentrating on business.

It did not, as Tyler had predicted, go smoothly with the board. Cassandra made an impassioned argument for Spencer-Hatten, and Shasta railed about the amount of money involved, but the numbers proved that Tyler's plan would not only guarantee an uninterrupted chain of supply, it would ultimately lead to substantial savings and growth.

Ty tried to listen to every side of every point of the debate, exercising patience he hadn't known he possessed. The arguing and the posturing endemic to his family continued as expected, but in the end even Cassandra voted in favor of Tyler's proposal, proof to his mind that Charlotte and the rest of the Jefford family were keeping him in their prayers.

Over that next weekend, thoughts of Charlotte and the others came to him constantly, and every time they did, he remembered the prayer that he had "caught" from Holt at the prayer meeting.

Lord, make me a man You are proud to call Your own.

He went to church on Sunday, realizing that being a man to make God proud required more than intention on his part. He couldn't just sit around waiting for God to create something in him that he did not actively pursue for himself. For the first time he became more than a mere observer. He really participated in the worship. He talked over things with God, too.

Still, something was missing. He kept thinking about that word *grace*. He mulled over the idea of talking to the pastor of his church about it, but he didn't even know how to broach the subject. If he could just talk to Hap then this confusion would leave him, but talking to Hap meant talking to Charlotte or, even worse, not talking to her, not seeing her. But wasn't that the case now?

He wondered if melancholy could kill a man.

Charlotte heard the creak of the screen door and quickly gulped back her tears, knowing that the night and the still, chilly air would amplify the smallest sound, even a sniff. Her brother's footsteps—she'd know them anywhere—scraped against the pavement as he walked toward his truck, but then they shifted, and she knew she'd been found out.

She should have gone to bed. She'd meant to as

soon as she'd told Hap and Holt that was where she was headed. Instead, she'd found herself sitting alone on the patio, steeped in self-pity. Grateful for the darkness of the shadow that sheltered her face from the stark revelation of the light at her back, she sat up a little straighter.

"What're you doing out here?" Holt asked, his shadow falling long and lean across the paving stones.

She tried to sound as if she hadn't been crying. "Just enjoying the peace and quiet."

Holt's shadow brought its hands to its hips. "You been crying over him."

"Him?" Her head bowed beneath the weight of pretense.

"What is it about Tyler Aldrich that's done this to you?" Holt demanded.

"I don't know," she answered softly, her voice wobbling.

"Well, it's not his money," Holt grumbled, "but just what it is I can't figure out."

She laughed mirthlessly, dashing tears from her eyes, and tried not to mentally run down a long list of what she liked about Tyler. "Actually, I'd like him a lot better without all that money."

Holt's feet scraped on the paving. "No, you wouldn't. It would just make it easier."

She shook her head, swallowing. "It's more than that. It's everything that goes with it."

"That could change," Holt said after a moment.

She dared not even contemplate the possibility. Instead, she calmed herself with the cold, hard truth. "I don't see how."

"You don't have to," Holt said harshly. Then his voice softened, though not without a touch of regret. "You ought to know that by now. We'll pray on it. All right?"

Stepping forward, he laid his big, work-roughened hand on her shoulder. Smiling, Charlotte trapped it against her cheek.

"All right."

On the second Wednesday evening in November, almost three weeks since he'd left Eden, Tyler stood looking out over the city at the distinctive Dallas skyline. He felt the emptiness of the apartment at his back. Sumptuous and far larger than a single man required, the Turtle Creek penthouse provided him with an upscale address, convenience and privacy, but in that moment he'd have gladly traded this place for a shabby little room with the furniture bolted to the wall, so long as that room was at the Heavenly Arms Motel.

Ty laid his forehead against the cool plate-glass window and spoke to God. "Help me here. I'm trying. I thought I knew what I was supposed to do, but now I'm just not sure."

He knew what he wanted to do. He wanted to go back to Eden and see Charlotte and Hap and Holt and Ryan, Grover and Teddy and Justus, too. Answers could be found there, he felt sure, but complications waited there, too.

"My feelings for Charlotte haven't gone away," he told God, "and it seems foolish to put myself into a situation where I can't expect anything but rejection and disappointment."

Leaving before had inflicted what had felt like a mortal wound, and it still ached. He suspected it always would. Lifting a hand, he pressed it against the center of his chest. His heart beat solidly against his palm, echoing into the hollowness inside him. Suddenly he knew that he didn't have anything to lose and everything to gain by returning to Eden.

Maybe he and Charlotte were not meant to be together, but the Jefford family had come into his life for a reason, and that reason had not yet been fully accomplished. Maybe his feelings for Charlotte were the price he paid for the work that God wanted to do in his life, and maybe he'd only now really opened himself up to what God wanted to do for him.

He took a deep breath and lifted his face to the night sky. Ambient light and pollution hid the stars, but that did not block the line of communication.

"All right," he said. "I'll go back if that's what You want. If it's not, well, I'm sure You can find a way to make that clear to me."

For some time, he stood there, feeling small but peaceful.

Strange how he found the most peace in those moments when he felt the least like himself, the least like the Tyler Aldrich of old. That Tyler was someone "important." This Tyler, the one he'd started to think of as the real Tyler, was just another soul in the great universe that he'd recently heard described as God's footstool.

The thought humbled him, but maybe that needed to happen. He certainly liked this newly humbled Tyler better than the old "important" Tyler. No doubt God liked him better, too, but Ty suspected that he had a way to go before either he or God could actually be proud of him.

He left from the office on the following Friday morning. This time he let everyone know where he could be reached and when he'd be back. Cassandra followed him out, making snide remarks and probing for information and weak spots.

"You're actually going back to Podunksville?" she demanded, on the way to the elevator.

"The name of the town is Eden, Oklahoma."

"You're blowing off work again to play country bumpkin."

Ty smiled. "Guess I just have the soul of a small-town boy."

"It's that woman," she declared, folding her arms.

The elevator door slid open just then, and Tyler stepped inside, saying nothing. He pressed the button for the first sublevel where he and a few others parked. At the last moment, Cassandra slid into the elevator car with him.

"She's no one," Cassandra said tartly.

Tyler clamped his teeth against an angry retort. He had to swallow before he could point out, "You don't even know her."

"I know her type."

"You *think* you know her type."

"You're an Aldrich!" Cassandra exclaimed. The elevator set down just as Cassandra stomped her foot. "You just like being a big fish in a small pond," she accused, trailing him as he walked out into the parking basement. "You throw your money around, and they fawn and fall all over you, don't they?"

The very idea amused him because it couldn't have been further from the truth. "These people are my friends, Cassandra," he said, moving toward the car and unlocking it remotely.

"Oh, please. Friends are of your own class."

He paused in the act of opening the driver's door and turned on her. "Class? *Class?* What is this, the 1800s?"

"You know what I mean!"

"Unfortunately, I do," he said, yanking open the door and dropping down into the driver's seat. "But let me tell you something. Not only are those people my friends, I am honored by them."

He reflected bitterly that he'd hoped Cassandra might somehow become the kind of sister that Charlotte was to her brothers, then he realized suddenly that for that to happen, he first had to be the kind of brother that Holt and Ryan were. He tried to think how Holt or Ryan might take leave of their sister.

"See you on Monday," he said stiffly, and then, almost against his will, he added, "By the way, I love you, even if you are a terrible snob."

With that, he closed the door, started the engine and drove away, leaving her standing there with her mouth agape and a look of complete shock on her face.

He felt some surprise himself. He hadn't planned to tell her that he loved her; he hadn't even realized that he did until he'd said it. In fact, had anyone asked him if he loved his sister, he'd probably have responded with a lot of mumbo jumbo and qualifications meant to evade any real answer.

Perhaps it wouldn't change anything, but he was glad that he'd said it. The very act of saying that he loved his sister had somehow freed him to do so. After all these years of fussing and fighting, he actually loved his big sister, and he intended to do a better job of it in the future.

He thought about that as he drove north, noting idly the changes in the landscape. With Thanksgiving almost upon them, the trees stood denuded. Even the dull, light brown grass had been swept clean of leaves by the swirling breeze that grew increasingly sharp the farther that he traveled. This time, though, he'd come prepared.

What he had not done was call ahead. It had never even occurred to him. Many times over these past weeks he'd reached for the telephone, hungry just for the sound of Charlotte's voice, but then he'd told himself that it wouldn't be fair to either of them. Oddly, though, when he'd made the decision to return to Eden, he'd never even thought of calling.

Now he wondered if she would want him to come. Others had said he'd always be welcome, but Charlotte had not. For all he knew, she might not even be there. He'd thought of her as tied to the motel, but nothing said she couldn't leave for a few days. Maybe God didn't intend for him to see her.

Gulping, Tyler promised himself that he would take whatever came. If it turned out that he could only spend time with Hap, then he'd spend time with Hap and gladly.

By the time he pulled up beneath the drive-through at the motel, he could barely wait to leap from the car, but he forced himself to walk sedately up the ramp and push through the door into the lobby. Hap met him in the middle of the floor, laughing and holding open his arms.

"Ty!"

They engaged in a warm hug punctuated with enthusiastic back pounding. "How are you?"

"Better just seeing you here," Hap told him.

"You feeling okay? Arthritis bothering you?"

Hap waved that away. "How come you didn't let us know you was coming? We'd have called out the troops to greet you."

Ty just shrugged. "How is everyone?"

Hap grinned. "*Everyone's* missed you," he said slyly. "She's in there laying the lunch table right now."

Tyler looked to the apartment door. He hadn't fooled Hap one bit, but he couldn't have cared less. He smiled. "At least my timing's good. I made it for lunch."

"Go on," Hap instructed with a jerk of his head.

Nodding his appreciation, Ty moved forward. His heart pounded harder with every step. He opened the door without knocking. Charlotte paused and looked up, the plate in her hand hovering over the table.

Tyler's knees went weak; he wouldn't have been surprised to find himself facedown on the rug the next moment. Instead, he somehow managed to step forward. She all but dropped the plate, and then she sat down hard in the chair she'd pulled out to give her access to the entire table.

Before he'd taken the next step Tyler knew that he needed this woman like he needed air and food and drink. He decided right then that he was going to have her in his life one way or another, even if it meant giving up everything in Dallas and staying here with her. First, though, he had to convince her that they belonged together.

From the look on her face, he figured he had reason to hope.

Charlotte laughed. Her heart had stopped when she'd looked up to find Ty standing there, but as he crossed the room her happiness bubbled over. Thrilled to the soles of her feet, she popped up again and went to meet him, mentally thanking God.

Over these past weeks, she'd wondered and pondered. Had she limited God by dismissing the possibility that He might mean for her and Ty to find a way to join their lives? It could only work, of course, if they were both totally open to God's will. She'd been thinking, too, about Tyler's understanding of that. She had, in fact, spent a good deal of time praying about it. Now, however, everything pretty much flew right out of her head.

She was so happy she hardly knew what to do with herself. Too happy. For once, she didn't care.

"You're here!"

He held her at arm's length, grinning down at her. "And hungry. What's for lunch?"

She laughed, blinking back the tears that burned behind her eyes. The past three weeks seemed like a moment to her now. Oddly, they'd felt like an eternity at the time.

"Homemade chicken noodle soup and crackers," she told him.

"Sounds good. Can I help?"

"You'd better." Beaming, she caught his hand and led him toward the kitchen, silently praying.

Thank You, Lord, but oh, what does this mean?

Something told her that only time would tell. God was in charge here. She would let things play out as He dictated and be glad that Tyler hadn't forgotten them after all.

They spent an easy weekend, doing not much of anything. Holt and Hap went out for catfish that night, while Charlotte and Ty stayed in. Ryan joined them, having a rare Friday off during football season, for pizza that Ty had delivered all the way from Waurika.

Ty turned down the opportunity to work off the extra calories with Ryan at the school gym the next morning. Instead he helped Charlotte finish her chores early so they could meander around the park, talking over the changes he'd made at the company and in dealing with his family.

She applauded his solution to the problem that had called him back to Dallas and tried to reinforce his instincts about dealing with his family by pointing out that no one could change anyone else, only oneself.

"You can't control what they do or say, only how you react to it."

"I hadn't thought of it that way," he admitted, "but it makes stellar sense."

She ducked her head, pleased, and he slung an arm about her shoulders companionably. Excitement shimmered through her. How could it be possible, she wondered, to feel such exhilaration and such contentment in the very same moment? The feelings persisted all through the evening, which they spent with the family, talking and joking and playing dominoes with Hap and his friends.

They went to church together the next day, and she couldn't help noticing how raptly Ty paid attention to everything that was said and done. After dinner, he had a long talk with Hap in the front room while she and Holt and Ryan cleaned up. Normally, she'd have left it to her brothers, but Ty had asked for this time alone with her grandfather.

Later, Ty suggested another walk, and they set off for the park once more, though evening had already settled in and he'd made it clear that he would be heading back to Dallas soon.

"Mind if I ask what you and Granddad were talking about?" she ventured when it became apparent that he wasn't going to volunteer the information.

He tugged at his earlobe. "Ah, I just needed some things cleared up."

"Was he able to do that for you?"

"Not sure yet." Ty slanted a wry glance down at her. "I'll let you know when I am."

She chuckled and gave it up. "Okay, then."

They walked a little farther before she brought up something else that had been on her mind. This weekend had been fleeting, and perhaps any time they managed to spend together would be, but she could not bear the thought of never seeing him again. She'd mourned when he'd gone away before, and perhaps she would mourn like that again. Nothing had been settled between them, and perhaps nothing ever would be, but she just couldn't let him go without knowing when she'd see him again.

"I'd like you to come for Thanksgiving."

He stopped, and so did she, turning to face him. His hands skimmed down the length of her arms. "I'd be delighted."

She dipped her head, more pleased than she probably should have been. Nothing about this situation had changed, after all. Heartbreak undoubtedly waited down the road, but Thanksgiving would be sweet.

"I realize it means driving up here two weeks in a row."

"That's true," he agreed lightly. "Maybe I deserve some consideration for that."

She laughed. "Like what?"

Cupping her face in his hands, he tilted her face up to his. "I want you to pray about us."

"Us?" she echoed weakly, her heart thunking.

He put his forehead to hers. "Charlotte, you have to know by now how I feel about you."

She caught her breath, heart pounding, and whispered, "The same way I feel about you, I imagine."

Smiling, he laid his nose alongside hers and nuzzled. "If you promise to pray about us, then I know you'll be thinking about us."

"You didn't even have to ask," she told him, slipping her arms around his neck and laying her cheek against his chest, "but I'm glad you did."

He hugged her close. Then they turned together and walked to his car. She felt pleased and apprehensive at the same time. Oh, how could this possibly work? Nothing had changed, nothing.

"I'll be back late on Wednesday," he told her, "so don't rent out my room."

"I wouldn't give up a sure deal," she teased.

He'd insisted on paying the room rent for this weekend even though no one had expected it. She had no doubt that he'd insist on paying again over Thanksgiving. Tyler Aldrich was a better man, she suspected, than he knew.

Again, she wondered about his spiritual state, dismayed to realize that she'd left it until too late. She'd been so concerned about what seemed to be happening between them that she'd let more important matters slide. Ashamed, she bowed her head.

He placed a kiss in the center of her forehead and got into the car. "See you on Wednesday."

When he turned out onto the highway moments later, she lifted a hand in farewell.

"I'll be waiting," she whispered, and this time she wouldn't let her silly heart obscure what was most important.

Chapter Fourteen

"Frankly, Mother, I never imagined you'd care where I spent Thanksgiving," Tyler said, crossing his legs and adjusting the drape of his slacks over his knee.

He hadn't been surprised when his mother, Amanda, had shown up in his office that afternoon on the day before Thanksgiving. She often came around with some complaint or other. The only surprising thing about it had been the complaint itself, so surprising that he hadn't known quite how to react at first. After a moment, he'd calmly walked her over to the sofa in the seating area of his expansive office and sat down beside her.

"Of course I care!" she exclaimed, but her gaze wandered away from his.

Her pale blue eyes, so like his and Cassandra's, reflected hurt, as they often did, but also something else. Guilt? Dishonesty? He couldn't be sure; he frequently found her difficult to read.

"You never said anything about us getting together for Thanksgiving," he pointed out.

"We're family," she insisted. "Thanksgiving is a family holiday."

"But we've spent many Thanksgivings apart." More, probably, than they'd spent together, although he didn't say so.

Even when he'd been a boy, his parents had been more apt to celebrate the holidays away than at home, often apart from each other as well as their children.

"Well, yes." She lifted her elegant, manicured hands and tilted her neat, platinum head quizzically. "But only when business or important people intervened."

So that was it. She wouldn't mind if the invitation had come from a business associate or someone she considered her social equal, but to her the Jefford family were nobodies.

Tyler sighed. "The Jeffords are very important people to me, Mother."

"That's impossible!" she scoffed, looking away.

Tyler relaxed against the tan suede upholstery and studied her. Slender and petite, her short, pale hair styled fashionably about her tastefully made-up face, Amanda Aldrich looked a good deal younger than her sixty-one years. Then again, she'd had a number of very expensive cosmetic surgeries to make certain of it.

"I assume you've been speaking to Cassandra about this."

Amanda glanced his way and lifted her chin. "She's right, you know. These people are no one."

"If that's so," Tyler said gently, getting to his feet, "then I want to be no one, too." Moving toward the door, he ignored Amanda's gasp. "You'll have to excuse me now. I have an appointment. Have a happy holiday, Mother."

Her face appeared stony when he looked back, but something about it gave him pause. Despite his simmering anger, he reached for kindness. "I'm sorry, Mother, but I've already accepted the invitation. We can talk again on Monday, if you like."

"I could understand if it was business," she retorted, folding her arms.

"Yes," he said sadly, "I'm sure you could."

The hour approached nine o'clock on that Wednesday evening before Thanksgiving when Ty parked the sports car in what he'd come to think of as its cubby hole next to what he'd come to think of as *his* room at the Heavenly Arms Motel. Leaving his bag in the trunk, he slipped his hands into his coat pockets and walked across the pavement to the lobby door.

For once, it appeared that his arrival had gone unnoticed, probably because he hadn't stopped beneath the drive-through. This gave him the opportunity to pause for a moment and study those on the other side of the window. Hap, Holt, Grover and Justus sat around the dominoes table, laughing and talking as Justus "shook" the playing tiles by stirring them with his hands. They looked so happy, these people.

Tyler thought of his mother and how *un*happy she'd looked when he'd left her. He wondered if his family had ever been happy. The Jeffords and their friends had all had their share of heartache and grief and little else, yet they had joy.

He'd tasted some of that himself, but only enough to

show him how bereft his life really was, and he wanted more. He wanted what the Jeffords and their friends had, and he knew that it started with their faith.

On his last visit Hap had given him a number of Bible verses to read, and Tyler had done so dutifully and repeatedly. He'd even gone out and bought a different translation of the Bible in hopes of better understanding what he read, but he still had questions. He meant to settle this grace thing in his mind before he did anything else.

Going inside, he smiled at the immediate eruption of greeting.

"Ty! 'Bout time you got here."

"Come join us."

"Yeah, Grover's gotta get home," Justus teased. "'Sides, I'd rather have you for a partner. When I lose I can blame it on you." Ty and everyone else laughed at that.

"Charlotte just went into the kitchen," Holt said at the same time that Grover got to his feet.

Ty held up a stalling hand. "Could you hold on a minute, pastor? I've got something on my mind."

"Why, sure." Grover sat down again, and Ty moved around to pull out the chair that Charlotte must have used to observe the game. "How can I help you?"

Ty shrugged out of his tan cashmere coat, draping it haphazardly over the back of the chair before he sat down, placing his hands on the table. "I always thought I was a Christian because I'm a member of a church," he began, noticing the way they exchanged glances around the table, "but I've come to see that it takes more than that. I'm just not sure what."

He saw the way Hap's arm slid across Holt's shoulders, recognizing the satisfaction in the gesture. He realized that these men had been praying for this very thing. They'd known something was lacking in him, and they'd quietly taken the problem to God. He felt a stillness inside himself and a surge of affection.

"Tell you what," Grover said, shifting closer. "What do you say I ask you a few questions? Then you can pray as you feel led. All right?"

"All right."

"Do you believe that Jesus is the Son of God?"

"Yes."

"Do you believe that He lived a sinless life on this earth?"

"I hadn't thought about it, really, but if He's the Son of God, then He must have."

Grover nodded. "And do you realize that He went to the cross blameless, laying down his life to pay the sin price for our sins?"

Tyler gulped. *Our* sins. "My sins, you mean."

He thought of all the angry things he'd said to his brother and sister and parents over the years. He thought of the callousness with which he'd often tended to business and the special treatment he'd expected, so many things he'd done wrong that they suddenly frightened him.

"Yours, mine, everyone's," Hap clarified. "He died for the sins of the whole world."

"Why would He do that?" Tyler wanted to know, understanding suddenly that this one issue lay at the bottom of his confusion.

"Because He loves us," Holt answered. "Think about

it. Wouldn't you give up your life for those you love? If they were in danger of eternal peril, wouldn't you say, 'Take me instead'?"

Tyler immediately thought of Charlotte. And Hap and Holt and Ryan, too. Surprisingly, he also thought of Cassandra and Amanda and Preston. Even Justus and Grover and Teddy. When he really thought about it, he knew that he'd take that step for them and others who came to mind. He'd never thought about someone else doing that for him, though.

Gratitude flooded him, and he seemed to have something in his throat, something he couldn't swallow away. "But I don't deserve it," he said.

"That's grace," Hap told him, "giving what isn't deserved."

Suddenly it all came clear.

"Do you know what it means to repent?" Grover asked, and Tyler shook his head. Grover briefly explained, "It means to recognize and turn away from, in other words stop doing, those things that displease God. Once you've made that decision, you need only ask for forgiveness."

"Then you never have to live apart from God again," Justus told him gruffly.

"Doesn't mean you won't mess up," Hap warned, "or have problems."

"Just that you'll be living in the grace of salvation," Grover said.

"And the power of the Holy Spirit," Holt added.

"And just asking begins that?" Ty said.

"Pretty much," Grover assured him. "It is a beginning of sorts, a new beginning."

Ty sucked in a deep breath and bowed his head. A moment later, he felt Hap take his right hand and instinctively offered Justus his left. He stilled his mind, and then he began to pray.

Charlotte gingerly pulled apart the paper bag that she'd just taken from the microwave and dumped the popcorn into a large green plastic bowl. She glanced at the clock, saw that the hour had just gone nine and wondered when Ty would arrive.

The counter behind her fairly groaned with covered dishes awaiting the food that currently stuffed the refrigerator, including the turkey, which sat ready for the oven. She'd have to be up early in order to get it in on time, but she wouldn't go to bed until Ty had come. She felt too excited to sleep, anyway. Nothing she could tell herself seemed to make any difference, a fact she found somewhat frightening.

She took up the bowl and headed back to the front room, tossing a couple of fluffy pieces of popcorn into her mouth and munching. She stepped through the apartment door, instantly aware of an odd stillness in the front room. For a moment, she saw nothing out of the ordinary. The men sat with their heads bent over the table, but they were not, she came to realize, studying their domino hands. They were holding hands.

She heard a familiar voice say, "Forgive me for all that. I'll do better with Your help."

Ty!

"And thank You for going to the cross for me," he went on. "Thank You for loving me. I never want to live apart from You again, Lord."

The bowl slipped away and hit the floor, no doubt because she'd covered her mouth with both hands to prevent herself from crying out and disturbing the prayer. She didn't hear another word that he said, but after a few moments, everyone lifted their heads and looked at her.

Tyler calmly swiveled on the hard seat of his chair, got up and came to her, a tender smile on his face. He cupped her cheek in one hand, then went down on his haunches and started sweeping up popcorn. She looked to the others in the room. Grover beamed ear-to-ear, while tears stood in Hap's eyes.

She burbled laughter and dropped down to her knees to help Ty gather up the spilled popcorn. "Sorry," she told the others. "I'll make some more."

Someone replied, several someones perhaps, but the sounds didn't register as words. With the popcorn back in the bowl, they pushed up to their feet. Holding the bowl by the brim with one hand, Ty reached for her hand with the other and led her back into the apartment and toward the kitchen.

"I didn't know you were here," she said quietly, sniffing.

"I only arrived a few minutes ago."

"It doesn't take long," she told him, "to give your heart to Jesus."

He chuckled at that. "Oh, I don't know. It took me weeks. Years, really, when you think about it."

She laughed giddily, and he squeezed her hand.

When they reached the kitchen, she dumped the popcorn in the trash. He lifted a dish towel and peeked beneath it at the cherry and pecan pies she'd baked that day. The aroma of freshly prepared dressing still filled the air. Pressing a hand to his flat stomach, Ty smiled.

"Smells wonderful, especially since I skipped dinner to get here sooner."

Delight shimmered through Charlotte. Quickly she turned toward the refrigerator. She would not taint this pure moment of joy by wishing for more than she knew was possible. "Let me fix something."

"No, you don't have to do that. Won't hurt me to go without, the night before the feast."

"A sandwich, at least," she insisted, taking the makings from the refrigerator.

He relented. "That would be great, thank you."

She slapped together the sandwich, all the time silently rejoicing for the prayer she had overheard. When she finished, she carried the plate to the dining table. He sat, and she hurried back to the kitchen to pour a glass of unsweetened iced tea. When she returned, she found him once more with his head bowed, but he looked up quickly, smiled and picked up the sandwich.

"Won't you sit with me?"

She pulled out a chair and watched him bite into the sandwich. "I know you're used to much finer fare," she began, but he reached out a hand and grasped her wrist, bringing her words and thoughts to an abrupt halt.

"Charlotte," he said, after swallowing, "some of the finest meals I've ever eaten have been right here at this table. Besides, I'd rather sit here eating a bologna sandwich with you than filets mignons with anyone else."

She looked down, warmth spreading through her. "That's a very sweet thing to say."

"Just the truth."

Blinking back tears, she let him eat in peace for a few minutes while she searched her heart. She'd been telling herself that God could not mean Tyler for her, and one of the facts upon which she'd based that conclusion had to do with his spiritual ambiguity. She just couldn't be sure that Ty truly shared her beliefs.

During these past few days, she'd prayed and prayed, as Ty had asked her to. Over and over again, she'd asked God to show her His will and she'd listed the reasons why she and Tyler could not have a future. Now she just didn't know what to think.

She couldn't deny that she cared for Tyler more than she'd ever expected to or that she missed him deeply when he was not with her. Still, they lived in different worlds. Didn't they?

Or did she just not want to leave her own personal comfort zone? If so, what did that say about her faith?

But no, she had to consider her family and their needs.

Shifting to the edge of her seat, she asked, "Can we talk about what just happened in there?"

His lips curled upward. "I'd be delighted to."

They talked for a long while.

"I really thought that joining a church was the same thing as being a Christian," he said at one point, "but after I got to know you and your family, I realized I'd missed something."

Charlotte had no doubt that Tyler had wholeheartedly turned his life and heart over to Jesus now, and her joy at that knew no bounds, but then he said something that deflated her a bit.

"I can't wait to get back to Dallas and talk to my

pastor now. I guess I wasn't comfortable going to him with this because I just didn't know what to ask him. Besides, he knows all of my family and many of our friends, and I guess that was part of it, too. I have to say that he's been pretty glad to see me hanging around the church lately. He's even spoken to me about serving on a committee with one of the church ministries."

Charlotte smiled, but inwardly she sighed. How could they possibly have a future together if he was meant to serve God in Dallas, and she was meant to be here for her family? When she thought about being with him, making a life with him, she knew she wanted that. But fitting into his world seemed…impossible… frightening, even.

She shook off the troubling thoughts and brightened her smile, determined to enjoy having him here. Thanksgiving seemed special this year because of Ty, and she wanted to concentrate on her many blessings, beginning with Tyler's growing faith. Everything else came second to that.

"So tell me," she said, changing the subject, "do you have any Thanksgiving favorites?"

He thought about it. "Hmm. Pumpkin pie, of course."

"Got it."

"Cranberry sauce?"

"Homemade by my grandma's recipe."

"Can't wait to dig into that."

"Anything else?"

"Well, football."

Charlotte laughed. "You came to the right place, then."

He carefully wiped away a spot of mustard on his

pinky finger before looking at her. "That's not what makes this the right place, Charlotte."

"No?"

Slowly he shook his head side to side. "Seems to me that anyplace you are is the right place." She ducked her head. "I thought about it all the way up here," he went on gently. "I've been thinking about it ever since my mother showed up at my office this afternoon to ask me not to come."

Charlotte jerked her head up, her brow wrinkled. "She asked you not to come?"

He nodded pensively. "We haven't spent all that many Thanksgivings together," he revealed, "and at first I thought her protests were just snobbery, frankly, but the more I think about it, the more I wonder if she's not frightened by the changes in me."

"Changes?"

He slid her a wry look. "Don't pretend I haven't changed since we met."

She thought about the stiff, all-too-charming stranger who had walked in there that first night and compared him to the friend sitting at ease at her table now. His entire countenance had cleared. Gone were the worries and cares that seemed to have burdened him before. She never wondered if he might be looking down his nose at her, never worried that he might mean ill for her friends or community. Her only fear was that she had come to care too much for him.

"I've changed, too," she admitted. "I thought I had all the answers once, and now…I just don't know anymore what God's will for my life is."

Nodding, Ty braced his forearms on the table. "We'll figure it out together."

Together, she thought, was the problem, but she nodded anyway. What else could she do?

Father in heaven, help me, she prayed silently. *I don't want to hurt this man, and I don't want to go against Your will. Thank You for bringing Ty to Your throne. Thank You for letting us make a difference in his life for You. Just help me figure out where to go from here. I don't want to love him if that's not Your will. I'm so confused. Help me do the right thing, even if that's giving him up.*

But what if that meant leaving here to go with him?

Obviously she still had some serious praying to do.

Could God really mean for her to leave Eden? Could Ty possibly be happy here?

She wanted to believe, wanted desperately to convince herself that God had brought Ty here for more reasons than his spiritual need.

As if that wasn't enough.

Chapter Fifteen

"Well, now, this just might ruin my whole day," Holt drawled, using his fork to pick something out of the hearty serving of dressing on his plate.

"What's that?" Charlotte asked, peering across the heavily laden table.

Holt held up a greenish-brown lump, slid a look at his sister and with a perfectly straight face said, "This piece of celery is at least three centimeters thicker than all the rest."

"Oh, you!" Charlotte picked up a green pea and threw it at him. Uproarious laughter filled the room to bursting.

Holt forked up a huge bite of the dressing and grinned over it at his sister. "Honestly, sis, this meal is as near perfect as it could possibly be."

Everyone agreed, including Ty. The table literally sagged beneath the weight of the feast she had laid before them. In fact, Tyler saw something he'd missed every time he stopped eating long enough to look around the table.

It was enough to make a man abandon healthy eating habits entirely, which is exactly what Tyler and everyone else did for the day, the most thankful day of the year. And, oh, how much they all had to be thankful for!

They'd stood around the table before the meal, four grown men and sweet Charlotte, linked their hands together and took turns praying aloud, praising and thanking the Lord for their many blessings. The festive, jubilant mood still infused them all, especially Tyler. He'd sat himself down and partook with all the enthusiasm of the Jefford men, teasing and laughing and groaning with pure delight.

Tyler couldn't have been happier or more at his ease. He felt, ironically, that he belonged here with these people, and for the first time he asked himself why he couldn't just stay here with them, with Charlotte.

Simply watching her interact with her family gave him great pleasure. Having her smile directed at him from time to time felt almost unbearably sweet.

Yes, he thought, *this is where I want to be. Let the company and my family take care of themselves.*

A pang of guilt surprised him. What would happen to all the people who depended on Aldrich & Associates for their livelihoods if he left the company to the care of his eternally bickering siblings? What would become of them, for that matter? How could his family ever hope to find what he had if he did not lead them to it, and how could he do that if he was not there?

The prayer that he had repeated so often whispered through his mind then.

Lord God, make me a man You are proud to call Your own.

Would such a man abandon the company that he had been charged to lead? Would he abandon his own family?

Tyler listened to the good-natured banter between brothers and sister and heard the unspoken affection and respect that they shared. These Jeffords valued family. Should he do any less?

Perhaps he wished to walk away from the Aldrich family, just put the fussing and backbiting behind him, but would that be right? Did he really even want that?

In all truth, what he wanted most was to feel the same tug of unquestioning love with his brother, sister and mother that Charlotte shared with her brothers and grandfather. Would leaving Dallas and the company achieve that? It didn't seem likely, but he no longer saw a way to live his life apart from Charlotte.

This day did not deserve such heavy thoughts, he decided, and he managed to push them aside. For the most part. He couldn't help wondering from time to time just how his mother, brother and sister were spending the day. They would not, he knew, be enjoying themselves as much as he was, and that saddened him.

No one could maintain a woeful mood in this company on this day, however. Eventually, even Holt, who seemed to have two hollow legs, called a halt. Pushing back his chair, he waved a hand in a sharp sideways movement.

"Enough," he declared.

"More'n enough, if you ask me," Hap corrected.

"More than enough," Holt agreed, rubbing his distended middle. "An embarrassment of riches, in fact."

"Well, then," Ryan proposed, clapping his hands together, "let's get this table cleared so we can get back to football."

"Oh, no," Charlotte protested. "Y'all go on. I'll take care of this."

"No, no, no," Holt insisted. "You cooked. We'll clean."

"Not necessary," she argued, getting up to begin gathering plates.

Tyler quickly rose and plucked up his own, holding it out of her reach. "I'll help her," he told the others.

Holt paused in the process of pushing his chair under the table. Ryan divided a look between Holt and their grandfather. All three of them turned near identical grins on Tyler and Charlotte.

"This is getting to be a habit, Ty," Holt drawled.

"Good habit," Hap inserted.

Ryan sent them both slightly censorious glances before stating firmly, "We'll all clear. If you two would rather wash and dry instead of watching the game, that's up to you. Otherwise, we'll all pitch in later. Well, me and Holt, anyway."

"That's right," Hap said merrily, limping and hitching his way toward the front room. "Got to be some compensation for getting old." Everyone chuckled. "I'll have the TV all warmed up by the time you boys get there. 'Sides, there ain't room enough for all these bodies in the kitchen."

The Jefford brothers shook their heads, grabbing up bowls and platters. Charlotte had sense enough to put down the soiled plates and hurry ahead of them to the kitchen, where she began getting out the necessary storage dishes for the leftovers. Tyler did his bit by gathering up the dirty plates and flatware and ferrying them to the kitchen counter.

In a surprisingly short time, the many leftovers had been safely stowed and the dishes stacked. Charlotte shooed her brothers toward the lobby, then turned to Tyler.

"You, too. I can take care of this."

"No, ma'am. If you're cleaning up, then I'm helping out, and nothing you can say will change my mind."

She looked at the stack of dishes regretfully, sighed and started to follow her brothers. Tyler stopped her with a hand on her forearm.

"I'd rather be right here up to my elbows in dishwater with you than out there with them, much as they tickle me."

She smiled, one corner of her mouth kicking up higher than the other. "What about the game?"

"They can play without me for once."

She relaxed back against the door frame. "Would you be there, actually at that game, if you weren't here?"

"Most likely."

"Why, then?" she asked softly.

"Why am I here instead of there? Or why did I come back at all?"

"Both."

He slid a finger down her cheek. "I had questions, and I knew I could find the answers here." Using his fingertips, he gently pushed her braid off her shoulder. "And then there's the sheer pleasure of your company."

An explosion of hoots erupted from the front room, evoking a smile and a glance in that direction.

"And theirs."

He gazed once again into her complex hazel eyes, noting appreciatively the bits of gold, silvery-blue and soft green. "But it's mostly you, Charlotte," he admitted in a husky voice. "You're why I'm here. And why I'll keep coming back."

She said nothing to that, but he saw a kind of fearful longing on her face that he knew only too well. He'd seen it in his mirror often enough these past weeks.

"Let's do some dishes," he said heartily, turning toward the sink and rolling up his sleeves. "I'll even wash if you want. In fact, I insist on it. I wouldn't know where half this stuff goes, anyway."

Charlotte laughed and reached around him to start the water. Tyler fought the urge to slip his arms around her and pull her close. It struck him then that just being with her like this, even though she was the sweetest thing he'd ever known, would never be enough. Stepping back, he watched her put in the stopper and squeeze in the liquid soap.

Make me a man You are proud to call Your own, he prayed. *I know that will be a whole lot easier if I can have Charlotte in my life, not just once in a while but all the time. I know there are problems with that, but please help me make that happen.*

Ty seemed wound as tightly as an eight-day clock from the moment he walked into the apartment that next morning. Grinning ear-to-ear, he could barely seem to stand still.

"All that food yesterday must've revved your engine," Hap noted over his second cup of coffee.

Tyler bobbed his head in agreement. "Yes, sir. I'm feeling pretty peppy."

He proved that statement by helping Charlotte with her chores. Even after that, however, he seemed bursting with such energy that he rushed her through lunch, saying repeatedly that he needed a good, long walk. Hap laughingly bullied the two of them into coats and sent them off.

Ty fairly danced across the pavement toward the park, skipping backward much of the time. His exuberance tickled Charlotte. He seemed so happy, and she chalked it up to his growing faith.

"Have you noticed how much of our relationship seems to revolve around food?" he asked at one point.

Our relationship. "What does that mean, I wonder?"

"It means that you're a very good cook, generous to a fault, welcoming, kind—"

"It means that there aren't very many places around here where you can get a decent meal," she interrupted with a chortle.

Empty tree branches clacked together on either side of the street, moved by a swirling breeze that held a damp, cold edge. The gray sky offered no cloud to threaten rain, however, and aside from the wind, the temperature remained lodged in the pleasant range.

"Okay, there is that," he allowed, "but that doesn't mean the rest isn't true, too. You are an excellent cook. Your generosity and kindness amazes me, and no one has ever made me feel more welcome. You, your family..." He looked around, waving an arm in an expansive gesture. "This whole town, really."

Her laughter wafted on the breeze. Why couldn't it stay like this? she wondered. The two of them, always.

And what if "always" is in Dallas?

She shook her head. Late last night she'd decided that she'd been getting way ahead of herself. Ty had asked her to pray about their relationship. He had said that he'd come back to be with her, and now he'd paid her extravagant compliments. That did not mean he would ask her to go to Dallas with him.

True, he'd inquired once before if she would ever consider leaving Eden, but that didn't mean he was making plans for the two of them. She could be agonizing over nothing. Why not just enjoy this time with him and let things play out as God willed?

Turning her face up to the sky, she said, "Have you ever noticed how God gives us glorious moments to get us through the dreary days?"

Tyler considered that for a few moments. "Honestly, the only truly glorious moments I've known have been right here, and I would definitely say those are from God."

She smiled. "You are really on the mountaintop today, aren't you?"

"It would seem so."

They walked on, chatting and laughing about a variety of subjects. Long before they reached the park they could see that the place was deserted. They strolled on, crossing the bridge to the gently rolling ground on the other side. The narrow stream at the bottom of the gully carried leaves with it, little brown and gold boats with crinkled edges.

While weaving their way through the trees, Tyler

kicked playfully at the leaves piled in drifts on the ground, a veritable bundle of energy. Suddenly he spun, grasping her lightly by the upper arms.

"I have to get something out of my system."

Staring up at him, she realized that he was seeking permission. "Go on."

To her surprise and delight, he stepped closer. His smile flashed in the instant before he dipped his head and kissed her.

Charlotte felt that kiss all the way to the tips of her toes. Instinctively, she lifted up onto them, her arms drifting about his neck. At length, he lifted his head and sighed.

Charlotte came back to the earth with a thud. She remembered the last time this had happened and that he hadn't seemed inclined to repeat the experience.

"Well, that was less than helpful," he muttered. Charlotte ducked her head, heat staining her cheeks. "Now I just want more."

Her gaze zipped up at that. "Tyler!"

"I know you're not the sort of woman to go around kissing every man she meets," he said, eyes glowing. "I also know that an innocent kiss is all you'd give any man, no matter how you felt about him."

"Except a husband," she blurted, face blazing.

"Since I heartily agree with that sentiment," Tyler said, his voice growing more solemn with every syllable, "I suspect there's just one thing for us to do."

She looked up. Was this the end for them, then, or the beginning? She feared the end, had tried to prepare for it, but something told her that he meant this to be a beginning for them, and she truly did not know what she would do about that. Cautiously, she tilted her head.

"What do you think we should do?" she asked.

"Get married."

Gasping, Charlotte stepped back with one foot. The other remained firmly fixed in place, which pretty well demonstrated how torn she felt. Half of her wanted to throw her arms around him and cry out, "Yes!" The other already grieved what she worried could never be hers.

"B-but how can we? You live in Dallas, and I live here."

"Logistics…" he began, but she cut him off.

"It's more than that! You know it is. We might as well live in different worlds! I don't know anything about society or fashion or suites at the football stadium!"

"Look," he said, stepping closer. "I don't know how it's all going to work out. I only know that I love you and my life will never be complete without you."

Something inside her melted, and one pertinent fact stood out among all the others. She'd fought against it, but she couldn't deny the truth any longer, not to herself, at least. "Oh, Ty."

He took her hands in his and went down on one knee, saying, "Might as well do this properly." Tears filled her eyes as he formally asked, "Charlotte, will you marry me?"

A sob slipped out of her. She hunched her shoulders as if she could call it back.

"Before you answer," he went on somberly, "you should know that the only way I'll live my life without you is if you convince me that you don't love me, too. Can you do that, Charlotte?"

She shook her head.

"Then I think you'd better agree to marry me, don't you?"

Staring down into his glowing, sky-blue eyes, she could not do anything else. Perhaps it had been only weeks since he'd walked into her life, but from the first moment she had known that God had brought him there.

She knew, too, that her love for him was stronger than her fears about leaving her family and fitting into his, fears that she'd insisted on interpreting as God's will. Even now she didn't know how this would turn out, but she knew that God would take care of it, one way or another, if she just had the courage to take what He offered her now.

Burbling with both tears and laughter, she managed to get out, "Yes, I do."

Tyler came instantly to his feet and drew her into his arms. "Thank You, God. Thank You. We'll work it all out, sweetheart, you'll see. I've been thinking that maybe I should move here."

Stunned, she drew back far enough to gaze up into his face. "But how would that work? What would you do?"

"Do?"

"To earn a living. You have to earn a living."

He lifted both shoulders, mouth flattening into a straight line. "Actually, sweetheart, I don't. Not really. I mean, money is something we'll never have to worry about."

"But can you be happy doing nothing?"

"I'm sure I'll find something to get into."

"What about your family's company?"

He sighed. "I don't know. That's troubling, frankly, but all I can do at this point is pray about it and wait for God to work it all out."

"You're right," she agreed, nodding decisively. "We should pray about it, starting right now."

Smiling, he squeezed her hands before looking around them. "There's the bench over there. Let's sit first."

They turned in that direction, arm in arm. A peacefulness seemed to settle around them, a rightness. Laying her head against his shoulder, Charlotte felt her fears recede and wonder steal in. She couldn't believe what had just happened. She had just agreed to marry Tyler Aldrich!

"I apologize for not being prepared," he told her.

She lifted her head to look at him in confusion. "What do you mean?"

He tapped the tip of her nose with his forefinger. "I've known since before I left here the first time that I'm in love with you, but I did not expect to ask you to marry me like this."

She squeezed his arm, admitting, "You broke my heart when you went away and I thought I'd never see you again." He covered her hand with his. "I thought that was the end of it."

"I didn't expect to return," he admitted, "but I couldn't stay away, and the more I thought about the two of us being together, the more I dreamed about it, prayed about it, the more right it seemed." His fingers stroked hers. "If I'd been prepared, though, I'd have a ring for you."

"Oh, that." She shrugged because she hadn't even thought about a ring. They had time for rings later. Right now they had other problems, but God would take care of those. If He meant them to be together, and He must, then everything would work out.

"Yes, that," Ty said. "As far as I'm concerned it's the next order of business."

She beamed at him. "Prayer first, ring second. Seems about right to me."

They reached the bench. He pressed a brief kiss to her lips before they sat down. Leaning forward, their elbows braced upon their knees, they clasped hands and bowed heads. Tyler spoke without prompting.

"Thank You, Father. Thank You for bringing me here to this woman. Thank You for making her love me. You've blessed me in so many ways, but this…"

He seemed unable to go on at that point. Heart swelling, Charlotte picked up where he'd left off, saying, "We're stepping out on faith here, Lord. Whatever You have in store for us, we'll face it together, trusting You to show us the way."

Ty spoke again, going on at length in a soft voice about his concerns for his family and their company. "You know I care about them, Lord, but Charlotte is my destiny. I see that now. I just want for my family what Charlotte's has. Help them see that."

Charlotte loved him all the more for his distress on their behalf, and she realized again how much the discord between him and his siblings and mother hurt him. She resolved silently to aid him in rebuilding those relationships. Family, after all, meant so much to her, and, daunting as the idea seemed, they would be her family, too.

They whispered together, "Amen."

Afterward, they lifted their heads to smile and kiss and finally to rise as one.

"Let's go tell Granddad," she said, suddenly giddy with elation.

Tyler laughed and slung an arm about her shoulders. "I confess, I don't think he'll be shocked."

"Or unhappy."

They went as quickly as they could, all but running. Arm in arm, they bumped and bounced and laughed and talked, brimming with joy and hope and love.

"I wonder if Holt could use a partner?" Tyler mused as they passed the oil pump behind the motel.

She glanced at him in surprise, saw the teasing glint in his eyes and shook her head. They both laughed. The oil field was not for him, at least not the filthy labor part.

"Something will turn up," she predicted gaily.

They rounded the end of the motel wing and crossed the grass to the pavement. Tyler's steps stuttered. Following his line of sight to the drive-through, she saw an expensive foreign luxury sedan parked there.

"Looks like something already has," he announced, suddenly solemn. "That's my sister's car."

Charlotte felt the bottom drop out of her stomach.

Chapter Sixteen

Tyler knew the moment he stepped into the front room that something serious had happened. When he'd seen her car there, he'd expected this to be nothing more than one of Cassandra's famous scenes, the sort she cooked up when she had nothing better to do than make his life miserable. One look at her told him otherwise.

His normally neat, perfectly coifed sister appeared unkempt, or as unkempt as he had ever seen her. Her shoulder-length hair actually looked rumpled, and the dark band that held it back from her face rested at an odd angle on her head. She needed to reapply her lipstick, and, even more alarming, a couple inches of the hem of her long, tailored, dark brown dress hung down. A matching thread trailed from the buckle of one flat shoe.

She'd come to her feet the moment that he and Charlotte had entered through the apartment door and now stood twisting her hands in an uncharacteristic show of concern. Still struggling to his own feet, Hap sent Tyler an apologetic glance.

"What's happened?" he asked.

Cassandra came forward, the lack of a pose indicative of her distress as she exclaimed, "Everything's a mess!"

"Describe 'everything.' No, wait. Describe the mess."

"For starters, we're facing a hostile takeover!"

"You're telling me that the company is being threatened by a hostile takeover?"

"Yes! And you have to stop it!"

Mind whirling, Tyler tried to make sense of this. As a privately owned company, Aldrich & Associates Grocery could only be taken over by an outside entity if one or more of the owners had yielded sufficient shares. He latched onto the first idea that made any sense.

"Spencer-Hatten."

"What? No!"

"You made some sort of deal with Spencer-Hatten, and it's backfiring on you," he accused.

"I didn't!" she insisted, her voice rising to a shriek. "I wouldn't!" For the first time in Tyler's memory, his cool, cryptic sister dissolved into tears. "I wouldn't," she insisted in a small voice.

Stunned, Tyler moved forward to place a hand on her shoulder. "Easy now," he urged gently. He waited until she sniffed and knuckled the tears from her eyes. "So tell me what this is about."

"Shasta," she answered succinctly.

Trust Shasta to make a nuisance of herself at holiday time. Ty sighed, thoroughly ashamed of himself. "I'm sorry I accused you."

Cassandra rolled a gaze up at him. "You had good reason."

He squeezed her shoulder, touched that she would admit such a thing. "What has our stepmother done now?"

"She's married Wilkerson Bishop."

Tyler needed a moment to get his mouth closed. "Wilkerson's eighty-four years old!"

"And our largest shareholder outside the family," Cassandra pointed out needlessly.

The implications were not lost on Tyler. "They still don't comprise a majority."

"They will if they get their hands on Ivory's share."

Frank Ivory had retired as the company's chief financial officer some two years earlier. Then, right before their father had revealed his cancer, he'd stripped Ivory of his seat on the board and awarded it to Shasta.

"Why would Ivory sell his shares to Shasta?"

"Apparently he's still upset about losing his seat, and Wilkerson is offering twice what the shares are worth."

Tyler put his hands to his head, stunned.

"That's not all," Cassandra went on, ducking her head.

Tyler steeled himself. "What else?"

"Mother's in the hospital."

Charlotte gasped, and Tyler's eyebrows shot almost to his hairline. "Why didn't you say so to begin with!"

Charlotte, God love her, stepped up and slid an arm about his waist, placing the other hand in the hollow of his shoulder in a show of support. Without even thinking about it, he reached up and hooked an arm around her shoulders.

Cassandra's chin began to wobble again. "It's all my fault."

"Your fault, how? Shasta's the one who—"

"Mother doesn't even know about that."

"Then what…" He shook his head, at a loss.

"It was something I said," Cassandra admitted. "She was going on and on about how we were losing you, and… It's just such a mess! She started crying yesterday and wouldn't stop. Preston finally called her psychiatrist, and he admitted her."

Tyler pinched his nose. "Great." This was all he needed, one of his mother's well-rehearsed nervous breakdowns.

"Then today when I heard about Shasta," Cassandra went on in a thin voice, "all I could think was that you have to come home!"

Tyler shook his head, feeling torn. He wouldn't have hesitated under other circumstances. He was still the CEO of Aldrich & Associates Grocery, after all, and it had been a long while since his mother had pulled one of these stunts, but now he had Charlotte to consider. Glancing at her, he saw the worried expression on her face and made his decision.

"I'm sorry, but I can't go back now. Charlotte and I have just decided to get married."

"Glory be!" Hap erupted, throwing up his hands.

"My place is here now," Tyler finished firmly.

Cassandra astonished him by again bursting into tears. Shaking her head miserably, she wilted back onto the sofa and covered her face with her hands.

Tyler tensed, momentarily at a loss. Half of him wanted to comfort his sister; half of him expected her to come up snarling. After a moment Charlotte gave him an insistent little nudge. Bowing to her superior knowledge in such matters, he eased himself down and perched on the edge of the sofa next to Cassandra.

"It's all right, Cass," he said, looping an arm around her. "You know how Mother is."

"I've never seen her like this," Cassandra said, dropping her hands and sniffing. "We had words, it's true. Nothing unusual about that, I know. But I said something I shouldn't have and she hasn't been the same since." Cassandra looked up tearfully, whispering, "I'd never have said it if I'd known how much it would hurt her."

Tyler tightened his embrace a bit, saying gently, "She'll get over it."

Cassandra shook her head, mopping at her face with her hands. "I don't think so, not if you abandon us." Suddenly she grasped his hand. "We need you! Mother needs you. The company needs you. We'll never be able to convince Ivory not to sell."

"Just offer him another seat on the board," Tyler suggested. "My sense is that's all he really wants. He can have my seat, actually. You won't even have to create a new one."

"And then what?" Cassandra demanded. "You're the voice of reason on that board. We're all lost without you! You have to come home. Now!"

He'd never thought to hear this. It warmed something inside him to know that his sister actually thought the family and company needed him, but he could not allow himself to be drawn back to Dallas now. Tyler knew what he had to do, and he had every faith God would work it all out for the best. Somehow.

"Cass, I'm sorry, but—"

"No," Charlotte interrupted, stepping forward. Hap made a sound like air leaking from a tire.

Tyler looked up. "Don't worry, honey," he told her, feeling a serenity, a sureness that would undoubtedly center his life from now on. "It's all right." And it was.

Even now, when God seemed to be answering his prayers concerning his family, Tyler understood that he and Charlotte could no longer be separated. They were one heart, joined by the generous will of a loving God, and whatever must be done, they would do together.

From now on Tyler would always try to deal with others, including his own family—especially his own family—with the same gentle, loving acceptance that the Jeffords had demonstrated to him, but without Charlotte by his side, he could only make half an effort at best. Together they would help his family to see that they needed God more than him or anyone, or anything, else.

He reached out a hand to this woman who made him more than he could be alone, this one woman in the whole world who not only completed him but who was undoubtedly God's will for his life.

"I know what I have to do," he said.

"Do you?" Charlotte asked, kneeling at Ty's feet. She exchanged a glance with Hap then looked into Tyler's eyes and saw love unlike anything she had ever dreamed of there. What a good man, not perfect by any means, but wholly surrendered to God, willing to do all that might be asked of him, no matter the personal cost.

How long had he worked and waited, yearning for the kind of acceptance his sister now offered him? How much responsibility had he shouldered, how many solutions had he found, how much regret and grief had he endured for this moment? She could not allow him to abandon that battle.

"We prayed about this not twenty minutes ago," she reminded him gently.

"I know, sweetheart, but I don't want you to think that my word means nothing. I said I'd stay, and I will."

"But is that what God wants, Ty? Don't you see? You told God how much you love your family and how you want them to have what you've found in Him, and this is His answer."

Tyler cupped her face in his hands and said exactly what she expected him to say. "Darling, you're my family now, even if we're not married yet. And you will always comes first with me."

"Yes, of course," she said, smiling through the tears that gathered in her eyes. She didn't know if she could do this. She only knew that she had to try, for Tyler's sake. She wouldn't think of how much she would miss Eden and her family, only of how much she loved him. *Oh, Father, help me,* she prayed silently. *Help me do this for Ty.* "And from this day forward you will always come first with me," she vowed, "but your place is in Dallas."

"I won't go," he insisted, shaking his head. "Not without you."

Charlotte took a deep breath, her heart beating a wild tattoo. "Then I'll just have to go with you."

Tyler seized her by the upper arms. "Charlotte, you don't mean that."

"I think I must mean it," she said, smiling and weeping at the same time.

"You see it's like this, son," Hap rasped. "God's got purpose for you in Dallas. Your family and your company need you, and if Charlotte belongs with you, then that's where both of you got to go."

Holt and Ryan walked into the room just then. Holt held a fork poised over a plate of pecan pie. "Both of who?"

Hap hitched around. "Ty and Charlotte's getting married."

Ryan pumped an arm in a whoop of approval. "Yes-s-s!"

"Who's this, then?" Holt asked, stepping forward to beetle his brow at Cassandra.

"Oh, this here is Ty's sister, Cassie," Hap said. Cassandra said nothing about the nickname. "She's a mite upset," Hap went on. "Their mom's in the hospital and some other stuff." Hap swirled a hand as if to say it was all too confusing for him.

"I'm sorry to hear that," Ryan immediately remarked.

Holt stared at his sister, and she knew his thoughts immediately. She pushed up to her feet and went to her brother.

"It isn't just that I love him," she said softly. "I love him enough to go where he has to go."

Holt's lips flattened, but then he cut off a big bite of the pie and gulped it down. "Ryan and me—" he grumbled, wiping a corner of his mouth with the pad of his thumb "—we figured this was coming."

"We have a plan," Ryan announced, grinning ear-to-ear.

"A plan?" Charlotte repeated.

"To take care of stuff around here," Ryan said, as Holt studiously forked in another huge bite of pie. "We've got it all figured out. We'll both pitch in. With some part-time help, we'll be fine."

"We can afford full-time if we need to," Hap mused, "especially if we throw in room and board."

Holt looked at what was left of his pie, a rueful twist to his lips. "Well, room, anyway," he amended with a sigh.

Charlotte wondered with dismay who would cook for them, but she knew they wouldn't starve. They could manage until they could hire someone. Nodding grimly, she swiped at the tears trickling down her face and whispered, "I love you all so much."

"But you belong with Ty," Hap rasped.

Tyler appeared at her side, sliding an arm around her waist. He looked down at her, and she read the troubled expression in his eyes. "Sweetheart, are you sure about this?"

"Yes," she answered. Then, because she could never lie to him, said, "No. What I mean to say is, I'm not sure how it's all going to turn out, but I think we have to do this. I think *I* have to do this." Fear of failing Ty coiled in her belly, but she ignored it, lifting her chin. It was time she stepped out on faith instead of just talking about it.

Tyler's gaze held more than a little worry, but he nodded, obviously relieved. She took joy in that.

"You better get moving," Holt told her, "before I decide I can't live without your pie." The quip fell flat.

She couldn't believe she was doing this, but she bullied aside her doubts and threw her arms around Holt. He held out the pie to protect it and pecked a kiss on her temple, but his tight smile didn't fool her. She knew he held back his tears with Herculean effort.

She went to Ryan next. "I hope you two know what you're letting yourself in for."

Ryan winked at Ty, teasing, "Anyone can make a few beds."

All her doubts rushed over her in that moment. "As if! It's not just making beds, it's—"

"I expect I know a thing or two about what it takes to keep this place running," Hap interrupted. "If three grown men can't do it, well, God'll provide."

"I know He will," Charlotte agreed, moving toward her grandfather with a heavy heart.

What a blessing he had been to her! Once she had thought her grandfather would forever be the center of her world. She had believed that anything that took her from there and him could not be right, but that was before Ty.

Oh, Father, don't let this be a mistake. Surely it shouldn't be this difficult!

"Granddad," she began, her chin trembling. He cut her off, engulfing her in a bear hug.

"I know what you're gonna say, sweet girl, but I never expected you to give up your life for me. I'm plenty old enough to be on my own. Me and the boys will work it all out. God's got something else for you to do."

"We'll be fine," Ryan said, joining the hug. "We have a plan. You go with Ty and help him out. Sounds like he needs it."

Holt pointed at Tyler then. "Speaking of plans, we're expecting to hear wedding plans as soon as your mom's able."

Tyler shook his head. "You're just going to trust me to take Charlotte off like this?"

The brothers looked at each other. "If we can't trust you to take her now, we sure can't trust you with the rest of her life," Ryan declared.

"Besides," Holt added, "we know our girl. Her we can definitely trust."

Charlotte hugged them both again, whispering, "Thank you."

"You just be happy," Hap instructed, nudging her to get moving. She couldn't think about that now. What if she could never be happy in Ty's world? She only knew that she would no longer be happy in her own world without him.

"Cassandra," Charlotte said, turning to Tyler's sister, her mind awhirl with a hundred concerns, "I'll need you to help me put together a suitable wardrobe as soon as possible. Can you do that?"

Cassandra blinked, looked at Ty, and then she smiled in a happily calculating manner. "I'd be delighted."

"Thank you." But her wardrobe was surely the least of what she faced, Charlotte knew. Whirling, she kissed Hap on his ragged cheek then rushed toward the apartment door, calling over her shoulder to Ty, "I'll throw some things into a bag and meet you outside."

Behind her, she heard Hap chuckle. "You best scoot, son. She's unstoppable once she's got her game plan on."

"Speaking of that," Ryan interjected, "you can expect us in your sky box at the next home game."

The last thing Charlotte heard before the apartment door swung closed behind her was Tyler's laughter. She wished that she could feel as happy and carefree as he sounded, but all she could do was gird herself for the battles ahead. How many, she wondered, before she could lay claim to any real peace in her life again?

Despite the doubts that crowded in on her, however, she clung to the hope of certainty. If the ground beneath her feet suddenly felt unsafe, then she'd just have to trust that angels would watch over her.

Chapter Seventeen

Charlotte felt strongly that Ty needed to see his mother as soon as possible, so they decided to drive straight to the hospital. Cassandra followed in her car. Along the way they spoke prayers for Amanda's well-being and Ty's wisdom in dealing with her. Once they reached the city, he pointed out landmarks relevant to his life, including the towering edifice in the distance, where he owned a penthouse.

"Just another word for a larger-than-average apartment," he commented mildly when Charlotte widened her eyes at the word *penthouse*.

Mentally gulping, Charlotte smiled and said nothing. Inside, she quivered with nerves, her stomach knotting painfully. She truly believed that she and Ty belonged together, but her new role in his life terrified her. The weeks and months ahead were bound to be difficult ones. Only with God's help could she hope even to get through them, but get through them she would. Somehow.

They left the car with a valet at the hospital entrance.

At some point Cassandra had fallen well behind them, but Tyler showed no concern.

"She knows her way around. She'll show up later."

He'd informed his sister via cell phone of their intentions, and she'd told him their mother's room number. Clutching his hand, Charlotte allowed him to lead her through the gleaming building to a central desk, where he spoke with a volunteer before being shown to a private elevator tucked into an out-of-the-way corner. They rode swiftly up to the correct floor. When they stepped off, a uniformed security guard nodded at them, and Charlotte's confidence abruptly faltered.

Gulping, she looked down at the jeans and sweater that she wore beneath her usual old quilted jacket. Why hadn't she at least exchanged her athletic shoes for flats? As if reading her mind, Tyler, still clad in his comfortable jeans and a simple shirt himself, dropped a kiss on her forehead.

She tried to put aside her fears and believe that God controlled the situation. Back in Eden, she hadn't doubted this was the right thing. She told herself that her place, now and forever, was at Tyler's side. She just hoped that she didn't embarrass him in any way.

They walked down a broad, shiny corridor that more closely resembled a plush hotel than any hospital Charlotte had ever seen. At the quietly bustling nurses' station, they were met by a distinguished, middle-aged man in a pristine white lab coat. His relief was clear.

Tyler introduced Dr. Olander, identifying Charlotte as his fiancée. The doctor quickly masked his surprise, but if Charlotte could have crawled into a hole at that moment, she would have.

After issuing congratulations and best wishes, the doctor got down to business. "I've never seen Amanda like this." As he spoke, he led them toward a door with the appropriate number affixed to it. "She's been weeping since she came in, and all she'll say is that she's a complete failure, especially as a mother."

Tyler dropped a perplexed look on Charlotte and pushed open the door. The "room" turned out to be a suite with a private sitting area.

Charlotte looked to Ty. "Maybe I should wait here."

He skimmed a knuckle across her cheek. "I know how hard this is for you, but I need you in there with me. If I thought I could handle this on my own, I'd never have asked you to come."

How could she refuse that? The doctor pushed into the inner room, announcing, "Amanda, Tyler is here."

He stepped aside, revealing a small figure in a high, narrow bed. That figure rolled to face them as they moved forward. Even without makeup, her white-blond hair sticking out at odd angles and swollen, red-rimmed eyes, she appeared much younger than her sixty-one years. One look at Ty, though, and she burst into noisy sobs.

To Charlotte's surprise, he did not immediately go to Amanda. Instead he looked rather helplessly at Charlotte. He seemed even more at a loss with his mother than he had with his sister. After a moment, Charlotte pantomimed a hug. He looked doubtfully back to the bed.

Finally, with Charlotte's hand still gripped in his, he walked forward, saying, "Mother, what is this about?"

Amanda's sobs rose to a wail.

Frowning at him, Charlotte gave him a tiny shove, indicating with a nod of her head that he should sit on the bed and moderate his tone. He looked somewhat desperate at that, but then he gingerly perched on the edge of the bed, saying, "It'll be all right. We're here now."

"We?" Amanda queried weakly, sniffing and looking up.

Ty tugged Charlotte closer, announcing firmly, "This is the woman I'm going to marry. Charlotte, this is my mother, Amanda."

The shock not only stopped Amanda's tears, it rounded her eyes and mouth to comic proportions. Forcing a smile, Charlotte remarked to herself that at least she now knew where Ty got those gorgeous eyes of his. The bedside manner was something they'd definitely have to work on, though.

"M-married?" Amanda's bleary gaze sought out Charlotte. "You're that Jefford woman, aren't you?"

"That's right," Charlotte answered, hoping her smile looked more cheery than it felt.

"I want you to tell me what brought this on," Ty said.

"First things first, though," Charlotte interjected gently, addressing Amanda. "Ty and I are going to pray for you. Then we'll all talk."

Amanda appeared stunned. Charlotte heard the door close softly behind them as the doctor slipped out. Heart pounding, she moved sideways to place both of her hands on Ty's shoulders and bow her head. Despite the distinct impression that Amanda did not follow suit, Charlotte's heart swelled as Ty began to speak.

"Thank You, Lord, for these two women. You know how much I love them and how much I need them. We all need Your guidance, and right now, my mother needs Your healing. Whatever's wrong, I know You can fix it, and while You're doing that, I ask You to make me a better son and a good husband, a man of whom You can be proud."

When he was done, Amanda lurched upward and threw her arms around her son, sobbing again. Tyler, thankfully, hugged her tightly, whispering, "It's all right. Please don't cry. Everything's going to be fine."

Suddenly, she grasped Charlotte's hand and fell back onto the bed, clutching at Ty. "Oh, son, I'm sorry for being so weak and stupid!"

Ty shook his head, smiling. "Amanda Aldrich may be a lot of things, but weak and stupid are not among them."

"Oh, yes, they are," she insisted. Her grip on Charlotte intensified as she switched her gaze once more to Charlotte's face. "I've been lying here making myself sick because I didn't think my son loved me." Her face crumpled, but she went on. "And why should he? I don't even know how to be a mother. I never have!"

Charlotte's heart lurched inside her chest. She'd been right to come. God was at work here, and He would surely work out everything else. Over time she would come to miss Eden and her family less and less, to love Ty and his family more and more.

"Now, now," Ty crooned, petting his mother's head.

"I'm sorry," she wailed, "but when Cassandra said that you'd told *her* you love her, I—I was so…so…*jealous!*"

"Mother!" Ty gasped, sounding a bit exasperated.

"Then I realized that maybe I'd never told any of my children how much I love them, and I *do,*" she squeaked. "I do!"

"Oh, Mom," Tyler said, gathering her close. He lifted a glance at Charlotte, his eyes speaking volumes. Charlotte nodded in acknowledgment. "It's all right," Tyler said, rocking Amanda slightly. "Everything's going to be different now, I promise."

She pushed back a bit then and in a slightly reproving voice said, "You've never called me Mom before." Then she looked up at Charlotte, adding, "I suppose I have you to thank for that, young lady." Lifting her chin, she whispered, "Thank you."

Charlotte laughed with delight. Relief and understanding swept through her. Maybe their lifestyles were as different as night and day, maybe she wasn't a fashion plate or from an influential family, but people were just people, after all, and every one of them needed the same things.

To her joy, she realized that she had more to offer Tyler and his family than she'd realized.

In many ways she'd just been marking time in Eden. Now she and Ty must forge a new world for themselves, for all of them. If she lost something precious in the bargain, well, it would be worth it. Besides, Eden would always be there for them. And they would never have to worry about having a room when they went to visit. With God's help, she could adapt. She must, for what other choice was there?

A palace, Charlotte thought with some dismay, glancing around Ty's sumptuous, elegant penthouse. He'd remarked earlier that *penthouse* simply meant a larger-than-average apartment, but the entire apartment that she shared with Hap back at the Heavenly Arms Motel would fit into just the master suite of this place.

Glass and shiny steel lightened dark, glossy wood,

black lacquer and rich burgundy, making for an undeniably beautiful decor, yet the place felt colder and emptier than even the most shabby room at the motel. She'd have preferred to see a bit of personal clutter, frankly, but even the enormous bathroom displayed all the hominess of an operating room.

Looked like she had her work cut out for her. But she could do this, she reminded herself. With God's help she would make this place a home.

"You don't like it," Ty said, leading her back to the living area after they'd settled Amanda into the guest room across the hall from Charlotte's.

It had been decided that Amanda would stay there with them after checking out of the hospital, at least for the time being. Later, Ty had suggested, Charlotte might be more comfortable the other way around, but the idea of moving in with his mother, even temporarily, filled Charlotte with gloom, which she struggled mightily to disguise. Fortunately, Cassandra and Preston had arrived just about then and were now spending a private moment with their mother.

"It's fabulous!" she insisted, lifting both arms to encompass the expansive room with its gorgeous furnishings, ceiling-to-floor windows and enormous, hidden television screens.

"Look," he said, coming forward to take her into his arms. "I never expected to live here forever. Actually, I always figured I'd wind up in a house in Highland Park, not some little town in Oklahoma. Just goes to show, huh?"

Charlotte blinked. "Do you mean that? You still plan to make our home in Eden?"

He drew back slightly. "Of course. Wouldn't you rather raise our family in Eden than here?"

"Well, yes, but what about your family?"

"I suspect we'll never be the same," Cassandra said, walking into the room, "and maybe that's a good thing." She'd changed into a teal silk pantsuit and twisted her hair up into a wispy, trendy clump.

Preston, Tyler's brother, followed in a somewhat more subdued, thoughtful manner. Charlotte had thought Ty to be the best-dressed man she'd ever seen, but Preston, whose thick, wavy, medium-brown hair seemed a perfect mixture of Cassandra's milky-blond and Ty's dark, chocolate color, might have been a male model. Charlotte wondered if she had ever been that comfortable in her clothes.

She tugged her mind back to matters of more importance. "What about your company?" she asked Ty.

"Please," Preston said, sounding bored as he dropped down into a leather club chair. "This is the twenty-first century."

Tyler tucked Charlotte close to his side and turned to his brother. "Meaning?"

Preston examined his fingernails. "You can run the company from anywhere. All you really need is a good Internet connection. DSL should do it."

Tyler rubbed his chin. "Actually, it would have to be a satellite connection."

Striking a pose, Cassandra shrugged negligently. "So you'll get a satellite link."

Hope rising, Charlotte looked to Ty. "Could we?"

Nodding, he mused, "Probably need a phone, too. The cell coverage leaves a lot to be desired." He looked at her. "It would mean a good deal of travel back and forth, I imagine."

Preston spread his hands. "So keep this place for when you're in town."

"Are you saying that you think I should continue running the company?" Ty asked pointedly.

Preston lifted an insouciant gaze. "Who else?"

"You didn't think you were going to get out of it that easily, did you?" Cassandra said, folding her arms.

Tyler looked between his brother and sister. "The two of you would have to take on more responsibility."

Something played across Preston's lips. "Think you can trust us?"

"Yes," Ty answered firmly.

"The infighting has gotten rather boring of late," Preston said, trying not to look too pleased. Crossing his legs, he dropped his gaze. "I'll do my best."

"I know you will." Ty looked at his sister. "Cassandra?"

She broke into a wide grin. "You know, it's just possible that we could make the best management team ever if we really put our minds to it."

"Amen," Ty agreed delightedly. He gazed down at Charlotte, his blue eyes glowing. "It'll take some time, you understand, to get things reorganized here, and then of course we have to find a piece of property around Eden and design and build our dream house."

"We have our whole lives," she told him, so happy she could burst. What a fool she had been to limit God in any way. All He'd ever required of her was surrender to His will. "But first things first, as you said earlier. We have a wedding to plan, remember?"

Smiling, Ty hugged her tightly. "How could I forget? And just so you know, I have recently discovered that I definitely do not believe in long engagements."

"That makes two of us then."

"Now," Cassandra said in a very businesslike manner, "I suppose the wedding should be in Eden."

Ty and Charlotte looked at each other. "At the First Church," he confirmed.

Charlotte beamed. "Grover will be so pleased."

"Just family and close friends, I'd think," Cassandra mused, "but of course we'll need to have a second reception here."

Tyler opened his mouth, ostensibly to object, but Charlotte elbowed him discreetly, aware that compromise behooved her and would henceforth be a large portion of her life. Besides, she would not pass up an opportunity to befriend her future sister-in-law. Her life, it seemed, had irrevocably changed in amazing ways.

"I trust you and your mother will take care of those details for us," Charlotte told Cassandra.

Tyler made a choking sound that quickly turned into a short cough. Less concerned with politesse, Preston baldly stated, "Try and stop them."

"You can count on us," Cassandra said to Charlotte, ignoring her brothers completely. Turning, she hurried back in the direction from which she'd come, muttering, "I hope Mother is not asleep yet."

Preston rose languidly. "I'm leaving before I get dragooned into helping out." He had just turned away when Tyler stopped him.

"Preston?" The younger man looked back. Tyler

stepped forward uncertainly. "I'd like to say something to you, something that should've been said long ago."

Preston smiled slightly. "I love you, too, bro." Then he walked away.

Elated, Charlotte went to slide her arms about Tyler's waist. "Things seem to be turning out better than I ever imagined."

"You can say that again," he told her, lifting his own arms about her. "I'll take you home tomorrow if you want."

"Hmm." She considered, feeling very much like a cat in cream. "Better wait on that. I think I have some shopping to do."

He laughed. "Buy anything you want. We'll start at the jewelers."

Charlotte sighed. "I'm afraid I could get used to this."

"I certainly hope so. Just like I got used to Eden."

The days passed in a whirlwind. It was more than a week before Charlotte saw her home again. They returned to Eden in a car laden with new purchases, and that did not count what Ty or Cassandra or Amanda had had shipped ahead or what would arrive later.

They'd planned the ceremony for the following Friday, the first Friday in December, and Charlotte had been gratified to find the church elaborately decorated for Christmas. She showed off her ridiculously extravagant ring and hung on to Ty as if he might disappear in a puff of smoke.

On Sunday evening, they took a lingering leave of one another. Ty had to get back to Dallas to tend to business there so he could afford to take time off for the honeymoon. Since she had no passport, they had decided on a very exclusive resort in the mountains of Colorado. Ty had promised her horse-drawn sleigh rides and skiing lessons.

He would return on Thursday with his family, a thought that made Charlotte's stomach cramp when she realized how primitive they were apt to find their accommodations.

She need not have worried. The Aldriches swept into town like traveling royalty and behaved just as graciously. Amanda had the rehearsal dinner and the reception catered, all the way from Dallas, in the church fellowship hall. Cassandra produced a mountain of lush poinsettias, sumptuous gold satin and thousands of twinkling lights, with which her personal decorator built a glorious bridal arch unlike anything Eden had ever seen. Preston's gift to them was a stringed quartet that produced hours of classical music.

The ceremony itself was somewhat unconventional.

Hap escorted Charlotte down the candlelit aisle of the packed church in her gorgeous new wedding gown. Her brothers met her at the altar and gave her hand in marriage, then stood at her side while Cassandra and Preston stood with Tyler.

Grover seemed somewhat overwhelmed, but as Hap would say later, "He got her done."

Charlotte stood with tears in her eyes and joy in heart to repeat her vows to Tyler and then laughed when Ty, the suave and debonair man from Big D, bobbled his own lines.

"Oh, forget it," he exclaimed. "I love you, Charlotte, with my whole heart, you and your family and my family and this whole town. The day I blundered in here was the most fortunate day of my life, and I praise God for it. With His help I'll make you the best husband I possibly can."

"You aren't apt to get a better deal than that," Justus Inman called from behind them.

Everyone laughed, and Grover quickly pronounced them husband and wife. After a long kiss that produced catcalls and more laughter, they ran back up the aisle, then stood arm in arm at the back of the church, watching their families file toward them.

"We're going to be so happy," she whispered.

"Yes, we are," he told her, hugging her close.

They watched Hap offer Amanda his arm, then hobble along beside her with his hitching step somehow matched to her elegant stride.

"All of us."

Laughing, they ran out into the December night, warm despite the chill of the evening, understanding just how richly God could and would bless His obedient children.

It went far, far beyond monetary things, from creation to salvation to the heart's desires.

And to think, Charlotte, said to her husband later, that she'd almost missed out!

Just by opening herself to it, by putting aside her assumptions and being willing to let God have His way, she'd received one of the greatest blessings of all.

True love.

Only that could build a bridge between two worlds.

* * * * *

Dear Reader,

Welcome to Eden, Oklahoma—God's country, land of oil! I grew up in south central Oklahoma. That's where I gained the foundation upon which my life is built, where I received the Lord and first dreamed of being an author. That's also where I met the love of my life.

I've tried to bring the feel and spirit of the place to you and to impart some of what I learned in the little church that my grandfather helped to build with his own hands. What better place to set a series about love and faith and the goodness of our Heavenly Father? It is, in many ways, a world apart. I hope you'll enjoy your visit there as much as Tyler Aldrich does and that you will be as richly blessed.

God bless,

Arlene James

Questions for Discussion

1. One of the great burdens in Tyler's life was the acrimonious relationship he had with his family, all of whom were fighting for control of the family company and wealth. Is great financial wealth a hindrance to healthy relationships? Why or why not?

2. Tyler had attended church his entire life, mostly for the sake of image. He never understood why he should really be attending church. Is his wealth a hindrance to his spiritual maturity?

3. It is often said that ours is not a God of confusion. Why, then, are committed Christians like Charlotte subject to confusion at times?

4. Until she fell in love with Tyler, Charlotte thought she knew God's will for her life. Yet, Ecclesiastes 3:10–12 speaks to the "seasons" of our earthly lives. In light of this, does God's will for our personal lives ever change? Is this what happened to Charlotte?

5. The Jeffords saw Tyler Aldrich as someone in need. As Christians we are taught to minister to the needy, but how do we define "needy," and is it possible for the financially wealthy to be as needy as the less affluent?

6. The Jeffords ministered to Tyler in a very personal fashion, but the average Christian does not have the

opportunity to mingle with the very wealthy. How can we, as Christians, go about ministering to the needs of the financially wealthy?

7. At one point, during a prayer service, Tyler feels "a presence." Is it possible in this day and age to feel the *physical* presence of God?

8. As Tyler fell deeper and deeper in love, his love for his family began to come to the fore. Is this because he was falling in love with Charlotte?

9. Tyler eventually found peace through surrender to Christ. Given his financial resources, he could have done much for the cause of Christ. Should financially wealthy Christians feel guilty about spending money on themselves or loved ones?

10. As Charlotte fell deeper and deeper in love, she began to question her understanding of God's will for her life. Is this because she had been fooling herself about her commitment to Christ?

11. Charlotte fought against allowing her emotions to guide her. Is it ever wise for a Christian to allow his/her emotions to guide him/her? Why or why not?

Her Small-Town Hero

Nay, in all these things we are more than conquerors through him that loved us.
—*Romans* 8:37

For Dad.
Rancher, builder, oil man,
businessman, salesman, auctioneer…
but first and perhaps foremost, roughneck.
I love you.
DAR

Chapter One

"Right here."

A slender forefinger pecked a tiny spot on the map spread out across the table in the little diner. Outside, rain drizzled down in a gloomy, chilly curtain, holding dawn at bay. Weather reports predicted a continuation of the current pattern of rain for northern Oregon, but Cara's concern centered more on what she would find south and west of here as they worked their way steadily toward Oklahoma and… She leaned forward, checking to be certain that her bleary eyes hadn't played her false. Yes, there, right next to Highway 81. Eden.

Her tired gaze backtracked wistfully the equivalent distance of some thirty miles to Duncan, following the tiny line that represented the silver, two-lane ribbon of road. None of the interminable bus trips of her youth had ever taken her farther than Duncan. She'd origi- nally planned to head straight for the town, thinking that she could find no better place to raise her son than that where she had known her happiest times, but then she'd realized that her brother Eddie would almost certainly think to look for her there.

So Eden it would be. Surely she could find sanctuary in a place with that name.

Next to her in a booster seat on the vinyl bench of the booth, her son, Ace, shoved away the remaining bits of buttered toast that remained from their shared breakfast and rubbed his eyes with two tiny, chubby fists before reaching toward her with a whine. Since his fussing the night before had prevented both of them from getting any real sleep, she knew exactly how he felt, but they dared not tarry another night in the Portland area. She hoped to make Boise, Idaho, before dinnertime and find a quiet motel off the beaten path where she and her little son could rest for the night before driving on.

After quickly folding up the map, Cara reached into the diaper bag that also served as her purse and removed several bills from her wallet. She placed the money on the table before sliding out of the booth, tugging on her short denim jacket and reaching for her son. Their clothing had proven no match for the chilly Oregon weather, but her limited funds prevented any but the most basic purchases. They'd just have to make do with layering. Ace, at least, seemed warm.

He laid his pale head on her shoulder as she reached for the diaper bag. She pulled up the hood of his tiny, gray fleece sweater before carrying him out into the fine rain. After belting him securely into his safety seat in the back of the small, greenish coupe for which she'd traded the minivan deemed suitable by her late husband and in-laws, Cara slid behind the wheel.

She would not regret the loss of the GPS guidance

system offered by the minivan or bemoan the state of the eight-year-old foreign car with which she'd replaced it. Instead, she told herself sternly to be thankful for the money she'd made from the trade, cash that, if carefully spent, would help her start a new life for herself and her precious son. Ace would grow up in the safety of a small town, cared for by his mother.

Cara started the car and gripped the steering wheel, suddenly beset by fear and doubt. Gulping, she told herself that she could do this. She'd come this far. She could do whatever she must for the sake of her child and a chance to live a normal, healthy life. With a new year but days away, she vowed that a new life would be her true Christmas gift to her child. He deserved a mother who provided him with a warm, supportive, affectionate and loving home. That required a strong woman able to make her own way in the world.

If only she knew how to be that woman.

Panic began to swell. Cara knew that she must find a way to protect and provide for her little son or watch him become another possession of his cold, controlling grandparents. But how? The task suddenly seemed too daunting for a woman on her own. Homeless, all but broke and on the run, how could she possibly give her child the life that he deserved and needed? Somehow, for his sake, she must find a way.

Help me! she cried out silently, wondering if her plea could reach through the great void that she felt. God had never seemed quite real to her, but Cara desperately wanted to believe that He existed, that He cared. She wanted to think that her late, beloved great-aunt had been right, that God noticed her distress and would respond to her prayers.

That was not insane. Was it?

She would not think of insanity or the clinic. She would pray instead, though she didn't really know how. Her aunt had always prayed silently with bowed head and folded hands, but the TV preachers sometimes stood with arms upraised, crying out. Surely something in between would work, as well.

Taking a deep breath, Cara whispered, "Dear God, please help me. For Ace. Please help me be what he needs, give him what he needs. Let Eden be just that for us. Amen."

Feeling no calmer but somehow stronger, she sat up a little straighter, looked into the rearview mirror and shifted the transmission into gear. Guiding the little car out onto the rain-washed street, she fixed her gaze on the road ahead.

Toward Eden and home.

Holt clicked the mouse and watched a new page open on the computer screen before dropping his gaze back to the ledger on the desktop. His grandfather was right. With the occupancy rate continuing high, the motel seemed to be doing well financially. Should they be forced to sell, and provided Holt could bring himself to ask that of his grandfather, they ought to be able to get a good price for it.

The Heavenly Arms had been Hap Jefford's livelihood, not to mention his home, for longer than the thirty-six years that Holt had been breathing. Hap had sunk his life savings into the place and often remarked that the hospitality industry offered the best of all worlds to a man with, as he put it, "the friendly gene." It also offered a great deal of work, most of which Holt's sister, Charlotte had managed until Thanksgiving of this year.

Now, at the very end of December, Holt felt like pulling out his hair in frustration. When he and his brother, Ryan had encouraged their sister to follow her heart, which meant relocating to Dallas with the man she loved, they had vastly overestimated their ability to handle the added responsibilities here, or even to hire help. Not a single person had replied to the employment ads they'd placed in area newspapers.

Holt pushed a hand through his sandy brown hair, aware that he needed a haircut, but when was he supposed to find time for that? His brother, Ryan, a teacher, coach and assistant principal at the local high school, could not be as available as Holt, who was self-employed as an oil driller. Ryan's many duties at the school meant that Holt had to shoulder the lion's share of the work around here. Motel issues now consumed his days, and his own business interests languished as a result.

He'd intended to have a couple new mineral leases signed before the end of the year so he could keep his crews busy exploring for oil, but New Year's Eve had arrived and he still hadn't moved on either one. Heartily sick of changing beds, he told himself that something had to give, and soon. They—*he*— had to have help.

Sighing, he dropped his head into his hands and silently went to the one source that had never failed him.

Lord, I'm stuck between a rock and a hard place here. I don't even know where to look next. There's got to be someone out there who wants this job. Even in this small town, there's got to be someone. Whoever it is, Lord, could You please hurry them along?

A chime accompanied the sound of the front door opening. Holt quickly finished his prayer and moved from the inner office out into the lobby area.

"Hello," said a breathy female voice as he walked through the door behind the counter.

A pretty little blonde in a closely fitted denim jacket worn over a figure-hugging double layer of yellow and white T-shirts stood before him with a baby on her hip, her golden hair curving in a saucy flip just above her shoulders. Deeply set eyes of a soft, cloudy gray regarded him solemnly from beneath gently arched, light brown brows. A pert nose, apple cheeks and a perfectly proportioned, peach-pink mouth in an oval face completed the picture.

Holt walked to the counter and looked down, far down. She stood more than a foot shorter than his six feet and three-and-one-half inches. Hitching the child, a blond, chubby-faced boy, higher on her hip, she shifted her weight slightly and offered a tentative smile.

"Hello," she repeated, dipping her head.

Holt mentally slapped himself, jarring his brain into sluggish activity. "Uh, hello. Uh, looking for a room?"

They had plenty to spare at the moment because of the holiday. The oil field workers who occupied most of the kitchenettes had all gone home to their families, and the truckers who usually filled the smaller units were off the road for the same reason. As a result, only a half-dozen of the twelve units currently held occupants, four by month-to-month renters and two others by out-of-towners visiting friends or family in Eden.

"Umm." The blonde nodded slightly and licked her lips.

"No parties," Holt warned. This being New Year's Eve, he wasn't taking any chances, though something told him he need not be concerned. For one thing, she had a baby with her. For another, she seemed rather shy. He watched her gather her courage.

"Actually, I'm more interested in that Help Wanted sign out there," she said.

Holt rocked back on his heels. He'd never experienced instantaneous answer to prayer before. It almost felt unreal.

So perhaps it was.

He narrowed his eyes while she hurried on in a soft voice.

"I—I'm looking for work, preferably something that would let me bring my boy along. Would this job, maybe, let me do that? I have a baby backpack, and he's used to being carried that way. He's quiet most of the time and…" She swallowed. "Look, I learn fast, and I'll work hard."

Holt didn't know whether to smile or scowl. Two minutes ago he'd prayed for help, and now here stood this strange woman, with a child, no less, and obviously desperate. He felt torn between sending her on her way and hiring her on the spot, a sign of his own desperation. As a man of faith, he couldn't discount the very real possibility that God might have sent her here, however. He stroked his chin, knowing that he had to interview her.

"Okay. First things first, I guess." He reached a hand across the counter. "Name's Holt Jefford."

She ducked her head and slid her tiny hand in and out of his so quickly that it barely registered. Holt took a job application from a cubbyhole beneath the counter. Placing the paper on the counter, he reached for a pen, then realized that the woman couldn't fill in the blanks while holding the boy. He turned the paper to face himself.

"Name?"

"Cara Jane Wynne."

He quickly wrote it out. "Birth date?"

"September first, 1983."

That made her just twenty-five.

"Address?"

She looked away. "The last would be in Oregon, b-but I used to live in Duncan." She slid a sad smile over him. "After my husband died, Oklahoma just seemed a happier place to be."

Widowed and homeless, Holt thought, jolted. *Well, Lord, I knew someone had to need this job.* "Let's use those addresses then."

She rattled them off, and he wrote them down.

"And how long did you live there?"

"Oh, uh, in Oregon, like seven years, I guess, and in Duncan until I was thirteen. Almost fourteen."

He made the appropriate notes, then looked up, but the instant their eyes met, she looked away again. "Job experience?"

Those soft gray eyes came back to his, pleading silently. "I haven't worked since I was in high school," she said in a voice barely above a whisper. "My husband didn't want me to."

"You must have married young," Holt said, without quite meaning to.

She nodded. "Eighteen."

"Ever worked around a motel?"

"No, but I can guess what needs to be done, and I'm not afraid of hard work."

"Can you use a computer?"

"Sure. But it depends on the program."

"Nothing too complicated," he muttered. "But what we really need is housekeeping, someone to clean the rooms, do the laundry and upkeep. And it would really help if you could cook."

A troubled expression crossed her face. "I'm no short-order cook, if that's—"

"No, no, that's not what I mean. See, this is my grandfather's place, and he needs somebody who can fix a decent meal for him at least once a day."

She visibly relaxed. "That I can do."

Nodding, he asked, "Any references?"

Once again, she avoided his gaze. "I don't know… I mean, it's just Ace and me now. M-my husband and I pretty much kept to ourselves."

Holt battled with himself for a moment. His every instinct told him that she was lying to him. A stranger without references or an address, he knew absolutely nothing about her. But she needed the job, and he needed the help. Besides, hadn't he just asked God to send someone? He looked at the baby on her hip and nodded, motioning toward the apartment door. He didn't know how anyone could manage the workload around here with a kid in tow, but that issue could be addressed later.

"Let's go talk it over with Hap."

She walked toward the end of the counter, speaking softly to the boy, who crammed his fist into his mouth and chewed. She had a petite figure, as those slim jeans showed, and tiny hands and feet, but she moved like a woman.

Stepping past her, he reached for the knob on the door that led into the small apartment where his grandfather lived.

"This way."

Holt Jefford pushed open the door to the apartment and stepped aside to let Cara and Ace pass. A tall, lean man with a ruggedly handsome face and intelligent, olive-green eyes, he made Cara nervous. Perhaps it had to do with the lies. Waves of suspicion had washed over her back in the lobby, but if he suspected that she'd lied, then why would he agree to let her speak to this Hap person?

Cara paused to look around, finding herself in a small private apartment. Unlike the warm, appealing lobby with its wood paneling and black leather furniture, this place appeared a bit dingy and cluttered, from the overstuffed bookcase against one wall to the old-fashioned maple dining set. Yet, it had a certain well-used hominess about it, too.

"Hap uses the front room as the main living area," Holt said, jerking a thumb over his shoulder to indicate the lobby. Three doors opened off the end of this room, which functioned primarily as an oversized dining area. "Bedrooms," Holt supplied succinctly. "Bath in between."

Cara nodded, uncertain why he'd mentioned this, before letting her gaze pick out details. A long narrow kitchen with incongruous stainless steel countertops opened off the wall opposite the door through which they had entered.

The acrid smell of burnt food permeated the air.

"Granddad," Holt called. "Company."

An old man limped into the open doorway, a spatula in hand. The faded denim of his overalls showed grease spatters, and his thinning yellow-white hair stuck up on one side. The two men shared a pronounced resemblance, although age had stooped the shoulders of the elder, whom Cara suspected had once been a redhead.

She found herself musing that this Hap must have been as handsome in his youth as his grandson was now. She met the welcome in those faded green eyes with smiling relief.

"And charming company it is," the old fellow rasped. Cara dipped her chin in acknowledgment, readjusting Ace on her hip.

"Granddad, this is Cara Jane Wynne," Holt said. "My grandfather, Hap Jefford."

Hap Jefford nodded. "Ms. Wynne."

"Cara Jane, please," she said, determined to make that name wholly her own.

At the same time Holt spoke. "She's applying for the job."

Hap's eyebrows climbed upward. "Well, now. That's fine." Hap limped forward, his left hip seeming to bother him some, and smiled down at the child chewing on his fist. "And who's this here?"

Cara hitched her son a little closer. "This is my son, Ace."

"Not a year yet, I'm guessing," the old man said pleasantly.

"He'll be ten months soon."

"Fine-looking boy."

Holt sniffed, and Cara felt a spurt of indignation—until she suddenly became aware of stinging eyes.

"Granddad, did you forget something in the kitchen?"

Jerking around, Hap hobbled through the doorway, Holt on his heels. "Land sakes! I done made a mess of our dinner. Again."

Holt sighed. No wonder he'd asked if she could cook. Cara knew that she had an opportunity here, if she proved brave enough to take it. She lifted her chin and crowded into the narrow room next to Holt, feeling his size and strength keenly. She tamped down the awareness, concentrating on this chance to prove herself.

"Maybe I can help."

Hap twisted around. "You can cook?"

"I can." She looked pointedly to the skillet, adding, "But it's been a while since I've even seen fried okra."

"Charred okra, you mean," Holt corrected.

Hap handed over the spatula with an expression of pure gratitude. "There's more in the freezer." He gestured at a large piece of sirloin hanging over the edges of a plate on the counter. "Do what you like with that. I set out some cans of sliced taters to heat in the microwave. Opener's in this drawer here. Anything else you need, just nose around. Holt will set the table while me and Ace get acquainted."

"Oh, no. Ace will stay with me," Cara insisted, looking down at her son. Too late, she realized that might have sounded rude, as if she didn't trust the old man. Then again, she didn't trust anyone. How could she? "I—I'm used to working with Ace close by," she said, hoping that would be explanation enough.

Hap traded a look with his grandson, and Cara held her breath until the old man nodded, smiled and said, "You and the boy will join us for dinner, of course." He somehow managed to make it an order without it sounding like one. Cara breathed a silent sigh of relief.

"Thank you."

"No need for that when you're cooking. We'll talk about the job later."

Nodding, Cara told herself not to blow this. It had been months since she'd cooked a meal, but surely she could manage this. Hap hitched himself past her and out into the other room, while Holt remained behind to lean a hip against the counter. Ignoring him, Cara sat Ace on the floor in a corner near what appeared to be the back door and removed his knit hoodie and the sweater beneath it. She took a small wooden toy truck from her jacket pocket and gave it to Ace before looking around her.

The apple-green walls and cabinets of pale, golden wood contrasted sharply with the industrial-grade metal countertop, but everything looked neat and clean if an odd mixture of the old and new, the professional and the homey. Noting the lack of a dishwasher in the small, cramped room, Cara glanced hopefully at the solid door next to the refrigerator.

"That goes out to the laundry room," Holt told her.

So, no dishwasher. She checked the sink. And no garbage disposal. Well, she'd survived a lot of years without those things.

"There's a big coffee can for scraps," he said, pointing to the cabinet beneath the sink. "It goes into the Dumpster out back when it's full. There's extra cans on a shelf above the dryers."

Nodding, Cara got down to work. She went to the freezer compartment of the refrigerator, moving past the tall man who watched her like a hawk. She found the okra in a half-empty plastic bag and a small box of frozen green beans.

"Okay if I use these?"

Holt glanced at the box of green beans, then at the boy now tapping the truck on the floor. "Sure. Use anything you want." With that, he moved to an overhead cabinet and began removing the dinner dishes, taking his time about it.

While Ace banged happily, Cara scraped the blackened okra and grease into the can under the sink, replaced the lid, cleaned the skillet and began looking in cabinets. Finally she asked, "Oil?"

Holt nodded at the tall, narrow cabinet doors across from the refrigerator. "In the pantry. Oh, and, by the way, there's a chance my brother, Ryan, will be joining us, too."

That meant three Jefford men, not just two, which explained the huge slab of steak. Cara removed her jacket, hoping he wouldn't notice the sleeveless tank tops that she wore in the dead of winter, and started heating the oil in the frying pan.

"Should I set a place for Ace?" Holt asked. "We don't have a high chair."

"No, that's all right," she answered without looking at him. "He'll sit in my lap, eat off my plate."

Holt went out, carrying dishes and flatware.

Cara's hands shook as she reached for the skillet, but a glance at her son stiffened her resolve. She could do this. She had to do this. Everything depended on it.

Chapter Two

Hap sat at the end of the table in his usual chair, reading from his Bible, when Holt carried the dishes to the table. He looked up, waggling his eyebrows and jerking his head toward the kitchen, but Holt didn't know what to make of Cara Jane Wynne yet. Shrugging, he began to deal out the plates onto the bare table. Charlotte had always kept the table covered with a fresh cloth and place mats, like their grandmother before her, but Holt and Hap had quickly found them a deal of work to maintain.

Hap crooked a finger, and Holt stopped what he was doing to lean close. "So? Tell me 'bout her."

"Not much to tell," Holt muttered. "She came in off the street, says she hasn't worked since high school and grew up in Duncan but last lived in Oregon. My guess is she's homeless and desperate." Hap made a compassionate sound from deep in his chest, and Holt frowned. "That doesn't mean she's trustworthy," he pointed out softly, then stiffened when she spoke from the doorway behind him.

"Excuse me. Are there serving dishes you'd rather I didn't use?"

Hap smiled and shook his head. "Use what you like. She that cooks gets to make the decisions in the kitchen, I always say."

"Okay."

Frowning some more, Holt laid the flatware, then went back to the kitchen to fill three glasses with ice and water.

Holt toyed with the idea of calling his brother to come over and evaluate Cara Jane. The satellite cell phones that their new brother-in-law, Ty, had given them for Christmas made it much easier to keep in touch, but Ryan often could not be called away from whatever activity currently required his supervision. As an assistant principal, history teacher and all-around coach, Ryan wore many hats. If they saw Ryan tonight at all, it would be briefly.

Holt could have used Ryan's input, but he understood only too well what it meant to be busy. His own drilling business and ranch and now the motel kept him tied up. Maybe, just maybe, Cara Jane was God's answer to that dilemma. He wondered if hoping so made him selfish or if not quite trusting her made him unfair. He didn't want to be either.

He took his time ferrying the glasses from the sink to table, making two trips of it. She never once glanced his way, but he found it difficult to take his eyes off her and the boy, who had pulled himself up and wrapped his chubby little arms around his mother's knees. Was she the poor little widow woman she seemed or something much more dangerous?

Holt felt sure that Cara Jane and Ace Wynne were going to be around until God had accomplished whatever purpose had brought them here. If that meant Holt could soon get back to his own life, so much the better, but he couldn't quite shake the feeling that all was not as it should be with her.

Cara placed the last platter on the table, Ace on her hip, and took a final survey of the meal: golden-fried okra, pan-grilled steak, buttered potatoes, green beans and carrots straight out of the can. Nothing fancy and nothing fresh.

You're not in California anymore, Cara.

Suddenly that warm and sunny place called to her. She'd left with no regret. Nevertheless, she suddenly found herself missing certain aspects of her old life, such as the warmth and sunshine.

Cara pulled out the chair and took a seat at the table, shifting Ace onto her lap.

"Gracious Lord God."

Hap's gravelly voice jolted Cara. She looked around to find the Jefford men with bowed heads. To her shock, Holt and his grandfather had linked hands. More shocking still, each of their free hands rested atop the table as if they'd reached out to her. Embarrassed, she pretended not to notice, holding Ace tight against her midsection and bowing her own head as Hap prayed.

"We thank You for this food and the pretty little gal You sent to cook it up for us. And thank You for bringing our Charlotte and Ty back safe from their honeymoon. We look forward to them coming home. You know we want only their happiness and Your will. Amen."

"Amen," Holt said. "Let's eat."

The two men practically attacked the food.

"My stars!" Hap declared, sliding a piece of pan-grilled steak onto his plate. "Will you look at that." He shot a grin at Cara, displaying a fine set of dentures. "Haven't had a piece of cooked meat I could put a fork in since our Charlotte up and married."

Over the course of the meal, Cara began to have doubts about her cooking, mostly because of this Charlotte of whom they spoke so glowingly. Charlotte, it seemed, was nothing less than a chef. They spoke of "good old country cooking" and such things as dumplings, chitlings and black-eyed peas.

"Speaking of black-eyed peas," Hap said, "good thing we're not superstitious."

"Why is that?" Cara asked idly, pushing Ace's hand away as he grabbed for steak and offering him a piece of carrot instead.

Holt braced both forearms against the tabletop and stared at her. "You grew up in Oklahoma and you haven't heard of eating black-eyed peas on New Year's for good luck?"

Cara dropped her gaze back to her son and tried not to tense, hoping the question would simply pass.

"Would that be New Year's Eve or New Year's Day?" Hap interjected. "Never was sure myself."

Relieved, she poked a green bean into Ace's babbling mouth with her fingers.

Holt stabbed potatoes with his fork, saying, "Well, if you want them for tradition's sake, I'm pretty sure there's a bag in the freezer, and since we don't believe in luck anyway, we might as well have them tomorrow as tonight, you ask me."

"You don't believe in luck?" Cara heard herself ask.

Holt looked up, eyeballing her as if she'd just beamed in from another galaxy. "As Christians, ma'am, we believe that God is in control of our lives, not random luck."

"Oh. I—I see." Except, of course, she didn't. God could not have been in control of her life or it would not have turned out like this.

Hap winked at Cara. "For tradition's sake, then. I like my black-eyed peas. Reckon if you stuck around you could rustle up a mess for us, young lady?"

Cara blinked. "Oh, I, um…"

"If you can cook beans, you can cook peas," Holt put in impatiently. "Just throw in a ham bone and make some corn bread."

"Now, Holt," Hap scolded mildly, "if it was that easy, we'd be doing it our own selves, wouldn't we? 'Sides, maybe she and the boy will be spending the holiday with family. Did you ever think of that?"

"Is that right?" Holt asked her. "You have folks around these parts?"

"No. No, I don't."

"Well, that's a shame," Hap said, shaking his head. "But if you got no family around, what brung you here? If you don't mind my asking, that is."

Cara opened her mouth, but Holt supplied the information before she had a chance to speak.

"Cara's a widow," he announced. "Looking for more cheerful surroundings."

Hap sat back in his chair, wiping his mouth with a paper napkin. "Now, that's a grief that I know too well." He looked Cara in the eye. "Both my wife and my son have passed from this world. You must have some family somewhere, though. They no comfort to you?"

"My parents are both gone," she said, which was technically the truth.

"No brothers or sisters?" Holt asked, sprawling back in his chair, which seemed too small to hold him.

She had the lie ready, but somehow it just wouldn't slide off her tongue. Besides, what harm could there be in at least admitting to Eddie? No doubt he was trying to track her down as they spoke, but the Jeffords wouldn't know that.

"A brother," she said, "but we're not close." Cara smoothed Ace's pale hair lovingly. "It's just us two really."

Hap shook his head. "It's a powerful sorrow when a father leaves a young family behind."

"Yes." Cara laid her cheek against the top of her son's head. "Ace was five weeks old when it happened."

Holt reached out a long arm and laid his fork in his plate. "Mind if I ask how your husband died?"

While she felt the shock that always came with the truth, she carefully masked her emotions. "He fell."

The two men traded looks, and Holt sat up straight again, looking uncomfortable now, his gaze going to Ace as he once more picked up his fork. "That's how my father died, too. He fell off an oil derrick trying to fix a pulley."

Cara took it that Holt's father and Hap's son were

one in the same. "They say he didn't suffer," she offered softly, swallowing hard.

Both Holt and Hap nodded at that. Apparently they'd been told the same thing.

"What'd your man fall from?" Hap asked.

"A highway overpass. He stopped to help a stranded motorist and somehow fell over the railing. No one's certain just how it happened," she said, still puzzled, "and the funny thing is, it wasn't like Addison to stop and help a stranger. Not like him at all."

Hap laid a gnarled hand upon her arm. "There are mysteries to which none are privy, and greater mysteries revealed to all. We must trust God with the first and thank Him for the last." Hap looked at Holt.

Cara sensed a certain reluctance in Holt, but she knew the moment had come to discuss business.

"The job requires long hours," he said. "It pays a salary on the first and the fifteenth." Holt glanced at his grandfather. "Plus room and board."

The figure he named didn't amount to much pay, but she wouldn't have to worry about food and shelter. "What about Ace? I need to keep him with me. If it's just housekeeping work, I know I could manage. He won't be any trouble to anyone."

"Well, there's housekeeping and then there's *housekeeping*," Holt said, and for the next fifteen minutes he detailed all that she would be expected to do.

It seemed overwhelming: beds to be made, laundry to be done, floors, bathrooms, draperies, dusting, sanitizing, even kitchens in some of the rooms. Every room. Every day. That did not include meal preparation or registering guests from time to time. But it did include Ace.

"We could give it a try," Hap said. "If the work and the boy together prove too much for you, we'll figure something out. It's not like you'd be on your own around here."

"Except for Saturday nights," Holt put in. "I take Granddad out for dinner on Saturday nights."

"Every other," Hap corrected, with another of those teasing winks at Cara. "Me and Charlotte, we always took turns with those Saturday nights. All you'd have to do is hang around here and watch the front desk."

That sounded doable to her. "I take it Charlotte used to work for you?" Cara asked carefully.

Hap chuckled. "Not exactly. Charlotte's my grand-daughter, Holt's baby sister. She up and married this rich fellow from Dallas."

"Work she did, though," Holt added. "More than I ever realized until I had to take over her job myself."

"Then essentially I'd be replacing *you?*" Cara exclaimed, pointing. Ace burbled something unintelligible and copied her gesture. Cara quickly pushed both their hands under the table, cheeks heating.

"That's the idea," Holt said dryly. He seemed to doubt she could do it. Just the way he swept his hard gaze over her seemed to pronounce her lacking somehow.

Hap waved a hand. "Now, now. Let's not get ahead of ourselves here." He pointed his fork at Cara. "You and the boy stay the night, take a good look around, think on it, and we'll all pray this thing to a conclusion. How does that sound?"

Cara smiled, feeling cautiously hopeful for the first time in months. "That sounds fine."

"Does that mean we get black-eyed peas tomorrow?" Holt asked, digging into his food again.

"Mmm, maybe some greens, too," Hap said longingly. "There ought to be a can in there. I hope there's a can in there."

"I think I'm not used to the same kind of cooking you're used to eating," Cara confessed.

"Oh, it's simple fare," Hap said, "nothing you can't manage, I reckon."

"It's sure to beat his cooking," Holt said, wagging his fork at Hap.

Hap pretended to take offense, frowning and grinning. "My cooking's what's kept these skin and bones together these past weeks, son, and don't you forget it. How many meals have you cooked since your sister married? Answer me that."

"None," Holt admitted. He grinned at Cara, grooves bracketing his mouth. Suddenly he looked heart-stoppingly attractive, sitting there in his faded chambray shirt that emphasized his strong, wide shoulders. "I like breathing even more than eating," he quipped and went back to doing just that.

"There you are!" Hap declared, slapping a hand lightly against the edge of the table. He looked cajolingly to Cara. "So do we get them black-eyed peas?"

"Black-eyed peas," Cara promised, gulping. "For tradition's sake."

But, oh, she thought, watching Holt chew a big bite of steak, *I could use just a little luck, too.*

* * *

Cara looked around the tiny, crowded bedroom with dismay. It still contained much that belonged to its previous owner: books, photos, various other keepsakes, even a yellowed set of crocheted doilies. An old-fashioned four-poster bed, dresser, domed-top trunk and wicker laundry hamper left only a narrow corridor of walking space around the bed.

She felt Holt at her back, watching her judge the room, and fought the urge to curl into a tight little ball. She'd hoped never again to live in someone else's space, meeting their standards rather than her own, always the outsider, never truly belonging or having control of her own life.

Hitching Ace a little higher on her hip, their outer garments clutched in one hand, she bucked up enough courage to say, "I think we'll be more comfortable renting a room for the night."

After a moment of silence, Holt replied, "I'll get a room key for you."

Relieved, Cara watched him stride for the lobby. After she'd taken a look at those frozen black-eyed peas—and thankfully found the preparation a simple matter of stewing in water for an hour or so—Hap had suggested Holt show her where she could stay the night. She'd never expected to be offered a room in the apartment.

A chime sounded as Holt crossed the room. Hap, who was stacking dishes in the kitchen, having insisted on helping her clean up after the meal, exclaimed, "Tell 'em I'll be right out!"

Just then the door opened and two elderly men appeared, their happy voices calling, "We're here!"

One of the newcomers wore dark pants and a white shirt beneath a sweater vest. More portly than the other, he boasted glasses with heavy black frames and a luxurious head of snow-white hair. The other, dressed in denim and flannel, possessed neither. Spying Cara and Ace, they stepped forward.

"Looks like y'all started the party without us," the flannel-shirted man said.

The other elbowed him and, without taking his eyes off Cara, commented, "Justus, your idea of a party is a bag of potato chips and a root beer."

"Yessiree-bob, 'specially if it comes with a purty gal." He nodded at Cara, eyes sparkling.

Holt laughed, and the sound resonated from the top of Cara's head to the very tips of her toes. He looked over one shoulder at her. "This is Teddy Booker and Justus Inman, two of the best domino players around. Otherwise, they're harmless. Fellows, meet Cara Jane Wynne. And the little guy's Ace."

Cara nodded, and the men nodded back, speculation lighting their eyes.

The chime came again, and Holt looked past them into the outer room. "Land sakes, Marie," he said, going forward, "is all that food? Come here and let me kiss your feet."

General laughter followed, during which a woman remarked, "Well, I know you poor things are still missing Charlotte, and it's no party without fixings."

Holt went out into the other room, followed by Misters Booker and Inman. Holt seemed an altogether dif-

ferent fellow than the one she'd known thus far, Cara
mused. Why, he could be downright charming when
he wanted to be.

She carried Ace to the table and began dressing them
both for the outside. She'd tossed on her own jacket and
had just pulled the sweater over Ace's head when Hap
hitched his way into the dining area, grinning happily.

"We're having a few friends in for dominoes," he announced. "That's our chief pastime around here. Figured we might as well usher out the old year that way.
You two are welcome to join us."

"Oh. No, thank you," Cara refused quickly, stuffing a
little arm into a sleeve. "He needs a bath and then bed."
The ripe smell of her son told her that he was more than
ready for a fresh diaper, too.

"I have your room key right here," Holt said, reap-
pearing. He looked to Hap. "Cara Jane thinks she'd be
more comfortable in a rental unit tonight."

"Sure," Hap agreed, heading off to join his guests.
"No charge, on account of that dinner. We got plenty of
space, and these jokers do tend to be a mite loud. You
change your mind about the party, though," he told her,
"you come on over, you hear?"

Cara nodded and smiled, tugging Ace's sweater
down. Hap disappeared into the other room, where
someone shouted, "Let the games begin!"

Holt closed the door behind him, saying, "I'm going
to put you in Number Six. There's just one bed and more
room for the portable crib that way."

"That's fine," Cara said, wrapping Ace's jacket
around him and gathering him against her chest. She'd
found sharing a bed with her little son like sleeping

with a whirling dervish. Pleased with the unexpected luxury of a crib, she reached for the key.

To her surprise, Holt slid it into his pocket before grabbing his coat from a peg on the wall. "I'll just see you settled in."

"That's not necessary. I don't want to keep you from your guests."

"Hap's guests," he said, shrugging on the leather-trimmed canvas coat. "They've got enough to make up a table. They won't miss me." He lifted a brown cowboy hat from another peg and fitted it onto his head, suddenly seeming ten feet tall. Nodding toward the kitchen, he said, "We can go out through the back."

Cara put on a smile and moved ahead of him, holding Ace closer to her chest to keep him warm. He babbled in a sing-song voice to himself as they stepped out onto the pavement, cold enveloping them.

Shivering, Cara hurried ahead of Holt to the car parked beneath the drive-though. At least, she told herself, they'd gotten a meal out of this and would sleep warm tonight. Tomorrow would just have to take care of itself.

Chapter Three

"I'll, um, move the car later, if you don't mind," Cara Jane said.

Holt shrugged. It seemed odd to him to leave the car sitting there under the drive-through, but a great deal seemed odd about Cara Jane Wynne. He reached into the trunk of her car for the two bags there.

"You can park your car in that space just to the left of the door to your room," Holt told her, hoisting their two bags. Neither of them, he noted, weighed enough to tax a child, let alone a grown man. A wise woman wouldn't pack more than she could tote herself, but Holt figured that starting a new life would require a great deal more than Cara Jane seemed to be carrying.

All that remained in the trunk was a lightweight baby backpack, which told him just how Cara Jane intended to manage her son while she worked. Trying to do such work with a baby strapped to her back seemed foolish to him, but he supposed she'd figure that out soon enough.

While he carried their bags to the room, Cara Jane

closed the trunk lid and went to rummage around in the car.

Opening the door, Holt entered and hit the light switch with his elbow. Leaving the door slightly ajar, he hoisted the bags onto the long, low dresser, then went to turn on the heat. The place could best be described as utilitarian, he supposed, but at least it was clean and neat.

She came in moments later carrying Ace, a stuffed diaper bag and a small plastic tub of groceries. Holt took the tub from her and closed the door so the place would warm up. Already the air that blew from the vent above the closet felt toasty enough to take the immediate chill off.

"Should be comfortable in here soon," he told her. Nodding, she dropped the diaper bag on the bed and turned to face him. "Furniture's bolted down," he informed her.

She shrugged. "Safer that way. Ace likes to pull up on whatever he can find."

"You're traveling light," Holt commented, waving a hand at the suitcases.

"I live light," she replied.

He had no idea what that meant, but he intended to make sure that she had a clear picture of what she would be getting into if Hap hired her. "A job like this requires hard work," he told her. "Take it from me."

"I understand."

"I'm not trying to discourage you, and God knows we can use the help. I just want you to be aware of what you'd be getting into."

"I appreciate that."

"I'm not sure you can," he said, rubbing his ear. "You and the boy want to come along, I'll show you one of the kitchenettes so you can get a better idea of what you'd be up against."

For a moment, he thought she might refuse. He had to admit that if he was standing here in nothing more than a jean jacket, he might have balked himself. Where, he wondered, was her coat? Didn't they wear coats in Oregon?

Cara nodded, held the boy close and headed for the door. Holt followed her out, pulling the door shut behind him and trying not to watch the sway of her hips.

Holt used his passkey to let them in the room next door and snapped on the light. The kitchenettes basically contained two rooms, pass-through closet and bath in one, bed, sitting area and tiny kitchen in the other. Cara stood in the center of the room, the boy on her hip, and looked around. Holt couldn't help noticing the way her eyes lit at the sight of that puny kitchen. Then she swept her fingertips along the arm of the tweedy sofa.

"It makes into a bed," he told her, "but because of the lack of space, it's usually folded up when we get here to clean, so you always have to check the sheets, even if only one person is supposed to be in the room."

"I see."

"Then there's the kitchens," he went on. "The regulars usually do their own dishes, but if they don't, you have to. The kitchens have to be meticulously cleaned to keep the bugs out."

"Good policy."

"Half our units are kitchenettes," he pointed out,

wanting to ruffle her for some reason. "The rugs have to be cleaned periodically, as well as the draperies."

"All right."

"Look," he said, "I'm an old roughneck, and I'm telling you, it's hard work."

She turned on him, her face stony. "Okay, I get it. You don't think I can handle the job."

"I didn't say that. I just want you—"

"To know what I'm getting into," she finished for him, brushing by on her way to the door. "Yeah, yeah."

Irritated, he caught her by the crook of the elbow. "I just think you should have all the facts before you make your decision."

She jerked her gaze up at him. "Are you saying that the job is mine if I want it?"

For an instant, he felt as if he might tumble head-first into those soft gray eyes. Abruptly, he released her and stepped back, clearing his throat. "I'm saying you should be fully informed. The rest is between you and Hap."

She flicked a doubtful glance over him and walked out into the cold night. He didn't blame her for not buying that. She, however, didn't know Hap. If Hap made up his mind to take her on, nothing his grandsons could say would make any difference, not that Holt wouldn't dig in his heels if he thought he should. He just hadn't really decided yet whether or not he would.

On one hand, Holt badly wanted the help she could provide. On the other, something wasn't right about her. Too pretty, too alone, too quiet, she set his every sense on alert.

He wondered, as he fetched the portable crib and

hauled it over to her room, just how he might go about running a background check on her. They'd never had to worry about things like background checks before, though Ty had suggested they consider it. Holt would speak with his brother-in-law about it. Meanwhile, he'd keep a close eye on Cara Jane Wynne.

Cara rolled onto her stomach and folded her arm beneath the pillow under her head, listening to the faint whir of the heater and Ace's easy breathing. He'd objected when she'd belted him into his car seat and moved the car after Holt had gone back into the apartment, but she hadn't wanted Holt to hear the awful knocking racket that her old car had started making earlier in the day. She couldn't help feeling foolish for having traded her dependable, almost new minivan for an older, high-mileage car, but she'd desperately needed the cash, which hadn't gone as far as she'd hoped. She certainly didn't want to give Holt Jefford a reason to question her good sense, so she'd waited until he'd gone to move the car.

After his bath, Ace had sucked down a bottle of formula then dropped off to sleep in no time, but she had not been able to. A giant clock in the distance seemed to be counting off the minutes—*ka-shunk, ka-shunk, ka-shunk*—while her mind whirled with the possibility of working for the Jeffords and all it involved. She kept thinking, too, about the kitchenette next door and imagining herself sitting down to that little bar with her son. It would almost be like having their very own place.

Cara thought back to her bitter disappointment upon realizing, on the heels of her husband's death, that the house in southern California had not belonged to her and Ace. Learning that it had been sold out from under her had sent her into a sharp decline.

Rolling onto her back, Cara cut off that line of thought. She and Ace were together and free of the past, and it was going to stay that way. No matter what she had to do, she would prove herself capable of making a good life for her son.

Provided she could make this job work for them.

Holt worried her. She couldn't escape the fear that he knew she'd lied. Thankfully the old man seemed more trusting. She'd prefer to concentrate on him, but she sensed that she must convince Holt, too, if she had any chance of staying on here.

Recalling words that Hap had spoken during dinner, she sat up and wrapped her arms around her bent knees. She felt the lonely weight of the darkness, heard the relentless *ka-shunk, ka-shunk* of an invisible machine and let the curious words wash over her.

"There are mysteries to which none are privy, and greater mysteries revealed to all. We must trust God with the first and thank Him for the last."

What had he meant by that? She would never understand Addison's death, but what "greater mystery" had been or would be "revealed to all" and why should anyone give thanks for it? She had never heard her aunt speak of such things, but no doubt the Jeffords could tell her. They seemed to be devout Christians, which only made her dishonesty seem worse, but she had to protect herself and her son.

"We believe that God is in control of our lives, not random luck."

Had God, she wondered, brought her here? She'd been praying a lot lately, and this certainly seemed the perfect place for her and Ace. For one thing, no one would think to look for them in the Heavenly Arms Motel in Eden, Oklahoma. Plus, this job offered not only a modest salary but shelter and food, as well, and the Jeffords seemed willing to let her keep Ace with her while she worked. If she could convince them to let her and Ace stay in one of the kitchenettes, it would be very nearly perfect, no matter how difficult the job might be.

Besides, she had the feeling that she might find answers here, answers to questions she didn't even know to ask yet.

If only she had the chance. If Holt would give her the chance.

Laughter filtered in from outside.

Feeling terribly alone, Cara glanced at the clock and saw that the old year had passed. *Ka-shunk, ka-shunk, ka-shunk.* Closing her eyes, she did what Hap had suggested and said a prayer.

Please let this work out for us. Please let this be the start of a new life, a real life, for us.

Needing reassurance, she leaned far to the side and peered over the edge of the crib at her sleeping son. "Happy New Year, sweetheart," she whispered.

Ace slept on undisturbed, so innocent, so precious, so deserving of love and protection and all the things that a good parent provided. She would be that good parent, Cara vowed. No matter what anyone else thought or said or believed, she would give her son everything she had never had, things that even his father had not enjoyed.

Somehow.

She settled down to wait for morning, one *ka-shunk* at a time.

Holt stretched, then sat up in the bed in his sister's room, the one in which Cara Jane might have slept if she hadn't been too proud or too wary or something. Thoughts of her had intruded far into the wee hours of the first morning of the new year, he realized as he swung his feet down onto the floor and stood. He had been too tired after the party to drive out to his ranch, and since Cara hadn't wanted to use this room, he'd figured he might as well.

While pulling on his clothes, he smelled bacon cooking. Hap—or someone—was making breakfast. Holt wondered if they had enough eggs in the house. He felt like he could eat a good dozen himself, despite the dinner and all the goodies he'd consumed last night. Bless Marie Waller anyway.

The pastor's wife had done her best to make up for Charlotte's absence these past weeks, sending over one dish or another with her husband, Grover, whenever he came to play at Hap's domino table, which was almost daily. Unfortunately, Grover suffered from diabetes, so those tidbits rarely included anything sweet, and Holt possessed a powerful sweet tooth. Maybe they'd get pancakes for breakfast if *someone* happened to be in the kitchen.

Hap happened to be in the kitchen, and by the time Holt got there, he'd burned the bacon.

"Does that look too done to you?" he asked, shoving the plate beneath Holt's nose.

"We've gotta get your glasses checked," Holt told him, taking the plate and sliding it onto the counter.

Hap grunted and handed over the spatula. "I reckon you better try your hand at the eggs this morning, then."

"You don't suppose the Garden's open, do you?" Holt asked glumly, referring to the café downtown.

Hap shook his head. "We could always ask Cara Jane to help out."

Sighing, Holt went to the refrigerator. "I don't know about her. Something's just not right there."

"She lost her man. All alone in the world with a boy to raise. That's what's not right."

"We don't know that," Holt grumbled, taking the egg carton from the refrigerator. "Why, for all we know, she isn't even that kid's mother."

"Have you looked at that child?" Hap scoffed. "If she's not his mama, then she's real close kin."

Holt had to admit that they favored each other. "Could be she's hiding out."

"From who? Not the law. That I won't believe."

Okay, she didn't strike Holt as a hardened criminal, either, but something about her didn't ring true. For one thing, he reasoned silently, a woman like her attracted men like honey attracted flies. If she'd hung tight back in Oregon, some fellow would have stepped up to take care of her and little Ace quick enough. Even if she'd loved her husband to distraction—and somehow he didn't think that had been the case—it didn't make a lick of sense for her to strike out on her own looking for someplace "happier."

"How do we even know she's widowed?" he asked, taking down a bowl to crack the eggs into. He preferred his eggs over-easy but that didn't mean he could cook them that way. Better to just scramble them and have it done with.

Hap considered, then shook his head. "I know that look too well. 'Sides, why lie about it? There's no law against leaving a husband. Even if she's scared of him, wouldn't it make more sense for her just to tell us that?"

"You mean, if he was abusive or something."

"Exactly."

Holt pulled open a drawer and took out a fork. "For all we know, she was never even married."

Hap humphed at that. "Don't strike me as that sort."

"Maybe not, but that would explain why she's not living off her husband's Social Security somewhere. It just doesn't add up. She hasn't been completely honest with us."

"No reason she should be, I reckon," Hap said, hobbling into the other room. "Maybe once she gets to trust us."

It seemed to Holt that his grandfather had that backward. How were they supposed to trust her if she didn't level with them about herself and her situation?

He cracked half a dozen more eggs and then took a certain pleasure in going after them with the fork.

Cara tapped on the window, her breath fogging the glass. Wearing the same clothes as he had the day before, Holt looked up from beating something in a bowl and reached out with one hand to flick open the door. His hair stuck up in disarray, and he needed a shave. Somehow that made him all the more attractive.

"'Morning," she muttered, sliding into the narrow

room sideways, Ace on her hip. The dark shadow of Holt's beard glinted reddish-gold up close, she noticed.

"Happy New Year."

"Oh. Yes. Happy New Year."

"Sleep okay?"

"Just fine, thank you," she lied. As if he knew that her conscience pinched her, Ace patted her chest before grabbing a fistful of the front of her aqua-blue T-shirt. "Except," she amended, "I keep hearing a giant clock in the distance."

Holt turned to lean a hip against the counter. "A giant clock?"

"Well, not tick-tock, exactly. More like *ka-shunk, ka-shunk*."

Holt chuckled, folding his arms. "That's not a clock, giant or otherwise. It's a pump jack on an oil well out back."

She goggled at him. "Oil well! But wouldn't that make you rich?"

Holt flattened his mouth. "Hardly. And it doesn't belong to us. A previous owner kept the mineral rights to the property."

"Ah." That hardly seemed fair, but what did she know about it? To cover her ignorance, she smiled and asked, "How was the party?"

He went back to beating what she now recognized as a bowl full of eggs. "'Bout like you'd expect for a room full of old folks and a domino table."

Since she'd never had experience with either, she said nothing more about that. "Is your grandfather around?"

"He is. You and the boy wanting some breakfast?"

"No. No, thanks. We've eaten already." Crackers, applesauce and warm cheese sticks, but Holt didn't need to know that. "I can finish that up for you, though, if you want."

"If you're not eating, it wouldn't be fair to let you cook," he grumbled.

"I don't mind."

He jerked his head toward the doorway. "Hap's in the other room."

"Your choice," she mumbled, stung. So much for winning his favor.

Slipping by him, she carried Ace into the dining room. Hap sat with his head bent over a big black Bible. He looked up, smiling, and nodded at a chair. She sat down with Ace on her lap. She heard the clump of Holt's boots as he stepped into the doorway behind her.

Ignoring Holt, Cara said to his grandfather, "I'd like the job, Mr. Jefford."

"Well, now, that's fine." Hap gave his head a satisfied nod.

"There's just one thing," she went on, heart thundering. "I'd like for Ace and me to have our own place. If we could stay in one of the kitchenettes, that would be great."

While Hap scratched his neck, Holt spoke up. "What's wrong with Charlotte's room?"

"It's too small," she said bluntly, not looking at him. "Ace would have to sleep with me all the time." She addressed Hap again. "I could pay something, maybe half, so you wouldn't be out the whole rent."

To her relief, Holt walked back into the kitchen.

"No need for that," Hap said, reaching out to pat her hand. "'Course, if we're full up and need the space, you and Ace might have to move in here temporarily. That room of Charlotte's is a mite crowded, but I'm sure she'll take all her stuff when she and Ty get their house built."

He went on chatting for some time about the house that Charlotte and her husband, Tyler, were planning to build in Eden, while Cara floated on a wave of relief and delight. When Holt came in with two plates of scrambled eggs, burnt bacon and white bread, Cara smiled brightly. Employed and with a place of her own, she finally let herself believe that this might work out.

"I'll see to those black-eyed peas now," she said cheerfully, rising to her feet and sliding Ace onto her hip, "and clean up the kitchen once you're done here."

Hap chuckled. "It's a holiday. The cleaning can wait till later."

"Thank you, Mr. Jefford."

"Call me Hap. We're one big happy family here. Glad to count you in."

Smiling, Cara nodded and started to turn away, only to be brought back down to earth with a thud when Holt said matter-of-factly, "I'll be needing your ID and Social Security number." He forked up a big bite of eggs before pinning her with his gaze. "For the employment papers." She felt the color drain from her face, even though she'd expected this. He seemed not to notice, digging into his food. "You can give it to me after you get the peas on."

She nodded before making her escape.

One more lie, she told herself. Just one more, and then everything would be fine.

Chapter Four

Holt lifted the employment forms from the printer tray and placed it on the desk in front of Cara Jane. "That's the last one. At least I think so. These are all I use with my crew, and I don't see why this should be any different."

"Your crew?" she asked, busy filling in the blanks.

Ace played beneath the counter at her feet, crawling back and forth and screeching from time to time. As he answered her, Holt couldn't help smiling at the sounds of a little one at play. "Roughnecks. I run a crew of roughnecks. Two crews, actually, and three rigs."

"Oh." She kept her gaze trained on the tax form in front of her. "I remember you saying something about being a roughneck last night."

He suspected that she didn't have the faintest idea what a roughneck was. "I don't usually work as a motel maid," he told her drily. "I'm a wildcatter."

This time she did look up. "Wildcatter?"

He leaned forward slightly. "A driller. For oil."

Comprehension finally dawned. "Oh!"

Holt frowned. Wouldn't a girl who grew up in Oklahoma know *something* about the oil business?

Eyes narrowed, Holt pointed to the signature line. "Just sign here. Then I'll need a copy of your Social Security card and driver's license."

She signed on the appropriate line and pulled her wallet from the diaper bag at her feet.

"So you don't actually work for your grandfather at all," she said, handing over the laminated cards.

Holt inclined his head. "Just helping out since my sister married. Well, before that, really. Since they got engaged at Thanksgiving. They didn't marry until December seventh."

"That's not much of an engagement," Cara Jane commented wryly, pushing back the desk chair and leaning forward to reach for Ace.

"Two whole weeks," Holt supplied, carrying her license and Social Security cards to the scanner.

She straightened, pulling Ace up onto her lap. "Goodness. I was engaged for two years."

Holt punched a button and looked at her as she stood, swinging the boy onto her hip. "Didn't you say you married at eighteen?"

"That's right."

He gaped. "Your parents let you get engaged at *sixteen?*"

Her gaze met his briefly. "Let me? I doubt they even noticed." She poked the boy in the chest with one fingertip, saying, "Don't you go getting any ideas, dude. You're going to college before you get married, just like your daddy."

Holt latched onto that tidbit of information. "So your husband had a degree?"

She glanced at him, wary now, and Holt could see her trying to decide what to tell him. Finally, she said, "He was a lawyer."

A lawyer? Holt thought of those two lightweight suitcases he'd carried into her room and the eight-year-old car from which he'd taken them. He put that together with her reaction and came up with…more questions.

"I thought lawyers usually made a pretty good living."

"So did I," she said.

Rubbing his prickly chin, Holt pondered this bit of information, remembering that she'd said her husband hadn't wanted her to work, even though they'd been married at least six years, by Holt's reckoning, before Ace's birth. Holt filed that away, allowing her to change the subject as he retrieved her identity documents.

"So," she said, a bit too brightly, as he handed them over, "you're not employed here, but I take it you live here."

"Here at the motel?" He shook his head. "Naw, I have a little place of my own, a ranch east of town."

"I see." Her expression changed not a whit, but relief literally radiated off her. "I guess that means you're, like, married."

Folding his arms, Holt asked, "Why would you think that?"

She lifted a shoulder, using both hands to anchor Ace on the opposite hip. "I don't know. Seemed like a reasonable conclusion for a man your age."

"What's my age got to do with anything? If you're thirty-six you must be married?"

"I didn't say that."

"Well, I'm not married," he told her, feeling rather indignant about her assumption, "which means I happen to be around here a lot. Every day, in fact."

She nodded at that, inching away. "Oh. I guess I'll be seeing you around then."

"Count on it," he told her, watching her snag the diaper bag then leave the room.

Even with the boy perched on her hip, she walked with a decidedly feminine stride. Holt shook his head, disgusted with himself.

A dead lawyer for a husband, engaged at sixteen, hadn't worked since high school, assumptions and secrets, and enticing, and he couldn't keep his gaze off her. Without a doubt, that woman was trouble walking. He just hadn't figured out exactly how yet. But he would. Oh, yes, he would.

Cara straightened, her arms full of rumpled linens, which she stuffed into the bag on the end of the cleaning cart. She took one more swipe at the newly made bed and hurried out to check on her napping son.

The backpack allowed her to tote him much of the time, but the thing became problematic when it came to certain chores, so she'd taken to hauling the crib from room to room with the cleaning cart. The portable baby bed resembled a playpen more closely than a conventional crib, anyway, and despite the cumbersome process, having her son within sight comforted Cara.

Unfortunately, she had no choice but to take the crib

into the apartment at nap time and let Hap watch over Ace while he slept. Since Hap could routinely be found at the domino table in the other room, that usually necessitated little more than an open door between the apartment and the lobby, but Cara hated not being able to watch over Ace herself.

After locking the room, she pushed the cart across the pavement to the laundry, then moved on through the kitchen to the dining area. Her heart jumped up into her throat when she saw the empty crib. Then she heard a familiar squeal, followed by men's laughter, coming from the front room. She raced out into the lobby to find Ace sitting in the middle of the domino table, surrounded by chuckling old men, while he clutched handfuls of dominos.

"Look there, Hap," Justus teased. "He takes after you, hogging them bones."

"That's my boy." Hap patted Ace's foot.

"You wish," Teddy crowed.

"He's getting in practice for when Charlotte and Ty start their family," Grover Waller, the pastor, maintained. Round and cheerful, Grover reminded Cara of an aging, balding cherub in wire-rimmed glasses and clip-on tie, but at the moment all Cara could think was that these men had her son.

As she rushed toward them, Hap turned his head to grin at her, holding out an empty bottle. "He's had him a little snack, Mama, and a dry diaper."

"Took all three of us to change that boy's britches," Justus told her, sounding pleased.

"Strong as an ox," Teddy confirmed with a nod.

Cara began plucking dominoes from her son's grasp,

her anxious heartbeat still speeding. "I apologize. This won't happen again. I—I'll pick up a baby monitor as soon as I'm paid, one I can carry around with me so I'll know the instant he awakes."

"No need, Cara Jane," Hap protested. "We don't mind watching out for him, do we, boys?"

"Not at all," Teddy said.

"Cheery little character," Grover put in.

"That's kind of you, but he's my responsibility," Cara said, gathering Ace into her arms. The relief she felt at simply holding him against her made the preceding panic seem all the more terrible. How could she have let him out of her sight for even a moment? Yet, she'd have to do the same thing repeatedly, for what other choice did she have?

Hap again patted Ace's foot, knocking his shoes together. "So long, little buddy."

Cara quickly carried her son from the room. She knew that she'd overreacted badly. Those old men meant no harm. They had no designs on her son. But Ace was her child, her responsibility, and she would give no one reason to question her ability to care for him.

Apparently her overreaction had been noted, for as she pushed the door closed, she heard Hap say, "She's mighty protective."

"Protective?" Justus scoffed. "You'd think we was trying to steal him."

"There's a story there," Grover murmured.

Carefully pushing the door closed, she laid her forehead against it. Ace tried to copy the motion, bumping her head with his. It didn't hurt, and he didn't fuss, but she soothed him with petting strokes anyway, sick at heart. Had she given them away? She shook her head. Impossible. These people had no idea who she really was. So they deemed her an overprotective mother. Let them think what they wished. Nothing mattered except keeping Ace safe and with her.

Except that they were bound to tell Holt how she'd reacted today, and that would be one more black mark against her in his book.

But she didn't have time to worry about Holt now. She had work to do. Sighing, she carried Ace out to the laundry room, got him into the backpack and returned to the apartment to fold up and move the portable crib.

One more room, and then dinner. And Holt.

He had not failed to show up for dinner the past two nights. On both occasions, he'd looked so weary that she'd have felt sorry for him if he hadn't watched her as though he expected her to pull a weapon and demand his wallet at any moment.

She held out the faint hope that he would have other plans for tonight, this being Friday. Didn't single men go out on the weekends in Eden, Oklahoma? Apparently not, because when she laid food on the table that evening, his big, booted feet were beneath it. As on the previous occasions, he barely spoke to her, just stared when he thought she wouldn't notice. She suffered through the meal in silence and hoped he would stay away the next time.

Not so. Even Hap expressed surprise when Holt arrived the next night. "It's not our usual Saturday night out," he exclaimed.

Holt brushed aside the old man's comments. "What of it? Still got to eat."

His brother, Ryan, arrived thirty seconds later. A big, bluff man with a good thirty pounds on Holt and dark, chestnut-brown hair and hazel eyes, Ryan greeted Cara with open delight.

"You are the answer to our prayers," he told her, holding her hand between both of his after their introduction.

Holt scowled and asked if Ryan would mind parking himself so they could eat. Ryan, who seemed to accept his role as younger brother with equanimity, sat. Hap prayed. Ryan then made friends with Ace, who occupied her lap as usual, while Holt scoffed down three pieces of grilled chicken and a truckload of macaroni and cheese before taking his leave again. At no point did he so much as speak to Cara, letting his nod suffice for both greeting and farewell.

Ryan, a very pleasant man, came into the kitchen later to sheepishly apologize for his brother. Cara pretended complete ignorance.

"I can't imagine why you'd think I'd be offended. I just work here."

"Work," Ryan said, "is a lot of the problem. You see, right now Holt's working too much. Well, he's always worked too much. It's just that now he's trying to catch up. My fault," he added with gentle self-deprecation. He then went on to explain that he had a hard time getting away from his responsibilities at the school, which had left Holt to take on the motel pretty much by himself. "Which is why I'm so delighted that you're here."

Cara didn't bother to point out that Holt obviously did not share that delight. Instead, she thanked Ryan, finished the dishes, picked up Ace and slipped out quietly. She couldn't help thinking, though, that it wouldn't hurt Holt to be nicer to everyone, including his brother.

With Ryan turning out to be such a friendly man, much like Hap in that regard, Holt's surliness seemed all the more pronounced. It smarted that he didn't seem to like her, so much so that she intended to keep her distance on Sunday, her one full day off. On Sundays the Jeffords "closed the office." Sunday, Hap had told her, belonged to God, though they'd rent to anyone in need of a room who wandered by.

Ace actually let her sleep in a bit that morning. After feeding him breakfast and watching a church service on TV, she thumbed through a magazine and finally stepped outside. The weather had turned surprisingly warm. On impulse, she packed a lunch of sorts from her meager provisions, loaded Ace into the backpack and headed for the park.

Separated from the motel grounds by a stream that wound through the gently rolling landscape, the park had to be entered via a bridge adjacent to the downtown area some three blocks to the east. Along the way, Cara explored the town.

There wasn't much to Eden, as far as she could tell on foot: some houses built before the Second World War, some houses built after, and just a couple blocks of old brick storefronts on the main street, which happened to be named Garden Avenue. Absolutely everything stood closed, everything except, of course, for the inviting little white clapboard church on the corner of Mesquite Street, which ended right at the back of the motel. The church appeared to be doing box office business, judging by the number of cars that lined the street and surrounded the building.

The sign next to the sidewalk identified it as the First Church of Eden and named Grover Waller as the pastor. The place had such a warm, inviting air, much like Grover himself, that Cara took note of the service times. Perhaps she and Ace would visit there next Sunday. Since she assumed that the Jeffords attended there, given their close association with the pastor, it might even win her some points. But not with Holt.

She'd learned the hard way how impossible it could be to win the regard of someone who had made up his or her mind not to like her. Her in-laws had hated her on sight, but Cara had tried to win their regard, nonetheless, without success.

Putting the little church behind her, she took Ace to the park, where they ate their lunch in solitary peace and sharp winter sunshine.

Holt paced the floor in front of the reception desk that next Saturday night. Cara had never seen him dressed to go out. He "cleaned up good," as Hap put it. Wearing shiny brown boots, dark jeans with stiff creases, a wide leather belt, open-collared white Western shirt and a similarly styled brown leather jacket with a tall-crowned brown felt hat, he looked like the epitome of the Western gentleman. All cowboy. All man. He'd gotten himself a haircut, too, which gave him a decidedly tailored air but did nothing whatsoever to blunt his impatience.

"You really don't have to wait," she said again,

bouncing Ace on her knee. "It's been almost two weeks. I can manage the desk until Ryan gets here."

In truth, she didn't expect to have to manage anything. The motel stayed full, or nearly so, during the week, but few guests strayed in during the weekends.

The last weekend had yielded only two rental opportunities, an older couple on their way up to visit relatives in Nebraska and a very young couple obviously looking for privacy. Hap had kindly but firmly turned away the last pair, saying only that he couldn't help them. Cara had learned a valuable lesson on how to handle an awkward situation that day.

"He should have been here already," Holt groused.

Cara opened her mouth to say that she was sure Ryan would be along soon, but just then, through the plate glass window, Cara spotted a now familiar late-model domestic sedan slow and turn off the highway into the lot. "There he is."

Holt spun to the window, bringing his hands to his waist. "It's about time." Striding to the end of the counter, he called through the open apartment door, "Granddad! He's here!"

"Comin'!" Hap called back, muttering, "Hold your horses. Always champing at the bit."

Cara ducked her head, biting back a grin. Hap Jefford had quickly endeared himself to her and her son. Witty, caring and cheerful, he seemed genuinely fond of Ace and had even taken over much of the laundry chores once he decided that Cara had "got the hang of things," as he'd put it. If not for Holt coming around to glower at her, she thought she'd be fairly content. She'd tried to be nice to Holt, but that only made him more dour.

"Now, listen," Holt lectured, splaying a hand against the countertop.

"Isssssn!" Ace mimicked, leaning forward to smack his hand onto the lower counter.

Holt looked at him, one corner of his mouth kicking up. He glanced at Cara, sobered and cleared his throat, drawing back his hand. "Just let Ryan handle things. If anyone comes in, he'll take care of them. You're still observing for now."

"Hap's already explained," she began, only to have him cut her off.

"If you need anything, you have our numbers." He made a face. "Well, mine, anyway. Granddad never carries his phone with him."

"Why should I?" Hap asked, limping through the apartment door. "I never go anywhere on my own."

"On your own what?" Ryan asked, stepping inside the lobby.

"On my own by myself," Hap said. "How you doing, Ryan?"

"Excellent, as usual."

Holt rounded on his brother. "You took your time getting here."

Ryan paused in the act of shrugging off his corduroy coat and glanced at his wristwatch. "It's ten minutes till six. What's the rush?"

"Oh, don't mind him," Hap counseled, limping over to ruffle Ace's hair. "He's got a burr in his bonnet. I say, a burr in his bonnet." Ace giggled and fell back against Cara's chest. She smiled up at Hap, who patted her shoulder affectionately. "There's pizzas in the freezer, and if you eat them I won't be tempted."

"Done," Ryan proclaimed, rubbing his hands together.

"Can we go?" Holt demanded. "I'm hungry."

"When was the last time you *weren't* hungry?" Hap asked, limping around the counter.

"I'm usually pretty good when I get up from the table," Holt grumbled as the two of them left the building through the front door.

Ryan shook his head. "That's our Holt, two hollow legs."

"Not to mention a hollow head," Cara muttered.

Ryan burst out laughing. "I'm beginning to wonder if that's not his problem, though I've never thought so before." He stood staring as if that ought to make some special sense to her, then he clapped his hands together. "I'm thinking we should dress up those pizzas. What have you got in the pantry?"

"Pineapple?" she suggested hopefully.

"Pineapple?" he parroted. "They eat pineapple on their pizza up in Oregon? Sounds like a California thing. You ever get down to California?"

Cara just smiled, but inwardly she cringed. When would she learn to watch her mouth? The jangle of the telephone saved her from any more uncomfortable questions and the lies she'd rather not have to tell in answer. Ryan reached across the counter and picked up the receiver.

"Heavenly Arms Motel." He threw back his head and laughed. "Charlotte! How you doing, sugar? How's Ty and the Aldriches?"

Cara rolled the desk chair back, giving brother and sister as much privacy as possible. She tried not to listen, even considered slipping out of the room, but Ryan stood there, leaning on the counter and looking right at her as if she were as much a part of the conversation as he and his sister. He smiled and chatted, enjoying himself.

Finally he said, "I love you, too, sugar. We all miss you like crazy, especially Holt, I think. Y'all coming for the big game, then? Excellent. Looking forward to it. My best to Ty."

He hung up, beaming. "Get this," he said. "My brother-in-law usually attends the Super Bowl live. This year, he's passing it up and bringing Charlotte home to watch the game on TV with the family." He shook his head. "Now that's true love."

"You really care for her, don't you?" she said to Ryan.

He chuckled and spread his hands. "Of course. She's my baby sister. I'm told you have a brother, and I'm sure he loves you, too. That's just how it is."

Like Ryan, she had once thought that Eddie must naturally care for her, but all she had ever been to him was a conduit to the Elmont money.

"You and your brother and sister seem to have a special bond."

"Yeah." Ryan nodded, smiling to himself. "I guess, after our parents died, we sort of banded together, you know?"

She wasn't sure she did, really. Cara and her brother had, for all intents and purposes, raised themselves. Usually Eddie had gone his way and she had quietly gone hers. They'd had little in common, except for Addison, who'd been buddies with Eddie in high school.

Something Ryan had said suddenly struck her. "Did

you say parents, as in plural? I was only told about your father's death."

Ryan passed a hand over his eyes and rubbed his cheekbone. Leaning both forearms on the counter, he drew a little closer and related the tale. "Yeah, Dad's death was a big shocker. You probably heard that he fell?" At her nod, Ryan went on softly. "Well, when our mother found out, she committed suicide."

Cara caught her breath. "Oh, I'm so sorry. I had no idea." Thinking of the moment she'd received news of Addison's death, she recalled the shock and the numbness, the uncertainty and the very great sadness. Part of that sadness, though, had been because she'd known she wouldn't really miss *him,* only the idea of raising their son together. "Your mother must have loved your father very much," she mused absently.

Ryan drew back at that. "I guess she did," he said, "but it marked Charlotte." He shrugged, adding, "Holt and I were already out of the house, young men. Charlotte was just thirteen and still at home, and she's never understood why Mom didn't think of her before she swallowed those pills."

Pills, Cara thought. She had more in common with Charlotte Jefford Aldrich than she'd realized. Neither of their mothers had cared enough about them to leave the pills alone. The knowledge saddened Cara and made her feel more kindly toward Charlotte.

Ace bucked and tried to slide off her lap, but she caught him up, hugging him tight. She loved him enough to put him first, and she always would. Thanks to the Jeffords, she now had a chance to establish herself as a fit guardian for him. If the Elmonts came calling, they would find no reason to again question her ability to care for her own son.

"That's why we're so happy God brought Ty and Charlotte together," Ryan said. "Next year, Ty wants to take all of us to the Super Bowl. Man, wouldn't that be something!" He shook his head. "Not that it'll happen, mind you."

"What makes you say that?" Cara asked. From what she'd seen and heard, Tyler Aldrich appeared to be a very generous and wealthy man, with the kind of money that even the Elmonts must bow to. If he wanted to take his in-laws to the Super Bowl, what was to stop him?

Ryan tapped a thumb on the countertop and considered. "You're right! You're here. You'll be an old hand at this by then. Why shouldn't we all go if we want to?"

Cara smiled. At least one of the Jefford brothers had confidence in her. Too bad it wasn't Holt. Irritated with herself, she tried to put him out of her mind. Why his approval continued to mean so much to her, anyway, she couldn't imagine. Besides, Ryan clearly had just as much influence with their grandfather as Holt did.

Determined that she would not subject herself to Holt's disapproval, Cara excused herself a couple hours later when his dirty, white double-cab pickup truck appeared in the frame of the picture window overlooking the highway. A sleeping Ace in her arms, she said goodnight to Ryan, left him to deal with the leftover pizza and slipped through the apartment and out the back.

She couldn't help feeling a little sorry for herself as she cradled her son in one arm and let herself into the dark, silent room. Despite her gratitude for the sanctuary she'd found here in Eden, it hurt to know that no one else in the world cared about her, not her brother, certainly not her in-laws.

At first Cara had thought being married would fill that void in her. Eventually, however, she'd realized that Addison really valued only one thing about her, that he could control her. She'd been his outlet for the control that his parents had exerted over him and his sister. That had been her sole function in his life.

When she'd at last been granted a child, she'd believed that things could change between her and her husband. Then Addison had died, and his parents had plotted to cut her out of her son's life altogether. To top that off, her own brother had been willing to help them, for a price, because that's all she'd ever been to him, a means to an end, a way to stay close to Addison, who would have dropped Eddie long ago if not for her.

The only person to ever really love Cara had been her great-aunt. Cara still missed her aunt deeply, and with tears in her eyes, she vowed to honor her aunt's memory by giving her son all that the *real* Cara Jane Wynne had given her, and at least one other thing that Aunt Jane had never thought or intended to share.

Her name.

Chapter Five

Holt guided his truck to a stop beneath the motel drive-through behind Ryan's sedan and killed the engine. Hap sent him a sharp glance, then grinned when Holt opened his door and stepped one foot down to the ground.

"I take it you're coming in."

"Well, of course I'm coming in."

"You don't always."

"So?"

Hap just shook his head and slid out on his side.

Why shouldn't he come in? Holt asked himself. He didn't always go haring off back to the ranch after dinner, and no one could say he did. Grumbling at the strange behavior of some folks lately, Holt strode ahead of his grandfather up the sloping walkway and into the building.

The TV played in a room lit only by it, a lamp and the glowing embers revealed by the open door of the potbellied stove. A replica of an 1890s model, the stove provided the cheery ambience of a crackling fire with less hassle and more actual heat than a fireplace. Ryan looked up from his customary spot on the sofa.

"Hey. Charlotte called. She and Ty are coming home for Super Bowl Sunday."

"That's good!" Hap crowed, hobbling past Holt on his way to his favorite rocking chair.

"Where's Cara Jane?" Holt wanted to know, ignoring the fact that his brother-in-law would give up a live Super Bowl game in order to bring Charlotte back home for a visit. Matters here seemed more important at the moment. If Cara Jane had waltzed out and left Ryan on his own to watch over things, Holt would be having a talk with her.

"She just took Ace back to their room," Ryan told him off-handedly.

Strangely deflated, Holt craned his neck. The thing seemed to have more kinks than a flattened bedspring tonight. "Why'd she do that? Some reason she didn't want to say good-night?"

Ryan sent him a blank look. "Don't think so. She'd rocked Ace to sleep and was just waiting for you two to show up so she could put him down for the night."

"Oh." Holt turned to stare blindly at the television set, trying to appear relaxed and unconcerned. "So, how'd it go?"

Ryan kicked back on the sofa, crossing his hands behind his head. "Quiet. Real quiet. And I don't mean just businesswise. She's not much for conversation, is she? I mean, we talked some, but it's not like she really says anything, not about herself, anyway." He grinned at Holt. "Fortunately, I'm able to carry a conversation all on my own. The two of you would probably bore each other to tears, though, given how little you each have to say."

Holt grunted at that. He didn't think of Cara Jane, or himself, as boring. Quiet, yes, but boring? No way.

"I'm a little concerned about her, though," Ryan went on.

Holt's attention perked up. "How so?"

Ryan looked to Hap. "She seemed, I don't know, sad. And doesn't she strike you as awful thin? I think she's lost weight since she's been here. The girl's no bigger than a child to begin with. Seems like a lonely little thing, too, despite the way she dotes on that boy. I don't think he got off her lap the whole evening."

Hap nodded. "She don't hardly give you a chance to get to know Ace or for him to get to know you. I could lighten her load a whole bunch just by watching over him sometimes, but she won't hear of it 'less he's napping." Hap shook his head worriedly. "I'm wondering how long she can hold up."

Ryan looked to Holt. "Maybe you and I ought to be taking a bit more of a hand, still."

Perversely, Holt had to bite his tongue to keep from telling Ryan to just back off and leave Cara Jane to him. He knew it wasn't reasonable and that rankled. He'd already had a talk with himself and God about his attitude toward Charlotte, and he didn't want to have to add Ryan to that list. He still couldn't believe what a load his baby sister had carried all those years, and God knew Holt wanted her happiness above even his own, but he couldn't deny that he'd felt a twinge of resentment at having to put his own work on hold in order to take care of what had been hers. Now, suddenly, he wanted to snap at his brother. And why? He knew the answer to that, and it had a lot less to do with Ryan than Cara Jane.

Narrowing his eyes, Holt wondered what she had been up to here on her own with his brother. Had she played on Ryan's sympathies? Maybe even tried to spark his interest? Ryan would be too trusting, too soft-hearted to properly judge the situation. He wouldn't understand how Holt could be so sure that Cara Jane wasn't being completely honest with them. Nope, this burden fell to him. So be it.

"I think I'll just check on things before I shove off," Holt announced, striding for the apartment door.

"You sure that's a good idea?" Ryan asked.

"I'll see the two of you later," Holt answered, as if he hadn't even heard the question.

"The boy was sleeping," Ryan began, but Hap cut him off, calling out a cheery, "Tell Cara Jane good night for me."

Holt kept on walking, right into the apartment and out the back door. He dashed across the pavement to her room, cold nipping at his ears and nose. If Cara Jane Wynne had designs on his too-trusting and too-amiable brother, Holt felt an obligation to find out and put a stop to it.

Of course, he'd felt the same way about Ty when he'd first realized that he and Charlotte might be interested in each other. Holt had feared that, with wealth almost beyond imagining, Tyler might consider Charlotte as nothing more than another plaything. In the end, Ty had turned out to be madly in love with Charlotte and willing to give up his whole world, family and career included, to make her happy. She'd refused to allow him to make that sacrifice. Thankfully, neither had to give up anything for the other. As it turned out, Ty would continue to run Aldrich & Associates even after he and Charlotte built their house and moved to Eden, and to everyone's surprise, the snooty Aldrich clan had accepted Charlotte with open arms.

Cara Jane, however, was nothing like Tyler Aldrich. Holt wanted to be fair, but whenever he came into contact with her, his every sense jolted to uneasy alert. He sensed that desperation hid beneath her quiet aloofness, and it made Holt wonder what secrets she held and to what lengths she might go to keep them hidden.

He stood in front of her door now, his hand fisted, but instead of knocking, he closed his eyes and reached for help, preparing himself for the encounter.

Father, You know I don't trust this girl, and I know that I tend to react in defensive anger to anyone who threatens my family. That serves no useful purpose for anyone. Help me here. I don't want to be unkind or harsh. I just want to protect my family and myself.

Himself?

Holt's eyelids snapped open. Yes, himself. All wrapped up in that small package lived a very pretty and compelling woman who made him aware of her as none other ever had. She took him back to a time when he'd thought he would marry and have a family of his own—until his daddy had died.

He'd taken up where his dad had left off, even hiring some of his father's old crew, and he'd accepted that God did not intend for him to marry and make a family of his own. Over the years, Holt had seen too many men crippled, broken down and even killed working on oil rigs. Sure, the odds had improved, but the chances of an accident were still too great. Besides, his brother, sister and grandfather needed him.

In all fairness, Cara Jane could not be faulted for making him think of a time when his life had seemed destined for a different path. He sucked in a deep breath of cold air and finished his prayer.

Help me be fair and insightful, Lord. Give me discernment so I'll know how best to deal with Cara Jane. Accomplish Your will in this and protect my family. Amen.

Calmly he lifted his hand and tapped on the door, mindful of the boy sleeping within. Seconds later he felt Cara Jane standing just behind that barrier. Backing up a step, he lifted his chin so his face wouldn't be hidden by the brim of his hat and she could see him clearly through the peephole. The chain snicked, and then the door opened a few inches.

Head bowed, she regarded him warily from beneath her brows. "Something wrong?" She sounded stopped-up, and he wondered if she might be getting a cold.

"I don't know," he answered. "You tell me. But do it inside, please. It's freezing out here." He bounced his shoulders up and down beneath his leather coat to emphasize that fact. She had to be chilly, too, standing there in nothing more than jeans and a tank top. Didn't the woman own anything with sleeves?

She turned away from the door, and he pushed inside, glancing around.

"Where's Ace?"

Cara Jane sent a fleeting, twisted smile over one shoulder. "In his room."

"What room?"

She moved toward the closet, crooking a finger at him. Basically, one passed through the closet area to the bath beyond, which could be closed off with louvered doors for privacy. She'd hung a blanket over the outer, open doorway into the closet and now pulled it aside. Puzzled, Holt walked across the floor to look behind the blanket.

The closet provided ample space for the small crib, especially since no clothing hung from the single rod overhead. The louvered doors that separated the bath area from the closet and the foot or so of space at the bottom of the blanket provided ample ventilation. The pebbled glass of the high window in the bathroom would filter sunshine into the space in the daytime, and the light in the toilet cell made a decent night-light.

Ace slept deeply in this makeshift nursery, a soft bundle of baby boy at complete peace with his little world. Holt's heart turned over in his chest. His mother might not be trustworthy, but Ace deserved only protection and consideration.

Backing out of the space, Holt took a look around and noted all the little ways in which Cara Jane had made this space a home for herself and her son, from the sprig of ivy falling over the lip of a water glass to the dish towel folded and fanned prettily across the bar counter. She'd fashioned a seat for Ace at the breakfast bar from an upturned cooking pot, a pillow and a woven belt arranged on a dining chair.

"Looks like you've settled in nicely," he commented, keeping his voice low.

Nodding, Cara Jane floated about the room and came to rest with her hands gripping the back of the dining chair she'd obviously chosen for her own.

"What's going on?" she asked.

Holt watched her study the hard wood seat of the chair. After a moment, he realized that she had yet to look him in the eye. She sniffed and made a swipe at one cheek, and suddenly he knew why she hadn't looked at him. He wandered over to the hide-a-bed sofa and sat down, just so she'd know that he meant to stay awhile. He removed his hat and turned it over in his hands.

Deciding that a direct approach would serve best, he asked, "Why are you crying?"

She shot him a wary look, moved around the chair and gingerly parked herself. "I don't know. Women cry sometimes."

He leaned back and crossed his legs, leaving the hat on his lap. "Last time Charlotte cried," he told her, "it was over Ty."

Cara Jane didn't appear to muster much interest in that, but she politely replied, "Oh?"

"Mmm-hmm. Never thought she'd see him again, I guess. That's when I started praying especially hard."

"And now they're married," Cara Jane said, a touch of asperity, or possibly envy, in her voice.

"Happily married," he confirmed.

Cara Jane gripped the seat of her chair with both hands. "Charlotte's very lucky. You all are." Spearing him with a tart look, she added, "Oh, that's right. You don't believe in luck."

"We're blessed," he admitted, tickled for some reason by her irritation, "and we know it."

"Do you? Even after the way your parents died?" He must have shown his surprise at that because she quickly added in an apologetic tone, "Ryan told me about your mother."

"I see." Obviously Ryan had more than carried his end of the conversation.

For a long moment, she said nothing, just sat there looking down at her hands, the palms turned up as if weighing the words she might speak. Her irritation gave way to wistfulness as she said, "It's odd, isn't it? Your dad fell to his death. My husband fell. Your mom took pills. My mom took pills." As if fearing she'd said too much, Cara Jane quickly tucked her hands beneath her thighs. "Not on purpose," she qualified. "My mom just liked to get high. She liked it so much it killed her."

Holt should have been pleased to learn something new about her, but instead he wished she hadn't told him, wished it hadn't happened in the first place, wished it didn't make him feel sorry for her. He especially wished he didn't have to know more, but he did.

"How old were you?"

"Seventeen."

Old enough to stay out of the child welfare system, he noted, not old enough to really take care of herself. A heaviness settled over him. He accepted it with the gravity it deserved, asking, "What about your dad?"

She waved a hand. "Last we heard he was living on the streets up in Vancouver, but for all I know, he could be anywhere. That was ten, twelve years ago."

No wonder she'd married so young. Mother dead of

a drug overdose, father gone. This information put Cara Jane in a somewhat new light. Holt acknowledged reluctantly to himself that he'd asked for understanding and God seemed to be delivering it bit by bit.

With an inward sigh, he commented, "Sounds like you had it pretty rough growing up."

Cara Jane nodded. After a moment, she confessed, "I loved school. I was safe there."

Meaning she hadn't been safe at home. Holt inhaled through his nostrils. "What about the summers?"

"My mother's aunt," Cara Jane answered instantly. "I don't think either me or my brother could have survived without her." Her lips curved wistfully.

"Where's your aunt now?"

The shutters came down behind her eyes, and she shifted on her seat. "Great-aunt," she corrected, "and she died a long time ago."

"What about your brother?" Holt probed, but apparently she'd reached the limit of her willingness to share because she stood then and moved to the door.

"My brother and I are not close. We're not all so lucky—" She broke off, ruefully bowing her head. "Blessed, I mean. We're not all so blessed as you and Ryan and Charlotte." She leaned back against the door frame and folded her arms, blatantly changing the subject then. "Did Hap enjoy his night out? I imagine you're both pretty tired by now."

Holt knew when he was being asked to leave. He got to his feet and walked toward her, his hat in his hands. "Hap always enjoys his night out," he told her. "Guess it's your turn next."

"My turn?"

He hadn't intended this, but suddenly it seemed like a very good idea. He'd learned something about her tonight. What might he learn given a little time with her in a purely social setting?

"If Charlotte were here, it would be her turn," he pointed out, "but since she's not and you are…" He let that trail off, pressing lightly, "You're not going to make me go to dinner next week by myself, are you? No fun in that."

Cara Jane lifted her chin. "But I have Ace."

"Bring him along," Holt told her, reaching around her for the door knob. She leapt out of the way, and he pulled the door open. "It'll be a night out for both of you." With that, he stepped onto the pavement and pulled the door closed behind him, giving her no chance to refuse.

Only then did it occur to him that he'd just usurped her Saturday evening off. But for a good cause, he told himself, an essential cause. Not only did he need to learn more about her, Ryan was right. She had lost weight. She didn't fill out those jeans quite as well as when she'd first arrived, and if he hadn't been trying so hard not to pay attention, he'd have noticed it sooner. This working herself to the bone had to stop, which meant that he would have to step in once more. Perhaps he could see her well fed while he pumped her for information.

Holt fitted his hat onto his head as he strode over to the apartment and let himself in through the kitchen.

He found Hap and Ryan at the dining table, eating leftover pizza. Hap dropped his piece when Holt blew into the room.

"Caught ya. You know you're not supposed to be eating that. Too much sodium."

Hap made a face. "You won't tell Charlotte, will you?"

Holt circled around to his usual chair and dropped down into it, snatching the pizza off Hap's plate on the way. "Nothing to tell," he said, cramming the first bite into his mouth. Pineapple. That was new. Not half-bad, either.

"Not now that you've eaten it yourself," Hap groused, and Holt grinned.

"You're in a better mood," Ryan noted, claiming a second piece for himself. "Guess Cara Jane's okay."

Holt shook his head. "Nope. You're right. Work's too much for her."

Hap sighed and sat back in his chair. "What're we gonna do? I'm telling you now, I'm not putting her and Ace out on the street."

"No one's suggesting that," Holt said, though he might have if she hadn't opened up just a bit. It hit him that she hadn't ever really said why she'd been crying, which made for one more mystery. "We don't have any choice except to pitch in until we can find her some part-time help."

"But we've already tried that," Ryan pointed out. "We couldn't find anyone to hire, and I couldn't free myself up enough to make any difference."

"Let me rephrase," Holt said, downing the last of Hap's pizza. He reached for the one remaining piece. "*I* will just have to pitch in until we either find her some help or she loosens her grip on the boy."

Hap rubbed his chin. "If you could just help her after

he gets up from his nap, say around three in the afternoon…"

Holt shrugged. "I guess I can manage that."

"And I'll be doing the dinner dishes from now on," Hap vowed, nodding his approval.

"No, I will," Ryan said, "and that includes the weekends, especially Sundays."

"Now how are you gonna manage—"

Ryan cut off Hap's protest with a raised hand. "I'll figure it out. It's only fair."

Hap looked at Holt, who shrugged again. Couldn't argue with fair.

"Speaking of Sundays," Hap said to Holt. "You invite her to go with us to church tomorrow?"

Holt made a face. "No, I didn't."

"I'll do it on my way out," Ryan volunteered, half rising from his chair.

"It can wait till morning," Holt insisted, focusing on his pizza. "She, um, looked like she'd be turning in when I left, so I'll ask her in the morning."

Ryan subsided, but Holt caught the look he traded with Hap. He started to protest, but then he thought better of it. Letting Ryan think he had personal interest in Cara Jane would be one way of protecting Ryan. Cara Jane could not be described as an open book yet, and until he knew a lot more about her, Holt decided, it seemed best for everyone concerned to keep her out of Ryan's way.

He didn't want to think about why that especially seemed best for him.

Instead, he bit off another chunk of pizza. The sweetness of the pineapple provided a nice counterbalance to the spicy pepperoni. "Where'd you come up with this?" he asked Ryan, knowing his brother's penchant for dressing up a frozen pie.

"I didn't. That was Cara Jane's idea. West Coast influence, I suppose."

West Coast? Holt asked himself. Definitely not the Pacific Northwest. He'd expect fish pizza from that part of the world, not tropical additions.

Questions and answers and more questions. Well, he'd never expected it to be simple with that woman, not from the moment he'd first laid eyes on her.

Dinner next week should prove interesting. Very interesting.

Chapter Six

Cara glanced at the door, a spoon poised to fill Ace's gaping mouth with a grayish glob of cereal. A second flurry of knocks had her inserting the cereal into Ace's mouth at the same time as she called out, "Coming!"

Rising from the breakfast bar, she reached over to shut off the television as she hurried to answer the knock. She liked to hear the hymns that played early on Sunday mornings. Slipping the chain, she opened the door. Hap and Ryan stood smiling at her.

"Mornin', sunshine!" Hap greeted her. "We heard the TV and figured you was up."

She started to smooth her hands down her cotton print bathrobe, realized that she still held the spoon and dropped her hands to her sides instead. "We're having breakfast."

"Won't keep you then," Hap said, adding with a wag of his thumb, "Ryan and me, we was hoping you and Ace might like to join us for church this morning."

"You already know the pastor," Ryan pointed out.

"Grover Waller," she supplied, nodding. "First Church, right?"

"That would be the one," Hap confirmed.

"Actually, I was already planning to go there this morning. I saw the church building last week on our way to the park."

Hap literally beamed at that news.

"No need to go on your own," Ryan said. "Holt will be along in a few minutes with his truck, and there's room enough for all of us."

She made a face. The last person she needed to be spending time around was Holt. "Oh, but we'd have to switch out the car seat and all that," she said, thinking quickly. "We'll just meet you there. Easier that way."

"If you say so," Hap told her. "We'll try to save you a place, but don't be late."

She thanked them, said the appropriate goodbyes and closed the door. Ace smacked the tabletop with one hand and reached for the cereal bowl with the other. Even as she hurried over to finish feeding him, she wondered if she really should go to church today. She couldn't seem to keep her mouth shut around Holt, and the more he knew about her, the more likely he was to disapprove. Keeping her distance seemed the best course, but really, how much trouble could she get into attending a church service? Besides, she'd already agreed to go.

In all truth, she wanted to go. She couldn't help being curious and even a little hopeful about it in a way that she couldn't quite peg. Her only experience with church had come during those summers with Aunt Jane, but she'd always felt somewhat out of place in a congregation comprised mostly of elderly folk, and those services had been nothing like what she saw on television, which tended to leave her with more questions than answers. Knowing Grover, however slightly, and Hap and Ryan and Holt, she felt instinctively that the First Church would be different from anything she could imagine.

It seemed foolish not to satisfy her curiosity, which had grown since she'd prayed for help just before she'd seen the Help Wanted sign here at the Heavenly Arms. Seemed like the least she could do after that was sit through a worship service, even if she'd have to do it in short sleeves and with Holt breathing down her neck.

"You two have done enough," Holt complained, waving his grandfather and brother toward the church door. "If you'd let me handle it, I'd have convinced her to ride along with us."

"Bullied her, you mean," Ryan corrected with a grin. "What's with you two, anyway?"

Holt ignored that last comment, making a sharp, slicing motion with his hand. "Just go on and save us a seat. If you can."

Where was the woman, anyway? As the others hurried into the church, Holt turned back to stand sentinel on the sidewalk.

So Ryan wanted to know what was with the two of them, did he? Only that Holt's every instinct told him Cara Jane had secrets that were potentially harmful to him and his family.

With a grimace, he admitted to himself that it was more than that. His head fairly buzzed every time he thought about her, bringing up emotions that he'd believed long buried. No one else needed to know these things, though. Once he'd uncovered her secrets, then he would decide whether or not to discuss his concerns with anyone else. That seemed fair to everyone. He wouldn't worry Hap and Ryan that way or cast undue suspicion on Cara Jane.

While scanning the area for her little car, his gaze snagged on a small figure striding toward him on the other side of the street. Correction. Two small figures, one carrying the other on her hip. He'd know that sleek, pale, moon-gold hair anywhere. The dress, however, caught him completely off guard. Putting a hand to the crown of his hat, he clamped his jaw to keep it from dropping.

Beneath her usual denim jacket, she wore a swingy little flowered confection that flipped and swirled about her shapely knees in flashes of vibrant pinks, oranges and purples as she walked. Coupled with the jaunty bounce and flip of her shoulder-length hair, the effect was nothing short of mesmerizing.

As she drew closer, he saw that her toes were bared by sandals, purple sandals with high platform soles and ankle straps. How she'd walked all this way in those shoes, he couldn't imagine. Moreover, not a stitch of that outfit could be deemed appropriate for this gray, chilly weather. She had to be freezing her toes off, but my, what toes they were, dainty and shapely and breathtakingly female, like everything else about her.

She hurried toward him, Ace clutched against her side with both hands. Holt went to meet her, torn between shaking her and draping her with his coat. He settled for sliding an arm across her shoulders and a scold.

"What is wrong with you? Wearing *that* in this

weather? I mean, isn't it pretty cool up in Oregon? Don't you have any warm clothes?"

She stopped and shrugged free of him, frowning. "Yes, it's cool up in Oregon." Tugging at the bottom of her jacket, she sniffed and turned her head away. "Maybe I'm impervious to the cold. Maybe I got so used to it up in chilly Oregon that I don't need such heavy clothing as you." She leaned sideways slightly and attempted to hitch Ace up a little higher on her hip while holding her skirt down at the same time.

Irritated as well as intrigued, Holt reached over and plucked the boy out of her grasp. He weighed more than Holt expected, too much for her to constantly carry around, and she clearly didn't like letting go of him, but Holt didn't particularly care at the moment. She had just lied to him through chattering teeth. But they didn't have time to discuss it now.

"If we don't get inside, we'll be standing through the service," he told her, not bothering to moderate his tone.

She clamped her teeth together, slashed a look at Ace and marched forward, arms swinging. Holt caught up in one long stride, unwilling to watch her walk away from him in that swishy skirt.

The opening strains of the gathering music reached his ears as they stepped up onto the broad stoop that fronted the building. At the same time, Ace reached up and grabbed the brim of his hat, tugging it down. Frowning disapproval at the boy, Holt removed the hat and used it to wave Cara Jane forward, his hand coming to rest in the small of her back as they pushed through the double doors into the church.

The place, as anticipated, was packed, and the congregation had already risen to sing the opening hymn. Ryan tossed them a wave from their usual pew up near the front of the building, but just then Agnes Dilberry scooted her brood down and made a place for them on the back row. Cara Jane reached up to take Ace into her own arms again, whispering that they would sit in the rear of the building so she could slip out in case he fussed. Holt didn't bother hissing back that she could always take Ace to the nursery in the other building. He already knew that she wouldn't let the kid out of her sight unless she had no other choice. Instead, he crowded into the pew next to her and accepted the open hymnal that Agnes passed to him, her eyes full of curiosity and speculation. Holt nodded his thanks.

Ace made a grab for the book and caught Holt by the wrist instead. Then the little fellow just sort of leaned and crawled his way right back into Holt's arms. Dismay flashed over Cara Jane's face, but Holt shifted the boy to his other arm to keep her from taking him back. Mama had to learn to let go sometime, and besides, the kid obviously liked him. Maybe she'd loosen her grip some after this.

She took the hymnal from him and held it open for them to share. He edged closer and resisted the urge to slide his arm around her. For one thing, he still held his hat in that hand, and one of the Dilberry scamps already eyed it covetously. For another, it surprised and alarmed him how natural the impulse felt. Befriending her until he knew that she posed no threat to his family was one thing; letting himself get caught up in something too personal for his own good would be nothing short of insanity.

Holt trained his focus straight ahead, the boy held tight in the crook of his arm, and tried not to think about how pretty she looked in that flowered dress with her pale hair flipping up against the tops of her slender shoulders and her dainty toes peeking out of those ridiculous shoes. She needed a good coat, he decided, preferably one that covered her from the top of her head right down to the ground.

Cara glanced around, surprised to find the church on the smallish side. The large, rectangular, flat-topped two-story brick annex in back made it feel like a larger place from the outside, but the inside told another story.

Constructed of pale wood from floor to ceiling, including the pews, the room felt somewhat bare, despite the many bodies crowding the unpadded pews. Only the bright, greenish-blue carpet covering the raised platform at the front of the building and the swirls of green, gold and blue glass in the tall narrow windows lent color to the space, while the crisp white altar, lectern and three armless chairs on the platform gave it a pristine feel. A brass cross stood upon the altar and before it sat a low, fresh arrangement of yellow carnations, white mums and ivy in a simple basket. Overhead hung airy fixtures of gleaming brass with tapered, frosted bulbs.

A young woman with light hair rolled into a tight knot at the nape of her neck enthusiastically played the dark, upright piano to one side of the dais while a tall, thin, pale man followed along on an acoustic guitar. The voices of the congregation, including Holt's smoky baritone, literally filled the space to overflowing, much to her son's delight.

Ace bounced in the crook of Holt's elbow, waving his little arms as if directing the cacophony of notes. His blue eyes danced in time to the music. That alone made Cara smile. The man at her side did not.

She should have known that she couldn't escape Holt just by refusing a ride in his truck. Determined to ignore his high-handed manner and enjoy herself, Cara drank in every face, sound and gesture.

After the song, they sat for prayer, announcements and more music. An older couple warbled a duet to prerecorded accompaniment. Ace stood on the edge of the pew between Holt's legs, Holt's hands fastened securely about his waist, and jigged up and down to the tune, alternately clapping and laughing. At some point Holt had slipped off his leather jacket and draped it over the end of the pew. He tried to balance the hat on one thigh while wrangling Ace. Cara quickly realized that if she didn't rescue the hat, she'd surely have to buy him another. Ace seemed so happy that she didn't want to bother him. Instead, she tugged the hat into her lap, placing it crown down as Holt had done. Shortly thereafter, she traded the hat for her son as Ace threw himself sideways into her arms.

She knew a moment of extreme embarrassment when the offering plate came by a little later. First, she hadn't thought to bring so much as a nickle with her, and second, Ace latched on to the polished brass platter with feverish possession. While her face glowed hot and she tried to pry his little fingers from the rim, Ace squealed his baby delight and hung on for dear life, threatening to spill the contents onto the floor. Holt came to the rescue, plucking the plate from Ace's determined grasp with a chuckle and then Ace himself from her lap. Cara telegraphed her thanks with a wan smile. Holt just grinned and shook his head. She found that grin disconcerting. Somehow his frowns and glowers seemed easier to deal with.

They spent the remainder of the service passing boy and hat back and forth between them until the action became so mechanical that Cara barely noticed, her attention riveted by the sermon. Grover Waller turned out to be unlike any preacher Cara had ever heard. He didn't preach so much as converse, and the conversation did not proceed one-sided, either. Those in the congregation often spoke up with a hearty "Amen" or a simple answer to a question posed from the pulpit.

"So that we *know*," Grover said at one point, "that Christ went to the cross as a sacrifice for the sins of… who?"

"Me," said one fellow.

At the same time, someone else called out, "Everyone!"

A veritable chorus of "Amens" accompanied both. Nodding, Grover lifted his Bible and read from it.

"'He Who did not spare His own Son, but delivered Him up for us all, how will He not also with Him freely give us all things?'"

Grover went on reading, but Cara's mind had begun to whirl with so many unanswered questions that she didn't catch much more of it.

Finally, Grover finished up with, "'For I am convinced that neither death, nor life, nor angels, nor principalities, nor things present, nor things to come, nor powers, nor heights, nor depth, nor any other created thing, shall be able to separate us from the love of God, which is in Christ Jesus our Lord.'"

Cara leaned forward, trying to soak in what seemed to her to be a mountain of knowledge contained in this one sermon.

"Do you get this, brothers and sisters?" Grover asked, laying down the Bible. "Nothing *created* can keep us from the love of God and the salvation that comes through His Son Jesus. What can then?"

"Sin," someone called.

"Our own unconfessed sin," Grover confirmed with a nod, "and our unbelief. Just that and nothing else."

Cara sat back with a *whump*. She believed, or at least she wanted to, but how could she believe in what she didn't really understand? And how could she confess what she must keep secret? She shook her head, so many questions crowding together inside of it, and felt the familiar weight of her son's hand on her cheek. Turning her head slightly, she puckered a kiss into his very sweaty little palm.

She realized suddenly that she should have peeled off a couple of his layers once they'd settled onto the pew, but she'd been so cold herself it hadn't occurred to her that Ace would quickly overheat in his warmer clothing. Practically shoving the hat at Holt, she pulled Ace onto her lap, but as soon as she began to tug off his outer layer, he started to buck in protest. It quickly became obvious that he would not give up even one layer without a fight. Exasperated, she did the only thing she could do. She stood and stepped over Holt's long legs into the aisle, heading for the exit.

* * *

Holt automatically drew his legs back when Cara Jane rose and stepped past him into the aisle. Only as she started for the door did he realize that she actually meant to leave the building, and only when she glared down at him did he realize that he'd reached out to stop her. Ace chose that moment to really kick up a fuss, squealing as he tried his best to squirm out of his mother's grasp. She made a dipping catch of Ace's suddenly eel-like body and surged forward, leaving Holt no option but to let go of her forearm. With heads turning from every direction, Cara Jane quickly slipped out of the building. Holt caught sight of Ryan's questioning gaze, shrugged and made his own escape as rapidly and unobtrusively as possible.

He paused on the broad stoop to cram his hat onto his head and toss on his coat. Cara Jane was already crossing the street when he stepped down onto the ground, but he loped off after her, surprised by how fast she could move with a squirming, howling Ace clasped to her chest. She'd covered half a block before Holt caught her.

"What's wrong with him?" he asked.

"He's overheated."

She kept walking, neither remonstrating with her son nor so much as glancing at Holt himself. He began to wonder why he'd come after her. Then he realized that her steps had begun to flag. When she heaved in a great breath of air, he reached out and snatched Ace out of her arms. Three things happened simultaneously: Ace shut up like a faucet turning off and reached up for the brim of Holt's hat, while Cara Jane stopped in her tracks.

Holt jerked his head back from Ace's questing fingers, coming to a standstill. This battle had to come sooner or later, he mused, might as well be now.

"Nope," he said firmly to the boy. Ace reached upward again. Holt shook his head, eluding those chubby but persistent hands. "No way, my man. Hat's off-limits." A third time he eluded capture of the hat brim by intercepting Ace in mid-grab. "Can't have the hat. No." Ace stared him in the eye for a moment, then crammed his hand into his mouth. Holt shifted around to face Cara Jane, dodging yet another attempt, this one somewhat wet. "No, and by the way, yuck."

Cara Jane hid a smile behind her hand. Once more Holt and Ace engaged in a mini staring contest. Finally Ace subsided with a sigh, his head sinking down onto Holt's shoulder. Triumphant, Holt addressed the boy's mother.

"I believe we have reached an understanding. I keep my hat, and he keeps his slime."

She threw out a nicely rounded hip and parked a hand on it, gray eyes sparkling. "Yeah? What's that rolling down the front of your jacket then?"

Holt looked down at the drool sliding down the front of his leather coat, at which point Ace reached up and neatly plucked the hat off his head by the brim. Proving too heavy for him, it promptly dropped to the ground. Chortling, Cara Jane lifted Ace from Holt's loose embrace and settled him onto her hip once more. Properly chastised, Holt swept up the hat and returned it to his head in one fluid movement, then pulled a handkerchief from his pocket and wiped the front of his coat clean. Falling into step beside Cara Jane, he wagged a finger at Ace.

"I've got your measure now, bud," he teased, "and you aren't to be trusted."

Ace grinned and lunged for him. Holt caught him with one arm and lifted off his hat with the other, while Cara Jane groaned, "Oh, brother. Here we go again."

"This time I'll trade you," Holt said. Holding Ace in the crook of his arm, he plopped the hat down on Cara Jane's head. She couldn't have looked more adorable if she'd tried.

"That's the trouble with babies," she said, rolling her eyes upward, "they pick up bad habits in a heartbeat."

Holt laughed. "Guess we did sort of set a standard back there, passing him back and forth like a sack of sugar."

She nodded and put her head down, the hat brim hiding her face from him. "You didn't have to follow us," she said. "I got him there, I can get him back on my own."

Holt shrugged. "The service was almost over anyway." He looked back, wondering how long before those doors opened and spilled people out. She shot him a wry, doubtful glance that made him say, "You're looking very pretty today. Cold, but pretty." Good grief, he was flirting with her, and now that he'd started he couldn't seem to find a way to stop. He eyed her head and quipped, "I especially like the hat. And the shoes."

She sputtered laughter, drawling, "Thanks. So glad you approve since someone told me they were inappropriate."

He hung his head at that. "Sorry. I didn't mean to

snap earlier. It's just that I see you standing around shivering all the time in sleeveless tank tops and now sandals and I have to wonder why."

She sighed and reached up to sweep the hat from her head, holding it in front of her. "I know. I just didn't pack the right things before we set out. Goes to show you how tricky memories are. See, in my head, Oklahoma is this warm, golden place of warm, lazy days."

"The lazy, hazy days of summer," he commented.

She smiled dreamily. "Mmm, with the crickets making their music and the screen door slamming. I remember shadows dark as ink under the trees." She lazily waved one hand side to side, adding, "I can still feel the fan blowing back and forth, back and forth, filling the whole house with the smell of blackberry pie cooling on the kitchen table."

"Peach," he said, hugging his own memories close. "My grandma made the best peach pie in three counties."

"Ah, but the blackberries were free for the picking," Cara Jane reminded him. "We'd drive along the country roads and take what spilled over into the bar ditches."

"But the best thing about summer," he declared, nodding, "is watermelon."

"Ooooh. Ice-cold, juicy watermelon," she agreed. "I ate so much one time, I had juice dripping off my chin and running down my chest. I had to be rinsed off with a water hose before I could go back into the house."

"Well, of course. That's why you can't eat watermelon in the house," he teased. "You have to eat it sitting on the back porch so you can spit the seeds into the dirt between your bare feet."

She laughed at that. "I can just see it. You, Ryan and Hap—about thirty years younger—sitting on the edge of the porch, eating and spitting and covered in sticky watermelon juice."

"Don't forget old Chuck," Holt said, grinning. "He was the best spitter of the lot."

"And who is Chuck?"

Some of the joy of the moment dimmed. "My daddy," Holt told her. "Charles Holt Jefford, but everybody called him Chuck."

"You're named for him," Cara Jane remarked softly.

Holt nodded. "Partly. Holt for him, Michael for my mother's father, Michael Carl Ryan."

She lifted a finger. "I see a pattern developing."

Holt laughed. "You do, indeed. My brother is named Ryan Carl Jefford. Grandpa Mike died when we were little bitty, and Grandma Ryan way before that. Mama worshipped Grandpa Mike because it was just the two of them, and then she worshipped Daddy after Mike was gone."

Cara Jane nodded. "It's funny how much we have in common, isn't it? My husband's name was Charles, and he was named for his father. Plus, my mother's parents died before I was even born."

Frowning, Holt said, "I thought your husband's name was—"

"Addison Charles," she supplied. "That's where Ace comes from. A for Addison. C for Char—" She stopped dead in her tracks, and suddenly Holt knew he'd stumbled onto another of her secrets. A for Addison, C for Charles...

"And E? What's E stand for, Cara Jane?"

"Edward," she said angrily, though which of them she was angry at, Holt didn't know. "For my brother."

"I thought you weren't close to your brother."

"That's right."

"So you named your son after a brother you aren't even close to?"

"You can always hope, can't you?" she demanded, reaching for Ace.

Holt swung away. Ace huffed against his neck, and that's when he realized that the boy had fallen asleep. He spread his hand across that little back and looked down at Cara Jane, feeling warm and protective and chilled and suspicious all at the same time.

"I'll carry him," he muttered darkly, wishing that every moment with her didn't end up tainted by distrust and suspicion.

They walked in silence the rest of the way and parted at her door with whispered farewells. Sighing, Holt headed back to the church, the keys to the truck heavy in his pocket and misgivings heavy on his heart.

Chapter Seven

"Here it is in Romans," Hap said, smoothing the delicate leaf of paper with his gnarled hand.

Cara had known that he would have answers for her. She'd wanted to ask the questions the day before right after the service, but Holt had so unnerved her that she'd thought it best to keep her distance until he'd gone. Then this morning Hap had announced that Holt would arrive this afternoon as soon as Ace rose from his nap to "help with the heavy work," as Hap put it. Cara had decided to speak to Hap about Grover's sermon during the lunch break, and he'd already clarified much that had confused her. The old man pecked the paper with the tip of his forefinger.

"Yep, this is the passage Grover read yesterday. Now what is it that's got you stewing?"

Cara shifted close, and he moved over to make room for her at the end of the table. Bending low, she started reading to herself.

"There," she said, placing her fingertip on the page. "What does that mean, 'His elect'?"

Hap bent low, adjusting his glasses, but even as he looked, he spoke. "Well, now, that just means believers. We'd say Christians these days, but the term wasn't in use back then."

Cara read the passage again, aloud this time, then went on to the end. "Huh. It doesn't say anything about sin."

Hap chuckled. "Well, now, it does and it doesn't. It talks about charges and justification, and those things have to do with sin, the committing of it and the forgiving of it. The point Grover was trying to make is completely valid, though. Here, let me show you."

His knobby hands flipped through the delicate leaves with swift surety. He took her through the book of Romans in a matter of minutes. Soon Cara's mind whirled with memorable phrases.

All have sinned and fallen short of the glory of God.
He is faithful to forgive.
He Who did not spare His own Son.
Confess with your mouth.

The last one bothered her greatly. "What does that mean?"

"In this case, it means declaring aloud that Jesus is your savior. In some other verses, it means to admit to your sins, your wrongdoings. That's the first step to salvation, admitting your sins and seeking forgiveness."

Saddened, Cara merely nodded and stared a little harder at the Bible. How could she confess her wrongdoings if it meant putting herself and her son in danger? She certainly wanted to. The longer she knew Hap Jefford and his grandsons, the more pronounced her guilt became, but then she'd think of the cold, doubtful look in Holt's eyes, and fear would overwhelm even her shame.

Restless and cranky, Ace kicked the wall next to the portable crib, letting them know that nap time had arrived.

"We better get out and let him sleep," Hap said, picking up the Bible. "We can continue this in the front room."

"Oh, no," Cara said, sidling in the other direction. "I have two more units to do." She jerked a thumb in Ace's direction. "I'll just get him down and head back to work."

Hap opened his mouth as if to protest, but the front door chime sounded, and he flattened his lips. "Best see who that is. Likely it's just one of the boys."

Cara didn't hang around to find out. Whether it was one of his domino buddies or a paying guest, she had work to do and thoughts to mull over, though what good might come of that, she couldn't imagine. This confession thing had her stumped. She couldn't even explain her predicament well enough to get answers without Hap or someone else tumbling to the very thing that frightened her most.

Feeling sick at heart, she went to the crib, bent and picked up her son. Cradling him against her chest, she carried him out to the laundry. After emptying both washers into the dryers, she took Ace back into the apartment, where she began to sway and croon. Drowsy as he was, Ace fought sleep for several long minutes before he relaxed into bonelessness. During that time, Cara kept thinking over and over how she could not be one of God's elect because she did not dare confess her sins. Much as she wanted the assurance that she did not live separated from God's love, she knew that if confession had to be part of it, she was doomed. For how could she tell anyone, let alone Hap or Holt, that she had run away from a mental institution?

Cara placed her palm against her son's forehead and felt the heat radiating off his skin. Irritable, Ace squawked and shoved her hand away.

"I can't go," she said, torn between disappointment and relief.

She'd managed to keep her lips sealed these past three afternoons while working with Holt, who'd been all things endearing, and she'd been looking forward to this midweek prayer meeting to which Hap had invited her. After all, God would still hear her prayers, wouldn't He, even if she couldn't confess her deception? He'd heard her before when she'd prayed for help. On the other hand, she wanted to confess so badly at times that she just didn't trust herself, not around Holt, at any rate, and especially not the friendly Holt who seemed so fond of her son now.

"What do you think it is?" Holt asked, smoothing Ace's hair with his big hand.

"Maybe we should be calling a doctor," Hap suggested.

"Office is closed," Holt pointed out. "We'd do better to take him to the emergency room in Duncan."

"He's cutting teeth," Cara said. "That and a case of the sniffles is all it is, but it's enough to make him too fussy for church. You two go on without us."

"Are you sure?" Holt asked, his brow creased with worry.

Cara almost laughed. Big, bad Holt Jefford. Let a kid steal his hat and he went all soft over him. She wished it didn't please her so much.

"He'll sleep and tomorrow he'll wake up fine."

"Well, if you're sure," Holt hedged.

"We'll pray for him," Hap declared.

"But meantime, if you need us, you call," Holt told her. "I'll set my phone on vibrate."

"We'll be fine," she insisted, settling into the rocking chair in the front room with Ace on her lap, "and we'll be right here holding down the fort when you two get home."

The men started for the door. Holt hesitated, looking back at her with a frown before following Hap out into the cold.

"They'll be fine," she heard Hap say. "'Sides, you got your phone. What'd we do before Ty got us them phones?"

She couldn't make out Holt's reply as they moved away. Then again, she couldn't make out much about him, period. First he'd been downright standoffish, even grumpy, now he seemed to be making an effort to be friendly. He'd been a lot of help, too, cleaning drapes and carpets and so on, those chores that went beyond the daily tasks. Seemed like someone was always pitching in these days. Ryan had done the dinner dishes on Monday and Tuesday.

"Only fair," Ryan had told her when she'd protested, "since I'm eating your cooking."

Hap had said pretty much the same thing when he'd

insisted on washing up this evening. He'd even gone so far as to claim that the hot, soapy water felt good on his arthritic hands.

Neither of them made her uneasy like Holt, did, though.

He still worried her with his pointed, perceptive questions and narrow-eyed stares, but it was more than that. She practically itched whenever the man came around, especially if he stood too close. She supposed it had to do with the times when she'd let down her guard with him and run off at the mouth, letting things fall that would be better left unsaid, like when she'd mentioned Aunt Jane and blurted the explanation of Ace as a nickname for her son.

At least she'd managed to cover, or so she hoped. E for Edward. Thank God she hadn't uttered the name Elmont. That information could lead to all sorts of trouble for her.

Ace stiffened up like a board in her lap, complaining about the mucus that clogged his throat and reduced his howls to croaks.

"Okay. Let's see if we can't get you a little relief."

Rising, she moved into the apartment, where she paused to shrug into an old corduroy coat that Hap had started insisting she wear. Even with the sleeves rolled halfway up, they covered all but her fingertips, but the big coat provided ample room for carrying Ace inside it against her chest. They hurried across the tarmac to their room to grab the little bag where she kept such things as baby vitamins and analgesic drops.

After she got the drops into him, cleaned his nasal passages and put the kettle on to steam atop the potbellied stove in the front room, Ace drifted off to sleep cradled against her in the rocking chair. His weight so numbed her arms that she carried him back into the apartment and laid him in the crib, thinking how much he'd grown in these past couple of weeks. He still slept peacefully an hour or so later when the men returned.

"How is he?" Hap asked at once, coming through the front door.

"Breathing easy and sleeping hard," she told him, tipping the chair forward as she got to her feet. "I'd better get him settled in for the night."

"I hate for you to wake him," Hap said. "Why don't you let him stay here in the apartment with me tonight."

"Oh, no, I couldn't," she insisted, shaking her head. "He'll expect me to be there when he wakes."

"But he and the crib are too much for you to manage," Hap began.

"I'll help her," Holt said, the front door closing behind him.

The protest rose automatically to her tongue. "No, no, that's not necessary."

He glowered at her. "I said, I'll help you."

She ducked her head in acquiescence, knowing that she'd have a difficult time getting the crib collapsed and across the tarmac with a heavily sleeping Ace in her arms. Irked, she followed Holt into the apartment where she slung on the corduroy coat. He moved to the crib, bent and easily lifted Ace into his arms. Hastily, Cara folded up the crib and together they moved through the kitchen and out the back.

Holt felt the warm little body snuggled against his chest and warmth seeped into his heart. The first time he'd held the boy, he'd marveled at his unexpected heaviness. Now, however, the little guy felt light as a feather. Holt supposed it was a matter of perspective. Ace no longer rated as a burden to be borne but, rather, someone to be shielded and protected. Holt wondered when that had happened.

Maybe it was seeing the usually good-natured imp fussing and unhappy earlier that evening. Or maybe it was simple proximity. Holt had come to appreciate the little scamp's usual sunny nature these past few days. It seemed to Holt that this boy needed the protection of an arm stronger than his mother's and so far as Holt could see, he happened to be the only one around capable of providing it.

That didn't mean Holt would be any less protective with his own family, however. He'd been protecting and caring for his family since the deaths of his parents, and he would not allow Cara Jane to hurt either of them. He wanted to believe that he had her all wrong, but Cara Jane *had* lied. Holt knew it, he just didn't know *how* yet.

He'd had real trouble staying in his chair while listening to Cara and Ryan chat in the kitchen earlier this week. The talk had been completely innocuous, all about how she'd prepared certain dishes and how she seemed to use fewer pots and pans than Charlotte did. The real problem had been how happy Cara Jane had sounded, how at ease the two of them had seemed with each other. Holt had wanted to march in there and demand that Ryan be as leery of her as he was himself, but he'd wanted to do that because he knew it would keep Ryan away from her.

The irony of the whole situation continually pricked

Holt. He *knew* that she lied. That ought to have been enough to repel any feeling for her. Instead, he found himself drawn to her, even admiring the way she went about her work and how seriously she took her responsibilities as a mother.

How, Holt wondered, had he gotten into this mess?

More importantly, how did he get out of it?

He'd asked God that very thing tonight, but silently, which reminded him of the promise Hap had made earlier.

"We prayed for Ace tonight," Holt told her as he waited for her to get out her key and let them into her room. "Everyone did. We put his name on the general list."

"Thank you," she said, turning the key in the lock and pushing the door open. "I appreciate that. I really do."

Holt followed her into the closet and waited while she set up the crib with quick, familiar efficiency. It bothered him that the boy didn't have a proper bed and that she had to drag that contraption around with her all the time. Besides, where would Ace sleep if a paying guest needed the crib? One had been enough before they'd acquired a resident infant. He decided he'd best discuss the issue with Hap and see if they couldn't come up with a more permanent solution, then it struck him that he shouldn't be thinking of permanent solutions until he knew the truth about Cara Jane.

He lowered Ace into the freshly made bed, then stood by while Cara Jane changed his diaper. The boy stirred, complaining with whimpers and kittenish growls, then promptly dropped off to sleep again the moment she covered him with a blanket. Holt and Cara Jane crept back out into the larger room.

"He'll sleep until the medicine wears off," she predicted.

"You got enough to see him through the night?" Holt asked.

"More than enough. Besides, with all those prayers, he could be well before morning."

"Take that much stock in prayer, do you?" Holt asked idly.

She nodded and bent to swipe a wrinkle out of the coverlet near the foot of her bed. "I'd be foolish not to, considering."

The statement sounded unfinished to Holt, so he had to ask, "Considering what?"

She shrugged off Hap's coat and plopped down on the bed she had just straightened, kicking off her shoes and tucking her feet up under her. Holt watched her decide how much to say. Finally, she answered him.

"I was praying in my car when I came upon this place."

"You don't say?"

"Maybe that's not how it's properly done," she went on somewhat defensively, "but it was quiet, Ace was sleeping, and I was driving, trying to figure out what we were going to do." She broke off and glared at him. "Well, you talk to other people when you're driving, don't you? I've heard people say prayer is just talking to God."

Holt held up a hand, palm out, in concession. "That wasn't criticism. It was surprise."

She ducked her head, saying in a small voice, "You don't think I pray? Maybe you don't think I ought to."

"Of course I think you ought to pray," he told her. "I think everyone ought to pray. Fact is, I was praying for help the very minute you first walked in the front door."

She looked as astounded as he felt, her spine going ramrod straight, lips parting. Then she laughed, falling backward. "You don't say?"

Holt couldn't suppress a grin. "Hey, that's my line."

She studied him for a long moment, her pale head tilting to one side, before she abruptly sat up, declaring, "That's why you gave me the job, isn't it?"

He wondered how careful he ought to be in answering, then decided not very. She was too bright not to have tumbled to his misgivings already. "That was a big part of it," he told her. "In this family, we believe in the power of prayer, so when I asked for help and then I looked up to find you standing there hoping for work, well, how do I argue with that?"

Her gray eyes lost their focus for a moment as she thought that over, then sharpened again as she asked, "You said that was part of it. What's the other part?"

"Hap. He loves this place, believes he's called to it, but he can't keep it going alone, and I was at the end of my rope trying to help him."

She nodded, gaze averted. "I'm grateful no matter why you did it."

He thought she might say more, but when she didn't, he did, just to keep the conversation going. "So where'd you learn to pray?" he asked.

She shrugged and picked at a thread on the toe of

her sock, which showed dazzlingly white against the dark bed cover. "My great-aunt was a praying woman."

"Not in church then," he said as much to himself as her.

She shot him a sharp glance, and then she lifted a shoulder. "My parents didn't like church. I guess they figured they'd have to clean up their act if they went to church."

"And your husband?" He didn't know why he'd asked; it just seemed important.

"Wouldn't even talk about it. His whole family thinks that church is just a scheme to get money out of them."

"Ah. I know those folks." Holt slipped his hands into his pockets. "They're the same ones who think the government ought to take care of the poor without bothering them about it."

"If I didn't know better, I'd say you'd met the…my in-laws."

"Can't say as I care to neither," he said, shaking his head.

"My sentiments exactly. The farther they are from me and Ace, the better I like it."

Holt's radar pinged. So she disliked her in-laws, did she? "I figured Charlotte would feel that way about Ty's family," he said conversationally, "but slay me if they don't fall all over themselves to please her. Could be because Ty's different since he met her, or different since he met the Lord."

"So he confessed, did he?" Cara Jane asked, face drawn into a woeful expression.

"Confessed?"

Her expression suddenly blanked. "His sins."

"Oh, I can testify to that," Holt told her happily. "I was there."

She seemed to wilt a bit, and it occurred to him that she must be tired. "I'll go and let you get some rest yourself."

"Thanks," she muttered, uncoiling her legs to get up and trail him to the door, "for everything."

"Carrying Ace over isn't anything," he said dismissively.

"It is," she insisted, "but I was thinking more about the help you've been giving me these past few days."

"That's no big deal, either," he told her magnanimously. "I just thought I should help out around here."

"I have to wonder why, though," she said just as he opened the door. The chill that flushed over him had less to do with the frosty temperatures than the cold edge of her voice. "It's not like I'm going to steal the curtains off the windows, you know."

He turned around in the open doorway, the hair on the back of his neck ruffling. "I never said you would." But he'd thought it a possibility, and she knew it.

Something flashed over her face, anger definitely, perhaps even hurt. "You," she said, "can be such a rat." Before he could even digest that, she put a hand in the middle of his chest and shoved. He reeled backward through the doorway, which she stepped into, blocking any re-entry. "You can tend to your own business from now on," she snapped. "I don't need your help anymore." With that, she shut the door.

He came within an inch of kicking it, but with Ace sleeping in the other room, he restrained himself. Confounded woman! She deserved his distrust, and he'd helped her in spite of it. He'd be boiled in oil before he helped her out again.

Halfway across the tarmac, he realized that was exactly what she wanted, him out of her way. He stopped and looked back at her door.

That woman read him like a book. He knew that she lied; she knew that he knew it.

It was even more than that, though, and he'd be foolish not to admit it. Something sparked between them.

For some surely stupid reason, that made him grin. By rights he ought to be appalled and plotting how to keep his distance while still somehow ferreting out her secrets, but that wasn't going to happen. He'd be here tomorrow, whether she liked it or not, and maybe, just maybe, that electric spark which so unsettled the both of them would eventually set off an explosion big enough that he'd finally learn what secrets she held so close.

Beyond that, he dared not even speculate.

Chapter Eight

"Is that an order?" Cara asked, keeping her tone light. She leaned slightly sideways, her hands linked together around Ace's waist to help balance his weight as he straddled her hip.

After almost a full week of working with Holt each afternoon, despite her every attempt to persuade him otherwise, she'd come to realize that his bark was definitely worse than his bite and that perhaps he did not actively dislike her, after all. That did not mean that he trusted her or that she could afford to trust him, and considering how much she was coming to actually like him, it seemed as necessary as ever for her to keep her distance. Yet here he stood on a chilly Saturday night, expecting to take her to dinner. She felt duty-bound to try to get out of it.

"No, it's not an order," he answered flippantly. "I don't give the orders around here, but that's not the point."

Cara rolled her eyes. "What is the point?"

"For one thing, you haven't been off this property since you got here."

"That's not true. I went to church last Sunday and to the park the Sunday before that, and last night I walked over to Booker's Store to buy diapers."

"You know that doesn't count," he retorted. "You need to get out, and you need to eat tonight, too, don't you? I certainly do." He pressed a hand to the center of his forest-green shirt, his eyes glowing deep olive in the muted light cast by the fixture outside her room.

"I can eat here. I've got food in the fridge." Bologna and yogurt.

"You're not really going to make me eat alone, are you?" he wheedled. "I don't like eating alone, and you won't like seeing the look of disappointment on Hap's face when he finds out you refused to take your turn for a Saturday night out."

She grimaced at that, instantly capitulating. "Not fair."

Holt laughed and stepped into the room as she turned and carried Ace deeper into the warmth. "Granddad has a way of worming into your affections, doesn't he?"

Cara nodded, resigned. "I mean, really, who could not like Hap Jefford?"

Holt gently pushed the door closed. "You'll get no argument from me on that score. Grandma always said the goodness of the Lord shines through him."

Cara thought about that, aware of a wistful envy, which she pushed away at once. Wishing did no good. She'd learned that years, decades, ago.

"Now," Holt said, clapping his hands together, "what

do you need? Coats? Diaper bag? A little arm-twist-ing?"

She laughed because he was being so charming and his usual high-handed self at the same time, a very dangerous combination. Oh, why hadn't she pled a headache or some other illness? But she knew the answer to that. Her lies were already eating her alive; she just couldn't bear another.

"Come on," he coaxed, "the Watermelon Patch is waiting."

The Watermelon Patch, she'd learned, was the local catfish restaurant. Justus called it a "dive," but even he vowed that better food could not be found around these parts. She acknowledged, if only to herself, a certain desire to see the place. Besides, she never won when it came to Holt. It irritated her, but the man always seemed to get his way. Maybe because she really didn't have the heart to fight him. Shying away from the thought, she waved a hand toward the dresser and the small satchel atop it.

"Um, I'd better stick an extra diaper into the bag." She looked down at her jeans and rumpled T-shirt. "And change my clothes."

"Naw, you're fine," Holt insisted, grabbing up the diaper bag.

She brought her free hand to her hip and gave him a blatant once-over. "I don't see you going out in your work clothes."

He set down the diaper bag and lifted both hands in surrender. "Okay. All right. Fine. Change, by all means. I'll watch Ace."

Miffed despite getting her way for once, she snatched

her car keys from the bedside table and tossed them at him. He trapped them with both hands in midair.

"Move the car seat instead."

He tipped his hat, lips quirking. "Yes, ma'am."

"It goes in the backseat," she lectured, "and make sure it's anchored properly."

"I'm on it." This time he pushed his hat down more firmly on his head. "Any other orders before I go?"

She just rolled her eyes at him. He went out the door grinning. She couldn't keep a smile from breaking out on her own face—until she remembered that she had nothing suitable to wear.

Holt had the child safety seat securely anchored in the center of the back bench of his double-cab pickup inside of five minutes and spent the next ten pacing back and forth beside the truck while his stomach rumbled.

Spinning Cara Jane's keys around on his index finger, he had to wonder why she never drove her car. Not only had she walked to church last Sunday—in sandals, no less—she'd admitted just minutes ago to having walked all the way over to Booker's Grocery west of downtown to buy diapers.

It had been spitting rain last night in near freezing temperatures, and thinking of her and Ace out on foot in that weather made the hair stand up on the back of Holt's neck. No matter what route she might have taken, at least half a block of it lacked a sidewalk, which meant she'd have had to walk on the narrow shoulder of the street, carrying Ace. All it would have taken was one careless driver, or even a good driver with a slick tire, and they could have had a catastrophe too horrible to contemplate.

The door opened and Cara Jane walked through it, Ace on her hip and the diaper bag hanging from her shoulder by the strap. Holt nearly swallowed his tongue.

She wore slim, pink pants, cropped at mid-calf, with a purple tank top, those flirty purple sandals and her denim jacket. With her hair tied back with a purple scarf and narrow gold hoops dangling from her earlobes, she looked like she'd just walked off a movie screen. It struck him suddenly how tan she was. Even now, in the dead of winter, her skin glowed pale gold.

At some point in her not-too-distant past, Holt mused, Cara Jane must have spent time in a tanning bed. He supposed that in the rainy northwest a tanning bed might not be such a bad idea to keep the doldrums at bay. Still, something about that scenario struck him as patently un-Cara Jane.

The notion flitted right out of his head as she strode toward him. She looked so good that just keeping a stupid grin off his face required all of his concentration. As she neared the truck with Ace, Holt dashed over and opened the back door for her. Then, realizing that she'd have to climb up inside to lift Ace into his seat, Holt promptly took over that chore, only to learn that buckling a kid into a safety seat required a degree in puzzle solving, especially when said child objected.

Cara Jane marched around the rear end of the truck, dropped the bag onto the floorboard and climbed up into the backseat on the other side to show him how it was done. While holding Ace in the seat with her forearm, she got the harness over his plump little shoulders, fit two pieces of metal together with one hand, positioned the latch with the other and somehow connected all three.

As soon as he heard that telltale click, Ace stopped struggling and settled down.

"Now you're cooperative," Holt teased, nipping the end of the boy's nose with the knuckles of two fingers. Ace favored him with a broad grin. "Whoa! Is that a tooth breaking his gums?"

"It is," Cara Jane confirmed in an I-told-you-so voice. She started backing out of the truck cab. Seeing how difficult that could be in those tall shoes, Holt jumped down and jogged around to help her, but she hit the ground just as he got there. She stumbled, her shoulder bumping him in the chest.

"Oops." He automatically closed his arms around her, steadying them both.

Instant awareness shot through him and apparently her, too, because they practically repelled each other, bouncing apart as if they'd both been hit with cattle prods. They each sought refuge in pretense, her smoothing her hair, him repositioning his hat.

Their aplomb somewhat restored, they both turned toward the truck, only to reach for the door handle in the same instant. The thing might have been electrified so quickly did they yank their hands back.

Finally, reaching wide around her, Holt gingerly opened the door and stepped back, hovering uncertainly until she'd climbed up into the front seat. He made his way around to the driver's side, where he paused long enough to close his eyes and blow out a steeling breath before getting this undoubtedly ill-advised venture under way.

Cara looked around at the ramshackle building, marveling that it hadn't fallen down around their heads already. A "dive," indeed. This place—which actually did sit in the midst of a currently barren watermelon patch about a half mile outside town—had been cobbled together with incongruent bits and pieces, some metal, some wood, some cement, some plastic. Nothing matched, not even the shingles on the roof.

The rough floors waved unevenly across heights varying by inches. Tables and chairs had been crammed into every available square inch of space, each and every one of them occupied.

The waitress, a hard-looking bottle blonde named Joanie, stuck their small party at a wobbly table that sat dead center of the passage between the two dining rooms, one of which contained an old-fashioned glass counter where the proprietor collected payment. Traffic had to squeeze by them, but at least the spot came with a high chair.

Ace loved the busy, humming place. He banged on the table with both hands, thrilled that he could make it tip, unless Holt, who sat across from him and on Cara's right, leaned on it with his elbows. He indulged Ace by keeping his hands in his lap. Cara's concern hinged more on her son's safety than his pleasure, however.

"I only see the one exit," she pointed out, leaning close to Holt in an effort not to be overheard, if one could be overheard in all this din. People talked and laughed, clinking their dinnerware and shouting across the crowded room at one another.

"That's because there is only one exit," he said in a false whisper.

"But what if there's a fire?" she muttered, an event that looked not only possible but entirely likely to Cara, given the smoke that belched from the stack pipe outside and the number of people crammed into the building.

Holt spread his hands, grinning at her. "Then there would be lots of exits. Cara Jane, Ace could punch his way through that wall right there." She had to admit Holt had a point. "Besides," he went on, "half the windows in the building would fall right out if you so much as tapped on them."

Someone behind her chuckled and exclaimed, "It's not a matter of *if* a fire breaks out, little lady, it's a matter of *when*. That's why they serve the drinks in these big old jugs."

"That's right," Joanie concurred, plunking down quart jars of iced tea. "In case of a fire, you just put it out your own selves with these."

The room bubbled with laughter. The locals obviously didn't worry overmuch about building or fire codes. Cara consoled herself with the idea that this place had been around for over thirty years, or so Hap's friends had said.

Joanie dried her hands on the seat of her skintight jeans. "How many?"

Cara looked up at the waitress in confusion. The woman had drawn her shortish hair into a ponytail so tight that it slanted her eyes. "How many what?"

"Pieces of fish."

"I'll have four," Holt announced.

"Not you," Joanie said, swatting a hand sideways. "I know how many you want. You always have the maximum."

"And then he eats everything else that's leftover in the building," someone who obviously knew Holt well put in.

Holt sighed loudly while everyone else laughed at his expense, but Cara could tell that he didn't really mind. He sat among friends here.

Joanie looked at Cara expectantly.

"How big are the pieces?" Cara asked.

"You're teeny. I'll just bring you two," Joanie decided, looking her over.

"Three," Holt countermanded. "I'll eat the extra."

Joanie cut her heavily lined eyes at him. "You sure you don't want to just go the limit on both plates?"

He spread his hands in easy capitulation. "Might as well."

"Four and four it is."

"Well, my cobbler's safe tonight," some fellow teased.

"I don't know," Holt said, deadpan. "I'm powerful hungry."

They laughed and made jokes all over the room about eating faster and guarding their food. Joanie, meanwhile, pointed to Ace.

"What about him, sugar? You want to order something for him? We got some applesauce, and Cookie will mash up some potatoes and beans for you, if you want."

"Applesauce," Cara decided, smiling wanly. "I brought along some jars of baby food anyway."

"I'll be right back with your corn cake." Joanie slid away, swimming a curvy path in and out among the tables.

"Corn cake?" Cara asked Holt.

"Best corn bread this side of Georgia," he bragged.

"Oh. I like corn bread," Cara said, brightening with the memory of Aunt Jane's sweet batter, baked or sometimes fried.

A chair scraped and a female voice asked, "You ever gonna introduce us to your girl, Holt?"

He jerked, then sent a look straight into Cara's eyes. That look said, "Sorry. I'll try to set the record straight." Cara surreptitiously sucked in a deep breath. He cleared his throat and half turned in his chair, hanging one elbow over the back of it.

"'Fraid I can't call her mine, Angevine. This here is Cara Jane Wynne. She works for Hap down at the motel, and since she's taken Charlotte's place, we figured she deserves Charlotte's night out."

A heavyset redhead in her mid- to late-thirties materialized at Cara's elbow, offering a surprisingly dainty hand. "Nice to meet you, Cara Jane. I'm Angevine Martin. I saw you in church on Sunday, but you were gone when we got out the door."

"Oh, uh, Ace got restless, so we left a little early."

"Ace, that's her boy there," Holt said with a wave of his hand. Winking at Ace, he added, "He likes singing and hats."

Angevine giggled, glancing at Holt's bare head. He'd left his hat in the truck, predicting correctly that there wouldn't be room for it inside, but the curving sweep of his hair showed where it could usually be found.

"Well, that's something y'all have in common," Angevine gushed. Then she shocked Cara by patting her on both cheeks. "I'm just so happy to meet you!" She patted Holt on the shoulder as she pranced back to her seat. "First Charlotte, now you. I guess Ryan'll be next. About time the Jefford kids started settling down."

As murmurs of agreement spread throughout the room, Holt sent Cara another apologetic look, but he said nothing more to refute the idea that the two of them made a couple. Cara understood from his expression that anything he might say would simply add fuel to the fire at this point. She tried not to cringe, but she'd gladly have crawled under the table just then. Fortunately, talk turned to descriptions of Charlotte's wedding, with comments flying about everything from the food to the decorations to the groom's family.

"Never seen the like," an elderly fellow said on his way to pay his check. "They came in here with caterers and florists and decorators." He flew a hand into the air, adding pointedly, "In limousines. Every one of 'em in limousines. They'll pro'bly build that new house with lumber shipped in by limousine."

He ambled off without waiting for any rebuttal, which wouldn't have come at any rate. Holt just chuckled and shook his head, while conversation abruptly shifted to the house that Charlotte and her new husband planned. One woman had heard that they'd bought sixty acres from a ranch west of town and were building a twenty-thousand-square-foot mansion.

"It's eight thousand square feet and thirty acres," Holt corrected. "They bought the Moffat place out east of the school grounds. Already pulled down the old house."

"That didn't take much, I warrant," someone put in, amidst gasps about the true size of the house.

"Nope. Just hooked a chain to the door lintel and the bumper of my truck," Holt confided. "Ty was going to send a wrecking crew, but I told him, 'Why bother?'"

Joanie brought the corn bread, still steaming from the oven. Holt set aside a piece to cool for Ace while someone asked whatever happened to Old Man Moffat. Several people debated the exact year of his death until Holt gave it to them around mouthfuls of buttered corn bread. Cara hadn't yet managed to split her piece, so hot it blistered her fingertips and so soft it fairly crumbled when touched.

"I remember because the drought was so bad that year they couldn't get the grave dug," Holt said to the room at large. "They called Daddy out to break up the ground with one of his big bits. It was the year before he died."

The atmosphere immediately took on a solemn feel.

"Good man, your daddy," a voice grated.

The sentiment echoed softly around the room.

"Good man."

"Good 'un."

Holt wiped crumbs from his shirtfront into his lap, but Cara knew memories of his father played fresh in his mind. On impulse, she slipped a hand beneath the table, intending to give him a slight touch on the knee. Instead, he dropped his hand just then, so she gave it a sort of fumbling squeeze. She meant it to be a simple gesture of sympathy and understanding, but Holt's long fingers closed over hers and suddenly they were holding hands, palm to palm. He never so much as lifted his gaze to hers, but their clasped hands hung there between them for several heartbeats while talk began to swirl around them once more and Cara's breath heated inside her lungs.

Joanie appeared, sliding plates and bowls and baskets onto the table, giving Cara the perfect excuse to break free. She quickly snatched up a corner of cooled corn bread and poked it into her mouth, humming with self-conscious appreciation. Just then, Joanie placed a bowl of applesauce in front of Ace, and everyone at the table reached for it.

Holt got to the applesauce first, sliding it out of Ace's grasp just before disaster could strike, leaving Ace with a smidge of applesauce on the tip of one finger, which Ace promptly popped into his mouth. Laughing, Holt scooted closer to the table, shunted aside his own food and spent a good five minutes spooning applesauce between Ace's smacking lips while Cara mashed big, meaty slices of fried potatoes with spoonfuls of pureed beef and peas.

Watching Holt feed her son touched Cara. No other man had ever done such a thing for him. Not his father, who'd seemed rather impatient and frightened of his tiny newborn son in the short time they'd had together. Not his uncle, who barely acknowledged his nephew's existence, and not his grandfather, who was much too important to be bothered with such things.

As soon as the last of the applesauce disappeared, Holt set to his own dinner while Cara split her time between feeding Ace and herself. It amazed Cara how much that man could eat, and it made her wonder if she shouldn't start cooking larger quantities. Her own meal tasted very good, but it was filling fare, which meant that Holt had plenty with which to gorge himself. No one seemed to think a thing of him eating off her plate.

"Waste not, want not," he quipped with a wink, helping himself to pieces of whole fish, potatoes and red beans, for which she'd never developed a taste despite her aunt's attempts to feed them to her. He did leave her half-eaten coleslaw untouched, though he scoffed down every bit of his own before lolling back in his chair, replete. By the time Holt had eaten his fill, Ace's head bobbed, his eyelids drooping to half-mast.

"Now I see why you don't like to eat alone," she teased. "One meal isn't enough for you."

"Nailed that, did you?" He patted his lean middle, adding, "I've about reached my limit tonight, though." He sat up straight again, glancing at Ace, just as Joanie delivered steaming bowls of peach cobbler. "I may even have to share my dessert with Ace."

"Oh, no, you don't," Cara said, pushing away her own dish. She just didn't have room. "No sweets for him. If you fill him with sugar he won't sleep tonight."

"He's asleep sitting up now," Holt pointed out, scraping back his chair.

"Guess you'll be wanting these to go," Joanie said, dropping the check and scooping up the cobblers again.

Holt nodded and picked up the bill. "I'll just settle this while you get Ace ready. Then we'll take our dessert and head out."

Cara rose to begin stuffing Ace into his outdoor layers. While she did so, folks kept coming by to offer personal welcomes.

"So good to meet you," said a complete stranger whose name had never even been mentioned to Cara.

"Hope you'll be happy here in Eden," a sweet-faced, elderly matron crooned. "Right fine little town."

"You couldn't do no better than to land with the Jeffords," pronounced a lipless fellow in a gimme cap and ragged coveralls. "Good people."

"You couldn't do no better than Holt, either," the plain-looking woman on his arm said. Cara opened her mouth to dispute the connection, then closed it again as the couple moved off.

"If you'll be wanting to get into the Ladies' Auxiliary, hon. I'll put your name up," Angevine Martin told her with a giggle just before she swamped Cara in a pillowy hug.

Cara hardly knew what to say to these well-meaning folk, so she just smiled and nodded and smiled some more. Joanie dropped off the cobbler in one large disposable cup. Holt returned at about the same time and hoisted Ace into his arms.

"Y'all come back now," a voice called, and Holt swept the owner a wave.

The trio started toward the door. Just then a young man half rose from his chair, cupped his hands around his mouth and bellowed, "Hey, Holt! Could you go back to wherever you got her and get me one?"

Cara's face instantly flamed. She felt sure it must clash with her outfit. Then Holt's strong arm ushered her through the door. At the same time he yelled back over his shoulder, "Sorry. One of a kind!"

They carried laughter with them into the cold air and, in Cara's case, a secret sense of delight.

She told herself that it would be foolish to hope for something personal with Holt Jefford. First, he didn't trust her in the slightest. Second, his lack of trust would be fully validated if he ever learned the truth. He would most likely hate her then or, at the very least, turn away.

She didn't even want to think about the third reason, but she forced herself to face it.

The day that the Elmonts discovered her whereabouts, she'd have to run again. How could she leave her heart behind her when she went?

No, it would be far better never to even start down that road.

She could only hope that it wasn't already too late.

Chapter Nine

Holt kept his arm looped around Cara Jane as he escorted her toward the truck, Ace snug in the curve of the opposite elbow. He told himself that it was because of the cold, but in truth he just liked having her close to him. That should have terrified him, but something else seemed to override his good sense.

For one thing, the assumptions of the townsfolk concerning a romantic development between him and Cara Jane didn't trouble him nearly as much as they should. The fact that he hadn't realized that everyone would figure Cara Jane for his girlfriend troubled him more than the assumption itself. He hated that she had been embarrassed by it. If he'd been thinking at all, he could have prepared her for what she would encounter, but he'd been too intent on getting information out of her to consider beyond that.

"I should've warned you about all the carrying on," he told her. "There's always lots of teasing and talk going back and forth. Everyone pretty much knows everyone else, so any newcomer is of interest."

"I understand," Cara replied, glancing around at the crowded parking lot, if an expanse of bare, dusty ground punctuated with trees, piles of debris and a propane tank the size of a small whale could be termed a parking lot. "Looks like the whole town's here tonight."

"Naw, just half of it," Holt quipped, relieved that she didn't sound offended by all the talk. "The other half came last night. This place is sort of the town's unofficial social club."

"I see. Tonight's crowd is certainly a friendly bunch."

"They are that," he agreed, but his conscience wouldn't let him ignore the real issue, so he added, "I just never realized how much interest there is in the romantic status of the Jefford siblings."

Cara shrugged, saying nonchalantly, "Obviously your sister's wedding is still in the forefront of everyone's mind."

"Obviously." He felt sure it was more than that, however, and he wanted her to be prepared, so as they reached the truck and he slipped his keys from his coat pocket, he said, "You can bet, though, that the main topic of conversation for the immediate future is going to be the two of us and this little guy right here, including his father and why he's out of the picture."

Holt looked down at her, saw the sad resignation behind those soft gray eyes and felt like a complete heel. He'd hoped to shake loose some new information by spending time with her, not to make her an object of speculation or, worse, gossip. Had he thought for two minutes about something other than his suspicions, he'd have known this would happen.

"I'm sorry," he said. "I should have realized what you were in for."

He kept expecting her to be upset with him, but she stood there between him and his truck, shivering inside her meager denim jacket, and broadcast forgiveness with a wan smile. A spark burst to flame inside his heart and spread warmth throughout his chest.

"Ace's father is dead," she said matter-of-factly. "It was a freak accident. He stopped to help another car broken down on a busy highway overpass. The witnesses all thought it was a woman driving, a young one, probably, which is the only thing that makes sense because I can't imagine Addison stopping otherwise. Then, somehow, he fell, and that's all there is to say."

Holt knew the truth when he heard it. He knew pain, too, even pain as layered as hers.

Nodding, he opened the truck and deposited a flagging Ace into his seat. Poor little guy didn't even bother protesting this time, just turned his head into the corner and closed his eyes. To Holt's surprise, Cara left him to perform the buckling process, hurrying around to climb up inside the front cab. Aware of how the cold must be affecting her, he joined her as quickly as he could, not at all offended that she turned to check his handiwork while he started the engine and got them moving.

They drove in silence for a moment before something she'd said triggered a thought. "Seems like that woman he'd stopped to help should've hung around after he fell, doesn't it?"

Cara shrugged. "I'm not sure she even realized it had happened. No one actually saw what went down."

"Huh. That doesn't sound a little suspicious to you?" he asked.

Cara turned her head toward him, meeting his glance. "I don't see why. The police did try to track her down, but the car turned out to be a rental."

"Didn't they follow up on that?"

"I can't imagine why they would, really. Addison didn't have any enemies."

"That you know of," Holt replied. Suspicion—or was it something else, something outside himself?—tightened his chest. He had to ask, "Have you considered other reasons for her behavior?"

Cara bowed her head, her face shadowed by the dim light from the dashboard. "You mean, that maybe he was cheating on me, that she was his girlfriend and had called him for help that day, then sped away after the accident because she didn't want it to come out?"

"Something like that," Holt admitted, his stomach starting to churn.

Cara looked out into the dark landscape passing by her window and softly admitted, "It was a distinct possibility." She looked at him. "But what difference does it make now?"

Uncomfortably wounded on her behalf, Holt fiddled with the temperature gauge on the heater, which had only just begun to blow tepid air. "I admire your attitude," he said, "but if you'll forgive my saying so, your late husband doesn't sound like much of a prize."

She leaned her head against the window, admitting raggedly, "Our marriage wasn't the greatest. But it wasn't the worst, either. It wasn't much of anything at all. But he gave me Ace. That's reason enough to grieve him."

"Yes, it is," Holt agreed gently.

The heater blew warmer now, so he turned it up, knowing that she couldn't be comfortable in those summer-weight clothes, clothes she could not have had much use for back in Oregon. If that's where she'd truly come from.

Truth and lies in one pretty little bundle, he thought.

He wished for everyone's sake that he could believe otherwise, that he could just accept what she'd told them and trust that nothing from her past would reach out to bite him and his family. Unfortunately, he just didn't know how to turn off the uneasy feeling that she hid something important.

All in all, he *had* learned new information about her tonight, he mused. He'd learned that she'd been hurt by her late husband and unhappy in her marriage but that she had managed to let go of her pain and be thankful for her blessings.

He could have done without that knowledge. It made him feel ashamed of his suspicions while doing nothing to lessen his concerns.

The rest of the trip passed in warm silence, both lost in their own thoughts.

After they arrived back at the motel, Holt carried in Ace for her. It had almost become a ritual with them, one he liked more than seemed wise, but he simply could not stand by while she struggled with the boy's dead weight and maybe even woke him in the process.

Cara Jane thanked Holt for his help.

"No problem."

It was their standard interaction lately, but as he was going out the door again, she suddenly said, "I had a lot of fun tonight."

That surprised him. He'd sensed her embarrassment and discomfort at times during dinner, and his guilt about that returned forcefully; he knew he'd be talking to God about it later.

For now, with his hand on the doorknob and the door ajar, he choked out, "Me, too."

"I know I'm the newcomer," she went on, "and a subject for gossip, but I somehow felt a part of the community tonight. Does that make sense?"

It made a lot of sense. Eden was a friendly town, and the Saturday-night crowd at the Watermelon Patch treated the place like one big community dining room. That Cara had felt a welcome part of that lightened Holt's conscience a bit and, at the same time, tightened his chest.

He turned to face her, a lump rising in his throat at the soft look on her face. He couldn't have gotten a word out to save his life, so he did the only thing he could think of. He leaned in and pressed a kiss to her forehead.

Before he could do worse, he quickly backed through the door, taking with him a trepidatious heart and the vision of her sweet, wistful smile.

Cara and Ace attended church with the Jeffords the next day. This time they rode in Holt's truck and sat up front in the usual Jefford pew. She'd argued that it might be wiser, considering the assumptions about the two of them, for her to make the trek on foot, despite the biting cold, and sit apart from the Jeffords, but Holt had decreed the plan pointless. Hap had dismissed the whole thing.

"People will talk," he'd said. "Let 'em. God knows the truth. Better than we do, even."

That did nothing to ease Cara's conscience. The more she got to know the Jeffords, the worse she felt about lying to them, especially to Holt. Her feelings for him had taken an alarming turn the night before, reinforcing her determination to keep as much distance between them as possible.

Holt had left his hat in the vehicle when they went in to church, a wise decision because, even though Cara had managed to maneuver Hap into a seat between her and Holt, Ace continually lunged back and forth between them. He treated Hap as a human bridge, often pausing during transition to dispense hugs and pats.

To Cara's relief, none of the Jefford men became impatient or seemed the least disturbed by the constantly moving little body. Ryan, sitting on the end next to Holt, even seemed to feel a little left out and at times tried to entice Ace onto his lap, but though Ace smiled at Ryan and flirted with him, he did it sitting with his back flat against Holt's chest. At least, Cara consoled herself, Ace was happy and quiet, and that allowed her to pay some attention to Grover's message.

It turned out that he was preaching a series from the book of Romans. She didn't understand much of what he read aloud, but she did get the premise that the created have no right to complain to the Creator about how they are made. Another idea, however, not only confused but troubled her, that those pursuing righteousness via the law "stumbled" by not pursuing righteousness through faith.

What did that mean, she wondered, to pursue righteousness through faith? And what was this law about which the writer spoke?

She needed to speak to someone about this, someone who might not become too suspicious if she hedged or changed the subject. As before, Hap would be her first choice, but after the last time they'd spoken of such things, she feared giving away too much with him.

During the final part of the service, when the congregation stood and softly sang while Grover gently exhorted those with needs to come forward for counseling and prayer, Cara felt an almost overwhelming compulsion to rush down the aisle and throw herself onto her knees, but she stayed put out of fear. Later, when she stood shaking hands with Grover, the notion of speaking to him in private hit her. When she quietly asked if that might be possible, he promptly suggested a time the next afternoon, then added that he'd take care of it with Hap. Feeling somewhat lighter, Cara went out to meet the others.

Holt had carried Ace from the building, seeming as comfortable as if the boy were his own. Cara's heart lurched when Ace lifted his hand to press it against Holt's mouth, as he often did with her. Holt first kissed Ace's palm then blew a raspberry against it, eliciting joyous giggles. Cara knew in her heart of hearts that Addison would not have been so easy with their son, that his affection would not have been doled out so unstintingly and without motive.

The sadness that had descended on her after that

first, terrified grief suddenly threatened to envelope her once more. Then Holt caught her eye, smiled and waggled Ace's hand in a wave.

Thank You, God, she instantly thought. *Thank You for my son. Thank You for bringing us to this place and these people.*

She wanted to ask that He allow them to stay, but after the lies she'd told these good men, she dared not ask for what she knew she did not deserve. For the first time, she began to wonder what she and Ace would do when they left here. They couldn't live forever in a tiny kitchenette. Ace could not grow up sleeping in a walk-through closet. Even if the Elmonts didn't find them, she and Ace would have to move on at some point. A growing boy needed a real home, and it fell to her to provide that. Somehow. Somewhere. She wondered how she could possibly do that on the run. If only the Elmonts had not filed for custody of her son....

Her shivers had less to do with the cold than the sudden bleakness that filled her.

Cara bowed her head, sitting forward on the edge of Marie Waller's flowered sofa in the living room of the modest parsonage next to the church. Ace played on the rug between her feet. After coffee, a plate of sliced fruit and cheese and a solid forty minutes of conversation, during which the pastor's wife had quietly disappeared, some of Cara's questions had been answered. She now understood that the Law referred to the Ten Commandments, and that only through grace could anyone hope to live up to its standard.

Unfortunately, receiving grace required confession

of one's sins, and she'd come no closer to being able to do that. All during the previous night, she'd wrestled with the possibility of confessing all, but that would only put the Jeffords in an untenable position. She couldn't expect them to keep her secret, so she could only confess if she could move on, but to where? To what? God knew she wouldn't get far on the money she'd managed to save thus far.

Grover had urged her to unburden herself to God, but she'd already done so, more than once, and somehow it only seemed to heighten her need to tell Hap and Holt and Ryan the truth. She felt trapped in a vicious circle of fear, guilt and lies.

Now, as the round, jolly pastor prayed aloud, tears leaked from Cara's eyes, welling up from her heavy heart.

"Father, You know Cara's burdens, and we're both trusting You to help her carry them. Help her see that her need for You is greater than whatever is holding her back from full surrender. Wrap Your arms of love and protection around her. Resolve these issues that are weighing so heavily upon her, and bring her fully into Your will for her life. Meanwhile, O God, make all of us who love You a blessing to her and Ace. In the name of Your Holy Son, Jesus the Christ, amen."

Sniffing and wiping her face, she gulped back her tears and took a deep breath before lifting her head. "Thank you, Pastor."

"I wish you could find the peace you're seeking," he told her gently.

She shook her head. "Maybe I just don't deserve it."

"None of us do," he insisted, "but thankfully that

didn't keep God from making a way for us to have it. You should know, in case you decide to talk particulars, that I'm bound to confidentiality by the sanctity of my office. Nothing you tell me will leave the room."

She fully realized that he meant what he said, but she thought of Hap and Grover's deep friendship with him and knew that she couldn't ask the pastor to keep her secrets. "I'll think about it," she hedged.

She bent and swung Ace up onto her lap to get him into his outer clothes. Once that had been accomplished, she drew on Hap's old coat over her denim jacket and rose. "Thank you for your time."

"I'll be praying for you," Grover said, taking her hand as he led her toward the door. "Whatever the trouble is, my dear, know that you have real friends here who will stand by you."

He could say that, of course, because he didn't know what it was that she dared not confess. Nevertheless, she treasured the fact that he'd said it.

"I appreciate that. Thank you again."

She hurried out onto the porch at the front of the house, smiled a farewell and shifted Ace onto her hip so she could descend the steps. The sky looked fittingly flat and gray, and a slicing wind swirled, clacking the bare tree branches and slashing any exposed skin to ribbons. She wished she'd worn Hap's old gloves or at least a scarf on her head. At least Ace was warm inside his layers and fleece hoodie.

Hugging him close, she crossed the street and turned toward the motel. She hadn't gone ten yards when she heard a vehicle approaching from behind her and then a beep. Turning, she found Holt lowering the driver's side window on his truck.

"What are you doing?"

"Heading back to the motel."

He put the truck in Park, got out and opened the back door before stepping up on the sidewalk and reaching for Ace. "Get in."

Cold, she yielded her son and trotted around to the passenger side. They'd agreed after church yesterday to take care of switching the car seat later, so the thing still sat anchored in the center of the back bench of his truck. Thankful for that, Cara basked in the warm air blowing from the heater while Holt buckled Ace into the safety harness.

Holt slid in across from her a few moments later, snapped his own safety belt and pulled the gear lever into the proper position to move forward, but then he paused with his foot on the brake, hung a wrist over the top of the steering wheel and turned to face her. "I can't believe you went out in this cold on foot."

"I had things to do," she told him defensively, stung.

"You should have waited for me to drive you wherever it is you needed to go."

"I didn't want to take up your time with it," she retorted.

"Then you should've taken your own car," he snapped.

Cara folded her arms mulishly. "I couldn't. The car is making an awful racket and I'm afraid to drive it, even a couple of blocks."

He just looked at her for several heavy heartbeats before facing forward again and depressing the gas pedal. "What was so important you had to go out anyway?"

She took her time answering that, mostly because she didn't want to lie to him. In the end she just told him without regard to consequences, muttering, "I wanted to speak to the pastor—I mean, Grover."

Holt shot her a glance, then carefully blanked his expression. "Okay. But why take Ace out in the cold when Hap's more than willing to watch him?"

Her defensiveness fading, she bit her lip, then had to admit, "I honestly didn't even think of leaving Ace with Hap."

"Well, it's time you started thinking about it." His expression softened, taking the sting out of his words. "You're not alone in the world, Cara Jane, whatever you may think."

The gallantry of that, coupled with her conversation with the preacher, threatened to move Cara to tears once more. She cleared her throat and said, "I'll keep that in mind."

Holt gave her a quick nod, then, "I'll take a look at your car first chance I get."

She bit her lip. "That's not necessary. After my next paycheck I'll—"

"*I'll* take a look at it," he interrupted, driving straight across the back lawn of the motel. "Then we'll see." He scraped a look over her, adding, "Ask me, you ought to be investing in a real coat and some winter clothes before you do anything else."

She hadn't asked him, and she knew she wouldn't be spending her hard-earned money on clothing for herself. She had no one but herself to blame for her inadequate wardrobe. Even though she'd had to sneak clothing out of the Elmont house over a period of days during her Christmas holiday furlough from the clinic, things that wouldn't be missed, she could have included some warmer articles. She just hadn't been thinking at the time, and now she paid the price by suffering the cold in order to accumulate funds in case she had to flee. The car being a necessity, she made no further protest about him taking a look at it; instead, she silently endured the jostling of the truck until it came to a stop next to the patio.

Thanking Holt for the ride, she slid out onto the ground. They both climbed up into the back from opposite sides to free Ace from his harness. Once unbuckled, however, he reached for Holt rather than his mother.

Cara told herself that Holt was nothing more than a fresh face for her son, but deep inside she feared Ace had become as fond of Holt Jefford as she had.

This was another complication that she had not foreseen. Indeed, the list of her failures seemed to grow hourly.

First, she hadn't appreciated the fact that Eddie would undoubtedly look for her around Duncan. Second, she hadn't planned for an emergency, like the car breaking down. Third, she'd underestimated the work involved in the job she'd taken on. If Hap and Holt and even Ryan were not good enough to pitch in, she'd be in way over her head by now. In fact, if her employers had been anyone else, she'd probably be on the street by now! In addition, she hadn't truly understood how arduous it would be to keep Ace with her all day long. Just the logistics of that were exhausting. Besides all that, she'd lied about her identity, where she'd grown up, where she'd come from, and why she'd struck out on this fool's mission to begin with, even about what she'd run away from. Worse, she hadn't counted on becoming so fond of the Jeffords that her conscience would get busy and eat her up like this.

It seemed to Cara in that moment that the best thing she could do was just hit the road again.

In a car that she didn't trust to drive another mile and with limited funds. Right.

No, she'd dug this hole by herself. She'd have to find a way to climb out on her own, too.

In the meantime, all she could do was pray that Eddie and the Elmonts didn't show up with a shovel.

Chapter Ten

Holt tossed the broken hunk of metal into the bed of the truck. He'd spent most of the morning figuring out the problem with the engine and getting to it. Now he had to find a replacement for the failed part.

After stripping off his filthy gloves, he tucked those into a green plastic bucket affixed to the inside of the truck bed by an elastic band. Next, he unsnapped and peeled off his quilted coveralls to cram them into the bucket on top of the gloves, leaving him standing in jeans and a white, long-sleeved insulated knit shirt. His hard hat went into the bucket last, becoming a protective lid of sorts.

Reaching into the rear compartment of the truck cab, he took out his heavy canvas coat and quickly donned it before sliding beneath the steering wheel. A billed cap, bearing the silhouette of an old wood derrick spouting the words "Jefford Drilling and Exploration," rested on the dash. He pulled that on, settling the bill just so, before turning the keys that dangled from the ignition switch.

The truck engine rumbled to life. As he wheeled the vehicle around the lot to the side of the drilling platform, he lowered the window and hung an elbow out of it.

"You men pick up around here, thread, dope and cap enough pipe to get us through the next couple days, then clock out and go on home. I'll see you in the morning. And don't forget to padlock the gate."

The crew waved a few grimy salutes and nodded their yellow hard hats. On one hand, it was busy work to keep them from losing a full day's pay. On another, with enough pipe threaded and ready for coupling and all hands on the deck when they started to drill in the morning, they ought to be able to make up for lost time, provided he got the engine up and running again.

Lots of drilling sites operated twenty-four hours a day, seven days a week, but those belonged to larger outfits that primarily serviced the major oil companies. Holt preferred to work for himself. He paid good money for geologists reports, made his own assays and negotiated his own leases on percentage, then sold any resulting oil to middlemen who, in turn, passed it to refiners. That meant sinking his own funds into the drilling operations, most of which came up dry. He had enough wells operating to keep the business going, though, with three portable rigs and two crews, one of which was punching holes up in the panhandle right now.

Holt prided himself on being able to offer steady work, with very little actual downtime. He took just enough of the profits to keep himself housed, fed and clothed, turned a good bit back into the business, banked as much as possible, and felt pretty good about providing incomes for a number of families. Working for himself meant doing a lot more than scouting leases and supervising operations, though. It also meant looking for replacement parts and working on his own equipment when the need arose.

He'd drive to Duncan in search of the part first, he decided, but if he couldn't find the thing there he'd have to head to Lawton or points even farther afield, which could make for a very long day, indeed. He used his cell phone to call the motel and let Hap know where he'd be. Hap had a dozen questions, so Holt spent almost the entire drive explaining the situation, including the fact that he'd leased his extra rig.

Though a cantankerous old thing, the third rig in his operation provided backup when another went down due to catastrophic mechanical failure of some sort. On the other hand, it mostly sat around in a field out behind his barn rusting and attracting field mice. He'd figured he might as well make some money off it, even if said money only went to repairing one of the two newer rigs.

With small operations like his, things went wrong about as many days as they didn't, but wrong could usually get made right in a relatively short period of time. Those days when nothing went right, Holt accounted as "patience" days, days the Lord set aside to teach him patience. Nobody had to tell him that he was a slower learner.

Today, he almost felt grateful for the distraction. He hadn't been able to get Cara Jane off his mind even for a minute these past couple days. He couldn't help wondering what she'd needed to talk over with Grover. She seemed open and curious about spiritual matters, but he doubted that she had a full understanding of them.

Could a Christian woman lie to his face? To Hap's? At this point, just one thing kept him from demanding some straight answers, the fear that he might actually have her entirely right—or entirely wrong. He couldn't decide which would be worse.

He sensed her disquiet. Something bubbled and roiled beneath that sweet, feminine surface of hers. Like a frightened bird poised for flight, she seemed to long for the warmth of the nest and yet fear it at the same time. On Tuesday, he'd asked her point-blank if she had something troubling her. She'd straightened, smoothed her brow with her wrist, her hands clad in rubber gloves, and looked him in the eye. He'd held his breath, but then her gaze had fallen away. She'd shaken her head and gone back to work. He'd wanted to fold her up in his arms, but whether to shake her or calm her to his touch as if she were an abused puppy he didn't know.

For the umpteenth time, he put her out of his thoughts. That lasted, mostly, right up until he found the needed part at, praise God, the very first place he tried.

Deciding that God must have deemed this a "take it a little slower" day, Holt tooled up Highway 81 to the drive-in burger joint and ordered a double cheeseburger, onion rings, extra-large cola and hot apple pie. The food hadn't even arrived when an electrifying impulse hit him.

Why not, since he had a little free time, drive by Cara Jane's old address? He could find it easily enough, and maybe just seeing where she'd grown up would offer some insight. Of course she'd supposedly left there long ago, but what did he have to lose? Someone might be able to give him some clue to the mystery that was Cara

398 Her Small-Town Hero

Jane Wynne. Besides, with his busy schedule, he might not have an opportunity like this again for a long while.

Half an hour later, he pulled over to the curb in front of a modest older home to polish off the burger and rings. The pie, he reasoned, would eat as good cold as hot. He cleaned his face with a napkin and got out of the truck to walk up the broken path to the low porch.

On the southeast side of town, the small house had been cheaply built back sometime around the Second World War. It had been minimally maintained. The hipped roof showed the most age, sagging in the center, but the original porch had been replaced at some point with a concrete pad that lent a contrasting air of permanence to the plain, square posts which held up the overhanging roof and clapboard siding painted a dull, uninspiring gray. The original front door had long since been traded for a dark, paneled, Spanish-style one that flatly did not belong. Lack of attention had let the yard go to dirt, except for the evergreen shrubs that flanked the walkway and an enormous cedar towering over all.

Holt knocked and shortly found himself greeted by a friendly young couple.

"I wonder if you might remember a girl who used to live here, a Cara Jane Wynne?"

As expected, they shook their heads and told him they'd recently rented the place from a Mr. Rangle.

"He might know her," the young man suggested.

"Or Mrs. Poersel might," the woman said, pointing next door to a better maintained white house with updated siding and gleaming metal roof. "Poor old thing's bedridden, but she loves to visit. Sent her nurse over here to invite me in before we even had the car unloaded. I'd guess she's been in that house fifty years or more."

Holt thanked them and walked next door. A jolly black woman in pink nursing scrubs and braids answered his knock, introduced herself as Gladys and let him ask his question before guiding him through a rabbit warren of musty knickknacks and worn furniture to a centralized bedroom and a thin, old woman who looked like she'd disintegrate if an errant puff of air should hit her. The house felt like an oven.

Mrs. Poersel half reclined in the center of a high, four-poster bed, wearing a frilly pink bed jacket and headband to contain wiry but thinning white hair cropped at chin length. A bed tray straddled her meager lap, and atop it rested a plate containing a sandwich. She was attempting to eat it with a fork and knife, her gnarled and spotted hands trembling with the effort.

Gladys walked around to the far side of the bed. "This young man wants to ask you about someone," she said, unceremoniously picking up the sandwich and sticking it beneath the old woman's nose.

Mrs. Poersel snapped off a bite, whereupon Gladys dropped the sandwich and left the room. Mrs. Poersel smiled at Holt while chewing punctiliously behind clamped lips.

He removed his cap and held it before him, saying, "Cara Jane Wynne? I understand she used to live next door."

Mrs. Poersel swallowed and broke into a smile so wide it nearly dislodged her dentures. "My, yes!" She rested her knife and fork on the edge of the lap tray. "I do miss her. What fun we had." She beamed up at him.

"Would you like a sandwich? I love a good sandwich, though they're hard to eat properly, aren't they?"

Holt had always figured that the proper way to eat something was the most obvious and efficient. "No, thank you, ma'am. I've had my lunch already. Very kind of you to offer."

Giggling, she asked, "Did you know about the berries?"

"The berries?" Holt shuffled his feet, momentarily lost; that or the heat was frying his brain. "Oh! You mean collecting blackberries on the side of the road?"

Mrs. Poersel laughed. "She could make the best pies in the world! Didn't you love her berry pies?"

Lost again, he could only glance around in the vain hope of enlightenment. "Cara Jane? At what? Twelve or thirteen? I—I thought she left here before high school."

Mrs. Poersel clapped her hands to her sunken, wrinkled cheeks. "I must mean later on!" Her dark eyes twinkled, the pupils so big that they barely left room for the irises. "No, wait. You're talking about the girl. Pale, pale hair? Sad smile." That sounded like Cara Jane, so he nodded. Mrs. Poersel laughed, reminiscing. "She used to catch lightning bugs and keep them in a jar. She'd run all around the yard, almost like one of them, flitting here and there. She was the daughter her aunt never had, you know."

"Her aunt?"

"Mmm. My very best friend in the whole world. Lived for that child. Well, someone had to care for her, didn't they? Whatever happened to her? Wound up like her mama, I fear."

"No, ma'am," Holt hastened to reassure the elderly

woman. "Cara Jane's just fine. She works for my grandfather and has a little boy of her own."

The old woman threw her head back in horror. "Cara Jane! Now, she never mentioned that boy to me." Shaking her head, she clucked her tongue. "I suppose I might have judged her." She suddenly looked to Holt, a beatific expression on her face. "Society's strictures have their place, and the Good Book is solid, but one does learn as one grows older to take a broader, kinder view."

Holt had the feeling that they were striving to communicate from alternate universes, but he bobbed his head and said, "Yes, ma'am."

"Now, Cara Jane, whatever her faults might have been, she was one for doing one's best, for making do and being thankful. But it's not enough for some. I gather her sister was like that."

"You mean her brother," Holt corrected, relieved to find that the Cara Jane whom he had come to know hadn't changed all that much from the Cara Jane remembered by her old neighbor.

"Yes, I suppose I do." The elderly woman's gaze wandered around the room as if seeing it for the first time. "There was a brother, wasn't there? Though mostly it was just the girl. Sweet little thing with that blond hair always hanging in her eyes. I wonder what became of her." Before he could remind her that Cara Jane worked for his grandfather, Mrs. Poersel gusted a great sigh and exclaimed, "I do so miss Cara Jane!"

"Maybe I could bring her to visit soon," Holt suggested. He wondered just how long the old dear would remain in this world; she looked that pale.

She hunched her thin shoulders. "Wouldn't that be

a treat!" Her gaze wandered off again. "My own children were older, you understand, but Mr. Poersel was still alive then. Did you know him? Worked fifty years in insurance."

Holt shook his head. "I'm sorry, no."

"Those were good times, if only we'd known it, but difficult for a single woman. What else could she do?" Mrs. Poersel shook her head and seemed to answer her own question. "Cleaning other people's houses was the only work she could get after the war, you know."

Holt felt sure they weren't speaking of Cara Jane now, but he just smiled. Gladys came back into the room then, walked over to the bed, picked up the sandwich and offered it to the old woman, who retrieved her knife and fork before taking another bite.

"Now you keep eating," Gladys instructed kindly, "while I show this young man out." She smiled at Holt, saying, "The least little thing tires her."

A glance showed the old girl all but asleep in her plate already. Holt thanked her for her time, but she didn't respond. Gladys smiled and turned him toward the door. "She gets awful muddled. Did you find out what you needed to know?"

"Yes, I think I did."

"That's good," Gladys was saying. "Then, you both got something out of it. I know she enjoyed the visit, even though it's not one of her better days. You come back some other time, she might be a little clearer."

"I just might do that."

"Don't you be too long about it," Gladys warned, adding with a smile, "You stay warm out there now."

He didn't think he'd ever be cold again. Sweat trickled down between his shoulder blades as he made his way out into the refreshing January air. Filling his lungs with the sweet, clean briskness, he set out jauntily for the truck. He doubted Mrs. Poersel would even remember him when she woke next, but he felt he ought to return with Cara Jane, out of gratitude if nothing else.

Mrs. Poersel hadn't made a whole lot of sense in there, but she'd confirmed to his satisfaction that Cara Jane had, indeed, lived in that house next door. And chased lightning bugs with a jar. He could just see her, skinny little arms and legs pumping, blond hair flying out behind her. As he slid into the truck, he remembered what Cara had said about her drug-addicted mother and Mrs. Poersel's comment about Cara Jane following in that parent's footsteps. Suddenly overwhelmed by gratitude, he bowed his head.

"Thank You, Lord. Because she didn't turn out like her mama. She's more like those lightning bugs than poor old Mrs. Poersel can imagine. Thank You for that."

After lifting up Mrs. Poersel and thanking God for finding the part he needed to fix the drilling engine, he ended his prayer. Then he peeled the paper wrapping off the fried pie and had himself a little celebration as he headed back to Eden.

Cara Jane decided to attend prayer meeting that evening, even though it clearly meant leaving Ace in the church nursery. Holt couldn't help feeling that they'd made progress. Not only had he confirmed that she had, indeed, lived in Duncan, she seemed to be loosening her grip on the boy just a bit. Holt supposed it was understandable, having lost her husband in a puzzling accident, that she would cling to Ace and want to keep him with her, but it was not always the wisest course for Ace himself—or for Holt. Once she felt comfortable leaving Ace in Hap's care, Holt could spend more time focusing on his own business.

She balked a bit when they handed off Ace at the nursery door.

"He's fine," Holt assured her, taking her hand and tugging her toward the fellowship hall and the sanctuary beyond it, attached via a narrow hallway.

Her steps lagged for a bit, then she fell in next to him, her hand never leaving his.

Holt smiled, thinking of that little girl who had chased lightning bugs with a jar and of the half promise he'd made to Mrs. Poersel. Given that, the statement that followed seemed entirely sensible.

"I drove by your old house today."

Cara Jane stumbled and nearly fell. He grabbed her with both hands, noting the sudden paleness of her face.

"Y-you did what?"

He tried not to frown, but alarm bells clanged inside his head. "I had to make a trip to Duncan and I drove by your old house."

She leaned back against the beige wall, and he could see her pulse racing in the throb of veins at the base of her throat. "Why did you d-do that?"

He shrugged, his hands still hovering about her upper arms. "Just wanted to see where you lived."

She gulped but managed a wobbly smile. "Never was much to look at."

He drew his hands away, tucking his fingertips

into the hip pockets of his jeans. "I spoke with a Mrs. Poersel."

Cara Jane gasped. "Mrs. Poersel is still alive?"

"Barely. How old is she, anyway?"

Cara Jane thought about it, her eyes flitting side to side as she appeared to calculate the years. "I'd guess mid-nineties anyway."

"She said she knew your aunt," Holt prodded.

"Yes." Cara Jane dropped her gaze. "The house actually belonged to her. My aunt, I mean."

"I take it they were good friends."

"Very good friends," Cara Jane confirmed with a nod, "although Mrs. Poersel was quite a bit older. How ironic that she should outlive my aunt by so many years."

"When did your aunt die?" he asked, trying to keep his tone conversational.

"Oh, before my fourteenth birthday," Cara Jane said.

"Is that why you moved away?" He sounded like an inquisitor, even to his own ears.

Again her gaze dropped. "Yes."

The piano began playing in the sanctuary. Cara Jane looked in that direction.

"Shouldn't we go in?"

"In a minute," he said, aware of a rising anger. Why did she do this to him? What was she hiding? Could he not have one full day of peace about this situation? "Mrs. Poersel would like to see you."

"Oh?"

That single syllable, false and wary and weak, told him how little the idea pleased Cara Jane. It didn't exactly thrill him, either. He'd thought that he'd settled something today, fixed at least one small piece in the puzzle, but the emerging picture suddenly made no sense to him.

"I have the feeling that sooner would be better than later," he told her firmly, "if you know what I mean."

Cara Jane swallowed. They both knew that she couldn't refuse. "I see."

Feeling a little ill now, he pressed on. "How about Sunday, between Ace's nap and the big game?" Hap had planned a Super Bowl party, partly because Charlotte and Ty wouldn't be joining them after all. Ty's mother had been rushed into gallbladder surgery, so naturally Ty and Charlotte had felt that they should stay close to her for the time being.

Cara Jane said nothing for a long moment, but the sound of singing reached them, and she looked once more toward the sanctuary door. He felt the longing in her, the yearning. "Fine," she said, sounding exhausted. Pushing away from the wall, she started for the sanctuary.

Holt watched her for an instant, torn between grim relief and keen dread. Then he followed her.

"Sunday it is, then."

"Sunday," she whispered.

He had the distinct impression that he'd just sentenced her to a cruel and unusual punishment. Perhaps both of them.

Chapter Eleven

Cara saw that she had entered the sanctuary at the front behind the piano. Avoiding eye contact, she kept one shoulder against the wall as she walked to the nearest empty pew and sat down on the end. Holt moved past and took the seat immediately behind her. Thankful for that much distance, she somehow managed to hold on to the edge of her composure, despite the trembling in her limbs.

She didn't sing, but she smiled at the woman in front of her who passed her an open hymnal. After the song, Grover rose to speak for a moment before dismissing them to small group. Cara, fighting off panic, barely registered a word, but she soon found herself being swept back the way she'd come, right into the large room they called the Fellowship Hall.

Earlier she had noticed that a shuttered window opened into a large kitchen along one side of the bland room. Of more immediate interest now, however, were the folding chairs arranged in circles of nine or ten seats. As people began filling them, Holt stepped up and lightly grasped her elbow.

"There's a mixed group forming over here."

She let him steer her to a chair and soon found herself sitting next to him and across from a couple about his age. The woman leaned forward and said a soft "hello." Angevine Martin came by, giggling and squeezing Cara's shoulder. Cara tried, hoped she'd managed, to smile. To her surprise, Holt took charge of the group.

"Any requests?"

A middle-aged man, sitting with arms and legs crossed, immediately began to speak about his impending divorce. He went on for several minutes, and Cara noted the soothing, supportive comments of the others, but she felt paralyzed, apart from the group.

Perhaps it was best that way, she thought tiredly. On Sunday next, her aunt's best friend would undoubtedly expose her lies and end her time in Eden.

Even in the midst of her terror, Cara tried to apply analytical logic to the situation, but the pall of doom hung so heavy over her that she could barely form coherent thoughts. Her wisest course might be simply to run, now, tonight, but the idea brought such enormous pain that the inherent fallacy of it seemed incidental. She had too little money accumulated, an undependable vehicle and not even a glimmer of a plan this time, but that all paled in comparison to her grief and disappointment. Her only option seemed to be to make that visit to Mrs. Poersel and endure whatever came of it, however terrifying.

God help me, she prayed in mechanical silence. *Oh, God, please help me.*

Several others around the circle voiced prayer concerns. Holt suggested that they pray silently then let him close them. Several people immediately slipped off their chairs and onto their knees, bowing their heads over the seats they had vacated. Cara followed suit and immediately felt overcome by a presence other than her own.

She began to cry out silent apologies to God, her tears flowing into the space created by her folded arms.

I'm so sorry! I didn't realize how hard it would be to lie, but what can I do now? Holt will report me, and even if he doesn't, I don't want to involve anyone else in my problems. I only want to make a good home for my son. Help me! Oh, please help me! I shouldn't have done it. I just didn't know what else to do. I'm so sorry. Please don't let Holt and the others hate me. At least if it all comes out, then You can forgive me, and I want that, but please, please don't take my son. Please don't let them lock me away and take my son. Oh, God, I'm so sorry!

She all but forgot about the others around her, until Holt jolted her into awareness by speaking aloud. With simple, homespun eloquence, he praised God for His mercy and kindness, addressed each request, mentioned several concerns of the wider church and even touched on some national issues.

Then he broke Cara's quivering heart, saying, "Lord, there's a lady in Duncan, Mrs. Poersel, who's about reached the end of her road. I ask You to ease her way, and I thank You for this touchstone to Cara Jane's past and pray that her visit will bring Mrs. Poersel the same measure of joy that she and Ace have brought to my grandfather and me." He went on to seek blessing for everyone in the room and their families. He asked God to use the church for His purposes and, as other voices in the background fell away, closed in the name of Jesus.

Cara hastily dried the last of her tears but kept her gaze averted as Holt's hand curled beneath her elbow, lifting her to her feet. He held her back with just a squeeze of his fingers as others began to move away. Some spoke to him, and he replied in jocular kind, until the two of them stood somewhat apart from the dwindling group.

Tilting her face up with a finger pressed beneath her chin, he looked down worriedly into her eyes. "Are you all right?"

She rubbed her nose, trying to hold back a sniff, and put on the best smile she could muster. "O-of course."

He frowned down at her, obviously not buying it. "I don't know what's eating you up inside, Cara Jane, but you've got to realize by now that my family and I will do everything in our power to—"

"You can't help me!" she declared, pulling away. Realizing what she'd said, she tried to cover. "B-because I don't need help. Besides, the Jeffords have already been generous enough."

Mouth flattened, jaw working, he shook his head. She could see his frustration, knew he bit back words he'd prefer to spew.

"I'm sorry, Holt," she whispered, daring no further explanation.

After a moment, he slipped an arm around her, turning toward the nursery wing. "Let's get Ace and go home."

Home, she thought bleakly. But only until Sunday.

She knew that she wouldn't run. She didn't have the heart. At least not before she'd seen Mrs. Poersel. After that, she didn't know what would happen, but she felt she owed that visit to her aunt's old neighbor. And Holt.

Over the next three days, Cara kept as much distance between herself and Holt as possible. By mutual agreement, they decided not to "repeat the mistake," in Holt's words, of their previous Saturday night out together. Both stayed in, Holt whiling away the evening with Hap and Ryan, Cara watching television with Ace in their room.

Work helped distract her mind from the agreed-upon visit with Mrs. Poersel, but it did not stop Sunday from coming. Cara skipped church, saying truthfully that she hadn't slept well the night before. What was the point in going when doom hung like a pall over everything and confession remained impossible?

All too soon, she found herself riding in Holt's big truck, Ace happily babbling to himself in the rear seat, as the miles fell away and her secret dread built. With no comfort to be found from any other source, Cara prayed in silence almost incessantly during that long drive, but as the truck turned off of 81 onto Bois D'Arc Avenue on the south side of Duncan, she lost the concentration required even for that. Morbid curiosity and desperate longing mingled with her dread as they made the familiar right onto 10th Street.

They crossed Highway 7 and drove past West Stephens Avenue. Much remained the same, but a new brick house had replaced the old Downing home. She marked another notable change as they passed West

Duncan. The hues were different. Once all the houses had been painted basic white. Now there were subtle shades of tan, gray and gold in the mix and even a smattering of more vibrant hues.

Holt parked the truck in front of Aunt Jane's house. Cara stared for long seconds at the dark, ugly door and cold concrete slab that had replaced the front porch. She much preferred the old wood porch and the door with the big window in it. The drab gray paint of the siding seemed to reflect her mood and confirm that this was not the same place she had known.

Saddened not to feel the tug of home, Cara opened the truck door and slid out. Oddly, despite the obvious changes, Mrs. Poersel's house seemed as familiar and solid as Cara's memories. Preoccupied, she didn't even realize that Holt had taken Ace from his car seat until they joined her.

"Her mind doesn't seem to wander so much as skip all over the place," Holt warned. "Don't be concerned if she doesn't recognize you right off."

Cara's lips curved wryly. The possibility of Mrs. Poersel failing to immediately recognize her counted as the least of her worries.

Holt's big hand came to rest in the small of her back, propelling her forward without actually applying pressure. Within moments, admitted by a competent and friendly private nurse, Cara found herself standing in Mrs. Poersel's hot, crowded living room.

It felt like a sauna, albeit a cluttered one. Yet, even the clutter retained something of Mrs. Poersel's natural elegance. Cara had always known that the kind neighbor's bric-a-brac items were the cheapest to be found, but that had not prevented them from assuming a certain dignified, even magisterial, ambience once placed by Mrs. Poersel's graceful hand.

Gladys, the nurse, arrayed in flowery purple cotton and athletic shoes, put her hands to her ample hips and smiled at them, her teeth white in her dark face, her many short, beaded braids clacking cheerfully.

"Well, now this is fine. Ya'll come on back. It'll make her day." She patted Ace's back, addressing Holt before moving away. "It's sweet of you to bring your family by, hon."

"Oh, we're not—" Cara began, only to break off as Gladys disappeared into the dining room, or what used to be the dining room. It had become, Cara quickly saw, a sick room, complete with four-poster bed, dresser and, lamentably, IV pole. Holt frowned at that IV pole, even as Mrs. Poersel—a smaller, frailer, more wisened version than the one Cara remembered—beamed at them from the bed.

"Sugar, that nice young man's come back with his wife and baby," Gladys announced, going to plump the pillows at her charge's thin back.

"Oh, actually, he's not my husband," Cara said quickly. Gladys turned a surprised look on her, prodding Cara to add, "He's my boss."

Holt turned his frown on Cara, stating flatly, "I'm not her boss. Cara Jane works for my grandfather."

Gladys chuckled. "Okay. Whatever you say."

At the same time, Mrs. Poersel reached out a cadaverous hand, asking, "Did you say Cara Jane?"

Cara put aside her embarrassment and stepped forward, announcing forthrightly, "It's Cara Sharp, Mrs. Poersel. Remember me? From next door?"

"Cara? Little Cara?"

Her face wreathed in a smile, Mrs. Poersel reached out for a hug with both arms, one of which trailed an IV line. Cara stepped forward, gingerly enfolding the fragile old lady. She felt less substantial than Ace, like autumn leaves swirling in the breeze. Cara straightened, tears clouding her vision, and heard Holt quietly ask the nurse, "How is she?"

"Not long for this world," Gladys announced baldly. "She'll soon be going home to Jesus. Won't you, old darlin'?"

Mrs. Poersel lay beaming against her pillows. "Not soon enough," she rasped. Then she moved her hands together weakly. "Cara. Oh, my child, you're here in her place. I can't thank you enough."

Cara bowed her head, cringing inside, wishing she hadn't come, so glad now that she had. She reached out to lightly clasp a finely knobbed and veined hand. "Can I do anything for you?"

Before Mrs. Poersel could answer that, Holt asked, "Are you in pain, ma'am?"

Mrs. Poersel looked at Gladys and actually laughed.

"Ain't modern medicine grand?" Gladys quipped. It had obviously become something of a joke between them.

"Not with this contraption," Mrs. Poersel said in cheerful answer to Holt's question, waving the IV line. "Mostly what I am is old. And glad to see Cara. So glad." Her gaze shifted to Ace. "Is it your baby?"

Cara glanced at Ace. Big-eyed, he stuck two fingers

into his mouth and warily looked around him. Holt had, thankfully, stripped him of his hoodie.

"Let me introduce you." Cara reached out, and Holt delivered the boy into her arms. She shifted him near the bed. "This is my son, Ace."

Mrs. Poersel studied him longingly. "Isn't he beautiful? Reminds me so of Albert."

"How is Albert?" Cara asked just to be polite. She only vaguely remembered Mrs. Poersel's rotund son.

"Waiting for me in heaven with his daddy," came the winsome reply. "Heart attack. Never did take care of himself. Cara Jane always said I spoiled him." Mrs. Poersel giggled and shrugged her delicate shoulders as if it were a great joke.

Cara was almost afraid to ask about the daughter, but she couldn't not do so now. She remembered Linda the best, though both Poersel siblings were decades older than her. "And Linda?"

"Very well. Retired." One gnarled, ivory hand wavered slightly. "Traveling the world."

"She just went to the church to drop off a cake for the fellowship supper," Gladys corrected with a smile, "but she's done some traveling all right. You name it, she's been there."

"Married well," Mrs. Poersel went on complacently, looking to Holt. "I hope she comes before I die." She fixed her gaze on Cara then, asking plaintively, "Will you pray that she comes home before I die?"

"I will," Cara said softly, glancing at the nurse, who merely shook her head. When Cara looked back to the bed, the sight of Mrs. Poersel with her hands folded and her snowy head bowed shocked Cara. Did the old dear expect her to pray at that very moment? Cara looked helplessly to Holt. He stepped up beside her an instant before his large, heavy hand covered her nape.

"Gracious heavenly Father," he said, his deep voice gentle and strong, "I thank You for Your loving kindness. Thank You for the place You've prepared for Your servant, Mrs. Poersel. I know You will welcome her with open arms in the company of her loved ones, but not until her daughter returns to this bedside. Thank You for Your generosity and patience in this, Lord, and for giving us this visit with an old and beloved neighbor. In the name of Your holy Son, amen."

"Eddie!" Mrs. Poersel exclaimed the moment Cara raised her head. "His name's Eddie, isn't it?"

Cara sneaked a glimpse at Holt, who seemed to accept this bizarre pronouncement with stoic calm. "Oh. Uh. My brother, you mean?"

"Cara Jane would be so proud of you both," Mrs. Poersel said. She smiled at Ace then, seeming to sink in on herself. "He's so beautiful. Makes me think of Albert."

Gladys sent them a meaningful look. Gulping, Cara nodded. "It was very nice to see you again, Mrs. Poersel."

"I miss her so," Mrs. Poersel sighed, her eyes closing. "All of them. I miss them all."

Holt slipped an arm around Cara, turning her toward the doorway with Ace. They navigated the crowded living room with Gladys trailing.

"Thank you all for coming," she said, standing patiently while Cara wrestled Ace into his hoodie. "You've made her last hours a little brighter."

Suspecting that Gladys had been nothing short of a Godsend to her old friend, Cara impulsively hugged the other woman, who surprisingly teared up.

"She done nothing but talk about your auntie since he's here last," Gladys said, waving a hand at Holt. "It's just the Lord's pure blessing that y'all came when you did. Now don't worry about her none. She's going straight to the mansions."

They parted with smiles and banked tears.

It hadn't been nearly as bad as Cara had feared. Sad, yes, and yet oddly uplifting, too. Glad she had come, unbearably relieved, she stepped out into the chill day.

"In my Father's house are many mansions," Holt said softly.

Cara faced him, the January temperature quickly cooling her overheated skin. "What was that?"

"It's from John 14," he told her, looking down into her eyes, "the very words of Jesus to His followers, the King James version. 'In my Father's house are many mansions: If it were not so, I would have told you. I go to prepare a place for you.'" He looked back to the house. "I'm glad to know her mansion is ready."

Cara marveled at this description of heaven. She could almost see Mrs. Poersel gliding through halls of marble and gold as if made for them, her earthly keepsakes replaced with valuables beyond description. Was Aunt Jane now living in one of those mansions that Jesus had prepared? A simple woman with simple tastes and simple wants, did she now enjoy unimagined luxury?

Yes, Cara believed she did.

And Addison? Her mother?

Cara closed her eyes, unable even to think the answers or to form the question that laid most heavily on her heart, the question concerning herself.

"When she speaks of Cara Jane, she means your aunt, doesn't she?" Holt asked, jerking Cara back to the moment.

Limp with relief, her emotions raw and her heart heavy, Cara could not lie to him again. "Yes," she answered simply.

"And Sharp is your maiden name."

"Yes. My maiden name."

Nodding, he ushered her down the steps and along the sidewalk, Ace snuggled against his chest.

"Thank you for bringing me here," Cara said once they reached the truck. She looked back at the house standing next to the Poersels', admitting, "I thought it would feel like home, but it doesn't."

"Is that why you were afraid to come?" he asked. Then, before she could even begin to formulate an answer, he mused, "Our fears never have as much power as we think they do." He tilted his head, as if listening to the sound of his own words again.

In that moment, she could almost, *almost,* believe them.

Holt was as disappointed as everyone else that Charlotte and Ty had not, after all, made the much-anticipated trip from Dallas for the big football championship game. Tyler had apologized profusely.

The family made do with an impromptu get-together of Hap's friends at the Heavenly Arms. Marie Wallace, Grover's wife, supplied her famous chicken lasagna, and Teddy Booker came with a Crock-Pot full of hot apple cider. It helped that Cara and Ace joined the party, with Ace happily beginning to lurch from lap to lap as soon as they arrived.

"Just like a real kid," Justus declared.

Cara blushed at this impolitic statement, compelling Holt to squeeze her shoulder. She'd been through a lot, seeing her old neighbor at death's door that afternoon. Receiving a smile for his efforts, he trailed her to the sofa and sat down next to her, remembering only as he settled himself how Charlotte and Ty had done the same thing and how everyone had known that they were drawn to each other even then.

He didn't want to be drawn to Cara. It hardly mattered now, for drawn he was. Once again buoyed by a visit with Mrs. Poersel, Holt lodged another tiny piece to the puzzle, a maiden name, and then put the whole mystery away to enjoy himself. Why not?

No one really cared a fig about the Super Bowl game except Ryan, but it gave them all something to do, something to celebrate, a reason to come together. Holt felt strangely content, oddly hopeful, and finally he faced the truth he'd been avoiding.

He wanted to let go of his suspicions and just trust Cara.

Cara Jane Sharp Wynne. He smiled, thinking of that little girl and the lightning bugs.

She seemed to enjoy the game, though she obviously knew next to nothing about football. Ryan proved only too happy to enlighten her, and she allowed him to do so with quiet indulgence. When Ace dropped off to sleep against Holt's shoulder, she rose, intending to take the boy out to their room and call it a night.

"You stay and enjoy your game," she urged, but with the boy already asleep in his arms, Holt wouldn't hear of it.

After carrying Ace out to the room, Holt worked quietly and efficiently with Cara to get the boy into bed. Then she turned, before he did, to move back into the outer room. Suddenly they stood face-to-face in the near dark, and somehow his arms were around her, those dainty hands of hers resting just above his elbows. He felt his heart stop beating and his head lowering toward her upturned face. At the last moment, Ace flopped over in bed, bumping against the wall, destroying the moment and restoring sanity. Holt cleared his throat as Cara glided away.

He took his leave quickly after that, and during the long night that followed, he pondered what he'd learned. It should not have been so important to him that her veracity had been proven, at least in this one area, by their visit with Mrs. Poersel. His relief felt entirely too profound, almost guiltily so, which meant that somehow he'd allowed himself to become attached to her.

Suddenly Holt could no longer be certain whose secrets were more dangerous, Cara's or his own.

Chapter Twelve

Holt finally found the time to take a look at Cara's car on Tuesday. Due to predicted precipitation, he parked the little foreign job beneath the drive-through at the motel for protection while he worked on it. He need not have bothered as the day turned bright and clear, if chilly. A quick adjustment stopped the clattering of a lifter arm, but he found another, more troubling issue that, had it manifested itself while Cara had been driving, could have resulted in disaster.

Though a pretty good mechanic in his own right, Holt knew he'd need help replacing a damaged pulley used by the serpentine belt that drove the engine. He called his old pal Froggy Priddy, of Froggy's Gas and Tire, the only mechanic's garage in town. Thankfully Froggy had little trouble getting his hands on the replacement part. An even greater blessing came when they discovered that they wouldn't have to completely remove the belt in order to replace the pulley. In less than two hours, they had adjusted the tension on the belt.

With the engine idling, Froggie crawled beneath the front end to check that all had been aligned properly, while Holt bent over the open engine compartment, tightening bolts and silently thanking God that Cara—he had stopped thinking of her as Cara Jane after their visit with Mrs. Poersel—had not found herself stranded or, worse, in an accident. As if summoned by the mere mention of her name to the Almighty, Cara appeared at Holt's elbow.

"It sounds wonderful!" she exclaimed, clapping her hands together. "The racket's gone!"

Holt straightened, smiled and nodded, tickled to see her so pleased, but when he opened his mouth to explain the greater ramifications of what he'd discovered, she struck him dumb by hopping up on tiptoe and throwing her arms around him in an exuberant hug.

"Mmm. Thank you so much!" She dropped back down onto her heels, grinning up at him. "You don't know how relieved I am. How much did it cost? I've put a little money back."

"Uh…" He couldn't remember what he'd been about to say to save his life. "It…needed an adjustment basically."

"That's all? Can I pay you for your labor, at least?"

"No. Uh-uh. No way."

Laughing, she clasped her hands together in the center of her chest before throwing him a kiss with a sweep of her arm. With that she danced away, beaming with gratitude.

He hadn't had a chance to tell her about the other issue, but somehow he didn't mind. So the repair would wind up costing him a couple hundred bucks. That made it a huge bargain, which he'd been quite willing to take on even before she'd stunned him with that affectionate display of gratitude. She'd seemed almost giddily happy since their visit to Mrs. Poersel, and he had no intention of dimming that smile, even if it did sometimes reduce his brain to a quivering mass of jelly.

Cara had disappeared into one of the waiting units when Froggy slid out from under the car, his lipless grin splitting his bland face ear to ear.

"Wonder how come I didn't get a big old hug?" he teased.

"'Cause you were under the car, nitwit." Froggy being one of Holt's best friends, the two traded regular barbs with genuine glee and false disdain.

Froggy sat up, dusting off his palms, back braced against the bumper. "Just as well. Kelly would break my head."

Kelly Priddy, Froggy's doting wife, clearly did not mind her husband's, well, froglike appearance, focusing instead on his good heart. She seemed to think all other women did the same, for she was known for her jealous ways, which Holt had always found rather funny. Suddenly, though, he had a better understanding of Kelly's motivation since he didn't much like the idea of Cara hugging Froggy as she had just hugged him.

"Tell you what we ought to do," Froggy said, getting up off the ground. "We ought to get together, the four of us. Kelly would sure like it, I know."

Holt smiled and agreed, liking the idea. Only later, after Froggy had gone, did it occur to Holt that he had no business even thinking of taking Cara over to the Priddy place as if the two of them were an actual couple.

Obviously his feelings for Cara had taken a dangerous path. Whatever she was, whatever the truth of her, she was not for him. He had to rein in these feelings, for nothing could come of them.

Cara had her path to walk, and Holt had his, as ordained by God above. Her path would, Holt suspected, eventually lead her to remarriage and a new father for Ace, but that wouldn't, couldn't, be him. His occupation, his calling, precluded marriage, as Holt knew only too well.

If he didn't feel quite as convinced of that as he once had, he chose not to acknowledge the fact, perhaps because he sensed that doing so could throw his whole world into a tailspin.

The first full week of February appeared to have been designed to test Holt's limits. The trial started on Sunday, right after church. Before that, Cara had seemed delighted with the world, happier and more relaxed than Holt had yet seen her. Afterward, she turned quiet and sadly contemplative, but none of his gentle prods prompted her to talk to him, and that left him feeling hollow and unappreciated. Then on Monday things really went haywire, starting with a sludge line at the drill site that backed up and gushed filth, blowing sixty feet of pipe out of the hole and missing the drill operator by inches.

The fellow's personal vehicle did not fare so well; a piece of pipe landed on the tailgate of his truck, crumpling it into a vee. Holt saw this as confirmation from God that drilling was no business for a family man, though fully half his crew, the drill operator included, were married with children.

After calling his insurance agent, Holt played plumber until he cleared the clog, wading through hip-deep slag to do it. That required hours of effort and left him so nasty he had to go home to his place to clean up before heading over to the motel.

He arrived later than usual by more than an hour and, to cap his day, found Cara and Ace in Room Five bawling their hearts out.

The sight of Cara sobbing as she jostled and petted her screaming son crushed Holt. He strode across the room, plucked the boy from her grasp and folded her to him with one arm, asking urgently, "What's wrong?"

As Ace sputtered to silence, hiccoughing and gasping, Cara pressed her face to Holt's chest. "I let him fall!"

Holt did a quick inspection of the boy, running his gaze over every visible inch. "Where did he hit?"

Sniffing, Cara reached upward. "His head."

Holt patted her shoulder, feeling paternal and a tad superior in the way of those who manage not to get caught up in a moment of hysteria, never mind how his heart had wrung when he'd come upon them. "Well, he's not bleeding and he's conscious, so it can't be too bad."

As if to confirm this prognosis, Ace sucked in a shuddering breath, laid his head on Holt's shoulder and stuck his hand in his mouth, drooling on Holt's neck.

"It's all my fault!" Cara wailed.

"If I'd been here on time…" Holt began, intending to comfort her, only to lose his train of thought as she clasped her arms around him, butted her face into his chest again and sobbed afresh. Sighing, he caressed the back of her head and let her cry, knowing that all those tears could not really be about a minor childhood accident.

Finally Holt sat her down in the only chair in the room, crouched at her feet with Ace on his knee and pushed away the strands of hair that had slipped from her ponytail. "Okay. Now what is this really about? Ace is fine, but you're making yourself sick over something. What's bothering you?"

She shook her head, not quite meeting his gaze even as she toyed with the edge of his shirt collar.

Holt sighed. "Last week, after we saw Mrs. Poersel, you were jubilant. This week, you're morose. I know something is bothering you, and it started with church yesterday."

In a small voice, she said, "I need to ask you something."

His heart thunked, but he kept his tone level. "Ask away."

Suddenly those soft gray eyes bore into his. "Can God forgive sins that you can't stop doing?"

Rocked, Holt shifted his weight, balancing on his bent toes. "God can forgive any sin that is confessed, Cara, but part of confession is turning away. By confessing our sins we acknowledge we are wrong and turn away from those wrong actions."

She didn't seem too happy with that explanation. "But what if you can't turn away? There are some things you just can't get out of!"

"Like what?"

Lips clamping, she looked toward the door. Ace

chose that moment to grab on to Holt's ear and twist it in a bid for his attention. Dredging up every ounce of patience he had left, Holt removed those little fingers with their surprisingly sharp nails from his person. At the same time he addressed Cara.

"You're going to have to trust me at some point, Cara."

That gray gaze zipped right back to his face. "Like you trust me?"

Holt felt as if he'd been kicked, and he didn't like it a bit. His psyche screamed about unfairness and justification. Every suspicion he'd ever had of her came roaring back.

"Give me a way to trust you, Cara," he demanded. "Anything." Questions too long pent up spilled out of him. "Why are your clothes more suited to the tropics than the Pacific Northwest? Why did your lawyer husband leave you destitute? Why were you scared out of your wits to go visit poor old Mrs. Poersel?" Cara turned her head away, silent as a tomb. "Why isn't your brother helping you?" he roared, growing more irate by the moment. "If you were my sister—"

"I'm *not* your sister!" she erupted, shooting up to her feet and sending the chair skittering. "I wish I were! Don't you think I'd rather be your beloved Charlotte than—" She bit her lip.

"What?" he urged, pushing up to his full height and shifting Ace to one side. "Than what, Cara?"

She looked at her son. "Alone," she said, her cracked voice draining away Holt's anger with that one word.

"You and Ace *aren't* alone," Holt vowed.

Taking Ace from him, she slid her hand over the

boy's pale head. "I might as well be," she whispered, whirling away. "Maybe it would be better if I was."

Knowing his temper had only made matters worse, Holt let her go.

"You're brooding," Charlotte said, her voice losing none of its censorial tone through the telephone.

Holt didn't argue the point. He could not get his exchange with Cara that afternoon off his mind. In what sin had she trapped herself, and why did she insist on carrying that burden alone? Didn't she know how much he wanted to help her, to trust her? Along with regret for losing his temper came indignation.

She had some nerve, not trusting him, after all he'd done for her.

In light of her stubbornness, he'd begun to think that he had no choice except to use every means at his disposal to figure her out, which was why he'd made this phone call.

"Are you done needling me yet?" he asked his too-perceptive sister. "If so, I'd like to speak to your husband."

Charlotte huffed and passed the telephone to Tyler. Some forty minutes later, Holt had instructions on how to run a detailed computer background check. He'd been careful not to mention Cara's name, which had undoubtedly left his brother-in-law with the impression that his concern centered on one of his roughnecks, but Holt didn't feel nearly as bad about that as he did about needing to find answers for the puzzle that was Cara.

Still, he dithered, torn between his need to know and his fear of knowing.

By morning, he'd all but convinced himself not to go through with it. Then, an hour or so before lunch, an overwhelming urge seized him. He left the rig site and drove straight to the motel. As expected, Hap and his cronies played Forty-Two at the table in the front room while Ace napped peacefully in the apartment and Cara tended to her work, leaving Holt free to slip behind the counter, retrieve Cara's employment file and seat himself in front of the computer in the office.

Holt didn't know exactly what he hoped to accomplish, but when Ty had told him how to use a popular satellite imaging site to check out physical addresses, he'd thought about how much relief he'd felt after stopping by Cara's old address in Duncan. Perhaps checking out Cara's previous address in Oregon this way would also ease his doubts.

Thanks to the lightning-fast internet connection, Holt located the necessary website within moments. He typed in the address and sat in amazement as the satellite beamed onto his screen an actual aerial photo of the site. He couldn't tell too much about it until he figured out how to zoom in, and then his hopes plummeted. Just in case he'd gotten something wrong, he went through the whole process again several times from step one, but no matter what he did that same image kept loading onto the computer screen.

For some minutes he sat there staring at the used car lot where Cara Jane Wynne had supposedly lived until widowed less than a year earlier. Clearly it had been decades, at best, since any residential structure could have stood at that address.

Sick at heart, Holt rubbed a hand across his forehead, trying to think of every possible reason why Cara might have found it necessary to use a bogus address. Suddenly he remembered making a photocopy of her driver's license. Flipping through her folder, he found the photocopy. Would the state of Oregon have issued a license with an incorrect address? Not likely.

Hands shaking, Holt looked up the Social Security number in her file, then went to the website that Ty had recommended. It took several tries for him to get the data that he sought, but when the necessary page finally loaded, he carefully read the information provided, information corresponding to the number that Cara had repeatedly written on her employment forms.

That number did, indeed, belong to Cara Jane Wynne. Unfortunately the Cara Jane Wynne to whom that number belonged had been born in 1926!

Holt dropped his head into his hands, close to tears and intending to pray, but his mind seemed frozen to the fact that the woman he knew as Cara Jane Sharp Wynne had assumed a false identity. The most logical explanation seemed to be that she'd assumed the identity of her late aunt. How else would Cara have known Mrs. Poersel? Holt realized that she'd used that knowledge to consolidate her position at the Heavenly Arms, and a tide of all-too-familiar anger swamped him. Before he even knew it, he was on his feet and striding for the door, intent on confrontation.

Hap, Grover and the others stopped what they were doing to watch him leave, but Holt said not a word. What could he say? That he'd known all along she was a liar? That he could have proven it weeks ago if he'd just had the nerve? That he'd somehow let himself drift in an agony of attraction and doubt?

He caught her preparing to enter one of the rooms. The smile with which she greeted him cut him to the quick, and that just ratcheted up his temper another notch. Striking a pose, he brought his hands to his hips, one knee cocked.

"So you lived at a used car lot," he accused without preamble. He'd intended to use a light, ironic tone but had been unable to prevent a sarcastic edge.

The color drained from her face, telling him that she hadn't just pulled that address out of thin air. She'd picked it on purpose. He tried to laugh.

"Guess there could've been a house there once, say forty years ago. But no problem, right, since you were born in 1926!"

She literally reeled, bouncing off the building at her back. He hadn't meant to shout. He'd meant to be as cold as steel, but his voice had risen out of control.

"Why, Cara?" he demanded. "Or is that even your name?"

She nodded mutely, and that he felt even the slightest relief infuriated him all over again.

"Where did you get the false ID?" he demanded, wanting her to understand that this went beyond mere lies.

At least she didn't deny it. "A-a man my h-husband knew."

"You've broken the law. You get that, don't you?"

"Y-yes," came her only answer. She glanced up at him then, her gray eyes wide and stark in her pale face.

Surprisingly, in the face of such woe and despondence, he found it difficult to hold on to his anger, but he couldn't just let it go. "Is that all you've got to say for yourself?"

Shaking her head, she croaked, "I'll clear out."

She left the housekeeping cart where it stood and stumbled away, hands clasped before her, shoulders hunched. He watched her go, his justifiable anger sliding into extreme frustration.

"Arrrrgh!"

Grasping tufts of hair with both hands, he waited. It was over. He'd proved her a liar, and that was the end of it.

Yet, the much-hoped-for relief did not materialize. Instead, frustration quickly morphed into dismay and then, suddenly, something very like panic.

Throwing back his head, he gazed heavenward, reaching out in wordless agony for understanding, enlightenment. When it came, he'd have rejected it if he could have, but truth was truth, and the awful truth was that he did not want her to go, could not let it be over.

He wanted her to stay. Even more than that, he wanted the truth, he wanted her to stay.

Bowing his head, he pressed the heels of his hands to his eyes and spoke urgently to God in his mind.

Now what? The lies are out there, and I'm still lost. Help me. Show me what to do. You've never failed me yet, Lord. Show me how to let her go. Or how to make her stay.

Swallowing, he started for her room.

* * *

She threw her clothing on the bed, mostly because in her urgency and terror she couldn't remember what she'd done with the suitcases. She had to get out of there fast, before she came apart or Holt notified the authorities. She couldn't take time to cry, to plan, to think. She had to go. Now.

Of course she'd known that it would come to this. For a little while after her visit with Mrs. Poersel, she'd lived in the happy dream of everything being okay, of her lies going undetected and Holt's suspicions of her dwindling into forgotten impulse. She'd gone to church on Sunday morning convinced that the worst lay behind her. Then Grover had spoken from the tenth chapter of Romans, sweeping away her relief and hope in the space of a few minutes.

Not only did the lies and secrets still exist, Cara had seen that they literally held her captive and would eventually destroy her.

Now they had. Or soon would if she didn't get out of there.

Closing an empty dresser drawer, she hurried into the closet and grabbed her son's things off the shelf, remembering only then that Ace slept in the apartment across the way. Panicked, she tossed his stuff at the bed and rushed toward the door, only to draw up short when it opened and Holt strode into the room.

He took one look at the bed, closed the door and leaned against it. "Stop it."

Steeling herself, she lunged forward and tried to push him out of the way. "I have to get my son!"

"Stop it!" he commanded again, refusing to budge.

"I only want to help." Seizing her by the upper arms, he shook her hard enough to snap her head back. "Don't you get it? I want to help."

She tried to push his hands away, teetering on the very edge of control. "You can't help! No one can. I have to do it myself. That's my only chance!"

"For what?" he demanded.

"To protect my son!"

She clapped a hand over her mouth, lest the whole ugly story fall out.

"From who? From what?" he pleaded, olive-green gaze darkened with concern and something else she'd rather not identify.

"I can't tell you." Too late she realized that his anger could be borne easier than his pain and disappointment, much easier than his caring. She shook her head, forced back the tears, and shut her eyes so she wouldn't have to see the emotion in his.

"Answer me one question," he begged, dropping his hands from her. "Are you hiding from Ace's father?"

"No! No. My husband is dead."

Until she saw Holt's relief, she didn't even realize that she'd looked at him. She slammed her eyes shut again when he reached for her. As his long, strong arms folded her against him, she cried out, afraid she might shatter. For a long moment, she tried to resist his comfort and the hope it offered, but both lures proved too great. She gave up and leaned into him, weak with need.

His large, capable hand invaded her hair, pressing her head against his chest. Listening to the beat of his heart, letting the heat of his body warm her chilled, raw nerve endings, she absorbed him, from his unique, earthy scent to the strength that defined him. In that moment nothing had ever seemed more dear, more sweet, more safe.

Knowledge coalesced. She understood in a blinding flash that she had misjudged him. Holt was not like any other man she'd known, not her absent, ghostlike father, not her scheming, selfish brother, not her arrogant, egotistical father-in-law, not her shallow, self-absorbed husband. Especially not her late husband.

Addison had never argued with her about anything; neither had he consulted her, even about her own likes and dislikes, which he had ignored as blithely as he'd discounted her concerns and hurts. She'd often wondered if she mattered to him as much as his stylish wardrobe and luxury car. He'd seemed to consider her nothing more than a convenience, an adjunct to his home, which hadn't really even been his but simply a way for his parents to keep their only son dancing to their tune.

No, Holt wasn't anything like Addison. Not only did Holt make his own way in the world, he did it without cutting corners and worked to assure everyone in his orbit the same privilege. Including her.

What was it then that disturbed her so greatly about Holt? Something more than just the fear that he would feel morally bound to inform her in-laws of her whereabouts colored her reactions to this man.

She had her answer a moment later when he tugged her head back and kissed her.

Until that very instant, she hadn't realized how long she'd been waiting for him to do that. When she found herself looping her arms about his neck, she understood how ardently she wanted this, how keenly she had hoped for it. Only then, as sweetness poured into her and her foolish heart sang, did she admit to herself that the problem wasn't Holt at all.

The problem was how she felt about him.

Chapter Thirteen

In the end she stayed simply because Holt asked it of her.

"We need you around here, Cara, in case you haven't noticed."

"I want to stay," she admitted shakily, not quite able to look at him after that kiss. "Just don't ask me questions that I can't answer, Holt, please." She didn't know how he'd found out that she'd faked her identity, but it hardly mattered. The only surprise, really, was that it had taken him so long.

She sat on the edge of the bed amid the strewn clothing and gazed determinedly at her hands. Holt stood beside the door, poised to exit, as if the need to touch might seize them both again unawares. She appreciated the distance and lamented it at the same time.

"Will you tell me your real name, at least?"

"No." Then, because she somehow needed him to know, she relented as far as she was able. "Cara Kay. Cara Kay Sharp. I won't give you my married name. Don't ask."

"Not Cara Jane then," he commented in a rueful voice.

"Cara Jane was my great-aunt," she told him, figuring he already knew. "I think I hoped by taking her full name to keep the best part of my old life and maybe even to be something like her."

"A good woman, then."

"The best I've ever known."

"Mrs. Poersel certainly seemed fond of her."

"They were very close."

"She raised you," he ventured cautiously. "Your aunt raised you?"

"Yes." Cara winced, finding it very difficult to lie to him. "And no. She was a great influence on my life, but I only spent summers with her. From as far back as I can remember until she died."

"Ah. That explains a lot." He rubbed a hand over his face, seeming weary and frazzled.

"You have to understand," she pleaded, gazing up at Holt. "Those were the best times of my childhood. They're all that got me through the rest of it. Aunt Jane sent the bus tickets, knowing my mother was always glad to get rid of us. Mom had to keep us during the school year. Otherwise she couldn't get the food stamps and other assistance, but in the summer we were Aunt Jane's. I always thought of it as going home to my real life."

His gaze seemed to turn inward. "You clung to the place and times when it all felt good, didn't you? That's why you came back to Oklahoma."

She nodded, slumping forward with relief. She had wondered if he could understand, given the caliber of his own family. Yes, he'd suffered loss and tragedy, but he'd had Hap and Ryan and Charlotte and even this whole town.

Eden, indeed. She wondered if he knew how clean and whole and safe and entirely beautiful this place seemed to her, with its ever-present pump jacks sucking the black oil from the earth, its streets named for trees and flowers and the park with its grand, whimsical bridge spanning a narrow, muddy stream. The three blocks of downtown, with its circa 1930s storefronts, felt like an oasis to her, an immutable place in a world of constant change. Why, the most modern building in town seemed to be the little city hall at the north end of Garden Avenue, but she hadn't seen the schools or any points east of Booker's old-fashioned grocery. Old buildings were not what gave the town its sense of community, however. That came from its friendly people. What she wouldn't give to be a real part of a town like this.

"I didn't want to lie to you," she told Holt in a small, wavering voice. "I don't want to keep secrets. I'm so sorry."

He opened the door a crack and stood staring through it for some moments before he faced her again. "Give me the driver's license and Social Security card so I can destroy them."

She would be trapped then. Oh, she could still run if she had to, but how would she find work? How would she support Ace?

"Give them to me, Cara," he repeated softly. "It has to end here."

Without further thought, she went to the bedside table and drew out her wallet, including every dollar of her savings, from the drawer. She handed over the whole thing and waited while he thumbed through it, extracted the cards and slipped them into his hip pocket before passing the wallet back to her. She snapped it closed and folded her arms.

He opened the door a little wider. "All right," he said, just that and nothing more. Then he left her.

Cara fell onto the bed, weak with emotion. She did not know what would happen next. She had placed herself and her son in Holt Jefford's large, capable hands. Now she could only pray that it had been the wisest course. But really, with her heart telling her to stay and nowhere else to go, what else could she have done?

When she finally dragged herself back to work, Holt had gone, and he did not return to help her that afternoon or any that followed for the rest of the week. Accepting Holt's absence as far less than she deserved, Cara left Ace to Hap's tender care in the afternoons and went about her business as best she could.

All else remained as it had been, with Holt and often Ryan dragging in to plant their feet beneath the dinner table, except that Holt would take himself off again as soon as he finished his meal, and Cara would pretend that her heart did not go with him.

Obviously he had said nothing to Hap or anyone else about what he'd learned, and for that she felt profound, if silent, gratitude. Just one question plagued her.

How long, she wondered, could it go on? How long before one of them broke beneath the strain?

* * *

"Hel-lo-o!"

That single word called out from the kitchen galvanized the entire dinner table. Three forks dropped and three chairs scooted back at the same time.

"My stars!" exclaimed Hap, as everyone got their feet. "It's Charlotte!"

A slight redhead appeared in the doorway just as Ryan, whose chair stood closest to the kitchen, reached it.

"Sis!"

Grabbing her up in a bear hug, he spun with her in his arms. Charlotte Jefford Aldrich laughed, then launched herself at Holt, who caught her as easily as he might have done Ace. With much laughter, he sat her on her feet. She turned with outstretched arms to Hap.

"Granddad."

The old man's chin wobbled, which was all it took to make Cara's eyes water. She'd been living on the edge of tears ever since Holt had learned of her duplicity.

After a long hug, Hap backed away, rasping, "You look fine. Marriage agrees with you."

Beaming, Charlotte took hold of the sides of her fine, brown tweed jacket, holding them out as she might a skirt, and turned in a circle, showing off expensive jeans and a rust-colored cashmere turtleneck that perfectly matched the lining of the jacket. Cara wouldn't have been surprised to see her decked out in satin and furs, given what she'd heard about the Aldrich fortune.

"Where's Ty?" Ryan asked, looking past Charlotte expectantly.

"Putting our luggage in our room. Assuming it's empty and our key still works."

Hap snorted at that. He usually kept the room vacant just for them. He turned to Cara, waving a hand. "Charlotte, honey, this here is Cara Jane and her boy, Ace. We told you about her."

Cringing inwardly at Hap's use of her aunt's full name, Cara rose as Charlotte reached a hand across the table, a smile warming her pleasant face. "Hello, Cara Ja—"

"Just Cara, please," she interrupted. Cara Jane seemed so false now, a constant reminder of her dishonesty.

"It's nice to meet you, Cara. I've heard so much about you and your son. All good."

That made Cara want to cry again, but she just smiled weakly and returned the compliment. "Oh, it couldn't be as good as what your brothers and grandfather have to say about you and your husband."

Charlotte laughed and squeezed her hand. "My family's prejudiced in that regard." She swept her gaze over the table, lifting her eyebrows at the chicken enchilada casserole and salad that Cara had made for Friday dinner. "This looks good. Is there enough for two more?"

"There is if Holt don't make his usual hog of himself," Hap declared, sitting down.

Holt rolled his eyes, going for extra chairs, while Ryan dipped into the kitchen for more plates and cutlery. "Why does everybody pick on my eating habits?"

"Maybe because we all envy you," said a newcomer, striding into the room. This had to be Tyler Aldrich, Charlotte's husband. Handsome in a bland, well-groomed way with dark hair and pale blue eyes, he beamed at the assembled group.

Hap came to his feet again. Tyler engulfed the old man in an affectionate hug and kissed him on the cheek. Holt hurried over to drop the chairs and pump Tyler's hand, while Ryan all but threw the plates onto the table in order to be next while Hap introduced Cara and Ace. Everyone sat down, rearranging to make room for the couple. Somehow Holt wound up sitting next to Cara, his arm balanced on the upper back edge of her chair.

Charlotte dished out meals for Ty and herself amid a babble of conversation concerning their unexpected arrival and Ty's mother's health.

"We thought we'd surprise you, that's all," Charlotte said.

"Mom's fine," Tyler supplied. "Scared us a bit until we figured out the problem."

"Ty's sister is looking out for her while we're gone," Charlotte added.

Ty looked at Holt meaningfully. "You wouldn't believe how those three women gang up on me. I cannot wait to get our house built here, even if my brother is threatening to move in with us to escape Mom and sis. Speaking of which, I have the blueprints in my car."

That launched the men into the subject of building. Charlotte, meanwhile, confided to Cara, "He doesn't mean a word of it. He adores his family."

Tyler pressed a kiss to her temple. "Especially you." He went back to his discussion, forking up bites of chicken enchilada between comments. Ty sat back, apparently replete, and turned his attention to Cara. "That was very good. Thank you."

Charlotte nodded, smiling. "I think I'll be needing this recipe."

"We'll trade then," Cara told her. "These guys are always asking for things I've never heard of before. What, by the way, is chicken and dumplings?"

"Chicken stewed with onions and a kind of batter that makes a rich sauce and thick lumps called dumplings," Charlotte explained. "I put peas in mine."

"Black-eyed peas again," Cara muttered. Hap and Holt erupted in laughter.

"It's green peas," Charlotte clarified, "but what is this about black-eyed peas?"

Hap waved a hand. "Cara just happened to join us on New Year's Eve."

Charlotte dropped her fork. "And no doubt you made the poor girl cook that very night!"

"Believe me, it was better than the alternative," Cara said. She flushed red the next instant. Thankfully both Holt and Hap laughed again, agreeing heartily, but that did little to ameliorate her embarrassment. "I'll, um, just clear the table and start the dishes," she muttered, reaching for soiled plates.

"I'll help," Holt announced, rising.

"That's my job," Ryan protested lightly from his chair.

Cara rose, shaking her head. "No, no. You two enjoy your visit with your sister. If you'll just watch Ace for a few minutes, I can make quick work of these."

"I'll help you," Holt said firmly, taking the stacked plates from her hands.

Charlotte and Ty traded looks. Then a smile spread

across Ty's face. "Lots to be said for doing dishes," he told Holt meaningfully.

"You would know," Holt retorted, carrying the plates into the kitchen.

Cara slid a puzzled glance around the table, took in the speculative expressions, put her head down and snatched up as many dirty dishes as she could carry before hurrying out after Holt. She found him leaning back against the counter, his big hands cupping its rolled edge. Only after she'd put in the stopper and started the water running did Holt speak.

"Ty used to wash dishes just so he could be close to Charlotte," he informed her.

Cara's heart thunked. "Oh." No one had to tell her that Holt's motives differed in regard to herself.

In confirmation of that fact, Holt softly said, "I just thought I ought to tell you not to bother servicing Number Eight while Charlotte and Ty are here. Like most newlyweds, they value their privacy."

Cara nodded and willed away her envy. "I understand."

As she squirted soap into the stream of running water, Holt reached beneath the sink for the scrap can, crowding close. She skittered out of his way, gasping, "What are you doing?"

He turned a frown up at her. "Helping clean up."

Cara looked at the pile of dirty dishes on the counter and shook her head. It hurt to know that he'd used this just as an excuse to caution her about maintaining the privacy of the newlyweds. No one had to tell her that he regretted that kiss. His absences had spoken volumes on that score.

"I—I'd rather you tended to Ace. He's missed you."
She felt lower than an inchworm, using her son to get
rid of Holt, even if what she'd said happened to be true.

Holt stared at her before plunking down the can on
the counter and leaving the room. A moment later, she
heard him exclaim, "Hey, little buddy, come along with
me."

She knew that he took Ace from his makeshift high
chair and carried him into the outer room. The others soon followed, though Charlotte first popped in to
offer assistance.

"Oh, no. This is what I'm paid to do," Cara protested. "Besides, your family's anxious to spend time
with you." After a pause, Charlotte smiled, nodded and
left her.

Alone in the kitchen, it felt to Cara as if she'd lost her
own place in the family, which was absurd. She'd never
had a place in the Jefford family. No matter how kind
the Jeffords had been, she was hired help, just as she'd
told Charlotte, and that position was precarious at best.

With that in mind, as soon as Cara finished cleaning, she went to fetch her son, declaring, "Bath time."

Ace stood on Holt's feet, giggling happily, his tiny
hands lost in Holt's much larger ones, while Holt moved
his knees up and down, pretending to march from a
sitting position on the couch. Cara picked up her son,
grasping him just beneath his arms. To her chagrin, as
she lifted him, the boy made a grab for Holt, one hand
closing in the fabric of Holt's shirt.

"You've got a fan there," Tyler commented laconi-
cally, sitting next to Charlotte on the opposite couch,
his arm about her shoulders.

"Yeah, we're real buddies," Holt said as Cara pried Ace loose.

He screeched as Cara swiftly carried him away from Holt. Nodding blind smiles in the direction of Charlotte and Tyler, Cara moved for the door, calling out, "Nice to meet you."

The usual, polite rejoinders followed her from the room. Holt did not. She didn't expect him to, which made her disappointment that much more difficult to explain.

Cara woke the next morning to the sound of something hitting the window. When she opened the door, what peppered her face felt cold and wet. She turned on the television to find a weather alert crawling across the bottom of the screen.

The long-predicted weather front had finally arrived, dumping sleet over New Mexico, Texas and Oklahoma. Authorities advised everyone to stay indoors and off the roads, but how many would have missed or ignored that warning? Cara looked out the window, unsurprised to find a strange car parked beneath the drive-through. It wouldn't be the last vehicle to stop at the motel that day.

Over the course of a few hours, sleet turned the roads and ground into one giant skating rink. Icicles grew from eaves and tree branches, tinkling like wind chimes in the frosty breeze. It soon became obvious that they had a real crisis brewing.

Before lunchtime, half a dozen other vehicles slid, literally, into the lot, two of them winding up in the ditch alongside the roadway. By early afternoon, tractor trailer rigs lined the road, leaving barely a single lane free for travel, had anything been moving. Those without sleeper compartments wanted rooms in which to wait out the storm. Fortunately, many of the regular oil field workers who bunked weekdays at the Heavenly Arms had set out the evening before for their respective homes, leaving some of the rooms contracted by the local oil companies free for rental. Those who'd slept in found themselves as stuck as everyone else.

"We'll have 'em stacked up like cordwood if this don't let up," Hap worried.

He sent Cara out to ask the remaining oil field workers to double up, freeing more space. Not ten minutes after she returned to the lobby, Holt showed up with a family of six.

"Found them stranded in their car behind a sand truck," he explained. The county vehicle had broken down right in the middle of the highway. "They've got someone out there working on it now, but I'm betting 81 is blocked for at least tonight."

Hap looked at the bedraggled couple and their four children, all elementary age or older, standing in the warmth of the lobby. "They can use Cara's room, but we don't have any more cots. Won't be enough beds."

"Or blankets," Charlotte added, coming in from the apartment. They'd all been scrambling to accommodate the refugees from the storm, but Charlotte had been a one-woman army, in constant motion with her auburn braid flying out behind her. "I've called Ryan on my cell," she reported, "and he'll take these folks over at his place if Holt can get them there."

Holt nodded. "What I don't know is whether or not I can get back out to my place. Took me all day to get into town, and the roads are worse now than when I started out."

"What I'm wondering," Tyler said, arriving just then, "is how we're going to feed this lot."

Hap whistled. "I'll call Teddy and Grover. Maybe they'll have some ideas."

"I'll get our things moved over here," Cara said.

"Good idea," Holt told her, nodding toward the front window. A man bundled against the cold tramped and slid on foot across the lawn. "Looks like we'll be needing it."

"Tyler and I can sleep in here," Charlotte volunteered, nodding toward the lobby, "so Cara and Ace can have my old room."

"Naw, you can have my bed," Hap said. "I'll sleep on one of the couches."

"I'm going to need the other," Holt informed them all. "For now, let's just get these folks over to Ryan's and everyone else moved. If we have to, we'll make other adjustments later."

The man pushed through the outer door just then, gasping and looking worried. "Can you put up two kids and two adults? My family's stuck in our car maybe a mile up the road."

Holt looked at Hap before addressing the harried fellow. "You come along with me." He nodded toward the family of six. "We'll drop off these folks, pick up your bunch, and the room will be ready when we get back."

The fellow closed his eyes in relief. "Thank you. Thank you."

"Thank God for snow chains," Holt said, going through the door.

"Where on earth did he get snow chains?" Tyler wondered aloud, as the party filed out.

"Eh, he keeps 'em in case he has to check on his rig and crew out in the panhandle," Hap explained. "They get lots worse weather out there than we do here. Usually."

Charlotte looked to Cara. "I'll help you move your things. Ty will take care of ours."

"Me and Ace will hold down the fort here," Hap said, waving them away.

Tyler had been spreading rock salt, which made walking across the pavement a little easier. Instead of hauling everything across to the apartment, however, Cara decided to take just what they'd need most and leave the rest in the trunk of her car, mindful of the cramped conditions in Charlotte's old room. With Charlotte's help, it didn't take long. Cara made a stoic, silent vow not to care, though it felt as if she'd lost her one true sanctuary.

"I'll come back and change the sheets," Cara said as they left, their arms full.

"I'll get the laundry started then," Charlotte said, "but I don't think we ought to be worrying about housekeeping until the roads clear. Folks can do for themselves until this passes."

"Now we just have to figure out how to feed everyone."

"Oh, I wouldn't worry about that," Charlotte told her with a smile.

Within the hour, Grover and Teddy showed up on foot with bags of groceries and the news that both Booker's store and the café downtown had opened and would remain so as long as necessary. Moreover, city workers were busy sanding and salting. The highways and county roads remained closed, but the city would soon be maneuverable, at least in the short-term, with more sleet predicted during the night.

Thanking God that she and Ace were safe from the storm, along with everyone else at the motel, Cara promised herself that would be enough for her. More, surely, than she deserved.

Chapter Fourteen

Outside, streetlamps softly illuminated a sparkling wonderland of trees, grass and buildings frosted in ice. Inside, with everyone hunkered down for the night, the Jeffords figured they might as well enjoy their time together. Despite predictions of more sleet and frigid temperatures, everyone could relax and wait out the storm.

The family sat down to a meal prepared by Cara and Charlotte. Hap spoke an eloquent prayer of thanksgiving and petition over it. Afterward, Hap smiled at those around the table.

"We couldn't have got through this day without every one of you."

Cara smiled. She'd felt very much a part of things all day long. They'd worked together side by side to handle the crisis, not just the Jeffords but the whole town.

They spent the evening playing dominoes and watching weather reports on the TV. To Cara's surprise and secret pleasure, Holt took it upon himself to teach her the game of Forty-Two, pulling her chair close to his and murmuring instructions in her ear. Laughter and a sense of well-being blanketed them all as surely as ice blanketed the ground outside. Nevertheless, Cara tried to maintain an emotional distance.

She dared not believe that, just because Holt knew some of her secrets and hadn't turned out her and her son, all would be well. The worst, to her shame, remained hidden and must continue that way. With that in mind, Cara and Ace retired for the night before everyone else.

The day's activity should have guaranteed both a sound night's sleep. Unfortunately, neither rested well. Ace had gotten too acclimated to the portable crib, now being used by a three-year-old in Room 12, and Cara could not completely relax for fear that Ace would roll off the side of the high double bed that they shared.

Morning found her bleary and aching, but the hot coffee and breakfast that Charlotte provided helped. Though reluctant—attending services these days just seemed to depress her—Cara got ready and tramped with everyone else across the lawn and up the street to the church. Normal Sunday dress yielded to necessity, which left her decked out in jeans, a sweater of Charlotte's, Hap's old coat and a pair of galoshes. The condition of the outlying roads naturally diminished the congregation, but nothing diminished the agony of guilt that Cara continued to carry in her heart, and as usual Holt noticed.

"You okay?" he asked quietly, trudging along beside her on the way back to the motel after the service. He carried Ace, as he had earlier.

Cara nodded, determined to feel only gratitude. "Yes, thank you."

"Are you two comfortable in Charlotte's old room?"

"We'll manage," she said, before succumbing to concern. "Although, I'd appreciate if someone could push the bed up against the dresser so Ace can't fall off it. Otherwise I don't know how I can put him down for a nap."

"I'll see to it after lunch," Holt promised.

He shifted the bed, with Tyler's help, as soon as they rose from the luncheon table. Charlotte, however, saw the real problem.

"We've got to clean this out," she decided. "I shouldn't have put it off this long."

"Oh, no. It's all right," Cara protested, "so long as Ace can't fall out of bed."

Charlotte wouldn't let it rest, however, bringing up the subject over breakfast the next morning. "There's just no good excuse," she stated flatly, "and it's not like we have anything else to do today."

"But it's a lot of trouble," Cara pointed out, "for temporary convenience." She'd thought about it during the night and decided that she couldn't, in good conscience, go on taking up rentable space, no matter how much it hurt to relinquish that little kitchenette, if Charlotte insisted on cleaning out her old bedroom. "So if you're sure about this, then Ace and I will make the move permanent."

Holt got up from the table and walked over to gaze into the bedroom, rubbing his chin. "I've got a smaller bedroom set at my place," he said. "We could swap them out. That would help a lot. Provided you girls approve."

"It's Cara's call," Charlotte insisted. "Maybe by the time we get all this junk emptied out, the roads will be

clear enough for the two of you to go take a look at it."
Abruptly, she snapped her fingers. "I wonder if Agnes
Dilberry's still got that crib for sale."

"I'll find out," Holt said.

"Me and Ace are gonna watch the reports," Hap announced, hobbling toward the front room. "One of you
bring him out to me."

Holt strode over and plucked the boy from his seat,
following Hap.

"Granddad sure is fond of that little guy," Charlotte
said, leaning her elbows on the table.

"I'm glad of that," Cara admitted.

"Not as fond as Holt, though," Charlotte went on.
"I thought Ryan was the one with an affinity for children, but you two seem to have worked a change in my
big brother."

Cara muttered, "Oh, I don't think it's anything we've
done."

Charlotte chuckled and confided softly, "It's not
just Ace. He follows you with his eyes every moment.
Hardly even tries to hide it."

He's probably afraid I'll steal something, Cara remarked to herself, bowing her head.

Holt reappeared just then, his cell phone in hand. "I
called Agnes. She'll have the crib ready for pickup soon
as the weather clears."

"Oh. Uh, I don't know," Cara began, thinking of
her meager savings. "How much does she want for it?"

"Why?" Holt asked. "You're not paying for it."

"But—"

"I'll let the two of you work it out," Charlotte said
airily, popping up and moving toward the bedroom.

"Just remember, big brother, you catch more flies with honey than acid."

Holt stared down at Cara. "I'm not trying to catch flies."

"Girlfriends, then!" came the retort from the bedroom.

Holt's gaze never wavered from Cara's.

Blinking rapidly, she opened her mouth to speak, but what was she supposed to say in light of his silence? After a moment, he followed his sister into the bedroom.

Cara felt stuck to the chair.

Why, she wondered, hadn't he spoken up? Why let his sister assume that they were linked romantically? Holt simply could not think of her that way, despite that one kiss, not now that he knew what he did about her. Could he?

Ridiculous! Holt told himself as the knot in his stomach tightened. What did it matter what Cara thought of his place? He'd proudly built the house nearly ten years ago, and he loved living out here in the middle of this quarter section, surrounded by his own land and his own cattle and his own things. He didn't care what anyone else thought of it. Except suddenly he did.

He took the turn off the narrow county road, the truck bumping roughly over the cattle guard. Beside him, Cara sat up a little straighter, her gaze avidly sweeping the area.

"Oh, this is wonderful," she said, but he imagined her comment had to do with being out and about after three days cooped up inside the motel. "I love the trees and the way the ground sort of rolls, even the barn. It's beautiful."

Holt relaxed somewhat as the truck barreled down the long, dusty drive. Okay, so she didn't hate the surroundings, not that it mattered. He was *not* trying to impress her. He didn't know what he was doing with her, frankly, only that he hated the air of shame and timidity about her lately. He ached for her sometimes, but he didn't have a clue what to do to help her. She'd lied, bought fake identity papers from some creep that her husband had known and wouldn't reveal why, even when confronted, but Holt had come to the conclusion that it must be for a good reason. He couldn't reconcile anything else with the woman and mother he'd found her to be, and he was sick and tired of trying to keep a "safe" distance between them.

The truck made the curve in the drive, and she gasped.

"You built this? All by yourself?"

He brought the truck to a stop in its usual spot beneath the carport and killed the engine. "Who told you?"

"Charlotte," she answered, opening her door with one hand and releasing her safety belt with the other.

A gust of wind whipped through the brief opening. Thanks to that dry wind every exposed expanse of road had been swept clean during the night, despite the frigid temperatures. Holt hurried to join Cara on the porch, where she huddled inside Hap's old coat, one mittened hand placed flat against the paneled door.

"Red!" she exclaimed approvingly.

"To match the roof and the barn," he admitted, reaching down to turn the knob and get them both out of that cruel wind. He'd never seen the need to lock up the place out here.

Her eyes wide, Cara tiptoed through the tiny foyer set off by spindles from the greater room. Head pivoting, she took in everything from the open living area with its spare leather furniture to the kitchen visible beyond the L-shaped breakfast bar and the empty dining space.

"I especially like the floor," she said.

Holt had laid every plank of the polished wood by his own hand. "Charlotte picked out the rugs," he told her, puffed up with pride.

Cara looked at the bandanna-patterned throw rugs. "I see you love red." He shrugged, inordinately pleased that she'd pegged his favorite color.

"How many bedrooms?" she asked.

"Two." He gestured toward the hallway branching off on his right. "And two baths." He pointed to a door in the back wall of the kitchen. "Laundry room's over there, and that…" He directed his finger to the glass-paned door off one end of the living area. "That's my office."

He knew the place must seem somewhat bare to her, especially when compared to Hap's apartment, but Holt found it easier to keep the place neat and clean that way.

"It must be wonderful to own your own home," she commented wistfully, "and to be able to do this all yourself." She spread her hands. "Amazing."

Holt bowed his head, smiling as much at his earlier nervousness as at her approval of his home. "Thanks," he said, adding quickly, "The bedroom set we could swap for is in here." As he led her down the hall to a door on the left, he asked casually, "You and your husband didn't own a house then?"

"We lived in a house," she said. "It wasn't ours, though. It belonged to my in-laws." He paused, and she leaned a shoulder against the cream-colored wall, smiling ruefully. "Decorated and maintained according to their dictates."

Holt raised his eyebrows at that. "But it was your home even if it was their house."

She shook her head. "Not really. Whatever they thought we should have, that's what we had. Whatever they thought we should do, that's what we did. What *he* did." She dropped her gaze, murmuring, "They're very controlling. I should have realized they held the deed to the house."

Holt goggled at that. "You didn't know?"

"Not until Addison died," she told him, folding her arms.

"Your husband didn't tell you that your house belonged to his parents?" Holt couldn't believe the subject hadn't come up between them at some point.

"Addison wouldn't have," she answered softly, "because he knew what it meant to me." She lifted her head then, explaining, "You see, my brother and I grew up in apartments, a whole string of them, each one more of a dump than the last." A wan smile curled her lips. "I thought Aunt Jane's old house was a palace until I married Addison. Then I found out that luxury does not make a home." She pushed away from the wall, saying, "If you must know, that little kitchenette at the motel is the closest I've ever come to actually having a home of my own."

"Then you shouldn't give it up," Holt stated, hating that she'd done so even temporarily.

She shook her head, smiling. "No, it's best this way. It will be easier all around, for Ace especially. Besides," she added, "it feels more like we—" Breaking off, she looked away.

"Belong," he said, finding the word only as he said it. She nodded, keeping her gaze averted. *Maybe that's because you do,* he thought. Waving a hand, he silently invited her to take a look inside the room.

She stuck her head in, looking over the sleek furniture. "This is nice stuff. Are you sure you want to give it up?"

"I don't ever use it. Besides, Charlotte's old furniture is much finer. It's just bigger and more ornate than my usual style."

Cara shot him a shy smile. "I think I prefer your style."

"Okay. We'll swap it out then."

Her glowing smile was all the thanks he needed, enough to tell him that he'd been kidding himself long enough. The time had come to face facts. He still didn't know if anything could or should come of them, but he could no longer deny that his feelings were fully engaged.

He knew that he would be spending long hours in earnest prayer about that, leaving it to God how it all ultimately played out. He could only hope that, when all had been said and done, no one would be the worse for it.

* * *

Charlotte and Ty took their leave on Wednesday, the day before Valentine's Day. Cara and Ace settled into the apartment, his new crib tucked into a corner of the bedroom. A high chair and baby monitor had been acquired from the Dilberry attic, as well the fine oak crib. Cara felt almost like a part of the family, but that did not prepare her for what she found when she walked out of the bedroom the next afternoon with a newly awakened Ace in her arms.

Holt and Hap stood shoulder to shoulder, the former in his Sunday best, the other holding a mixed bouquet of flowers and a huge, heart-shaped box of chocolates.

"Happy Valentine's Day," Holt said. Cara promptly burst into laughing tears.

"Couldn't let the day go by unnoticed," Hap rasped, handing over the goodies. "Now go get yourself changed. Holt's taking you out on the town."

"Oh, but—"

"Grover and Marie are coming over with dinner, so don't be worrying none about me and the boy," Hap insisted.

"Charlotte left something in the closet for you," Holt told her. While Cara stood with her mouth open, he took Ace from her, adding, "And by 'town,' Hap means Lawton."

"That's fifty miles away!"

"So we'd best get an early start." With that, he turned her by the shoulder and gave her a little shove. Cara dithered for a moment, but then she rushed back into her room, excitement filling her. To think that they'd all done this for her! Hurrying to the closet, she found the garment bag hanging from the rod. She'd wondered why that had been left in there but had assumed that it contained some memento of Charlotte's. Opening the bag, she found a long-sleeved black velour knit dress with a square neckline and a pair of black velvet mules with kitten heels.

Blessing Charlotte for her generosity, Cara threw off her own clothes and went to work. Twenty minutes later, she stepped out of the bedroom, her heart pounding. With the use of a rubber band and a few pins, she'd managed to put up her hair in a simple twist with a spray of wisps coming out the top. Her plain, gold hoop earrings and a small pendant added a touch of glamour. Because she was shorter than Charlotte, the sleeves of the dress puddled at her wrists and the slightly flared skirt reached almost to her ankles, but Cara didn't think that mattered any more than the shoes being a couple sizes too large.

Both Holt and Hap stood up when she entered the room. Now Holt came forward with a crooked elbow. "Beautiful," he said. "Elegant. Perfect."

Cara beamed, and she kept beaming all through the evening.

The drive, filled with lighthearted conversation about Charlotte's recently improved sense of style, proved shorter than Cara expected. Perhaps, she mused, it had something to do with the company. Holt had made reservations at one of the finer restaurants in Lawton, so Cara soon found herself following a smiling young waitress through a dimly lit room tastefully decorated against a backdrop of oak planking and black lacquer. As they wound their way through tables dressed with black linens and red roses, Cara felt Holt behind her, his hand riding gently against the small of her back.

Compared to some of the restaurants Addison had frequented back in California, the place would probably be thought fairly pedestrian, but Cara appreciated the quiet atmosphere and the aura of privacy that came with it. Holt stepped up and quickly pulled out her chair for her as the waitress placed their menus on the table. Taking his seat opposite her, Holt laid aside his menu without even looking at it.

"You seem to know what you want," she noted, skimming her gaze over the heavy parchment page of her own menu.

"I do, yes."

She looked up into his warmly glowing eyes. Something shimmered between them, but she pushed it away. Best not to let her imagination run away with her. This amounted to an act of kindness on his part, not a declaration of romantic intent. She sat up a little straighter. "You've been here before then?"

"Nope." After a moment, he looked down, smoothing his napkin across his lap. "I took a look at the menu on the internet."

"Ah."

He folded his hands together. "Had to be sure it was the right sort of place."

"The right sort of place for what?"

"For a beautiful woman and a special occasion."

Cara caught her breath. She dared not take his sweet words too seriously, however. They were not sweethearts. This was just Holt taking care of her as he took care of everyone around him. His kindness and generosity moved her, though, misting her eyes. She looked back to the menu, saying softly, "Thank you."

"It's my pleasure," he told her. "This is nice. To tell you the truth, I can't remember the last time Valentine's was anything but just another day to me."

Cara remembered all too well her last Valentine's Day. Hugely pregnant, she'd sat home alone while Addison had claimed to be entertaining important clients. He'd come in long after she'd gone to bed and seemed peeved in the morning because she hadn't been appropriately thrilled with the wilted bouquet of flowers that he'd left on the kitchen counter the night before. Even sitting here in a borrowed dress and shoes that were too large, she felt special and pampered by comparison.

She tried to derail those feelings, knowing that they were unwarranted and dangerous, but Holt's smile and easy manner disarmed her. Now that he knew her true identity, he'd been generous to a fault. She almost missed the old suspicious Holt. At least she'd had no doubt where she'd stood with him. If he ever learned the whole truth about her, his generosity and thoughtfulness would undoubtedly turn to disdain. She prayed that never happened.

After a leisurely dinner, Holt surprised Cara yet again by announcing that he had prepurchased movie tickets via the computer. As he escorted her out of the restaurant, he remarked repeatedly that he hoped he'd made a good choice. Nothing she said seemed to lessen his concern on that score.

Once they arrived at the movie theater, Cara began to understand where that surprising angst came from, as it quickly became evident that he'd never laid eyes on the place before. He seemed somewhat befuddled by the electronic ticket checker and a tad overwhelmed by the multiple offering of the many screens. Finally, they found the correct theater and excused their way past a long row of early arrivals to take the only pair of remaining seats.

The film, a comedy, kept them both in stitches. It was not one that Cara would have chosen, but she found it surprisingly charming, almost as charming as the man at her side. Once as they were both reeling with laughter, their shoulders collided. Holt casually slid his arm around her, and there it stayed. She refused to read anything into that, but she could not deny that she felt protected, even perhaps, just a little bit, treasured.

They left the theater chuckling over their favorite bits, so the ride home began in laughter. As talk dwindled, however, Holt switched on the radio, filling the truck with dreamy music fit for the occasion. By the time they arrived back at the motel, Cara floated on a sea of relaxed delight.

Holt accompanied her as far as the kitchen, but there in the dark, he drew her to a halt, pulling her into his arms. She went willingly, no longer able to pretend that the occasion and the evening had not affected them. Her heart clutched tight in a fist of emotion. She told herself that she deserved this moment, to believe in the possibility of romance. What if… But good sense refused to be ignored. A man like Holt did not indulge himself frivolously, and he might well regret this one small incident.

"Holt," she whispered, "are you sure about this?"

He pressed a finger to her lips. "I've already said everything there is to say to myself about it."

"In that case…" She twined her arms around his neck, lifting her face. "Thank you for tonight."

They kissed for a long while. It wrapped around them like a warm blanket, that kiss, bundling them together in a way that neither could quite explain. Afterward, they simply stood together, her head tucked beneath his chin. Finally, he pulled away, leaving her there in the warm, silent darkness, at peace for the first time in far, far too long.

It wouldn't last, of course. Sunday's sermon brought the same crushing sense of guilt that had haunted Cara from the first, and Wednesday's prayer service left her once more in silent, aching tears that seemed to destroy the careful, joyful truce in which she and Holt had been operating. He grew frustrated with her on the way home to Ace and Hap, who had stayed in because his arthritis had worsened with the continuing cold weather.

"Why can't you get it through that pretty little head of yours that I only want to help?" Holt demanded of her as they swept into the apartment through the kitchen door. She only shook that "pretty little head," biting her tongue against a snappish reply, before walking straight into disaster.

Chairs scraped back from the far side of the table, a figure rose, leaving Hap seated in his usual chair, a worried expression on his long, weathered, beloved face.

"Cara, honey," he rasped. "This fellow says he's come to take you and Ace back to California. I told him there must be some mistake."

Cara stared into the glittering eyes of her brother,

and a scream gathered in her chest, a wail of grief and betrayal, but she locked it inside. She had known. All along she had known that it would come to this. Her sins had finally caught up with her.

Chapter Fifteen

"No mistake," Eddie said, grinning like the scheming cad he was. "Right, sis?"

"How did you find me?" she asked with the calm that came from accepting one's doom.

Eddie smugly rocked back on his heels. As usual, he wore too much cologne and a cheap, orangey-tan jacket over rust-colored pants and a matching T-shirt, his light brown hair slicked back from his face to curl at his nape.

"Wasn't so tough. Couldn't be any doubt where you'd head. I just drove by Aunt Jane's old house, and this nice young couple there told me a guy had come by looking for information." He slid a glance a Holt, who seemed frozen in place. "Said he wore a cap with a company logo and the words 'Jefford Exploration' on it. Took a little while to put two and two together and come up with the Heavenly Arms Motel." He looked around him then, a thinly veiled sneer curling his lips. "You come down in the world, sis."

"Don't you dare!" Cara hissed angrily.

"Seems to me we ought to take this to the front room before someone accidentally wakes our boy," he said.

"Our boy?" Eddie queried avidly. "Ace is here?"

"Of course Ace is here!" Cara snapped. "Where else would he be except with his mother? Where he belongs."

"Well, now," Eddie said. "That's a matter of opinion, isn't it?"

She had no doubt of Eddie's opinion on the matter. Sick with dread and dismay, she made herself face Hap. "Actually, if you don't mind, I'd like to speak to my brother in private."

Hap glanced at Holt, who took a half step forward. After a moment, Hap nodded. "You just holler if you need anything."

She turned away, intending to take Eddie out the back through the kitchen and across the lot to her old room, where they could be assured of privacy. Perhaps, she thought wildly, if she could just keep him quiet for a bit, put him off somehow, she might find a moment to run. Sickened at the prospect, she could not so much as look at Holt, even when his hand shot out and fastened around her wrist.

"Cara? Are you sure about this?"

Eddie appeared in front her, wearing his jolly, buddy-to-the-world smile. "Hey, I'm her brother, man. Didn't she ever mention old Eddie?"

"Is that true? Is he your brother?"

"Yes, unfortunately, he is."

"He-e-ey," Eddie protested mildly.

Flaying him with her gaze, Cara ground out, "Just don't let him anywhere near my son."

"Don't worry," Holt said, releasing her.

She finally chanced a glance in his direction and found him staring a threat at Eddie. She loved him for that. Who was she kidding? She'd loved Holt for a long time already. This just gave her one more reason to regret whatever must come, one more way to break her heart.

Brushing past Eddie, she led the way out of the apartment. He made comments about the weather—too gray and too cold—as they crossed to the room. She let him in, then stood back and waited.

"Man," Eddie said, turning in a slow circle in the midst of her room. He shook his head, looking up at her from beneath the rise of his brow. "Even the clinic beats this dump, wouldn't you say?"

"No, I wouldn't," Cara told him. "Not that it matters. I'm not going back."

He shrugged and slid his hands into the pockets of his slacks, sneering down at the sofa as if to say he wouldn't dare sit there. "Not willingly, maybe."

Chilled, Cara folded her arms. "You can't make me go back, Eddie."

"No," he conceded, his tone light, unconcerned. "But the Elmonts can." He pegged her with a look then. "They've got a commitment order, Cara. They can come after you anytime they want. But it's not too late."

"I'm not going back," she repeated, hating the hint of desperation in her tone.

"We can still fix this. All the Elmonts care about is getting their grandson back. You come with me and everyone wins."

Cara let out a bark of derisive laughter. "And how do you figure that, Eddie? I really want to know."

"Simple." He spread his hands. "We negotiate a nice settlement, with visitation rights, for guardianship, and Ace grows up in the lap of luxury. That's better than them winning full custody in court, isn't it? I can even fix it so you don't have to go back to the clinic."

"That's very big of you, Eddie," she said sarcastically. "And just what is it that you get out of this benign arrangement?"

He waved a manicured hand. "Man's got to earn a living. You cut me in on the settlement, say fifty-fifty." He looked her in the eye then, adding, "Or there's always the finder's fee. Your choice."

"The Elmonts have offered a reward," she guessed, not at all surprised.

"Chicken feed compared to what we can take them for," he said urgently.

"You mean for what we can sell my son for!" she erupted.

He shrugged, cool as a cucumber. "Call it what you want. They're just two loving grandparents willing to give up a fortune to insure the well-being of their only heir."

"What?" Cara gasped. "Their *only* heir?"

"Didn't you know? They cut out Addison and his sister the day he told them you were pregnant. They always intended to raise the boy. Addison would have arranged it himself if he hadn't died like that."

"For a price, no doubt!" Cara spat, reeling. Was there no limit to her late husband's greed and self-centeredness?

"Look, you can't blame Addison," Eddie said. "You know how the Elmonts are."

"Controlling, manipulative. They have to own everything and everyone around them."

"And they've got the money to do it," Eddie confirmed. "But, hey, beats a shabby fourth-floor walk-up and an old lady more concerned about her next fix than dinner, you know? At least, that's the way I figure it."

"You talk like it has to be one or the other," Cara argued. "Didn't Aunt Jane show you that there's another way?"

"Aunt Jane," Eddie scoffed. "What was it about her that got to you? She never had anything in her whole life, not even her own kids."

"She had love, Eddie. She had love to give."

"Love," Eddie echoed dismissively. "That and five bucks will get you a decent cup of coffee." He waved a hand. "Well, it doesn't matter now. Old girl's gone, and the Elmonts are coming." He thumped himself in the chest. "I'm your best shot of staying out of the loony bin now, kid, and you know it." He winked and added, "Has old Eddie ever steered you wrong?"

Cara shook her head, not in answer to his question, but in wonder that he had never appreciated what Aunt Jane had offered them, someone to love and be loved by. That and that alone had saved her from following in their mother's footsteps. Maybe that was all she really had to offer her son, too, but it would be more than the Elmonts could give him with all their money.

"You think about it," Eddie said, patting her shoulder.

Those were the same words he'd used when urging her to date Addison way back when, though she'd known even then that she was too young, too vulnerable. She had listened to him once, but never again. Poor Eddie. He just didn't understand that he'd used up every bit of his credibility with her then.

He moved to the door, saying, "I'm going to find me a bite to eat. Then we'll talk again." He wagged a finger at her. "You think on it, and then you'll know I'm right."

With that, he went out the door, leaving her to fall to her knees in silent, frenzied supplication.

"I'm telling you, it's a wonder they didn't cart her off in a straitjacket," Eddie said, shaking his head. "Wailing and screeching. I mean, okay, it was a shock. The man was dead." Eddie shuddered. "Falling like that." He bounced his shoulders up and down as if shaking off the willies. "Let that be a lesson to you, hey? Don't stop on an overpass to help some chick change a flat. I mean, call a wrecker, for pity's sake. Right? Am I right?"

From his seat on the edge of one of the black leather couches in the front room, Holt traded a significant look with his grandfather, ignoring Eddie's question—and everything else about the man that he could. Holt feared that if he paid too much attention to Cara's brother, he'd rearrange Eddie's face for him.

"So you're telling us that Cara's in-laws had her committed because of her grief over her husband's death?" he probed.

"Well, no, not right away. She went into the clinic willingly at first."

"At first."

"Yeah, you know, because of the shock."

"Of her husband's death."

"That and finding out she didn't have any place to live, I guess."

"No place to live?" Hap asked, tilting his rocking chair forward. "Why wouldn't she have anyplace to live?"

"Because the house belonged to the Elmonts," Eddie said, as if it were the only sane assumption.

Holt bowed his head, remembering what she'd said about that the day he'd taken her out to his place. She'd been so impressed by what he'd built for himself, what no one could take away from him. When he thought about how hard she'd fought to claim that little kitchenette out back for her and Ace... He swallowed and sucked in a deep, calming breath.

"Look, she's my sister and all," Eddie went on in that insufferably reasonable tone of his, "but you can understand why the Elmonts want custody of their grandson. It's a wonder they didn't cart her off in a straitjacket that day, and it's not like they wouldn't let her ever see Ace again."

Holt tamped down his temper. "Uh-huh."

"Between you and me," Eddie went on, sliding to the edge of his seat and leaning forward, "there's a reward. Twenty-five grand. I wouldn't bring it up, but you've been so good to her, hiring her off the street and all. And after the way she's had you on—Cara Jane Wynne, hoo, boy—you ought to have something for your trouble." He sat back and crossed his legs, pinching the crease in his slacks. "I'll hook you up with that. Be glad to do it."

"And what about your sister?" Hap demanded, clearly wondering if he'd heard right.

"Don't worry about her," Eddie counseled. "I'll negotiate a generous settlement for her."

"In return for custody of Ace," Holt said, his temper beginning to slip.

"They'll send her back to that clinic," Hap declared, looking to Holt.

"She'll be well taken care of," Eddie confirmed.

Holt pushed up to his full height. "I see."

Eddie smiled. "I knew you'd get it. Cara would, too, if she was in her right mind."

"There's just one thing I don't understand," Holt said.

"What's that?"

"How is it, with everything that she's been through, Cara turned out to be so sweet and hardworking and good," Holt asked, calmly reaching down to yank Eddie up by his shirt collar, "while you became such a creep?"

"Hey!" Flailing his arms, Eddie resisted only minimally as Holt propelled him toward the door.

Hap, bless him, rocked up to his feet and hobbled swiftly across the room. "Here, let me help you." He shoved open the door, grinning at Holt as he thrust Eddie through it. "Interesting to meet you, Mr. Sharp," Hap called as the door swung closed. "Real interesting. What do we do now?" he asked Holt, ignoring Eddie's indignant shouts.

Holt glanced at the door. "You mean, since we can't give Eddie Sharp the beating he deserves?"

"More's the pity," Hap grumbled. He shook his head. "Poor girl. She can't fight folks like that on her own."

Holt grinned. "Which is surely why God gave Ty all that money."

"And gave us Ty!" Hap added, laughing. He pulled himself up straight.

"I'll go find Cara while you call him," Holt said, heading for the apartment.

Hap turned toward the office, chuckling. "Them Elmonts just *think* they got money."

"And Eddie Sharp isn't." Sharp, that was. In fact, unlike his sister, Eddie Sharp couldn't have been much duller.

He found her on her knees, weeping. Pulling her up, he sat her on the couch, dried her tears and sat beside her.

"Where's Eddie?" she asked, sniffing.

"On his way to California by now, if he knows what's good for him."

She scoffed. "Eddie always knows what's good for him. But what makes you think he'd leave?"

"I threw him out."

She goggled at him. "You did what?"

"Threw him out. It's the least I could after I led him right to you," he muttered.

"Don't blame yourself for that," she said, wincing. "You wouldn't have gone there if I hadn't lied to you. Thank you for getting rid of him, by the way."

"Actually, Hap helped. He opened the door."

Her jaw dropped. When Holt told her what Eddie had said, though, she began crying again. What could he do but put an arm around her?

"No, no. It's all right. I only want to hear your side of the story now."

She told him in fits and starts between tears and

fortifying breaths. They had delivered the news of Addison's death in one breath and told her that she would have to leave her home in the next. Ace, they had said, could stay with them. Tired from having struggled through the night alone with a colicky infant, Cara had simply come apart.

"I couldn't think, couldn't take it all in."

Holt shook his head and pulled her close against his side. "Who could blame you?"

She had gone of her own accord with the doctor summoned by her in-laws, and that, she said, had been her first mistake. "I thought it would appease them and give me somewhere private to get over my grief while I figured out what to do."

They'd brought a nurse to care for Ace. It hadn't occurred to her that they meant to keep him, until her "temporary respite" had turned into an actual commitment.

"They told me that I had no choice, that it would look better if I signed the papers rather than forced them to petition the court on my behalf. I decided to go along, thinking I'd get back home to my son sooner that way."

"So you essentially committed yourself for treatment," Holt surmised.

"Yes. Later, when I was served with papers saying that the Elmonts had filed for full custody of Ace, I realized what a mistake I'd made."

Her protests had only made matters worse.

"If I gave in to my anger, they told me I was behaving unreasonably. If I wept, they concluded I was depressed. When I begged, they essentially patted me on the head and told me to concentrate on 'getting better.'"

"And meanwhile, the Elmonts had your son."

Eventually Cara had learned to play the game, to give the staff at the private hospital what they wanted in order to "progress." She'd finally won supervised visits with her growing son, and then, thanks to an astute and sympathetic social services caseworker, weekends and holidays spent with him at the Elmont home. But the deck had been stacked against her, and with no financial resources to enable her to fight via the courts, Cara had done the only thing she could do; she'd run.

"I stashed what clothing I could for the two of us, whatever wouldn't be missed."

Holt chuckled and shook his head. "No wonder you showed up outfitted for the summer. What I don't understand is how you managed to fake your identity."

It seemed simple when she explained it. "I'd once overheard Addison mention a man in Oregon who could provide fake documents. So that's where I headed first."

In an unguarded moment, she'd taken Ace, jumped into the minivan that the Elmonts had deemed appropriate for a mother and driven north. Once there, she'd sold the van and used the money to buy a used car and false documents.

"My husband did me two favors," she said. "Three, counting Ace."

"He told you where to get a driver's license and Social Security card with your aunt's name on them," Holt surmised.

Nodding, she added, "And he put the minivan in my name. It wasn't cool enough for him to own, you see. Oh, he acted all magnanimous about it, pretended that buying it was all his idea, but I knew the Elmonts had purchased it as a reward for us providing them with a grandchild."

Armed with a new identity, she'd struck out for Oklahoma, the only haven she'd ever truly known. Realizing that Eddie would surely think to look for her around Duncan, she'd chosen Eden, based on its name alone.

"Just picked it out on a map. How stupid was that?"

"Not at all," Holt told her. "I suspect God was guiding you even then."

"I don't know about that," she said, shaking her head. "I just couldn't let the Elmonts raise my son. He'd turn out just like his father, dancing to the Elmont tune, willing to do anything for a buck, building his life on shallow image and foolish ideas of success."

"You did the right thing," Holt told her.

She looked at him in surprise. "You think so?"

"Absolutely."

She stared at him for several moments before giving her head a decisive nod. "My one regret, really, is that I have to do it again."

He pulled back a little, frowning down at her in confusion. "Do what again?"

She turned woeful eyes up to him. "Surely you see that I have no choice. I have to disappear before the Elmonts get to us."

"No," he said, quite calmly, he thought.

"I can't let them take Ace!" she exclaimed, leaping to her feet.

"Of course you can't," Holt agreed, rising to face her.

"But how can I fight them?"

"We," Holt corrected. "The question is, how can *we*

fight them? And the answer is, with every resource at our disposal."

"You don't hate me?"

"Hate you? Of course I don't hate you." He watched hope blossom in those soft gray eyes before they slowly filled with tears again. "It's okay," Holt promised. "It's all going to work out."

"It's not that," she squeaked.

"Then what is it?"

She swiped at the tears streaming down her face, and choked out, "Grover."

"What about Grover?"

"I'm ready," she managed, gripping his sleeve. "I'm finally ready to say that prayer."

She covered her face with her hands and sobbed. Holt pulled out his cell phone. He couldn't be certain what this was about, but he had the feeling that Grover would know. As for himself, he had no doubt that he'd do anything she asked of him from now on, importune Ty on her behalf, summon the town pastor, pray the moon down right out of the sky, whatever she needed.

In a way, he felt an immense relief. The secrets had been uncovered, and knowing why she'd done what she had, he couldn't fault her. Indeed, he applauded her courage and initiative. Yes, he feared for her, too, but he trusted that right and truth would win out, with God's help, and surely God was with them.

Cara might not think so now, but Holt would forever believe that God had guided her eyes the day she'd perused that map and let her gaze settle on Eden. He had no doubt at all himself now. He should have trusted, the

very first day that she'd walked into the place, that she
was the answer to all his prayers.

Grover arrived within minutes. Cara and Holt barely
beat him to the lobby. She went at once to her knees,
so anxious was she to unburden herself fully at last,
barely noticing when Hap handed Holt the house phone.
With Grover and Hap beside her, she spilled her sins
at God's feet, begging His forgiveness. She dared not
ask for His help, after all that she'd done. It was enough
that Holt and Hap seemed willing to forgive her and
lend their aid.

She still couldn't believe that, in the end, she
wouldn't have to pack up and flee with her son. Eddie
would be back, and the Elmonts wouldn't be far behind
him. But she wouldn't think of that just now. Nothing
mattered just then but unburdening her heart and, at
long last, getting right with God. The rest could wait.
For a bit.

After several minutes of conversation with Grover
and then more prayer, during which she did ask Jesus
into her heart, vowing her belief and acceptance, Grover tried to give her reason for hope.

"You're not alone now, Cara. Never again. And you
need not have waited. God knows your heart, honey. He
knows you acted out of fear and concern. Even now the
Holy Spirit is lifting up your troubles to the heavenly
Father with groans too deep for simple words. He'll
work this out. You'll see."

"He already is," Holt announced, appearing in front
of her. He squatted at her feet, bringing himself eye
level with her as she sat on the couch between Hap and

Grover. "I just got off the phone with Tyler. He'll have an attorney for us in the morning."

Cara put a hand to her head, teetering on the edge of relief so great it seemed unbelievable on one hand and a world of all-too-familiar concern on the other. "I—I can't pay a lawyer."

"Not to worry," Holt stated flatly.

Cara shook her head. "You don't understand. The Elmonts have money, enough to make it very, very expensive to fight them."

Holt just smiled. "You don't understand. Tyler says he can't contribute more than a couple million to start, but that we should give him a few days."

"A couple million!" Cara yelped.

Holt shook his head. "Personally, I don't think it's going to take anything like that, but let's talk to the attorney before we reign him in. Okay?"

Several seconds ticked by before she could wrap her mind around what was happening, and even then she couldn't quite believe it. "But why?"

"Why what?"

"Why would Tyler do such a thing?"

Holt traded looks with Hap, who rasped, "Why, because he can. What else is all that money for, after all, if not to do good?"

"But why do this for *me?*" she persisted.

"Because we asked him to," Holt said bluntly.

"But I lied to you!" she argued. "I used you."

"I don't see how you used us," Hap rasped, shaking his head. "You've done more than your fair share of work around here, more even than what we hired you for."

"As for the other," Holt said, "you only did what you felt you had to do. No fault in that."

Stunned, Cara could only gape at him for long moments, and then she began to sob again, too grateful for words. She knew that the nightmare had not ended, only taken an unexpected turn, but to her everlasting relief, no one even mentioned calling a doctor.

Chapter Sixteen

Holt turned the truck into a small, old-fashioned gas-oline station. Flanked by a sheet metal fence meant to conceal a salvage yard and boasting only two pumps and a single garage bay, the circa 1950s building bore the title of Froggy's Gas & Tires. The place looked closed, however, and Cara had a difficult time believing that Holt had bullied her out into the cold just to show her where she could buy gas for her old car.

"What is going on?" she asked, the tension of the past two days making her tone more sharp than she'd intended.

"Distraction," Holt answered, driving right past the station and across the lot to a small clapboard house beyond. The light above the uncovered stoop came on as the truck drew to a halt. Holt killed the engine and shifted sideways in his seat, facing Cara. "Froggy and Kelly Priddy are friends of mine. You met them briefly at the Watermelon Patch."

"Froggy?"

"It's a nickname, but he prefers it to his given name of Filmore. He helped me fix your car, by the way."

"And we're here because of that?"

"We're here because we've been invited over, and I thought you could use the distraction, so I accepted."

Cara didn't know whether to be touched by Holt's concern for her state of mind or indignant at his highhandedness. Before she could decide what her reaction would be, the door of the tiny, hip-roofed house opened and a man appeared in the doorway. Squat and lipless, he'd obviously earned his unusual nickname by appearance, but the effusiveness of his greeting instantly endeared him to Cara, who set aside her irritation and followed Holt's lead by getting out of the car. Froggy jogged across the square stoop and down the steps to pound the much taller Holt on the back.

"Come on in out of the cold! Kelly's heated some cider. Got them fat little cinnamon sticks in it and everything."

He bounded back up the steps and into the house. Holt waited until Cara reached him, then climbed the three steep steps at her side and ushered her inside. Kelly Priddy met them with steaming cups containing the aforementioned cinnamon sticks. As plain as her tidy living room with its white walls and nondescript brown furnishings, Kelly stood perhaps an inch or two taller than her squat husband, her straight, light brown hair flowing over her plump shoulders. The bangs gave her a girlish air even before she giggled, showing front teeth with a slight gap between them.

In short order, Cara found herself seated next to Holt on the sofa while Froggy took the only chair and Kelly parked herself on the matching ottoman to one side. The television played softly in the background while they sipped their cider and chatted. Cara took the opportunity to thank Froggy for working on her car.

"Aw, Holt's helped me out more than once, I can tell you."

"Still, it was my car, and if I can ever repay the favor in any way," Cara began. At that point, Kelly bounced up to her feet and waved a hand at her, turning toward the open doorway between the living area and kitchen.

"Come tell me what you think about this."

With a bemused glance at Holt, Cara set her cup on the side table and rose to follow her hostess. A moment later, she found herself standing in a small eat-in kitchen. The square table and four chairs with red seat cushions had been shoved up against one wall to leave as much space as possible, but the room still felt crowded. Kelly regarded the window over the sink, or, rather, the colorful curtains hanging over that window. On closer inspection, Cara saw that the "curtains" were actually just lengths of fabric that had been draped over the rod.

"Coordinating or contrasting?" Kelly asked, tapping her forefinger against her chin.

Cara looked around the room again, noting the red towels that hung from the oven door handle and the red frame of the clock on the wall. "Coordinating," she decided, pointing to the cherry-print fabric in the center of the window rod. "But if you want contrast, you might try banding it in the yellow."

Kelly Priddy threw up her arms. "Brilliant! But why not the green?"

Cara tilted her head. "Too Christmasy for every day, don't you think?"

Kelly smacked herself in the middle of her bangs. "Duh. So, do you sew?"

Cara shook her head. "Never learned."

"I'll teach you," Kelly announced, reaching for a bowl of potato chips on the counter. "Let's give the guys some snacks, then I'll show you the bedroom so you can see what I've done in there." She winked at Cara and whispered, "Froggy likes a fancy boudoir. Romantic cuss."

Fancy turned out to be big flower prints, ruffles and lace. Cara managed to keep a straight face as Kelly explained how she'd created the various elements in the room. Amazed by the level of expertise in the workmanship if not the frilly decor, Cara soon found herself caught up in laughing conversation, which continued even after they rejoined the men. With every word and gesture, Kelly told Cara how much she adored her odd-looking husband. As the sentiment seemed entirely mutual, Cara could only envy the Priddys.

She and Holt departed several hours later with hugs from Kelly and handshakes from Froggy. "Good night, and thank you!" she called one more time as Holt handed her up into the passenger seat. When he slid beneath the wheel a few seconds later, she thanked him, too. "I guess I needed that to keep my mind off Eddie and the Elmonts," she admitted, "but next time try asking, why don't you?"

"Good advice," he said around a grin.

Too bad he didn't take it.

* * *

Five long days after Eddie blew her carefully constructed little world apart, Cara at last sat across the desk from one David Hyde in his Duncan law office, Holt beside her.

A stout man of middle height with frizzy gray hair, Hyde wore a huge college ring on one hand and a narrow wedding band on the other, along with golf clothes. Clearly they had interfered with his plans for the day, but he listened to the whole ugly story as if fully prepared to give them his undivided attention for as long as it took. After what felt like hours of questions, replies, notes and instructions via the intercom to his assistant in another room, the attorney gave it to them straight.

"I'm not familiar with California law. We're researching that now. But according to Oklahoma statutes, since the commitment was voluntary, we only have a few problems." He ticked them off, along with their possible solutions, everything from psychological evaluations to the most important consideration, a stable home environment for Ace. "For my money," he went on, looking them square in the eyes, "the easiest, quickest, most unassailable fix is for the two of you just to get married."

Cara bit her lips to prevent her gasp from escaping, while David Hyde went on, pointing out the obvious benefits of such an arrangement.

"It's one thing to fight a single woman for custody of her child," he concluded, "another to destroy a family. Make yourselves a family, and you've created a fortress of sorts. Then we fight from a strengthened position."

Finally, he sat back, waiting for their response.

Cara gulped, keenly aware of Holt's silent presence, and marshaled together the only possible reply. "I'm afraid you've misconstrued the relationship between Mr. Jefford and me."

"He's right, Cara," Holt interrupted, taking her hand. "Fighting a married couple is a whole lot different from bullying a single mother. We should think about this."

Appalled, she shook her head. Supporting her was one thing. Convincing his brother-in-law to bankroll her legal battles went far beyond anything she had a right to expect. She would not allow Holt to take this to absurd levels. She got to her feet as calmly as she could and stuck out her hand for Mr. Hyde.

"Thank you, sir. I feel much better knowing that you're on this."

"My pleasure," Hyde assured her, and she didn't doubt it a bit, considering what Tyler must be paying him. Holt, however, did not figure into this. How could anyone expect him to saddle himself with a wife and child just to help her win a custody suit?

Poor Holt. He'd only begun to make peace with the lies he'd known about when the whole truth had exploded in his face. She couldn't let his guilt at unwittingly leading Eddie to her dictate his future.

Though aching inside, she walked out with her head high and eyes dry. Later, when Holt broached the subject again, she had to turn her face away in order to maintain her composure.

"It makes sense, Cara."

"Not to me."

"Look, if getting married will put a stop to this nonsense—"

"This subject is closed," she interrupted sternly. "And that's all I have to say on the matter."

He gave up, and they drove back to Eden in silence.

Holt sat slumped over the dining table, his head in his hands. He felt all prayed out and still in shock over everything that had happened. He'd spent the first three of the past five days keeping Eddie Sharp away from Cara and Ace. Eddie had not, as hoped, returned to California, but he hadn't had enough nerve to approach Cara again, either. That respite, Holt knew, would not last. Time was running out. Eventually Eddie would give up and summon the Elmonts. It would undoubtedly be best, as Hyde had pointed out, if they were married before that happened. That way Holt could fight for her. Apparently, though, Cara just didn't see things that way. What hurt him most about that was the cool, resolute manner in which she had refused Hyde's suggestion.

"I'm afraid you've misconstrued the relationship between Mr. Jefford and me."

Holt had been shocked to hear Hyde's blunt suggestion that they marry, but he'd immediately seen the sense of it. In that moment, it had even seemed inevitable, the absolutely correct end to all that had gone on before, but it appeared that he had "misconstrued" the woman's feelings for him. After that meeting in the lawyer's office, Cara had refused even to discuss the idea of marriage to him, and that had hurt Holt right into his own silence.

Ryan clumped into the room. "There you are! Granddad and I were waiting for you to get back and tell us what the lawyer had to say. Where's Cara?"

"In her room."

"This doesn't sound good," Ryan muttered, coming to brace his hands on the back of the chair at the end of the table. "Tell me everything."

Holt did, including the lawyer's suggestion that he and Cara marry.

"So what's the problem?" Ryan asked, pulling out the chair and sitting down. Holt glared at him, partly in surprise, partly in anger. "Don't look at me like that," Ryan drawled, "and don't try to tell me you aren't wild about the girl. We've all seen it."

Holt felt his ears heat and quickly looked down at his hands. "It's not that simple."

"I don't see why not. Unless you've still got that stupid idea about the oil business being too dangerous for married men."

Holt stared more than glared this time.

"Did you think we didn't know?" Ryan chuckled and sat back, draping an arm over the back of the chair. "That's it, isn't it? Tell me something. When was the last time you or any of your men had to go up top on a rig?"

"Falling isn't the only danger," Holt grumbled. "We blew two full lengths of pipe recently."

"So? Everyone will be more careful now, won't they? Check everything twice, I'm sure." Holt looked away, because that was precisely what they were doing. "What about truck drivers, Holt? Lots more of them die every year than roughnecks. What about firemen? Policemen? Soldiers? Are those jobs only for single men? I don't think so."

Holt didn't think so, either. He knew his conviction about staying single had more to do with the grief and fear that he'd somehow held on to when he should have turned it over to God instead. That didn't solve anything, however.

"I'm not the issue. I made it clear I was willing to marry her."

Ryan reared back in his chair. "Willing? That must have thrilled Cara right down to her little bitty toes."

"Look," Holt snapped, "Cara is the one who doesn't want to marry me. All right?"

"Well, I don't know. Is it all right with you?"

"If that's the way she wants it," Holt muttered.

"What about what you want?"

"That apparently doesn't figure into it."

"Maybe she doesn't know how you feel about it."

"How could she not?" Holt demanded, surprised by his own anger. "After everything I've done, everything that's happened, how could she not know?" He rose, suddenly too worked up to stay in his chair. "I mean, I knew. Okay? I knew from the very beginning that she wasn't being truthful with us, but I kept it to myself."

"And why was that, I wonder?" Ryan asked.

"What difference does it make?" Holt retorted hotly. "She lied, and I kept mum. With every inconsistency that cropped up, I kept it to myself. I *protected* her!"

"Of course, you did," Ryan commented idly. "That's what you do, protect the people you care about."

"Exactly! And if that wasn't enough, what about after I found out she'd faked her identity? I kept quiet about that, too." He thumped himself in the chest. "I stood by her. Even though she wouldn't trust me with the truth, I stood by her! I'd still be keeping her secrets if not for that brother of hers. Then it all blows up, and what do

I do? I get her every bit of help I can find her, that's what?" He folded his arms, finishing glumly, "And now that she's got the whole family in her corner, she doesn't need me anymore."

"So what are you saying?" Ryan asked. "That Cara's an unscrupulous, immoral, ungrateful—"

"No!" Holt shouted, throwing up his hands. "You know better!"

"Then what's really keeping you and Cara apart?" Ryan demanded, slapping his hands down against the tabletop.

"She doesn't love me!" Holt roared, thinking it obvious. Ryan straightened. "She doesn't love me," Holt repeated miserably.

Ryan folded his arms, a smug look on his face. "Oh, really? And I suppose Cara told you that?"

"Don't be ridiculous."

"Oh. Of course. That would be too obvious. Like you telling her how much you love her and Ace."

Holt winced. "Just stop it."

"Better yet, you stop with this 'willing' nonsense and tell her how you really feel," Ryan said. "Now would be a good time."

With that he turned aside, revealing Cara in the open doorway to her bedroom, her eyes wide with shock as she clung to the casement, Ace on her hip. They were the two most precious things in his own personal world, Holt realized, and they just stood there staring at him.

Cara held on to the doorframe for support, her heart pounding so hard that it threatened to knock her off her feet.

Earlier, she'd lain on her bed with Ace sitting in the curve of her body and once again tearfully poured out her heart to God. The whole thing had felt a little shopworn, frankly, as if God had sat there on His throne shaking His head in strained patience, asking what more she wanted from Him. She'd wanted solutions; He'd given her solutions, and then she'd complained that they were not to her taste? She had wondered petulantly if having a husband who actually loved her was too much to ask. It had never occurred to her that Holt might be questioning her feelings for him.

"Is that what you think?" she asked. "That I don't love you? After everything you've done for us, h-how could I *not* love you?"

He spread his hands. "But you told the lawyer that he had misconstrued—"

"Your feelings!" she interrupted. "I was talking about *your* feelings."

"*My* feelings? Why do you think I was there with you? Why do you think I've done the things I've done, why I couldn't just let it go and tend to my own business?"

"Because that's just the kind of man you are, Holt," she said, "a good Christian man with a big heart and broad shoulders that you expect the whole world to lean on."

"Oh, please! I've followed you around like some pathetic, adoring hound." He shoved a hand through his hair. "Everyone else has seen it! Why not you?"

"Because I'm me," she said, thumping herself in the chest. "I'm the escapee from the loony bin, the liar, the schemer." She shook her head. "A lousy schemer, but a schemer, nonetheless. I'm not what you thought I was, Holt."

"No, you're not what I first thought you were," he admitted, "but you're twice what I dreamed about. You and Ace, you're more than I ever dared want, more than I ever dared ask for. And, the truth is, Cara, God brought you here *to me*. You're mine! And I'll be hanged if—"

She never knew what he'd be hanged for. She somehow got across the room before he could tell her, and then he didn't have to, not with words, because he was kissing her, both her and Ace wrapped in his strong arms.

At some point, Ryan began to laugh, prompting them to pull apart enough for Cara to gaze up into Holt's warm green eyes. "I don't deserve you," she whispered.

"Hoo, I'd better marry you before you come to your senses," Holt crowed joyfully.

"I'm serious, Holt," she insisted solemnly. "I do love you. How could I not? After everything you've done, you're already my hero. But I don't want to be rescued. That's not what marriage is supposed to be."

"Sweetheart," he said, "it's not about that. I'd planned to ask you as soon as the other issues were resolved. Then when the attorney suggested it, I thought… I thought how wondrously God works, dropping my heart's desire right into my lap like that. Then when you just dismissed the whole idea out of hand, I can't tell you how disappointed I was."

"Oh, Holt. I couldn't bear the thought of forcing you into something you didn't want. I was afraid you felt guilty about leading Eddie to us when the fault was mine all along."

Cupping her face in his big, capable hands, he pressed her forehead to hers, saying, "It's not about fault, not yours, not mine. God's been in charge here all along, honey. God knew, even before I did, how much I wanted, needed, you and Ace. He gave you Eden for a destination. He put your finger on just the right spot on that map. And He made sure that I was desperate enough to hire you when you walked in right off the street. Did you get that? *I* need you."

"Good grief," Ryan quipped, "I think he's about to give up the big brother cape."

Cara giggled. Holt dropped his hands from her face, his arm sliding around her shoulders as he turned toward his brother. "Okay, so maybe I have a little bit of a big brother complex."

"Ya think?" Ryan stepped up and clapped Holt on the shoulder, adding, "That wasn't a complaint, by the way. No one's ever had a better big brother than you."

"Thanks," Holt drawled before dropping his gaze to Cara once more. "But that's not what this is about. That's not what *we* are about. My wanting to marry you doesn't have anything to do with heroics. This is about you and me belonging together."

"Amen," Ryan agreed. Reaching for Ace, he winked at Cara. "Personally, I've always thought what this family needed was a cute blonde sister-in-law and an adorable nephew." With that, he hoisted a chuckling Ace over his head.

"Heh, watch it," Hap said, limping in from the front

room. "That's my grandson you're tossing around like a sack of grain there."

Cara pulled away from Holt and went to Hap. "You heard."

He looped an arm around her, reaching out for Holt with the other. "I'm old, but I'm not deaf, sugar. I heard, and I just have one thing to say. Let's get this show on the road."

Laughing, Cara hugged him. Holt's long arms embraced them both. Ryan carried Ace over to get in on the action, beaming ear to ear. Cara had never felt so loved, so included, so much a part of a something, so right.

She understood now what God had been telling her earlier. Her every problem had been solved. Her prayers had already been answered, with blessing heaped upon blessing until all the world could not hold them as they spilled out and ran over. God had kept His hand on her all along, from the very beginning. The Elmonts were not a problem; they were just a means He had used to get her here, to this man and this family, where she belonged.

They planned the simplest of ceremonies for the following Saturday, the first day of March, delaying only that long so Charlotte and Ty could whisk down from Dallas to be there.

Charlotte, God love her, came on Thursday morning armed with a trunkful of dresses. From that bounty, Cara chose a formfitting, cream-colored knit chemise with a flowing overlay of dusty pink lace, the sleeves of which ended in fluttery, bell-shaped cuffs. They dashed to Duncan for cream-colored heels and a simple bouquet of pink roses.

Only the day before that Holt had insisted on buying a lovely diamond solitaire to go with the simple gold bands he and Cara had chosen for wedding rings. He'd also come up with, all on his own, a handsome black suit, white shirt, black-and-red pin-striped tie and black cowboy boots. Most astonishingly, he'd managed an almost identical outfit for Ace.

Cara informed her brother by telephone on Friday morning of the impending nuptials. He did not offer to walk her down the aisle as he had at her first wedding. Indeed, she'd hung up while he was raving about the fortune that could still be wrangled from the Elmonts, if only she'd "listen to reason."

How the whole of Eden had gotten the news about the wedding, Cara didn't know, but when she showed up at the church with Charlotte and Ty, who had dismissed her effusive thanks for his generosity with a heartfelt hug, the parking lot literally overflowed. Cars lined both sides of the streets in every direction. Cara couldn't have been more pleased. She only hoped that the ladies of the church, who had volunteered to prepare a meal for the reception, had gotten together enough food for all these people.

The only sad moment of the morning had come when Holt had sent in a copy of the Duncan paper, folded to the page that contained the obituary of Mrs. Poersel. Yet, it somehow seemed fitting that their wedding should take place on the same day as the old dear's funeral. Cara's only regret was that she and Holt couldn't be there. She didn't think her aunt's old friend would mind.

Now she stood with Charlotte in the freshening breeze, the barest hint of spring ruffling their skirts, and at last felt the serenity of that golden haven she had come seeking. Cara stepped off toward the church, and Ty rushed forward to open the door to her future.

Charlotte looked resplendent in a pale, minty suit that brought out the green flecks in her hazel eyes, her long auburn hair hanging down her back. Cara had twisted her own hair into a sleek roll on the back of her head, anchored with pink rose buds and white baby's breath. Charlotte had loaned her a set of genuine pearls for jewelry.

Having agreed to act as Cara's matron of honor, Charlotte preceded her down the aisle at a stately pace. They had chosen to forgo music, but Hap was there to escort Cara, his eyes misty and his dentures on display. Ryan, whose single duty as best man was to hold Ace, stood next to Holt before the altar.

Grover made an eloquent business of the rites, but both Cara and Holt were content to repeat the time-honored vows without inventive deviation or embellishment, while Froggy Priddy slipped around with a camera in his role of self-appointed photographer. Afterward, neither could stop smiling as they stood together in an impromptu reception line while their uninvited but very welcome guests streamed past them at the front of the church to the fellowship hall beyond. The very last to offer his congratulations turned out to be, to their surprise, none other than David Hyde, the attorney.

"Tyler didn't think you'd mind my showing up,"

he said, "especially since this seems like such a good time to give you this. It came by special messenger this morning."

Cara watched as he pulled an envelope from his inside coat pocket and handed it to her. A glance at the return address showed it to be from her former in-laws, but to her surprise, the envelope was addressed to Holt. Curiosity more than anything else piqued her interest, but she dutifully handed over the letter to her new husband.

Holt considered but a moment before tearing open the envelope and removing two pieces of paper. He glanced at the smaller of the two before passing it to Cara, who quickly realized that she held in her hand a check for twenty-five thousand dollars. That "finder's fee" of which Eddie had spoken! She digested that while Holt quickly read the letter, which he then handed back to Hyde.

"What does it say?" she asked, passing the check back to the attorney, too.

Holt slid his arm around her waist. "They respectfully request that I urge you to consider a formal visitation agreement, a very generous one. For them." He smiled down at her. "So they can see their grandson and heir."

Cara closed her eyes and leaned into him. It was over. She'd won. They'd won. Ace would grow up with every advantage that a loving Christian home could provide.

"I suppose the check is their way of sweetening the deal," Holt said with a chuckle, pulling her close. "As if it could get any sweeter."

"What should I tell them?" David Hyde asked, tucking the folded letter back into the pocket from which it came.

Cara looked at her husband and smiled. "Tell them we'll pray about it."

Nodding, Hyde held up the check. "And this?"

Holt shrugged. "I don't know." He looked down at Cara. "What do you think, wife?"

She considered. "Well, you did find me. Sort of."

"And I'm keeping you," he declared, pulling her closer still. She laughed and kissed his cheek. "Hey, maybe we should send it to Eddie," he said. "I mean, fair's fair, don't you think?"

"Poor Eddie," Cara said. "I'd hate to think that was all he'd get out of this."

"It does seem like a pittance compared to what we have, doesn't it?" Holt said.

Cara looked to David Hyde. "Make it our wedding gift to him, then."

Hyde just smiled and shook his head before slipping the check into his coat and walking away.

In the moment they had to themselves, before good manners would compel them to join the reception in the fellowship hall, Cara laid her head on her husband's shoulder and thought about what he'd just done, how easily he'd let go of that check. She knew that her son, not to mention her heart, would always be safe with Holt.

My hero, she thought, just before she winged a prayer of humble gratitude and growing wonder heavenward.

"Ready to celebrate, Mrs. Jefford?" he asked, folding her arm around his.

"With you," she answered. "Always."

* * * * *

Dear Reader,

Have you ever allowed guilt to separate you from God's blessings? I have—while God stood ready to supply my needs! All He requires is that we let go and let Him. As both Cara and Holt discover, that seems difficult—until we understand what we're holding on to instead of God.

Are you holding on to guilt, fear, pride, pain or intentions/ goals instead of God? Guilt can be deserved, fear justified, pride misplaced, pain real, intentions good, but anything that keeps us from letting go and letting God is harmful.

As Scripture says, let us conquer our woes overwhelmingly through Him. Sometimes that means laying it all on the line for truth, which is precisely what must happen in the final book of this series, *Their Small-Town Love,* coming in February 2009. I hope you will enjoy Ryan and Ivy's journey to love and truth.

God bless,

Arlene James

Questions For Discussion

1. What does it mean to conquer difficulties through Christ? (See Romans 8.) What did it mean in Cara's case? In Holt's?

2. Holt is an active Christian; in light of that, is Holt's suspicion of Cara understandable? Necessary? Why or why not?

3. None of Cara's clothes are appropriate for Oklahoma weather. Would this make you suspicious of who she is and where she came from? Why or why not?

4. Holt's grandfather Hap welcomes Cara, a stranger, into their lives. Would you be as welcoming of a stranger as he? Why or why not?

5. Cara believes that she cannot publicly confess her deception, and therefore cannot receive God's forgiveness. Do you agree?

6. Exodus 20:1—17 and Deuteronomy 5:6—21 give us what we know as the Ten Commandments. Exodus 20:16 and Deuteronomy 5:20 use the same words to convey what we think of as the ninth commandment—"You shall not bear false witness against your neighbor." Does Cara break this commandment? Why or why not?

7. What impact does Aunt Jane have on Cara? Why does her influence not lead Cara to a full understanding of the mission of Christ? Should it have?

8. Holt eventually comes to realize that he continues to allow himself to be affected by his past. Has this ever happened to you? What did you do to change things?

9. Cara is extremely protective of her son, Ace, going so far as to carry him on her back when she's cleaning motel rooms. Is she justified in doing so? What would you have done in her position?

10. Because Holt is an oil rigger, he believes that this prevents him from getting married and having a family. Do you agree with him? Why or why not?

11. Does Holt's visit with Mrs. Poersel soften him toward Cara's situation? How?

12. Cara assumes that Holt wants to marry her in order to provide protection for her and her son. Is this an acceptable reason for marriage? Why or why not?

SPECIAL EXCERPT FROM

Love Inspired

Read on for a sneak preview of
THE SHEPHERD'S BRIDE
by Patricia Davids, the next heartwarming story in the
BRIDES OF AMISH COUNTRY *series*
from Love Inspired. Available April 2014.

Carl King scraped most of the mud off his boots and walked up to the front door of his boss's home. Joe Shetler had gone to purchase straw from a neighbor, but he would be back soon. After an exhausting morning spent struggling to pen and doctor one ornery and stubborn ewe, Carl had rounded up half the remaining sheep and moved them closer to the barns with the help of his dog, Duncan.

He opened the front door and stopped dead in his tracks. An Amish woman stood at the kitchen sink. She had her back to him as she rummaged for something. She hadn't heard him come in.

He resisted the intense impulse to rush back outside. He didn't like being shut inside with anyone. He fought his growing discomfort. This was Joe's home. This woman didn't belong here.

"What are you doing?" he demanded.

She shrieked and whirled around to face him. "You scared the life out of me."

He clenched his fists and stared at his feet. "I didn't mean to frighten you. Who are you and what are you doing here?"

"Who are you? You're not Joseph Shetler. I was told this was Joseph's house."

She was a slender little thing. The top of her head wouldn't reach his chin unless she stood on tiptoe. She was dressed Plain in a drab faded green calf-length dress with a matching cape and apron. Her hair, on the other hand, was anything but drab. It was ginger-red, and wisps of it curled near her temples. The rest was hidden beneath the black *kapp* she wore.

He didn't recognize her, but she could be a local. He made a point of avoiding people, so it wasn't surprising that he didn't know her.

"I'm sorry. My name is Elizabeth Barkman. People call me Lizzie. I'm Joe's granddaughter from Indiana."

As far as Carl knew, Joe didn't have any family. "Joe doesn't have a granddaughter, and he doesn't like people in his house."

"Actually, he has four granddaughters. I can see why he doesn't like to have people in. This place is a mess. He certainly could use a housekeeper. I know an excellent one who is looking for a position."

Pick up THE SHEPHERD'S BRIDE
wherever Love Inspired® books and ebooks are sold.

Love Inspired®
SUSPENSE
RIVETING INSPIRATIONAL ROMANCE

FOR THE CHILD

Foster mother Noelle Whitman adores the little girl she's caring for. Noelle has terrible memories of her own foster care experience and vows to do right by this child. But when the girl's father, fresh out of jail for murdering his estranged wife, arrives for his daughter, Noelle is worried. The former SWAT team member insists he was framed. But moments later, someone shoots at Caleb, and the three are forced on the run. Protective and kind, Caleb is nothing like the embittered ex-con she expected. And learning to trust him may be the only way to survive.

TOP
COPS

WRONGLY ACCUSED
by
LAURA SCOTT

***Available April 2014 wherever
Love Inspired books and ebooks are sold.***

LIS44591R

LOVE INSPIRED HISTORICAL

OPEN TO LOVE?

After refusing to give in to an unwanted engagement,
Alice Hawthorne is determined to stake her own claim during
the Oklahoma Land Rush. But when she meets Elijah Thornton,
can the preacher convince her to open her heart?

BRIDEGROOM
BROTHERS

The Preacher's Bride Claim

by

LAURIE KINGERY

Available April 2014 wherever
Love Inspired books and ebooks are sold.

LIH28259

Love Inspired

Cowboy, wanderer… Father?

Nate Lyster and Mia Verbeek are in perfect agreement—that letting someone new into your heart is much too risky. Left on her own with four kids, Mia can't let just anyone get close, while wandering cowboy Nate learned young that love now means heartbreak later.

But when a fire turns Mia's life upside down, Nate is the only one who can get through to her traumatized son—and her heart. If Nate and Mia can forget the hurts of their pasts, they might get everything they want. But if they let fear win, a perfect love could pass them by….

A Father in the Making
by
Carolyn Aarsen

Available April 2014 wherever
Love Inspired books and ebooks are sold.

Find us on Facebook at
www.Facebook.com/LoveInspiredBooks

LI87878

A wave of terror washed over Morgan Smith when she heard the tapping at her window. Someone was outside the caretaker's cottage. Had the man who'd tried to kill her in Mexico found her in Iowa?

Though she'd been in witness protection for two months, her fear of being killed had never subsided. She'd left Des Moines for the countryside and a job at a stable because she had felt exposed in the city, vulnerable. She'd grown up on a ranch in Wyoming, and when she'd worked as an American missionary in Mexico, she'd always chosen to be in rural areas. Wide-open spaces seemed safer to her.

With her heart pounding, she rose to her feet and walked the short distance to the window, half expecting to see a face contorted with rage, or clawlike hands reaching for her neck. The memory of nearly being strangled made her shudder. She stepped closer to the window, seeing only blackness. Yet the sound of the tapping had been too distinct to dismiss as the wind rattling the glass.

A chill snaked down her spine.

Someone was outside.

If the man from Mexico had come to kill her, it seemed odd that he would give her a warning by tapping on the window.

She thought to call her new boss, who was in the guest-house less than a hundred yards away. Alex Reardon seemed like a nice man. She'd hated being evasive when he'd asked her where she had gotten her knowledge of horses. She'd been blessed to get the job without references. Her references, everything and everyone she knew, all of that had been stripped from her, even her name. She was no longer Magdalena Chavez. Her new name was Morgan Smith.

The knob on the locked door turned and rattled.

She'd been a fool to think the U.S. Marshals could keep her safe.

Pick up TOP SECRET IDENTITY *wherever*
Love Inspired® Suspense books and ebooks are sold.